KING·PENGUIN

JUMPING THE QUEUE

Mary Wesley was born near Windsor, England. Her education took her to the London School of Economics, and during the war she worked in the War Office. She has also worked part-time in the antique trade. Mary Wesley has lived in London, France, Italy, Germany, and several places in the West Country. She now lives "rather a hermit's existence" in Devon, where she has written five novels. She has previously written for children and claims that her "chief claim to fame is arrested development, getting my first novel published at the age of seventy."

JUMPING THE QUEUE

Mary Wesley

A KING PENGUIN

PUBLISHED BY PENGUIN BOOKS

PENGUIN BOOKS
Published by the Penguin Group
Viking Penguin Inc., 40 West 23rd Street,
New York, New York 10010, U.S.A.
Penguin Books Ltd, 27 Wrights Lane,
London W8 5TZ, England
Penguin Books Australia Ltd, Ringwood,
Victoria, Australia
Penguin Books Canada Limited, 2801 John Street,
Markham, Ontario, Canada L3R 1B4
Penguin Books (N.Z.) Ltd, 182–190 Wairau Road,
Auckland 10, New Zealand

Penguin Books Ltd, Registered Offices: Harmondsworth,
Middlesex, England

First published in Great Britain by
Macmillan London Limited 1983
Published in Penguin Books 1988

LIBRARY OF CONGRESS CATALOGING IN PUBLICATION DATA
Wesley, Mary.
Jumping the queue/Mary Wesley.
p.   cm.
ISBN 0 14 01.0827 0
I. Title
PR6073.E753J8   1988
823′.914—dc 19   87-30839
                        CIP

Printed in the United States of America by
R. R. Donnelley & Sons Company, Harrisonburg, Virginia
Set in Melior

JUMPING THE QUEUE

1

All week Gus had been fussed by Matilda's unusual activity. He stomped round the house peering in through the French windows, craning his neck through open doors, eyes bright, head to one side, listening. She could hear his feet slapping on the brick path as he moved from the kitchen door to the window. Soon he would leap onto the garden table, look in, try to catch her eyes. He did this inelegant jump flapping his wings, hitting them against a chair as he strained for the table. His blue eyes met hers.

'Gus, I have to make this list, it's important.'

The gander throttled gentle anxious noises in his throat, flapped his wings, raised his head, honked.

'Shut up.' She tried to ignore him, concentrating on the list: *any trouble with the pump Peake's garage they know its vagaries. For ordinary electric work Emersons in the High Street, telephone in book in kitchen table drawer.*

Gus honked louder, slapping his feet on the wooden table.

'Shut up!' Matilda shouted without looking up. Butcher, baker, post office, garage ,doctor, dentist. They won't want those. Vet – they won't need him, solicitor, bank, police. They would perhaps only need these. She checked the telephone numbers, put down her pen and went to the window.

'Oh Gus.'

He nibbled her ear, making crooning noises as she stroked his cool neck sliding her hand from his head to his breast, feeling the depth of his feathers, their beauty and strength, parting them with her fingers until they touched the warm breastbone. Affected by her touch Gus excreted onto the table.

'What a way to show love.' Matilda moved away to the kitchen. Guessing which way she was going the bird jumped off the table and half ran, half walked to the kitchen door where he stood peering in, knowing he was not allowed inside the house.

Matilda ran water into a bucket. The telephone rang. Gus honked.

'Hullo, hullo, I can't hear you.'

'This is Piers.'

'Yes, John, how are you?'

'Haven't you had your phone mended yet?'

'No.'

'You should. It's months since that dog bit it, broke it.'

'What?'

'I said it's months since –'

'He hated the bell, the noise hurt his ears, so he jumped at it, bit it.'

'You should get it mended, it won't cost you anything.'

'Oh.' Matilda ran a finger over the sellotape holding the machine together.

'He's dead anyway.'

'I can't hear you.' She smiled at Gus in the doorway shifting from foot to foot.

'I said he's dead.'

'I heard you. What do you want?'

'I want to know how you are.'

'I'm all right, John.'

'Piers.'

'All right, Piers. It's awfully silly to change your name at your age.'

'It's always been Piers.'

2

'John to me. This call's costing you a lot. What do you want?'

'Are you coming to London?'

'Don't know.'

'Do you good to have a change.'

'I'm going to have one.'

'Going somewhere nice?

'I can't hear you.'

'Get the phone mended.'

'What?' She waved to Gus.

'Heard from the children?'

'Yes, no, fairly lately.'

'Matilda.'

'Yes?'

'Get the phone mended, it's dangerous, you might need it urgently.'

'Mind own biz.'

'What?'

'Goodbye, John.'

'Piers.'

'All right, Piers.' She replaced the receiver, lifted the bucket out of the sink and sloshed water over the table stained by similar previous events. The wet wood steamed in the sun.

'Like some maize?' She stood looking down at Gus. 'Come on then.' Gus followed her while she fetched the maize. She threw a little on the grass. The gander ignored it.

'Gus, you must eat.' She sat down and the bird climbed onto her lap. 'Eat, you fool.' She held the bowl. Gus ate a little, pushing the corn about with his beak while she stroked him, pressing her hand along his back then curving it round his breast. 'You must keep up your strength for all those pretty ladies. You will like them, you know you will.

You wont't be lonely with them.'

Gus got off her lap to stroll about cropping grass before coming back to stand behind her, leaning his neck over her shoulder, twisting it to peer up into her eyes.

Matilda sat looking down the valley, tired, trying to think whether there was anything left undone.

The house was scrubbed, polished, hoovered, the beds made up with the best linen. Silver, brass and copper shining. Stores in the cupboards and larder. Bills paid, desk tidy, list of the whereabouts of people and things they would need all written, every spider captured and put outside before its web was destroyed. All done. Only the picnic basket and bathing things to get now. And Gus.

'Such a betrayal. I can't help it, Gus. Geese can live to be thirty or more. I can't wait. You will be all right.'

A landrover drove up the lane, stopped by the gate. A man got out. Matilda stood. Gus honked angrily, the rims of his eyes showing red. Matilda shook hands while Gus hissed and threatened the man's ankles, his neck stretched out, head low.

'Good afternoon. He's a fine bird. I brought a sack.'

'Oh yes, you said. You said that would be the best way. Would you like a drink?'

'No thank you, I'd better not. If I get this fellow loaded up I'll be on my way, then he'll have time to get to know his harem before dark.'

'They won't hurt him?'

'No, no, no, a gander rules his geese. They haven't heard of women's lib.'

'He rules me –' The man nodded, unsmiling, looking down at Gus.

'Your other gander?'

She glanced away. 'A fox got him. I think I told you.'

'Yes, of course you did.'

4

'Gus, don't!' The man sidestepped as Gus pecked his calf. 'I'm so sorry.'

'That's all right. Thick trousers. I keep them all shut up at night now. He'll be safe.'

'He's always slept in the scullery.'

'Well yes, but he will get used to his shed, stable actually, stone floors, geese are messy birds. I hose them down, the stables.'

'I slosh water over the scullery floor, it's got a drain in the middle, a sort of grating.' What a stupid conversation. Couldn't he get on with it and go? 'Shall we get him into the sack?'

'Okay. You pick him up as you know him, put him in. That's right. I'll tie this round his neck so that he can't hurt himself. Ouch! That was sharp.'

'He's frightened.'

'Yes, of course. There we are. I'll take him now, he'll be all right, don't worry. Soon he'll be with his harem. Six of them.'

The man carried Gus to the landrover, put him over the tailboard. Gus did not stop honking as the man drove away.

'Fucking harem. I must be mad.' Matilda went indoors, poured herself a stiff whisky, switched on the radio for the weather report. High pressure continuing over the Atlantic, very hot, very dry.

The telephone began to peal again. Matilda went up to the instrument and pulled off a strip of cellophane, letting it ring until it tired. Now the picnic. She took a basket and put in butter, rolls, a slab of rather runny Brie, some peaches, a knife, a corkscrew, a bottle of Beaujolais.

'Right,' she said out loud. 'Right, I'm ready then.' A final look round the house, appallingly clean, strange. She shut the windows and the front door, picked up the basket.

A spider of vast size scurried in at the kitchen door across the floor and under the dresser. 'You win.' Matilda stepped out carrying the basket, locked the door, put the key under the bootscraper where only a fool would leave it for any fool to find. Into the garage, into the car, start it up, drive off. 'If you exist keep an eye on Gus. See that he is all right. Please.' Matilda prayed without faith as she drove fast down the lane which led to the main road. A god with wings was a credible God but not in the guise of a man driving a landrover. Matilda trod hard on the accelerator. The noise of the engine failed to drown the sound in her mind of betrayed honking.

In the empty house the telephone rang to an audience of one spider.

2

She switched on the car radio to drown the sound in her mind. I will not think of it. I will suppress it, forget it, bury it as I have done with other things all my life. Go away Gus, go away. She turned up the sound.

For many days now she had carried her transistor about the house and listened as she scrubbed, swept, hoovered, polished, dusted. As she worked she had heard Mozart, Beethoven, Bach and Brahms, pop and pop and pop, the news. Rumours of war, violence, here, there and everywhere, only it isn't war now, she had thought, it is Guerillas, often pronounced Gorillas, who bomb, shoot or kidnap, hijack planes and trains. An active lot these Guerillas/Gorillas, forever in the news, by no means unsympathetic, full of ideals and always on the hour every hour between quiz games or music, *Woman's Hour, Listen with Mother,* the news and weather imperceptibly changing as the days passed and she startled spiders, catching them in a tumbler, putting them out of doors before destroying their webs. The weather hot, continuing hot, traffic jams on the motorways, the French industrialist kidnapped from his home, the vanished bride on her honeymoon – perhaps she had realized her error, fled – and the Matricide. The police hunt for the Matricide and the Vanished Bride followed her upstairs and down as she dusted and swept, lifting the transistor from one piece of furniture to the next.

She had considered matricide. Why was killing your mother so special? Worse than killing your wife? Your child? Worse than being a Guerilla/Gorilla? He looked quite nice in the photo they showed on the box. Six foot two, they said, brown eyes, fair hair, large nose, speaks with an educated accent. One would hope so from a person who had weathered Winchester, Cambridge and the Sorbonne. One would hope so but just as able to kill his mother as the Guerillas were able to blow people up, shoot them down. A lot of Guerillas had also been to the Sorbonne or Harvard or Oxbridge.

Matilda had thought, as she put clean sheets on the beds, that anyone with any gumption was capable of anything if brave or annoyed enough. She, when she had a mother, had often longed to kill her to stop the incessant prying and interfering, the possessiveness. Poor Matricide she had thought vaguely, her mind turning to her own children. Did they? Would they? They would like to, she decided, noticing that there was now a talk on roses purring out of the radio. They would like to but they were not among the brave – possibly Claud. Yes, Claud –

He had, this Matricide, killed his mother with a tea-tray. Marvellous! A heavy silver tea-tray. How nice to be rich. Had he when a child toboganned down the stairs on a tea-tray? Perhaps people who went to these posh educational establishments didn't.

The spiders were a great worry. Old cottages were full of spiders of all sizes, some as large as a mouse when they scurried across the floor at night, others tiny, found in the mornings in the bath with wistful legs. Anyway, it being August and the Silly Season, the media babbled on about the Matricide every day, though it was true not quite so much latterly, rather favouring the Bride. He had not been seen since he left his mother's house after banging her on the head with the tray, not been seen so not been caught.

'Makes the police look silly,' Matilda had said to Gus feeding him his midday mush. 'Makes the police look idiotic, doesn't it?' Gus had made his throttling noises and Matilda had gone back to sweeping away her house's character. 'Dirt of ages,' she had hummed to a religious programme. 'Dirt of ages made by me! Oh, how filthy I do be.' Well, it was all clean and tidy now, Matilda thought, as she drove, and although it's latish, not sunset yet. Not quite yet, time enough for my picnic. I have tidied myself out of my house with the spiders. I betrayed Gus. Now I can have my picnic in peace, delicious Brie and Beaujolais unbothered by God in trousers. Petrol. It would be stupid to run out of petrol. She drew in at a garage and waited. No attendant came.

'It's self-service,' a man called to her, easing himself into the driving seat of his car and adjusting the safety belt across his stomach.

'Oh hell!' Matilda felt shame. 'Bloody hell!' She got out of the car flushing with hate.

'Excuse me, could you – I can never manage, would you fill her up for me, please?'

The man there to take cash, give change, watch that there was no hanky panky came slowly out of his glass box. He exuded contempt, the chauvinist swine.

'How many?'

'Fill her up, please.' Matilda waited by the glass box watching the man jiggle with the petrol pump, push the nozzle roughly into the tank, stand idly as the liquid gurgled in. Sexy in a dreary way, she thought. Inside the glass box the man's radio was playing. 'Here is the news.' She listened to the weather, still fine and hot. The Prime Minister – the Common Market – the airport strike –

the bomb alert – the hijack in Italy – the kidnapping in France – the five sightings of the Matricide seen in Los Angeles, Hong Kong, Bermondsey, Brighton and Kampala. High pressure over the Atlantic would continue for some days –

'Any news?' The man came back.

'Only the usual stuff. What do I owe you?'

The man named the price. Matilda paid exactly counting out the change, which seemed to irritate the man.

'Sorry. I thought it would help.'

'Ah, you remind me of my mother, she's pernickety too.'

Matilda felt insulted. There was something bourgeois about being pernickety.

'Do you want to murder her?'

'Sometimes.' The man laughed. 'Only sometimes.' He was counting the money. 'Guess he did away with himself. Here, you gave me 10p too much. Got remorse poor sod.'

'Oh, sorry.'

'Your loss not mine.'

'Not quite as pernickety as you thought.'

'No.' The man grinned. 'Did they say what ransom those French kidnappers are asking?'

'I didn't hear. I don't think it said. Why?'

'Good way to make a packet.'

'Yes, I suppose so. Well, goodbye. Thank you.' Matilda got back into her car, leaving the safety straps unused. They hung dusty and twisted. She was afraid of them, afraid of being tied down, tied in. She checked that her picnic basket and bag were safe – bathing suit, lipstick, comb, pills for hayfever, pills.

'The Pillage'. Rather a bad pun but it had been funny in the context he had used it in. 'Now then,' Matilda muttered, starting the engine, 'don't think of *him*, don't think of Stub and don't think of Prissy, think of anything else, Gus, no, not Gus. That fat man tying himself in so carefully. Did he feel loved and wanted? For crying out loud, how could he be wanted, so fat and ugly?' She drove fast but carefully, not wanting an accident. The radio was playing pop. She turned it off and began to sing:

'Pop, pop, poppity pop
They all pop in and
They all pop out
Pop is the name of the girl inside
She sells the ginger pop you see!'

Why had her grandmother told her not to sing it? Was it vulgar or was there some hidden indecent Edwardian meaning? What silly things she remembered from child-hood. She went on singing, 'Pop,pop, poppity pop. Must pay attention here, not miss the turning' – which led by devious lanes to the cliffs from where she would walk to the beach.

'They all pop in and –' here was the turning, a lot of cars waiting to get out onto the main road, people hot and sunburned, tired after too long a day on the beach, on their way home to supper, tea or the pub.

As she swung the car into the lane she caught the eyes of a holiday dog hanging his head out of a car window.

'They all pop out
Pop is the name of the girl inside
She sells the ginger *pop* you see!'

Matilda didn't want to think about dogs. Suddenly she realized why her grandmother did not like her to sing the ditty. Miss Renouff, blue eyes and shingled hair, had

11

taught it to her. Grandpa had cast an appraising eye in that directions. All dead now of course. All popping over for that lot.

The lane twisting between tall banks led to the cliffs. She parked the car in the cliff car park, took out her picnic basket, swung her bag over her shoulder, locked the car.

All round her families with children were packing into their cars, getting ready to leave. Matilda picked her way past waste paper, lolly sticks, torn cellophane and remains of picnics, tipped – but not into the wire baskets provided. She wondered whether to pause, collect a few Coca Cola tins and beer cans and put them into the basket, but the jibe 'pernickety' still rankled. She kicked a can with her espadrille and watched it merrily roll.

All the way along the cliff path she met weary holiday-makers returning.

'Pop, pop, poppity pop, I shall have the beach to myself,' she hummed, strolling neither fast nor slow, carrying the basket with the Brie, the rolls, the peaches and the Beaujolais swinging along downwards, twisting and turning down from the top of the tall granite cliffs to the beach and the sea sighing gently over the sand to stroke the line of pebbles until they rattled. The tide was up, would soon turn and drag itself out across the sand leaving it clean and smooth for her feet.

Matilda paused at the bottom of the cliff path. Three lots of people were getting ready for the long climb up. One group was having a last swim. Matilda had seen them before, knew their routine. They would soon be gone. She walked along the stones enjoying her rope soles. At the far end of the beach she stopped by the favourite rock. Here she would sit in the sun and wait. She put the basket in the shade and undressed, pulling on the bathing suit, deciding to swim before the picnic. It was early yet. It would be light for a long time.

Out to sea a boat sailed slowly across the bay. She could hear the voices of the people on board and a dog barking. The boat had a blue sail.

Not wanting to wet her hair she walked into the sea and swam slowly, breast stroke, no effort, her body received by the wonderfully warm sea. Here so often they had swum, paddling out slowly and chatting with the same closeness as the closeness of bed but unleavened by sex. Matilda, swimming gently, savoured the memory of long swims, the easy talk, the intimacy, remembering conversations wrapped in water, their heads close, bodies floating. A long way out she turned to look at the cliffs which were so like Sounion.

Down the zigzag track came a party of people, young, lithe, noisy. They laughed and talked among themselves. They carried armfuls of rugs, carrier bags, spare sweaters. In jeans and T-shirts they were beautiful and young. Two girls danced down the track swinging a bottle of wine in each hand. Their voices carried across the water.

'Bobby and Vanessa collect the driftwood. We'll get the fire for the barbecue going while you swim.'

'Super, it's so warm we can sleep down here.'

'Super, super.'

'I shan't sleep, I shall watch the moon. Super.'

'I shall watch Vanessa.'

'Super.'

'Let's swim naked.'

'Super.'

'Not yet, there's someone in the water.'

'Oh, bugger, is there?'

'Yes, but she'll soon be gone.'

'Oh yes. Oh, isn't it super.'

Cold, sick with disappointment Matilda swam for the

13

shore, trusting her arms through the unwelcome sea no longer hers.

Slowly, bitterly she dried herself. The barbecue party had settled fifty yards away. Fifty yards and the beach was half a mile long.

'I'd meant to use that flat rock she's on as a table but she's on it. It's got useful dips which hold the food. I mix the salad in one of them.'

'She'll be gone soon, don't worry. It's a super rock, just the job, super.'

Matilda slowly rubbed her legs, pushing the towel down to her ankles, up, then down again.

'I thought we'd have it to ourselves, it's always empty at this time, everyone goes home,' the boy arranging the fire grumbled.

'We will. It's super. She wont't be long, she's drying herself, look.'

Matilda rubbed her arms, looking out to sea where the boat with the dog on board sailed slowly, the sail turning purple. The barbecue party moved continuously, bringing driftwood, fidgeting, throwing their long young limbs about. Their inane voices carried in the clear air.

'Shall we swim now or later?'

'I want to swim naked.'

'Super! Why not?'

'Well –'

'She'd go more quickly if we stripped.'

'Super. Do strip Bobby – go on.'

Matilda pulled off her bathing suit and dried herself standing on the hot rock, baked all day in the sun.

'Christ! She's stripped. D'you think she heard us?'

'No, of course not. She's old, she can't have.'

'Old people aren't necessarily deaf.' The girl called Vanessa spoke crisply.

14

'Oh Vanessa, you are so witty, why don't you strip?'

'I'm not beautiful enough or old enough not to care.'

She meant me to hear that, Matilda thought, sitting down on the warm rock. That girl would murder her mother without hesitation if she thought she wouldn't be caught. There's no passion in that voice. I bet the Matricide has passion.

'I want that flat rock as a table. I had it all planned.' The voice held a whining note.

'She'll be gone soon.'

'Yes, poor old bird.'

Feeling the rock warm on her bottom Matilda reached for her shirt thinking. 'Yes, I'll be gone soon, you despoilers of my beach.'

Pulling her shirt on and buttoning it slowly she suddenly wept, remembering this rock with – well, with him her love, he lying back, his hips in one of the hollows, his crane-like legs stretched long and thin towards the sea, grey hair falling back onto the rock, the colour of the granite and the hair merging. Or of watching him stepping slowly along the edge of the water like a heron, unhurried, thoughtful, beaky nose, grey hair, elongated legs, flapping his arms to tease Stub who barked to attract his attention, to make him play, and the children tailing heel and toe along the sand, pressing in toes to form a pattern with Stub's paw marks, Stub who dearly loved swimming and even once with Gus who had become so emotional he'd messed all over the rock and the car going home. Matilda let herself pee allowing the hot urine to flow into a dip in the rock. She stood up, dried between her legs, pulled on her jeans, zipped them.

'She isn't wearing knickers,' a girl's voice hissed. 'Fancy, an old person like that!'

Matilda picked up her bag and slung it over her

shoulder. She remembered she had a sweater in the car and was glad. She took up her basket feeling the weight of the Beaujolais. It would be heavier by the time she got back to the car park.

'Goodnight – there's your table.' she said, moving off away from the barbecue party and the rock gently steaming.

'Oh. Goodnight. Thanks. Super.'

'Have a good time.'

'Thanks, we will.'

'Do you think she was listening to us?'

'Of course she was, the old bitch.'

Matilda grinned, walking barefoot along the sand.

3

A long haul up the goat track. That voice – 'one more twist, one more turn – nearly there, nearly there now.' Voices linger in the mind long after the face blurs. The muscles of her thighs hurt as they always did. Her breath came short, her heart beat. A matter of honour not to stop, however slow one went, until the top. She remembered another very steep path at Le Brusc down to the pebbles in the cove, no sand there, and the hair-raising climb at Pedney Founder where they hauled themselves up clutching at clumps of thrift.

What madness to bring Gus here. Still, he had adored the sea even if he had hissed and honked all the way up the cliff. Stub had barked running ahead and then run back to encourage them. The top at last. Matilda set down the heavy basket, dropped her bag and sat gasping, her legs trembling. Away on the horizon the boat sailed almost out of sight, below on the beach the young people had the fire going, the food laid on the flat rock. Two girls were swimming in water as clear here as in Greece, their hair streaming behind them. They were naked. Their distant voices cried 'Super! Oh, it's super!' Super for some. Would he lay the salad on the rock and would a girl cry, 'Oh Bobby, what a super salad dressing. What did you put in it? I've never tasted anything like it, it's super.'

Her heart steadied, her breathing slowed. Matilda looked at the view. She was humming a Brandenburg Concerto now. Away to the west were other beaches but all with easy access and car parks. What to do?

Back to the car.

She shouldered her bag, picked up the basket, walked along the cliff, strolling slowly. The was heaps of time. The tide must go out, pause, and come in again. She had to fill in time. That was all. A little more waiting didn't matter. The car smelt of hot metal. Matilda opened the windows, started the engine and drove slowly to the town down the steep streets to the harbour car park. With difficulty she found a place. She locked the picnic basket in the car and set off to wander round.

The town wore its summer face: shops with souvenirs, striped awnings, clusters of buckets, spades, beach balls, racks of pictures postcards, the harbour full, every mooring filled. Now was the time for yachtsmen to come ashore, drink long, talk loudly in the pubs, boring on in yard-arm voices. Matilda strolled slowly among the people, observing the fat women in tight trousers or bikinis. They did not seem to mind their bulges burned red by the sun. Nor did the men, their shorts held up by tight belts biting into beer stomachs, mind their shape.

The fat and middle-aged were predominant by the harbour, wandering along with peeling noses, thighs sore from rubbing together. She turned up the main street, glancing in at the shop windows. A group of people stood staring at a television shop. The colour sets were showing the news on BBC and ITV.

'I wonder what he's saying?' A small child holding his mother's hand tugged. 'Come on Mum, I'm tired.'

'Just a minute love, let's see the news.'

'You can't hear it –'

'I like that girl announcer, she's lovely.'

'I like the man best.'

'Oh look dad, that must be the Matricide.' A teenage

girl in shorts pointed. 'He doesn't look like a murderer.'

'Murdered his mother, a right bastard.'

'Oh Mum, I'm tired. Can't we go home?'

'Wait a minute. There may be a new photo.'

'They've shown the same photo ever since he did it. You'd think a bloke like that would have lots of photos done.'

'I like the way she does her hair. D'you think that way would suit me, Mum?' the girl questioned.

'Ask your Dad, dear.'

'I'm tired,' whined the small boy.

'I expect with all that money he's had a nose job done by now.'

'A nose job?'

'Well anyone would recognize that great hooter.'

'Oh.' Mum sounded pleased with the idea. 'You're clever, Dad.' Dad looked gratified.

'Big hooter like that stands out a mile, don't it? So he has a nose job sharpish. That's what I read in the paper anyway, either a nose job or he's done away with himself.'

'If he had any decent feelings he'd have done that.'

'Oh Mum, I'm tired – '

'Come on, son, I'll give you a ride.' The father hoisted the little boy onto his shoulder. 'Up you go!'

'Oh look, look, they're shooting! Wait a minute, wait.' The child craned down from his father's shoulders to watch a scence of violence, bodies falling, ragged men lying legs astraddle firing guns. 'Oh look, that one's dead.' He sounded joyful. 'Look at the blood.'

'So's the Matricide's Ma.' The father started up the street carrying the boy who looked back towards the silent television, craning his neck to see death happening.

'D'you think our Mr Antoine could do my hair like that, Mum?' the girl urged.

'Don't see why not, dear. You ask him when we get home. He'll charge, mind.'

'Oh I don't mind.'

Matilda stood idly watching the man talking and pointing to the weather chart which had circles all over it in which were written 'High'. Up the street she heard the husband say to his wife, 'Bring back hanging, that's what they ought to do.'

'Hanging isn't good enough, Dad.'

'Got to catch him first, haven't they? Shouldn't be difficult with that great hooter.'

Matilda turned back down the street remembering a pub which was relatively quiet. She would sit there and rest.

At a corner shop she bought a paper and strolled along entertaining speculations of that tired child grown up murdering his dreary mother at some future date. Why not? Children like that, perfectly commonplace children, became Guerillas and shot people.

Finding the pub with an unoccupied seat outside she ordered a whisky, sat down to wait and read her paper.

The paper was not one she was used to. She read an article on fashion, another on diet, an account of a footballer's divorce, several accounts of rail, motor and plane crashes, a new earth tremor in Guatemala. On the last page but one the usual photograph of the Matricide, now supposed to have reached Japan. He did not, Matilda thought, seem to have such a very huge nose, nothing out of the ordinary, not much larger than Tom's. The photograph could be anybody. She sipped her whisky, looked at her watch. Still early. A lot of people about, a lot of time to creep by.

Poor man. She looked at the photograph. The country was full of large noses, large cocks too. 'My God, I feel tired,' Matilda muttered, not even hungry, too tired to eat. What frightful waste of Brie. Mustn't get drunk, she thought, but one more whisky won't hurt me.

She took her empty glass to the bar. As she waited to be served she observed the people sitting round the tables or standing talking. She listened to the topics of conversation. A group of three men and a pretty girl were discussing a couple called Jeffrey and Sally. Sally had upped and left Jeffrey and gone to Ibiza with Johnnie, whose wife Vanessa had moved in with Chris.

'Which Vanessa?' asked one of the men.

'The dark one, you know her, the one they call the Dark Filly.'

Everybody laughed and chorused, 'Oh, that Vanessa,' understandingly.

'But what about Sally when she comes back?'

'She hasn't a leg to stand on. She's been having it off with Charles for a year, everybody knows that.'

'But Chris doesn't.'

'No, Chris doesn't.'

'They only mind about the money. There aren't any kids.'

Gossip, thought Matilda, paying for her whisky, never varied much. She edged back to the door, noting three conversations about sailing, two about cars, another husband and wife complex. Nobody, she thought as she regained her place outside, was talking about plane, train or car crashes, terrorists, Guerillas or Earthquakes. They were so saturated with horrors they were immune to catastrophe.

Her watch said 8.30. Time creeping on. She put her whisky on the table, not wanting it now, and sat with her legs stretched out watching the passers-by.

On the whole, she reflected, the human race was unbeautiful although some of the girls in long skirts, were lovely as they passed, holding their lovers' hands, looking up into the ordinary faces of their men who, whether their noses were large, snub or crooked, were transformed by the girls' love to beauty. Matilda remembered Gus's beak and sighed. 'A great hooter.' She wondered how he was faring among the strange geese and took a sorrowful sip of whisky.

Stub's nose had been long, sad, black, Prissy's a tender pink. Matilda allowed her thoughts a brief recollection of those companions, very brief, for to think of Stub and Prissy made her think of Tom. There, the thought was there. Tom, Tom, Tom, she said in her mind. Tom, Stub, Prissy, all dead. She had said it to herself. Dead, dead, dead, those three and Gus she had betrayed. Matilda had another sip of whisky and looked down towards the harbour.

I am a great betrayer, she thought. That is my sin. I am not a sticker. I betray from laziness, fear and lack of interest.

Beyond the harbour the sea was growing dark, on board the boats were lights and laughter. The sailors had returned from the pubs to cook their suppers.

Matilda stood up, leaving her whisky unfinished, pulled her bag over her shoulder. Inside the bar the musak was turned up and with it rose the decibels of conversation as she started down the street. The voices cried, 'Ignition', 'It's only the money!', 'If we altered the spinnaker', 'I really think a Jag is best never mind the Japanese'. Matilda went down to the harbour.

She reached the bridge where the river joined the sea. Peering over the parapet she could see that the tide was up, about to turn. A feeling of intense excitement almost made her cry out. She gripped the parapet, stared down at the water, secret, black; soon with the tide running out there would be ripples, as sweet flowed into salt to be drawn out to sea, swing west with the current far beyond the cliffs, round the bay a long way out under the sickle moon.

Suddenly she felt furiously hungry.

She looked at her watch, luminous in the dark. Too late. She felt cheated.

'No Brie, no rolls, no Beaujolais. Damn' muttered Matilda, 'Damn and blast!'

She only realized she had spoken aloud when a man, also leaning over the parapet, shifted his feet. She felt fury. What business had he here, how dare he invade her privacy?

Would he go away? He must. There was nothing to keep him here unless, she thought with a sinking heart, he has a tryst. He is meeting his girl. Curse him, she thought. Curse him and his girl. She looked at him sidelong, not turning her head. He looked dreadfully tired. He couldn't be meeting a girl as tired as that. He leant on his elbows, his face in his hands, obviously exhausted. A car passed, driving slowly across the bridge, heading away to the country beyond the town. The man did not move or look up. Perhaps he was drunk. Matilda risked a quick glance. Tall but slumped with depression.

Oh God! Matilda thought to herself, he's going to throw himself over! The selfish brute, he bloody well mustn't. I shall just stay until he goes. She willed him to move, to leave, to push off.

A boy and girl came walking so closely entwined they nearly tripped each other up. They stopped in the middle of the road to kiss, their bodies clenched. Matilda, exasperated, willed them to move on but they continued kissing.

The man paid no attention, leaning lost in thought on the parapet.

Perhaps he's drugged, Matilda thought.

A police car came crawling slowly. The driver gave a little toot. The boy and girl looked up, faces dazed with love.

'Oh piss off,' called the girl, moving to one side out of the boy's arms. 'Piss off,' she yelled.

The constable beside the driver wound down his window. 'Now then Brenda, now then –'

'Piss off.'

'I'll tell your dad,' called the constable. The driver laughed.

The boy lifted two fingers. 'Come on,' he said to the girl. 'Bloody fuzz.'

'Fucking public here. Come on then, Eddy.' The girl retwined herself round the boy. They moved awkwardly away.

Matilda's heart beat in heavy thumps. She moved along the parapet closer to the man. Two yards from him she said in a low voice, apologetic:

'I'm dreadfully sorry but I saw your face in the lights of the police car.'

'Yes?'

'They'll be coming back.'

'I daresay they will.'

'Well, I recognized you –'

'Yes.'

'Are you going to throw yourself over?'

'It had occurred to me.'

'Well, are you or aren't you?'

'I haven't made up my mind.'

'Oh.'

'I was undecided.'

'Well, I wasn't. I'm just waiting for the tide to be right. You are rather – '

24

'De trop?'

'Yes.'

The Matricide laughed, leaning against the parapet. 'So sorry.' He choked with laughter. 'So sorry to be in your way. I'll move if you like.'

'Put your arm round me. The police car's coming back. Quick.' The Matricide put his arm round her shoulders.

'Round my waist, you fool. My hair is white but it looks fair in this light.' Matilda pressed her face against him. 'I look young in the dark.'

The police car crawled by, the constable talking on the car radio. 'No, nothing Sarge. Willco. Roger. Out.'

'They do dearly love their radio.' He bent back a little.

'You haven't shaved.'

'Haven't since –'

'Well, I think that's silly. The first thing they expect is for you to grow a beard and have plastic surgery to your nose.'

'D'you realize I killed my mother?' he said gently.

'Of course. Lots of people long to. You just did it.'

'Oh.'

'Oh hell!' exclaimed Matilda. 'I've missed the tide. Damn and blast!'

'I *am* sorry.' Sarcastic.

'Well it's too late. I can't now. You have to be exact about these things,' she said angrily.

'If you'd jumped –'

'Yes?'

'I would have tried to save you.'

'How ridiculous. Interfering.'

'You saved me just now.'

'That's instinctive.'

'What now? I'm in your hands. Hadn't you better take me to the police?'

'If that's what you want you can go by yourself. Are you hungry?'

'Starving.'

'Come on then, I've got some Brie in the car – I was going to picnic first. Brie and a bottle of Beaujolias.'

'Sounds tempting.'

'Put your arm round me and your head against mine.'

'I'm rather too tall.'

'Don't make difficulties, it isn't far.' They walked in a loverly way to the car park.

4

Matilda unlocked the car. 'Get in,' she said. 'I'll get the food.' She reached for the basket on the back seat. 'Could you uncork this?' She handed him the bottle and corkscrew.

'I think so.' In the dark he fumbled, holding the bottle between his knees. Matilda buttered a roll and spread the Brie. The cork popped.

'Go ahead and drink. I haven't a glass. I wasn't bothering for myself –'

'But – '

'Go on, take a swig. I'm all right, I've been drinking whisky, waiting for the tide to turn, for it to get dark.'

He drank, tipping up the bottle. Matilda watched his profile. Not such a very large nose after all.

'The way the papers write about your nose you might be Pinocchio.'

'That was marvellous.' He handed Matilda the bottle and took the roll. 'Thank you.'

Matilda watched him eat. After cramming in half a roll he ate slowly.

'There's some salad and a peach. Cyrano de Bergerac too.'

'Really?' He sounded amused.

'Yes, really.'

'What's your name?'

'Matilda Poliport.'

'Married?'

'Widow.'

'Sorry – sad.'

'One gets used to it. No, that's not true, one never does.'

'My name is Hugh Warner.'

'I'm glad to know it. I must have heard or read it but for two weeks you've just been the Matricide on the radio and television. Have another roll? Your photo's in all the papers.'

'Thank you.' He took another roll. 'That your dog? Surely you were not going to leave her behind?'

Matilda looked down. Looking into the car a canine face, paws just reaching the car window.

'Not mine. I have no dog.'

'She looks dreadfully hungry.' He held out half his roll. The dog snapped at it, gulped, retreated a few paces.

'Now you've done it.'

'Done what?'

'Got yourself a dog. Can't you see she's lost? Look how thin she is. If you looked at her paws you'd see they are sore. That's a lost dog.'

'We can take it to the police when you take me.'

'I'm not taking you, you can manage by yourself.'

'Look pretty silly if I walk in and say "Hi, Constable, I'm the Matricide and here's a lost dog, will you arrest us."'

They began to laugh quietly at first then in great whoops. Tears trickled down Matilda's cheeks. She watched him feed the last roll to the dog, bit by bit, luring her into the car until she sat on his knee and licked his face.

'Look at her paws. Poor little thing, oh poor little thing.' The dog licked Matilda's face also.

'Well?'

'Well?'

'I'm still frightfully hungry. Will the police feed me, d'you think?'

'Not for hours. They ask questions first.'

'Oh dear,' he sighed, stroking the dog, tipping up the bottle for another drink. 'That was delicious.'

'Any left for me?'

He handed her the bottle. She drank, tipping it up three quarters empty, her eyes looking over to the black water in the harbour reflecting the lights from the town. She finished the bottle and reached back to put it in the basket.

'Here's a peach.' He ate. The dog watched him.

'You wouldn't like fruit.' His hand fondled the dog's tatty ears. 'She's a frightful mongrel,' his voice tender.

Matilda wiped her face with her handkerchief, tidied up the remains of the picnic. 'She's lost and unwanted. I think we can skip the police.'

'Ah. You are soft.'

'Absolutely –' Matilda began to speak then stopped, remembering Gus. 'No, I'm not soft. I don't know what I am. I hate. I hate. I'm full of it.'

'Pretty soft sort of hate.'

'It would be difficult to resist, just look at her.' The dog now lolled between them, her body relaxed, sore paws hanging down, small black eyes moving from one face to the other.

Matilda tried to think. She had failed to carry out the planned picnic. 'I've missed the tide,' she mewed.

'You can try tomorrow.'

'Not with this dog and –'

'And?'

'All that planning gone to waste.'

'Carefully worked out, was it?'

'Yes.'

'So sorry.'

'No good being sorry,' Matilda said brisky. 'No good us just sitting here.' She switched on the engine. 'I daresay you'd like a bath.'

'A bath would be thrilling. They have them in the nick I understand.'

Matilda switched on the headlights, drove out of the car park up through the town. Her passenger did not speak.

On the outkirts of the town Matilda saw a corner shop still open. She stopped the car. 'Won't be a minute.' She got out, went into the shop and bought several large cans of dog food, two pints of milk, a carton of eggs. 'When I get back to the car he will be gone,' she thought. 'Perhaps he will take the dog. It would be an intelligent thing to do; nobody is looking for a man with a dog. If he's gone I shall go straight back to the cliffs and whether that barbecue is going on or not, I shall swallow my pills and swim out, though washed down with milk isn't as fine as washed down with Beaujolais, but if I swim fast the pills will work on their own. My plan will work after all.'

She took the carrier bag back to the car. Hugh Warner was fast asleep holding the dog in his arms. Matilda restarted the car. She sensed her passenger was awake though he did not speak.

They drove out of the town past the bus station, the railway station and the police station. Matilda grinned to herself momentarily, forgetting her resolution.

'It's about ten miles.'

'I see.'

'You can have a bath and go to bed or you can go to bed and have a bath in the morning. There's food in the house.'

'I'd love a bath.'

'Okay.'

'If you have a razor?'

'Yes.'

'A bath and a shave, how civilized. My feet are sore like Miss here. What shall you call her?'

'Folly,' said Matilda.

'A very good name.'

They drove along the main road. When she reached the turning leading to the hills she said: 'I live in an isolated cottage. It is not overlooked. I am a solitary person, people do not often come. You will be as safe as it is possible to be.'

'You are very kind.'

'I hope you appreciate my tact in not asking you why you killed your mother.'

'I do, immensely.'

'Good.'

'And I hope you will also appreciate my tact in not asking you why you had planned your suicide.'

'Oh I do, I do.' Matilda began to laugh again. Sitting on Hugh Warner's lap, Folly wagged her tail. Her problem at least was solved.

5

The back door key was under the bootscraper where she had left it. Matilda opened the door and, switching on the light, walked in.

'What a spotless kitchen.' Hugh, carrying the bag of food, followed with Folly at his heels.

'It's rather untidy usually.' She felt the Rayburn which was still warm, opened its door. In the fire box embers glowed. 'I expected it to be out.' She threw in sticks and a few larger pieces of wood, opened the damper. The fire flared and she put on coke. 'Could you feed Folly? Don't give her too much. The tin opener's on the wall.'

Hugh opened a tin. 'Is there a dog bowl?'

'There on the shelf.' Matilda handed him Stub's bowl. 'I bet she's thirsty.' She filled the water bowl and watched the dog drink while the man spooned out food. 'That's enough. Too much will make her sick.'

They watched the dog eat. Matilda sighed and muttered.

'What did you say?'

'I said "another hostage to fortune" – I had just got free.'

He looked at her curiously.

'If you give her a run out at the back I'll get us some food. She may not be housetrained. It's a walled garden. She won't run away.'

'What about me?' He snapped his fingers for the dog.

'You needn't run any more tonight. You can eat and sleep.'

He went out with the dog.

Matilda went upstairs to switch on the immersion heater and turn down the bed in the spare room. She opened the window and leaned out. In the oak tree up the lane an owl screeched. There was no other sound but the stream trickling over its stony bed. She felt terribly hungry. In her bedroom she opened windows and let in the warm night. The house caught its breath and came to life.

In the kitchen the man sat slumped in the beechwood chair, the dog at his feet, nose straining towards the stove. He said: 'She's a good little dog, your Folly.' The dog pricked her ears but looked at neither of them.

'She's yours, not mine. I'll get something to eat. Could you manage an omelette?'

'Lovely.'

'Salad?'

'Yes please.'

'You'll find wine in the larder. The corkscrew's in that drawer.' Matilda took a torch from the dresser and went out into the garden, shining it along the rows of vegetables, choosing a lettuce.

The sky was a mass of stars, windless. Were Vanessa and Bobby still on the beach? Had the barbecue been a success? The torch focussed on a toad crawling slowly across the brick path, his eyes golden. With concentration he pulled first one long back leg up then the other. He knew his destination.

She laid the table, broke eggs, made a salad, found biscuits and butter, poured the wine, cut bread.

'It's a bit cold.'

'It doesn't matter.'

The eggs sizzled and spluttered in the pan. She cut the omelette in half and tipped it onto their plates.

They ate in silence. Matilda felt strength return slowly. Their plates empty, they sat looking at each other across the table, sizing one another up.

Matilda saw a man of thirty-five, she knew his age from the radio. Large nose, large mouth, light brown hair, not fair as the papers said, brown eyes, thick eyebrows, stubbled face drawn with fatigue, good teeth, a few definite lines.

Hugh saw a woman in her fifties, blue eyes, very white hair, arched nose, good teeth, slightly runaway chin, sensual mouth.

'You don't look like a Major.'

'They confused me with my brother; he is a Major. I expect he will be furious, bad for his image.'

'Is he fighting Guerillas?'

'He is actually. Why?'

'Such a lot of fighting. I don't approve.'

'Pacifist?'

'I just don't like violence.'

'I –'

'You hit your mother. It may have been justified.'

'What makes you think that?'

'The choice of weapon. A tea-tray. Really!' Matilda began to laugh. 'Oh dear, I'm drunk. So sorry. It's the anticlimax. I was worked up, was all prepared – I was ready.' Folly put her paws on Matilda's knees and buried her face in her crotch sniffing deeply, pressing her jaw against Matilda's thighs. She stroked the dog's head.

'Silky.'

Hugh Warner yawned.

'I'll show you where you sleep.' Matilda stood up. 'This way.'

He followed her upstairs.

'Here's your room, the loo, the bath. Sleep well.' She left

34

him abruptly. Folly followed her back to the kitchen.

Matilda poured the last of the wine and stood drinking it, trying to think. Her head was looping the loop. with tipsy care she cleared the table, washed up, put everything away, stoked the fire once more and tipped the ashes into the bin outside the back door. Followed by the dog she went upstairs, undressed and got into bed. Without hesitation the dog got up on the bed and settled, pressing into the small of her back. Matilda thought, I shall never sleep, I'm drunk, and fell asleep instantly, her mouth open, snoring.

Along the passage Hugh Warner soaked in a boiling bath, sat up and shaved, then ran in more hot water to soak again. He washed his hair, his hands, his feet, his whole exhausted body until finally, when the water cooled, he dried himself and crawled naked into the bed assigned him and lay listening to the night sounds.

A stream somewhere near.

Owls.

Traffic a long way off.

Snores. 'Down the passage my hostess snores.' Relaxed for the first time for weeks, he smiled. What folly. He turned on his side and slept.

Half an hour later Matilda sat up in bed screaming, soaked in sweat, trembling. Folly licked her face, wagging her tail.

'He's a murderer, a murderer, he murdered his mother.' Speaking this aloud made it true. She shivered, the sweaty nightdress cooling to clamminess on her body.

'Fuck!' She tore off the nightdress and sat hugging her knees.

'Poor little dog.' Matilda stroked her. 'You will be all right now.' She switched on her bedside light to look at the time. 'Three o'clock, soon be dawn.' She lay back, pulling the sheet round her neck. The dog settled again.

If my picnic had gone according to plan I should be floating by the lighthouse. Time from now on is borrowed. The thought pleased her. She noticed from the taste in her mouth that she had been snoring, got up, rinsed her mouth with cold water at the basin then went back to lie on her side, mouth shut, breathing through her nose. How conventional to wake up and scream, how strong her upbringing. The man must have had a reason to kill his mother. Louise would, Mark could, Anabel certainly. Claud. Not Claud. Something would make him laugh or more probably he would not bother.

Time was I would have killed mine, Matilda thought, only Tom came along. It's all in the mind, she thought drowsily. It is ridiculous to scream about it. Was I not brought up not to scream? Who am I to judge? I was going to kill tonight, suicide is murder.

Hugh Warner was too deeply asleep to hear Matilda's screams. Across the British Isles the police were alert for a man answering his description. At airports and channel ports travellers' passports were examined with care. At 4 a.m. a bored journalist in Cairo filed a message that a man answering Hugh's description had been seen heading south.

Only Gus, the betrayed, shifted restless, unable to settle among the geese, utterly at a loss, anxious, disorientated, lonely.

6

Matilda thought best while occupied. Now, kneading dough, her mind came alive.

She and Folly had come down early, Folly trotting into the garden while Matilda made coffee. It was still very hot. Through the open door she could hear the hum of insects, birds singing. Away up the hill a cow cried for the calf recently taken from her. Far off a shepherd was driving sheep – she could hear the harassed bleating, the barking dogs. Folly now sat in the doorway listening.

Matilda heated up the coffee and sat at the table while the dough in its basin rose in the warmth by the Rayburn. Upstairs her visitor slept, she supposed, though he could quite easily have gone on his way while she slept. She hoped he had gone, it would be the best thing. She did not wish to be involved. Sipping coffee Matilda thought, I do not wish to get involved. Then, to be truthful: I would like to be involved and as I am why not enjoy it.

She wore a blue cotton dress, an old friend. Her legs and feet were bare, her hair still damp from washing.

About now the boat crew, probably a mackerel fisherman's, should have caught sight of her body, fished her out to bring her ashore, sent for the police and the ambulance. Matilda frowned, trying to recollect whether drowned people sank for a few days then surfaced, or floated for a few days before sinking. Not knowing bothered her. Why had she not found out this simple fact?

She divided the floury dough into four, smacked the

loaves into four, pressed each with the back of a knife and put them in the oven. She would buy another bottle of Beaujolais, more butter, more Brie, another peach.

'I shall take you to the Lost Dogs Home.' Folly twitched her tail. 'But I shall have to wait for the tide to be right.' The dog wagged cheerfully. 'I do not want to grow fond of you.' The dog looked away. 'You should have gone with him. He picked you up. You are his, not mine.' Matilda listened to the silence of the cottage, certain that the man had gone. Not knowing whether the man was there or not, she felt in limbo, not wanting to readjust to living. She felt anguish choking her, cheated, for her mind had been prepared for death. She felt especially angry at the prospect of cleaning the house all over again, all those spiders.

Automatically she took the bread from the oven. If he had gone she would do as before, clean the house, weed the garden, pack her picnic, do it all again in a month. This time there would be no barbecue on the beach; the young people would have gone, their holidays over. If he had not gone she would phone the police. No, not that. They would ask questions. She would be involved. She could just imagine the questions. He would have to go off on his own before anyone saw him. She would ask him to go.

When the telephone pealed she felt fear leap in her throat. She watched the instrument as the bell jangled. Then she picked up the receiver, pinched her nose between finger and thumb and said:

'Ullo?'

'Can I speak to Mrs Poliport, please?' John's voice, crisp and terse.

'She's not here.' Only John again.

'When will she be back?'

'She didn't say.'

'Has she gone away?'

'She may have.'

Who is that?'

'Mrs 'Oskings.'

'Mrs Hoskings who –'

'I clean for Mrs Pollyput. From time to time I clean. Mrs Pollyput she don't like cleaning.'

'I daresay not.'

'Not's the word. Who shall I say called? I'll write down. You should see the spiders.'

'Piers, just Piers.'

'Like at the seaside?' Matilda, holding her nose, snorted.

'Yes, like at the seaside. Write it down, please.'

'Just a minute. I'll get a pencil – sir –' added Matilda to add credence to her role. 'Oh, here's a message from her. Shall I read it to you?'

'Yes, please do.'

' "Dear Mrs Hoskings." Pretty writing Mrs Pollyput's got, hasn't she?'

'What does she say? Read it.'

'Okay. Dear etcetera, you won't want that twice will you? No. Well it says, "gone away for a change. I'll let you know when I get back. Help yourself to anything you think might spoil from the garden." '

'Is that all?'

'Yes, that's all Mr Pier. D'you think she'd mind if I took the raspberries, the birds will get them else. Shall I –'

John rang off. Matilda released her nose and sniffed, wriggling it up and down like a rabbit. Piers. How ludicrous John calling himself Piers. Piers rang a distant bell far back in her mind. Piers? No, it meant nothing, recalled nothing, it couldn't. Why this insistence on Piers? Sir John sounded all right. Claud said it was snobbery, that

John was a common name. Claud had bet Anabel ten pounds John would be elevated in the Birthday List, not the New Year's, it being the more recherché of the two to enter the lists as Sir Piers in June rather than hustle in in the New Year when everyone was too hung over to notice. Not that he will allow anyone to fail to notice. 'He will never get further than a knighthood in his occupation. Decorous recognition for services rendered. No life peerage for the likes of he.' Claud's voice in her mind, always that note of affectionate mockery to keep one at arm's length, his arm's length, Claud's. No good trying to get close to that one. A slippery character, Claud, the more lovable for his inaccessibility. Standing with one hand on the rail of the Rayburn, Matilda thought of her youngest child. No hook there to hold her, however tenuously. Why did his saying 'occupation' in that tone of voice, almost as though John –

'What a superlative smell.' Hugh stood in the doorway looking in.

'You made me jump.' Matilda pretended to jump. He grinned.

'No wonder nobody recognized you,' Matilda said. 'You don't look like your photo at all in daylight.'

'I have rested. Besides –'

'Besides what?'

'I told you that photograph is one of my brother. He really has a huge nose but now he's grown a moustache it's not so noticeable.'

'The Major?'

'Yes. There's been a mistake, a mix-up.'

'Why hasn't he said?'

'He's abroad. He may not know, he might even be loyal.'

'She was his mother too.'

'He inherits.'

'Oh.' Pause. 'Like some breakfast?'

'Please.'

'I was thinking I should call the police.'

'Shall you?'

'No.' Matilda, getting coffee, had her back to him. Neither spoke for a while. She put a loaf and butter on the table, marmalade in its pot – Cooper's.

'If it were not for your interference I should be happily dead by now.' Rage suddenly choked her, tears blinded, the hand carrying the coffee pot trembled.

'It was you who interfered with me, you silly bitch. "Put your arm round me," you said, "put it round my waist." Like a fool I did. I was going to fill my pockets with stones and go into the river like Virginia Woolf.'

'You hadn't made up your mind.'

'How do you know?'

'You said so – you implied.' Matilda leaned across the table screaming at him, white with sudden fury. 'You were shilly-shallying. *I* had it all planned and you spoilt it. I could kill you.'

'Do. It will save a lot of trouble. Poke that knife into my guts, then you can push off and have your picnic, drown the dog as well –' He too was shouting, handing her the knife she had pressed on the dough.

They glared at each other with hatred. The dog whimpered.

'Are we having a row?' Hugh sat back.

'Yes. I'd forgotten what it's like. It's ages since –' Matilda pushed back her hair. 'I'd forgotten about Virginia Woolf and the stones. I must remember.'

'They would prevent you swimming very far.'

'Yes.'

'Your plan was probably best for you.'

41

'Was?'

Hugh glanced at the dog who wagged, placating, unsure.

'Eat your breakfast. It's ages since I had a row. Makes me feel sick, my legs are trembling.'

'Soon passes.' Hugh helped himself to marmalade. 'Delicious bread.'

Matilda stood by the stove, breathing hard, watching him eat. The kitchen clock ticked. It would need winding tomorrow.

'If anyone comes to see me go through that door into the scullery. It leads to the woodshed.'

Hugh looked up, munching.

'If you want to go further cross the garden to the copse. It's thick, nobody can see you by the stream, nobody goes in there, I don't allow it.'

Hugh's eyes were on her face.

'I don't allow fishermen or hounds in there. It's mine, private, people know.'

'Do they pay attention?'

'Oh yes. Gus found a boy there once and terrorized him. I tied him to a bush and left him for hours. He was scared stiff – told all his friends. It worked.'

'Sounds a bit ruthless.'

'There's a badger set in there. The boy was planning to bring his friends and bait them.'

'I see.'

'So you'd be absolutely safe in the copse.'

Hugh nodded, helping himself to more marmalade.

'Or if you're upstairs, keep from the windows and go up into the loft.'

'The loft?'

'It might be raining.'

'You think of everything.'

'I'll try.'

'Why the hell should you?'

Matilda shrugged. 'I meant to be dead by now. It doesn't matter what I do, if it's any help to you.'

Hugh looked at Matilda for a long time then said: 'You and your husband must have made a formidable pair.'

'I betrayed my husband.'

'Gus?'

'Gus? Gus is a Chinese Goose, a gander – I betrayed him too.' Matilda wept while Hugh laughed.

7

Hugh looked away from Matilda, finding her tears embarrassing. Betrayed husbands come two a penny, he thought, but a goose – that's different. The dog, sitting with her nose towards the heat of the Rayburn, glanced over her shoulder. She had bright little black eyes. She wriggled her haunches, getting closer to the warmth. He wondered where she came from, who had abandoned her.

'Have you got any money?' Matilda retrieved his attention.

'Not an awful lot. I cashed a cheque – er –'

'After killing your mother?'

'Yes.'

Matilda sniffed, whether from contempt or to stop the last tear he couldn't tell. 'I have quite a lot in London but –'

'You can't go there, the police –'

'I suppose not.'

'They will have your money.'

'No, it's hidden in a safe place.'

'You sure?'

'Yes, I have a cache.'

'I can lend you money. I can cash a cheque, overdraw if need be. I can fetch your money. I'd like to.'

'That would put you to a lot of inconvenience, danger.'

'I'd like it. It would amuse me. It would be fun.'

'Law breaking.'

'No more to me than parking on a yellow line.'

'An adventure?'

'I suppose so. Have you a passport?'

'Yes. I was going to Greece after visiting my mother. I've got my passport and a bit of money. I left my bag there though.'

'How much? Count it.'

Hugh pulled his wallet from his back pocket and started counting. 'Nearly two hundred.'

'That won't get you far. How much do you have in London?'

'Two thousand in cash.'

'Well then.'

'To get it I –'

'I'll get it. I've told you. Trust me. I'll go to London. You stay here and keep hidden. I'll fix you up with food. Keep out of sight. The rest's easy.'

'I need clothes.'

'Yes, the whole world knows what you are wearing. There are some of Tom's, a few things of Mark's and Claud's which they left here.'

'Your husband's?'

'He wouldn't mind. He didn't die here, he went to stay with a friend in Paris –' she paused.

'And the friend was Death?'

'That's who it turned out to be.'

'He must have been very lonely without you.'

'Perhaps. No, no, I don't think lonely.'

'Dying on his own.'

'Don't say that, you have no right.'

'Why didn't you go too?'

'I never went to Paris with him. I had responsibilities here, things to do.'

'Such as?'

'The children, our animals.'

'I thought they were grown up.'

'They are. They weren't even here. It was –'

'What was it?'

'What right have you to catechise? What business is it of yours?'

'None. Idle curiosity, I suppose.'

'Well,' Matilda burst out. 'I don't like Paris. I never went there with him. I didn't want to put our dog and cat in kennels. I just didn't want to go. If I had I would have looked after him, not let him drop dead in the street, don't you see? I know I betrayed him, of course I know. They found his pills in his hotel. If I'd been there – damn you, what right have you?' Matilda felt despairing, angry. 'I always saw that he carried his pills.'

'You saved my life. That gives me the right. Folly and I have every right. We belong to you.'

'No.'

'Yes.'

Hugh buttered another piece of bread, fished in the pot for marmalade. Matilda stood with her back to the stove watching him pour more coffee, drink.

'How do you know I won't betray you? As a good citizen I should.'

Hugh grinned. 'I don't think you belong to the W.I.'

'That's not necessarily respectable.'

'Of course it is. You don't, do you?'

'No.'

'Well then.'

Matilda sighed.

'And these children – where are they?'

'Louise is married. She lives in Paris.'

'Didn't you want to see her when your husband –'

'Not particularly. Mark is in business – he centres on Hamburg. Anabel is always on the move, I never know where she is. Claud lives in America.'

46

'Do they come to see you?'

'They telephone sometimes. They don't really want to speak to me or I to them. What would we say?'

'So they won't have to talk to you at your funeral?'

'That's about it.'

'So you thought you'd meet the Mutual Friend?'

'It seemed the sensible thing.'

'Sensible.' He stressed the word.

'Yes, sensible. Without Tom I've no attachment to life. The children don't want me. I was left with our dog, our cat and Gus. The dog died four months ago, the cat was caught in a gin and died of blood poisoning. Gus could live another twenty years. I've found him a good safe home with geese. I've thought it all out, left everything tidy. There's nothing left for me here. I'm off.'

'But why? You can get another cat. You've got another dog.'

'That dog's yours not mine.'

'I doubt it.'

'Oh yes, she is. You picked her up. I don't want her.'

They both turned their eyes on the dog who sat with her back to them, ears laid back.

'We are embarrassing her.' Hugh snapped his fingers. The dog jumped gratefully onto his knees.

Before Hugh could speak Matilda said hurriedly:

'To people like me animals are hooks to hang one on to life. Think of the thousands of people hanging on because of the dog, the cat, the budgie. Think of all those thousands only hanging on for no other reason as they grow old, miserable, useless, bored. I bet your mother –'

'Her cat died in May. It was a smelly old thing.'

'But it didn't murder her.'

'No, there is that.'

'And she didn't replace it?'

47

'I tried to give her a kitten.'

'And she refused?'

'Yes, she did. She was sentimental about –'

'Old Smelly?'

'Yes. How d'you know I called it Old Smelly?'

'She didn't want to be hooked any longer, not once her company had gone.'

'I don't know.'

'No, you don't. She didn't want any more hooks. She didn't want old age, arthritis, falling down, losing her teeth, her balance, her hair, her memory, her wits. She didn't want dependence on other people, becoming a bore, growing incontinent –'

'She was very spry for her age, not at all incontinent.'

'So am I for mine, but I'm not waiting for all that: it's against my principles; creaking joints, fatigue, clicking teeth, brown spots, wrinkled bottom.'

'Bottom?'

'Of course, one wrinkles all over. I'm for the last fling – the ultimate.'

'Ultimate what?'

'Adventure. Fun. Experience.'

'That's a serious statement if you are talking about death.'

'Of course it is. I don't suppose your mother had exactly thought it all out. You saved her the trouble with your tea-tray.'

'Her tea-tray, she inherited it from her father.'

'How pedantic you are. I was starting off in good shape and got interrupted.'

'Sorry about that.' Hugh stroked Folly's ears.

'That dog is yours, as Old Smelly was your mother's.'

Hugh shook his head. 'No.'

'What future had your mother?'

'There was nothing really wrong with her.'

'And nothing really right.' Matilda pounced. 'Why should you and the Major bother? You would have put her into an old people's home and forgotten her.'

'Probably.'

'That's what I can't face; losing my faculties and being put away into a safe place. I am leaving everything tidy, I'm off for my picnic, swimming out while the swimming's good. Now you've turned up and spoilt it.'

Hugh laughed. 'That's tough.'

Matilda's anger switched to merriment. 'I think you did your mother a very good turn. One good bang with a heavy tray and Whoops! she's gone. No more worries.'

Hugh winced. 'She had no worries.'

'How do you know? Sure, she had her memories. "She lives with her memories," people say. I hear them all the time. How d'you know she liked her memories? People don't necessarily like memories. Christ!' Matilda cried, 'of course they don't. Old people are like empty paper bags. You blew yours up, gave it a bang, and pop, that was the lot, her lot anyway.'

'And yours?'

'You've interfered.' Matilda pulled on her espadrilles. 'I'd better stop talking and go to the village, buy the papers, cash a cheque, do some shopping.'

'Very practical all of a sudden.'

'I am practical. Keep out of sight, won't you? I'll leave your dog with you. Don't answer the phone.'

'A loss to the W.I.'

'They don't think so.'

'Show me the house before you go.' Hugh stood up, towering above Matilda. 'You are the same height as my mother.'

'I don't want to think about her any more. I'll show you

round.' She led the way. 'Here, in this front room if taken unawares you can hide in here or here. They are the old fireplaces, cupboards now for logs for that.' She gestured to a pot-bellied stove in the middle of the room. 'You can get right up the chimneys to the roof. Claud did once. He got filthy.' Hugh stooped and went into one of the cupboards. 'Can you stand upright? You are taller than Claud.'

'Yes.'

'Claud once locked Anabel in one and Louise in the other and went out for the day.'

'How did they get out?'

'Mr Jones heard their screams. He was passing, luckily for them. You've seen the kitchen and scullery, come upstairs. Mr Jones is my only neighbour. No bother. If you see anyone coming you can hide in those cupboards or in the one in my room, it's huge. Anyway I always know when someone is coming, Gus honks.'

'But I thought –'

'Oh God!' Matilda's eyes filled. 'I'd forgotten. How could I? He's not here, he's climbing onto all those geese, covering them, whatever it's called, or is that only for horses?'

'I don't know. I believe geese copulate.'

'I hope he enjoys it. He's had a sexually deprived life.'

'I shall keep my ears alert.'

'Yes, do that.'

'You do worry about your goose.'

'Gander. Yes I do, of course I worry. If you'd seen him in that sack driving away –'

'The cupboard upstairs.'

'Oh yes.' She led the way upstairs to the room from which he'd heard snores reverberate. 'Here's the cupboard. It's deep, it goes on for miles behind those

50

clothes.' She pushed an open palm against hangers. 'Behind these there's lots of room. It's L-shaped, turns to the right, almost another little room.'

Hugh peered in. 'What's that?'

Matilda leant forward, her hair brushing his face. 'Ah. Claud's fancy dress.' She took a hanger off the rail and slipped a caftan over her shoulders. 'Look.' As she turned her back he saw the back of the garment was painted with a skeleton. 'He had castanets and clicked them.' She began to dance, making the skeleton move eerily. Hugh drew back in vague distaste. 'He scared the girls.'

'Why should he want to do that?'

'It was Louise, she had –' Matilda pulled the caftan round her.

'She had – what? What had she done?'

'I always think of it as the Postman's Ball. Louise was – poor Louise was going with the postman. She had planned to have him for herself. Yes, I think she had. I know she had. It was to be the postman. He wasn't the postman then. They were all at school together. It's a long time ago. I expect he's forgotten – I mean Claud – the postman wouldn't forget, one doesn't, does one?' She paused, looking at Hugh, pulling the caftan over her shoulders, putting it back on its hanger. She repeated, as she hung the caftan on the rail, 'One doesn't forget, does one?'

'Forget what?' Hugh looking down at her, thought that her skin was good for her age, smooth, hardly lined.

'One's first love. One never forgets one's first love.'

'I suppose not.'

'Claud is homosexual. The postman wasn't even pretty. I don't think he knew until Louise started making jokes, sly digs.'

'Not nice of her.'

'None of her business, was it?' Matilda shook her head.

'Well, behind that fancy dress there's miles of cupboard. All the garden cushions are in there for the winter. It's very clean, I've just swept it out. I've kept Claud's dress, some of Louise's and Anabel's things too. I borrow them occasionally.'

'Do they wear them when they visit you?'

'They don't visit. I have kept them in case they'd like them when I'm dead. Some of those clothes of Anabel's are dateless and Louise always buys wonderful material, she could use it to cover cushions, couldn't she?'

'Yes.'

'The boy's clothes are in your room, mixed up with Tom's. I thought –'

'What?'

'I thought I wouldn't tidy Tom away quite as much as myself. It's me they don't come and see.'

Hugh said nothing. Matilda closed the cupboard.

'If really pushed you can go up that ladder to the attic. I even cleaned that.'

'Thank you.'

'Have some more coffee before I go to the village.'

'Thanks.' Hugh followed her downstairs, noting that she walked like a dancer, straight backed.

'Are you a dancer?'

'No. I used to do yoga at one time.'

'So did my mother. She stood on her head and sat in the lotus position, all that.'

'Wasn't brisk enough to avoid that tea-tray.'

'She was frightened,' Hugh expostulated.

'I bet she was.' Matilda, reaching the kitchen, poured the coffee into a pan to reheat.

'Help yourself. I'm off.' But she lingered in the doorway, obviously wanting to say something more. Hugh looked enquiringly over the rim of his cup. 'You must think I don't love my children from the way I talk about them.'

'You seem a bit – well, casual.'

'They will like me better out of the way, the girls especially.'

'Why?'

'They think I love Claud best. Those dresses upstairs are dresses he pinched from them. Claud is far more beautiful than either Louise or Anabel, far more attractive.'

'You said he is gay.'

'In more ways than one.' Matilda laughed. 'He went to a party in one of those dresses in the days when boys wore their hair long. He snitched all the girls' fellows, quite disrupted Anabel's life – it was a dreadful evening.' Matilda grinned reminiscently. 'Louise had the big feller – she called him her "feller" – he went over the moon and as for Anabel's boy – well –'

'What happened?'

'Claud lives in New York.' Matilda turned on her heel and went off leaving Hugh sitting at the table, holding a cooling cup of coffee, wondering about her. With the kitchen knife in his other hand he tapped a tune on the deal table, trying to remember his actions of the last days. Then, followed by the dog, he left the house and let himself through the gate into the wood, walking along the stream until he found a patch of sunlight and sat down to watch it cunningly run and circle over the stones. Stroking the dog, who came to loll beside him, he reviewed the jumble of thoughts and terrors which had accompanied him ever since he killed his mother. They could perhaps be looked at clearly now that he had stopped running. He was puzzled that he had run at all. Why had he not stayed? Why take flight, leaving the tray flung down beside her dead body? She had looked peaceful, composed, happier than he had seen her for a long time, certainly happier than during the preceding moments when she had been in a state of extreme terror.

The extraordinary moment with the tray was clear enough, but he was still puzzled by his actions afterwards, his instant flight to his car, leaving his mother, the tray flung down beside her. She was dead. What seemed callous was that he had stopped at the bank in the town to cash as large a cheque as he could without drawing attention to himself. To be overcome by panic was unforgivable. He had driven to London, left his car in Hans Crescent then taken the Knightsbridge tube. Since then he had been on the move, expecting every minute a hand on his shoulder.

The sound of the stream was mesmeric. Hugh dozed. Matilda might not belong to the W.I. but she was capable. 'I'll go back presently and they'll be there. No more running.'

When Matilda came back with her shopping and the papers she found the cottage empty. Her feelings of relief were equal to her sense of disappointment. She was not used to ambivalence, it worried her. She looked closely in the looking glass above the sink, trying to read her feelings in her face but it was the same face as usual, a mask for whatever feelings or thoughts there might be inside this middle-aged face which was neither young nor old, neither beautiful nor ugly, just her face as usual which protected her from the prying world.

8

Matilda laid the papers on the kitchen table, put her shopping away, sat down to read. The Matricide no longer rated the front pages. No mention of him in the *Guardian*. She had not been able to buy either *The Times* or the *Daily Telegraph*, only the *Mirror*, the *Sun* and the *Express*.

'Thought you didn't read the *Express*, Mrs Poliport,' the postmaster, Mr Hicks, had remarked, taking her money.

'Fascist rag.' Matilda smiled. 'Very occasionally I like to see it, keeps the mind open to read lots of papers.'

'I read the local.'

'Yes, that tells you all you want and it's unbiased.'

'That's so.' Mr Hicks, a stout bald man, gave Matilda her change. 'Is there anything else, Mrs Poliport?' He pronounced it 'Pollyput' as did most local people.

'Oh, I nearly forgot. I need a dog licence.'

'A dog licence?' Mr Hicks had been astonished. 'I thought –'

'I know, I said never again. I know I did. I'm weak. It's a mongrel from the Lost Dogs, just a little mongrel.'

'Said you didn't want another dog, didn't want to be tied.'

'I know. I changed my mind. There it is.'

'You were offered that Boxer, pure bred.' Mr Hicks could be seen thinking even less of her than usual.

'Well, this is a mongrel. How much is the licence? I forget.'

Mr Hicks had found a licence form. Matilda could hear him presently telling Mrs Hicks that Mrs Pollyput got a mongrel from the Lost Dogs when she could have had that Boxer almost free. They would sigh together over her folly.

'I shall call her Folly.' Mr Hicks was writing slowly, breathing hard through his well-picked nose, wide-nostrilled. 'Hairy as a fernfilled grotto.' Tom's voice from the past. None of her family liked Mr Hicks. Louise said he steamed open letters, Mark that he had bugged the call box outside – an unusual flight of fancy for Mark. 'How else could he know so much about everything?' She tried to hear Mark's voice but failed. Perhaps one only heard the voices of the dead? Anabel claimed that he had put his hand up her skirts at the school sports, a thick fingered hairy hand slowly filling in the form. Mr Hicks had all the time in the world.

'Folly, eh? And how is Claud?' Mr Hicks knew all about the postman's reign in Claud's affections and never hesitated to put in a reminding pin. Matilda, waiting for the man to finish writing the few words and find the date stamp, leafed through the paper.

'No sub-post offices robbed lately,' she said brightly.

'Busy murdering their mothers.' Mr Hicks brought the date stamp down hard on the dog licence. 'There's your Folly all legal.'

Matilda interpreted this as a quick dig against sex between consenting males. 'I don't feel matricide and robbery go together somehow. I haven't seen anything that he robbed his mother, only that he killed her.'

'Only!' Mr Hicks, still holding the dog licence between finger and thumb, stared at Matilda through his thick lenses which hid his piggy eyes, 'Only! That sort of man doesn't need to rob, he's rich, isn't he? A toff who went to Winchester and New College.'

'What a delightfully old-fashioned word – a toff.' Matilda regretted the days of long ago when sub-post offices were not guarded by barriers of glass. Mr Hicks, holding the licence in his horrible fingers, was safe. He held her in his power, fixed her with his glittering glasses. She could not snatch the licence and so she must wait for him to pass it through the hatch. Had those fingers pried up Anabel's parts? One could never tell when Anabel was lying, she was a compulsive liar whose highest flights of fancy often turned out to be true.

'Lots of our Trade Union leaders went to New College, Mr Hicks.'

'But not to Winchester.' Mr Hicks was studying the licence. 'That school should be closed. It breeds more commies than any other school in England. I read it in a book.' By 'book' Mr Hicks meant magazine. Matilda bit her lip.

'Your party too, Mr Hicks.'

'My party?' Mr Hicks, fingers holding the licence, rested behind the glass as he leaned on the counter to see her better.

'Fascist – anti-nig-nog.' Matilda could just reach and take the licence without seeming to snatch. 'Thank you so much, Mr Hicks. Lovely day.' She left the shop regretting her anger, for he would know, as he always knew everything, that she was angry and he would wonder why. Very likely he would set about finding out.

She took the licence from her purse and stuck it on a hook on the dresser. If the murderer had taken Folly with him it would be more money wasted. She perused the papers.

Nothing in the *Sun*. She turned to the *Express*. Ah, here was something. *Matricide's car found at Harwich. Search for him intensified in Scandinavia.* Fru Sonja Andersson from

57

Copenhagen had identified the killer on the ship. Why had she not reported her suspicions to the Captain? She had not been sure at first, but now she was asked, as were some of her fellow-passengers, she was sure and so was the friend travelling with her.

Bully for you, Sonja Andersson. The *Mirror* had in its inner page *Matricide in Porn Capital*. Goody! Matilda, hearing a step, looked up.

'I thought you'd gone.'

'I thought you'd have a Panda car waiting.'

Folly greeted Matilda enthusiastically.

'I bought her a licence,' she said shamefacedly.

'*She* trusts us.'

'Mm, puts us to shame.'

'Anything in the papers?'

'Yes, your car's been found at Harwich and you were seen by passengers on the boat to Denmark. How's that?'

'My car? Where?'

'If you left the keys in it somebody's pinched it.'

'That's very helpful.'

'Look, *Matricide in Porn Capital*. That's helpful. Nothing in any paper except the *Express* and *Mirror*. Your story is stale; they've run it into the ground.'

'Maybe, but the police –'

'They never give up but other things take their time. Look, here's a story of a wife's disappearance. Naked. Just her footmarks in the sand leading inland, uphill away from her clothes and her honeymoon husband.'

'Aahh.'

'And this one. *Man ate dog for bet. Mr Hooper of Saxon Lane, Hertford, killed his wife's spaniel dog, skinned it, roasted it in butter and ate it with caper sauce.* Says it tasted rather strong.'

'The British public won't like that.'

'*Interviewed last night Mrs Hooper said, in tears, I shall divorce him.* Of course she must.'

'You're making it up.'

'I'm not.' Matilda handed Hugh the paper. 'Could you manage some bread and cheese and salad? I don't usually eat much lunch.'

'When I've recovered from the roast dog story.'

'No worse than Matricide. I'll pick a lettuce.' She paused in the doorway, her face in shadow. 'Incidentally, why did you do it?'

Hugh blushed. 'I'll tell you some time, not now.' He bent down, embarrassed, stroking Folly's ears.

'Please yourself.'

'And you can tell me why you really planned your picnic.'

'Easy – but not now either.'

Together they shied away from their fear and horror, their pain and remorse.

We have quite a lot in common, Matilda thought wryly as she chose a lettuce, pulled spring onions and radishes.

'How tall are you?'

'Why?'

'Clothes.'

'Oh, six foot one or two if I hold myself straight.'

'If you've finished eating you had better come up and change your clothes. I'll burn yours.'

'Why? I'm not so desperately dirty.'

'It isn't the dirt, it's the description. All England, all Europe for that matter, knows you are wearing blue socks, suede shoes, fawn corduroy trousers, a check shirt, red and white, a red scarf round your neck and that you wear your watch on your right wrist.'

'How exact.' Hugh took off his watch. 'There's a sunburn mark.'

'We'll rub in shoe polish. Come on.'

59

Touching Tom's clothes Matilda felt detached. A year ago she could not have opened his cupboard or chest of drawers without gulps of hysteria. Now she picked out a white T-shirt, a blue pullover, pants, jeans, and handed them to Hugh. 'Try his shoes for size.' She pointed to a row of shoes. 'Give me your clothes.'

Hugh changed, dropping his clothes onto the floor while Matilda stood looking out of the window.

'How do I look?'

'Changed.' She eyed him carefully. 'Tom was very dark. He was thin like you.'

'I think I've lost weight on the run.'

'I daresay. Here's his watch. Put it on. It's a cheap Ingersoll, goes like a bomb and tells you the date.' She strapped it round his left wrist.

'What shall we do with mine?'

'I'll put it in the bowl in the hall. It's full of unwanted stuff, anything small and broken. We'll hide it under the world's nose.'

'How much nose does the world put in your door?'

'Very little. I can't help the occasional person. Nobody comes regularly. Tom and I put people off. They got the message and left us alone.'

'And when he died?'

'One needn't encourage people. Everyone comes to the funeral, then they leave you alone.'

'The children?'

'They have husbands or lovers. They came once or twice dutifully. I could see my grief bored them. Mothers are not supposed to be in love with your father – there's something indecent about it. They adore love and sex for themselves but for parents it's unnatural.'

'I see.'

'Do you?'

60

'Well, yes, I do. I'm not your child.'

'You could be if –'

'Only if you'd been a child bride.'

'You flatter me. Actually Tom and I never stopped squabbling in front of the children so they thought my grief hypocritical.'

'Quarrels are often an indication of love.'

'Tell that to Louise, Mark, Anabel and Claud.' Matilda picked up Hugh's discarded clothes. 'Found any shoes that fit?'

'These sneakers are fine but my feet are bigger than his.'

'Perhaps it will be safe to keep your own.' She was doubtful.

'They are a very common make.'

'All right, then.'

In the kitchen Matilda cut up the discarded clothes and fed the bits into the Rayburn. Hugh sat watching her profile as she worked. What have I let myself in for? he wondered. He tried to place her among the women of his world and failed.

In the afternoon sun the garden shimmered with heat.

'I shall have to water my vegetables. There's been no rain.'

'I'll help you.'

'You might be seen.'

'Couldn't I be a visitor?'

'It's not normal for me to have visitors.'

Matilda, putting the last sock into the Rayburn, sat back, her hands folded in her lap, silent.

People do shy away from the slightly loopy, Hugh thought. They don't know what to say. If they are harmless they leave them alone. Watching her lids droop, he wondered whether sitting upright she would snore.

They sat companionably, both tired by the emotions of

the past days.

It was Folly who heard the footsteps, first pricking her ears and looking from Hugh to Matilda. Hugh listened. Someone coming — a child on bare feet? Footsteps coming rather slowly from the copse. Was it a trick? A spy? Whoever it was, was coming on steadily. Folly growled. Hugh half rose then sat down again. He was cut off from the passage door by Matilda and could be seen through the open door from the garden. The footsteps were on the flagstones now. Matilda's head jerked up. She cried out, rushed to the door. The footsteps stopped.

'Gus!' Matilda sprang out, swooping down in a birdlike movement. Her arms and Gus's flapping wings made patterns in the sunlight. Gus raised his proud head, honked loud, then laid it across Matilda's lap. She gathered him into her arms.

'Gus, oh Gus! How did you get here? Oh Gus, it's more than ten miles – your feet –' She stroked his neck, his back, his breast. She examined each foot. 'You hero!'

Hugh brought a bowl of water. The gander dipped his beak in the water, raised it high, looking at Hugh with an enraged blue eye.

'It's all right, Gus, he's a friend.' Gus snipped quickly at Hugh's wrist and dabbed his beak at Folly who backed into the house, tail between her legs. 'She's a friend. Oh Gus, I betrayed you.' Matilda sat inelegantly, her legs apart, skirt riding up. Gus made throttling noises, weaving his sinuous neck against her throat, nibbling her ears, tweaking her hair.

'He's made a frightful mess on your skirt.'

'That's love.'

'Will it wash off?'

'It doesn't matter. It's marvellous to have you back. We need you.' She looked up at Hugh who was grinning. 'We

62

need him to protect us from prying eyes. Mr Hicks, for instance.'

'Who is he?'

'The postmaster. He's an inquisitive menace, dangerous.'

Hugh noted that Matilda had said 'we'.

9

Watching Matilda with Gus, Hugh wondered whether they were as beautiful as Leda and the Swan. This up-to-date version touched him. Matilda, bare legged, in a crumpled dress, stroking the bird, her hand sliding down his neck from head to breast, her white hair flopping forward over his head while he nibbled at her ears. Now and again the bird stopped his attentions to peer at Hugh and hiss.

'There's some maize in the scullery. Could you find it?'

Hugh brought it, holding out a handful to the bird. Gus snipped his forefinger in a painful grip. Hugh kept his hand still. Gus held on while Hugh waited. After a while the bird released him and began to eat. Matilda watched the blood returning to Hugh's finger.

'He won't do that again.'

'I hope he won't, once is enough.'

'He will terrorize Folly.'

'I think she will be all right. She's not very brave, a rabbit scared her in your wood.'

'Let's see.'

In the room behind them Folly sat anxiously on the chair by the Rayburn.

'I think he will ignore her.'

'She will keep out of his way.'

'Doesn't he have a new owner?'

'Oh Lord!' Matilda sat up. 'He will come over to tell me Gus is lost.'

'He may telephone. Couldn't you telephone first?'

'Yes.' Matilda was examining Gus's feet. 'He doesn't seem footsore.'

'Could he have flown?'

'Not the world's greatest flyer. He can fly but doesn't.'

'The stream?'

'It goes nowhere near – oh yes, it does, it comes down from the reservoir and he was at the farm at the far end of it. That must be it. You clever, clever Gus.'

'So diddums swam and paddled the whole way home – '

'I know I'm soppy.' Matilda got up, eyeing the goose mess on her frock. 'Frightfully hard to get the stain out. Lucky this dress is old. I'll telephone.'

Hugh listened as she went indoors. He could hear her dialling. The dial whined six times. Not 999, not the police. The gander, having finished the maize, began preening. In the house Matilda was talking. After a few minutes the receiver was replaced with a bang. Hugh waited. The gander finished preening and tucked his head along his back, letting himself sink down on the path.

Hugh looked at the watch on his left wrist. Twenty-four hours ago he had got off a train and taken a bus to the port.

'What are you thinking about?' Matilda sat down beside him.

'What did the man say?'

'He said Gus was no good, attacked his geese, killed one. He *was* rude, said Gus is no gander, no good to him, and will I send a cheque for the damage! I said I would and to bugger off.'

'Wouldn't do for the W.I.'

'I told you.'

'Not a very successful betrayal.'

'No. What were you thinking just now?'

'How I was twenty-four hours ago.'

'Tell me.'

'I had been on the move since I killed my mother. I thought I might get to France, might meet someone with a boat who would take me across. That's what I thought early on. Then I decided it was all too silly. I'd wait until dark and go out with the tide. The police have been no help at all.' Hugh laughed. 'I've discovered how to run away successfully in this country.'

'How?'

'For starters you don't mind whether you are caught or not. You never hurry. You ask the way, if possible from a policeman. He will obligingly tell you. I even went into a police station and stood by a wanted poster of myself and asked the way to the bus station. They gave me a lift in a Panda.'

'Where was that?'

'Salisbury, I think. If you run you are chased. If you wander about unworried nobody bothers.'

'You were just lucky.'

'No. The nearest I ever got to getting caught was when you started helping me.'

'Thanks!'

'I do. But now I don't want to be caught. I'm dead scared.'

'Oh.'

'I keep thinking you will send for the police. I thought when you went to the village that you would get them then, that I would find them waiting when I came back from the wood. I thought just now you might dial 999 not the goose man. I'm sorry.'

'Nothing to be sorry about. I'm a great betrayer.'

'Not really.'

'Half of me is. I hoped you'd be gone, taking Folly, when

I came back from the village. I thought having a dog with you would be splendid camouflage. I didn't want to get involved and then –'

'Then?'

'Then I thought I do want to be involved, it's fun.'

'Fun? Who for?'

'Me. I've had no fun for years.'

'I wondered whether you were mad.'

'Menopause?'

'Yes.'

'No way – beastly expression – but it applies, it's true. This is fun, let's make a success of it.'

'Harbouring a murderer is a criminal offence. Don't be frivolous.'

'Don't be so conventional. People are conventional, we can't do without them. In your case, in my life, I've no room for it.'

'Oh.'

'If you want to go to the police yourself or throw yourself into the sea –' Matilda flushed, getting angry.

'And what will you do?'

'Kill Gus, have Folly destroyed, wait for the tide to be right and swim out as I'd planned.'

'Such despair.'

'We have equal despair. Your despair could cancel mine, that's all.'

'Blackmail now.'

'If that's what you like to call it.'

They stared at one another with horror.

'We are getting a bit near the knuckle,' Hugh murmured.

Matilda nodded.

Feeling their tension, the dog had got down from the safety of the chair and sat between them, managing to press her bony ribs against each of them. She shivered a little, eyeing Gus, but more fearful of losing Hugh and Matilda.

'It's all right.' Hugh stroked the dog's head. 'Nothing to worry about.'

'Sorry to be nervy.' Matilda was apologetic. 'It's Mr Hicks. There's something very unpleasant about that man. Maybe Anabel wasn't lying.'

'About what?'

'She said he groped up her skirts years ago. We couldn't believe her, but I don't know. He frightened the children. Today he made me uneasy. He pries through pebble glasses.' Matilda shivered. 'A goose walking over my grave. Not you, Gus, not you.' She looked at Gus, folded compactly in sleep. 'Horrible Mr Hicks was one of the first on Louise and Anabel's list.'

'What list?'

'They took a great interest when they were about fifteen and eleven in the population explosion. It was about then Louise joined the Conservative Party. They hung a sheet of foolscap on the wall by the clock and listed people they would eliminate. Mr Hicks was high on the list. They ran out of actual people rather soon or changed their minds and reinstated them, but Mr Hicks and Charles Manson were constants. It became a little macabre. I objected.'

'Little girls?'

'Little girls, yes, but I found Tom often agreed with them. They switched from actual people to kinds of people. The list included spastics, lepers, brain-damaged people. Claud wrote in brain-washed, and Louise started it again – the very old, all the handicapped, all Communists. Then Anabel decided Berlinguer was rather dishy and stopped playing. Louise took the list up to her room and carried on alone. A world without weak or

68

imperfect people is, she thinks, she still thinks, a better world. She's a Fascist, my child.'

'And your Tom's.'

'Yes, of course. Oh well.' Matilda shook herself. 'Louise is one of the reasons I was picnicking. It would be intolerable to be looked after by Louise, however right she may be about Mr Hicks.'

'Have you a terminal illness?' Mention of the picnic suggested this reason to Hugh.

'Haven't we all?' He could see by the set of her jaw he would get no other answer.

10

That evening there was a thunderstorm which solved the
problem of watering the garden. Clouds gathered about
six o'clock while Hugh and Matilda watched the news on
television.

The pound was down - the Bank of England had
intervened.

The meeting in Brussels –

The E.E.C. –

Unrest in Spain, Ethiopia, the Middle East, Africa –
Cambodia –

China –

Students –

The earthquake in Central Asia –

The C.I.A. –

Our correspondent in Beirut reports that the Moslems and
Christians –

Mr X, the honeymoon husband of Perranporth told the
police that –

Mrs Y, the owner of the dog eaten by her husband was

arrested by the police this morning and will be charged with grievous bodily harm –

Our correspondent in Cape Town reports Hugh Warner, the Matricide, was seen at the races by an intimate friend Mrs Vivian Briggs –

Here the television blanked out, lightning flashed, followed by a clap of thunder.

Matilda got up and tried a light switch. 'Power cut,' she said and tried the telephone. 'That's gone too. Who is this intimate friend, Mrs Vivian something?'

'I've no idea.'

The rain came down in noisy torrents. Outside the kitchen door Gus honked, defying the elements. Folly crept under the dresser.

Matilda ran round the house shutting windows against the rain whistling down venomously after holding off for so long. Thunder crashed overhead, then cracked and burst simultaneously with the lightning. She found candles to light the kitchen. Hugh drew the curtains. Gus stood in the doorway and Matilda let him into the scullery and closed the door to the garden. Hugh lit the candles.

Matilda stood with her back to the stove, her arms crossed, hugging herself, her dress stained with goose mess, her feet bare. In turn she warmed each foot against the stove, standing birdlike on one foot. Her hair was swept into a crest. She looked, he thought, like a print he had once bought of a Polish Fowl.

When the centre of the storm had moved a little way off Matilda asked again: 'Mrs Vivian something?'

Hugh shook his head. 'No idea.'

Some girl friend of yesteryear, thought Matilda. Some

woman who would enjoy saying at parties, 'Oh, Hugh Warner – of course I know him well –' attracting attention to herself by dubious name dropping. It was the sort of thing Anabel did. She let her mind dwell briefly on her daughter and found her wanting. Anabel craved attention, always had, and so too did Louise who got more, being more beautiful than her sister. Two beautiful daughters, two good looking sons, thought Matilda. They shall find nothing of me to pick over, no surprises. Let them go on with their erroneous ideas. She smiled.

'What's the joke?'

'I was thinking of my children.'

'Funny?'

'I have left no secrets for them to pore over – burned my letters, destroyed all clues. I shall leave them nothing but a shed snakeskin.'

'You look like a Polish Fowl.'

'They are very rare nowadays.'

'Yes?' Hugh was delighted that she knew what a Polish Fowl was.

'A white topknot, sometimes known as the Tufted Hamburg.'

'Extinct,' said Hugh, laughing.

'Like me.' Matilda smiled. 'I am almost extinct.'

'Shall we have a bottle of wine? It would pass the time.'

'Okay.' Matilda took a candle to the larder. Hugh watched her bend down, reaching for a bottle, and thought that for her age she had good legs, a good bottom. He opened the bottle, poured the wine. Matilda sat opposite him in the candlelight. Overhead and all round the hills the thunder groaned and rumbled. The rain spat down.

'I am an habitual liar,' Matilda remarked conversationally. 'I find it almost impossible not to embroider.

Anabel is as bad.'

Hugh nodded.

'When I said Tom went to Paris to meet a friend and you said he went to meet Death I thought that sounded so good I'd let it go. I lied by default. In fact I don't like Paris. Tom knew there was no question of my going with him. When he wanted to go to Paris he went on his own. The friends he was meeting were his friends, not mine. Neither Tom nor I thought he would meet death. That was not in our plans at all. He had a heart attack in the rue Jacob – dropped dead.'

Hugh stayed silent.

'The children were all grown up. They had their lives. We were busy still with ours but – ' Matilda pushed her hair away from her face, drank some wine. A slight draught made the candles flicker. Her eyes looked dark in their sockets. 'But Tom and I were aware of what was coming. Tom called it "*La dégringolade*". He could not bring himself, as I do, to call it disintegration. You looked surprised when I talked of a wrinkled bottom. However well and fit you are the flesh grows old. We had been young together, loved, fought, had children, ups and downs, a tiring, insecure life but not a boring one. We talked to each other, Tom and I. We decided when we were still in our prime not to allow ourselves to crumble into old age where you are dependent on others, your powers fail, you repeat yourself, you become incontinent. The children try their best, then put you into an old people's home with nothing to look forward to but the geriatric ward. That is what we both minded about age, the keeping alive of useless old people. He and Louise used to have a game: how many children could eat if old people were allowed to die? Millions.'

Hugh watched her drink more wine. Presently she went on.

73

'We decided we would leave no mess behind, nothing for the children to quarrel over. We would leave no messages, we would not let them know us once we were dead. Our children were not interested in how we had lived or felt, so our letters – when we were in love we wrote many letters, people did – we would destroy them. If they are ever interested it will be too late, we said.'

'Rather nasty of you.'

'D'you think so? We didn't mean it, well, he didn't. Tom was not a petty person. I am. I would have liked the children to have been interested in us but they were only interested in Louise, Mark, Anabel and Claud.'

'Are they interesting people?'

'To themselves, certainly.'

Hugh was afraid he had interrupted the flow but Matilda went on.

'Sex had a lot to do with it. We thought when sex was no longer fun, no longer essential, we would push off. The great thing for us was to go together, to time it right. Our death must come while we still slept well, ate without indigestion, still made love, while, in Muriel Spark's words we were still "in possession of our faculties".' She sipped her wine, holding the glass with both hands, her head raised, listening to the thunder. 'We were not prepared to put up with terminal illnesses. It seemed to us that the responsible thing was to end our lives at the right moment, go while the going's good.'

'Responsible?'

'Yes. Socially responsible in the same way as birth control.'

'Wasn't it selfish?'

'Certainly not. We planned to save other people trouble as well as ourselves. It was unselfish.'

'I see your point.'

74

'There were other things. We planned not to have another dog or cat when ours died.' Matilda cast an irritated eye toward Folly sitting facing the Rayburn, ears cocked, listening. She sighed and made a defeated gesture.

'Suddenly Tom died without me, before we were ready, while we still –'

'Still?'

'Still were enjoying life. We weren't ready. I should have swallowed my pills then, looked sharp about it. But I have betrayed him. I'm still here, damn it.'

'You were about to have a stab at it last night.'

'You deflate me, mock me. It wasn't just a stab, it was the real thing. I had tidied myself away. In my mind I was as good as dead.'

'Okay. What about Gus? What about that heroic bird coming back to find an empty house?'

'It never occurred to me that he would.'

'And it never occured to you and Tom that he would drop dead in the rue Jacob, did it? A fine pair, I must say.' Hugh drank his wine, refilled Matilda's glass.

'You are detestable.'

'And I murdered my mother.'

'How much do you mind?'

'It's difficult to say.'

'Why?'

'She wasn't particularly happy. She never had been satisfied with anything. She was a frightened person –'

'I bet she was, with you about to bash her to death.'

'It wasn't me she was afraid of, it was –'

From the scullery Gus set up a loud honking. There was a rat-tat-tat at the door. Matilda gestured toward the inner door. Hugh went through to the hall where he stood, heart thumping. Folly barked shrilly.

'Who is it?' Matilda shouted.

'Only me, Mrs Pollyput, only me. Constable Luce.'

'She did betray me,' thought Hugh. 'The crafty bitch, keeping me talking, telling me that tripey tale.'

'Came to see if you are all right, been a power cut in the valley.'

'Here too.' Matilda sounded cool. 'Come in. Like some coffee?'

'Powerful honk that gander's got. He's a good watchdog.'

'Yes, he is.'

'Got a new dog I see.'

'Yes, I licensed her today. Coffee? Tea? Wine? I'll get another glass.'

'No, thank you. I must be on my way. Just wanted to see you were all right, you living all alone here. Must be lonely.'

'I love it.'

'So they tell me. My wife wouldn't do it. She thinks you're brave.'

'Or mad perhaps.'

'No, no, what an idea –'

'My children think I'm crazy.'

'Do they? Well, it's for you to suit yourself isn't it?'

'Yes.'

'Nice little dog. She's only a puppy.'

'She might be. I got a licence to be on the safe side.'

'Sensible that.'

'I've always been scared of you since you caught me with the car untaxed.'

'It was duty. I was sorry to do it so soon after Mr Pollyput's death.'

'That's what made me forget. Sure you won't have a drink?'

'No thank you, Mrs Pollyput. I must be going. I was going to call in on Mr Jones.'

'He'll be hiding under the bed.'

The constable laughed.

'Goodnight,' Matilda called, watching the policeman get back into his car. She shut the door. 'You can come back now, he's gone.'

They sat again at the table. Hugh refilled their glasses. 'I took mine out of the room with me.' He glanced at her sidelong.

'How clever. I didn't think of it. I offered him wine.'

'I heard you.'

'Where were we?'

'You were telling me about your well-planned death with Tom after your successful loving life together.'

'You sound acid.'

'Did you love him?'

'Of course I loved him. There was never anyone else. He was my first and only love.' As she spoke a puzzled expression flitted momentarily across her face.

'What is it?'

'Something I can't remember.'

'Another man?'

'I don't know. How odd. How strange. Why should I suddenly think –'

'What?'

'Some tussle, a sort of thrill. Good Lord, I can't remember. It must be something I've heard or read. It wasn't me, one of the girls perhaps or a friend. Something happened at a party in Bloomsbury. Not important.'

Hugh didn't believe her.

'Where did you meet Tom?'

'At a party in Kensington.'

'And you fell in love and lived happily ever after.'

'Yes.'

Hugh tipped his chair back and laughed.

'It's not possible to believe.'

'Why not?' Matilda snapped. 'Ask around, ask our friends.'

'No need,' said Hugh. 'It's a good story but it won't wash.'

Matilda looked blank.

'A person like you,' explained Hugh, 'with a happy past, nothing but lovely memories does not just walk into the sea.'

'I should have thought it rounded everything off nicely,' Matilda now was sour.

'Either,' said Hugh, watching her, 'you had a happy surface life, even deceiving yourself, or you didn't care except for your animals.'

'What!' Matilda almost spat at him.

'I've seen you with Gus. That's genuine feeling. You are trying not to let yourself love Folly here.'

'I shan't.'

'There you go. So passionate.'

'Well, animals –' Matilda left her sentence airborne.

'Animals are easier to love than human beings. Animals give you their whole heart, animals don't betray. Shall I go on?'

'No. I think I shall get us some supper.'

Hugh watched her moving about the kitchen, laying the table, preparing vegetables, rubbing garlic onto steak, grinding the pepper mill.

'I believe your Tom had somebody else in Paris.' Hugh watched the hands twisting the pepper pot.

'Oh no.'

'I suppose yes. Why don't we tell one another the truth? We met near Death, why don't we tell the truth as good Catholics do on their deathbeds?'

'It would be original.' She put down the pepper pot.

78

'So he had someone else in Paris.'

'Yes, he did.'

'You could have done something – gone with him, murdered the girl. I'm supposing she was younger than you.'

'Much younger.'

'He would have got over it. Did you know her?'

'Yes. Yes. I thought so.'

'So?'

'I did murder someone once.' Matilda looked at Hugh across the table. 'I never think of it. It was so quick.'

'So why not the girl in Paris?' Hugh wondered if this crazy woman who looked like a bird was lying.

'One could never kill one's own child.' Matilda's voice was low.

'Was it Anabel?' Hugh felt shock.

'Louise.' Matilda put the steaks under the grill.

'I thought she was happily married,' Hugh said stupidly.

'I never said happy. She was only happy fucking with her father. You like your steak rare?'

'Rare, please.' He breathed in hard.

'And do you like French mustard or more Truth with your steak?'

'I should like mustard and the story of the murder you did commit.'

'All right, as we are into Truth. It's not as interesting as incest.'

'But longer ago?'

'Much longer ago, almost forgotten.'

11

When the telephone rang Matilda lifted the receiver and listened, her jaws working on a mouthful. Hugh listened too.

'Hullo?'

'Matilda, your phone was out of order.'

'There's been a storm. What do you want, John?'

'Piers.'

'Look, I've never called you Piers in my life. What *is* this?'

'My name is Piers. Call me Piers.'

'Okay. What do you want?'

'I've got to go away. I want to know if you are coming to London.'

'I might.' She swallowed the steak and held the receiver away from her ear. Hugh listened to the pedantic voice at the other end.

'Do make up your mind.'

'I can stay somewhere else.'

'You always stay here. I'd like to see you.'

'That's nice of you, John.'

'Don't tease. When are you coming?'

'I'll think. I'll let you know. I have to arrange for the animals.'

'I thought the dog and cat were dead.'

'They are. Their names were Stub and Prissy, John. They had names.'

'Well then? Come on, Matty, don't dither.'

'I'm not even going to try to call you Piers if you call me Matty.'

'Sorry, Matilda.'

'I'll let you know. I'll phone.' She grinned. 'You wouldn't exactly call this an adult conversation, would you? Think what it's costing you, Piers. Goodnight.' She put down the receiver. 'I can fetch your money if you like. How would that be?' she asked Hugh.

'Marvellous.'

'Will you tell me where it is?'

'Yes.'

'My steak's cold. Damn! I'll give it to Fol-de-rol.' She cut the meat into small pieces.

'You were going to tell me about your murder.'

'So I was. It will give you a hold over me perhaps. John "Piers" knows about it.' She fed the bits of steak to Folly who took each piece delicately.

'Did your husband know?'

'No, come to think of it, he didn't. It never arose. Only John knows.'

'What happened?'

'It was that terrible winter after the war. You'd be too young to remember.'

'I don't. My mother talked of it.'

'I was nineteen, just married. First love. Marvellous. So great it hurt, every nerve raw with love. We had rushed into love, into marriage, headlong. It was gorgeous. I was pregnant with Louise. We were the only people in the world. Then I found he'd had this woman. She was older than him. She was all the things I wasn't. Well dressed, well read, travelled, sophisticated, good looking, sexy, funny, educated. She never let go of anyone she had once had. Once hers he was hers for evermore. She tormented me, showed me up naïve, unsure,

81

inexperienced, unsafe. Tom used to laugh, said she didn't matter, never had, but I could see there was still a bit left over. If she jerked the lead he'd go back. I saw her do it to other men. Their girls could do nothing.' Matilda made a cross with her knife on a smear of butter. She seemed far away.

'What happened?'

'What? Oh! Yes, what happened. London was thick with snow. I was trying to get home to Chelsea from Marble Arch. All the buses were full. I couldn't get a taxi. It was dark, freezing hard, snowing, the ducks standing about on the ice. The snow blotted everything out. I walked through the park. Then, as I walked along the Serpentine towards Knightsbridge barracks, there she was. We were nose to nose in the snow. She laughed when she saw me. Her face lit up with pleasure. "My Tom's little wifey," she said. "Does he let you out alone?"'

Matilda laid her knife and fork side by side and looked across at Hugh. 'It annoyed me.'

'So?' He studied her face while she paused.

'So I hit her.' Matilda was now back there, standing in the snow by the Serpentine. 'I hit her as hard as I could. She was taller than me. She slipped down the edge onto the ice, tried to get her balance, slid on out, then, crack, she went through, disappeared.'

'What did you do?'

'I waited for her to pop up but she didn't. I suppose she went sideways under the ice. I ran all the way to John's house. He lived off Sloane Street in those days. He was in when I banged on the door. I told him what I'd done. He'd just got in, he was shaking the snow off his bowler and swishing his umbrella. I remember that clearly. He's a fussy old bachelor, wants me to call him Piers now. It suits him, his new job. He's hoping to get a knighthood. Sir

Piers would be grander than Sir John. I tease him.'

'What did he do?' Hugh suppressed a longing to kick her shins.

'Oh. He made me sit down, gave me a stiff brandy, listened to what happened, then said I was not to tell Tom, ever. He asked me if anyone had seen it happen. I didn't think so. It was snowing so hard I couldn't see more than a few yards, in fact I'd hardly seen her fall though the ice, I only really heard it. Well,' she stood up, 'that's all. John took me home to Tom in his car, said he'd overtaken me in the street. Tom was pleased to see me. I cooked dinner. It was steak, I remember that, black market. It was delicious.'

Hugh allowed the pause to lengthen.

'I suppose the snow covered your footprints.'

'I suppose it did.'

'When was she found?'

'When it thawed, weeks later. Tom read it in the paper at breakfast. He said, "Oh look, old Duplex is dead. Found drowned in the Serpentine." Old Duplex was her pet name, her real name was Felicity.'

'What did you say?'

'I can't remember. I remember it being quite obvious he didn't care one way or the other so I had no remorse.'

'And Sir Piers?'

'He's like the grave. He's never referred to it. Funny fellow.'

'Was he in love with you?'

'John? He's not capable of love. He's cold.'

'The police?'

'John clammed up and I forgot all about it. I've never told anyone until now.'

'It's a good story.'

'Yes,' said Matilda kindly, 'a good story. You see, anybody can commit murder. It's chance really.' She could see Hugh didn't believe her or was uncertain.

'You are uncertain of my veracity.'

'A bit. It seems odd you should meet this Felicity woman alone in Hyde Park in the snow.'

'Not really. She used to follow me to make me feel uncomfortable. One never knew when or where she would appear. She did it to other women whose husbands had lain with her. It was her hobby to make us feel insecure. John told me. I remember now when he gave me the brandy he said, "A lot of girls will be the happier. You must not let it worry you. Promise." I'd forgotten that. I promised – put it right out of my mind.'

'Can you do that? Put things aside.'

'One has to.' Matilda looked bleak. 'I put Louise aside. How else could I have gone on living with Tom? He needed me, I needed him and Louise –' Her voice trailed, leaving Louise up in the air. She got up and began clearing the table.

'Let's have some coffee and you tell me where your money is hidden. I'll stay a night or two with John and fetch it for you. Is it somewhere difficult to get at?'

'No, it's under the carpet on the staircase up to my flat.'

'For everyone to tread on?'

'Yes.' Hugh smiled.

Matilda's laugh rang out in delight.

'How original.'

'It was my brother's idea, some of it is his. Tax evasion.'

'So he –'

'No, he won't. My mother had just heard he was missing in Guerrilla country.'

'Dead?'

'For his sake one hopes so.'

'Oh, Guerillas/Gorillas. Your poor mother. Maybe I'm right, she was lucky. Did she love him?'

'He was her whole life.'

'There you are then, you did the right thing.'

'She could have loved me more.'

'Too big a risk, I think.' He could see Matilda's thoughts straying where he could not follow. 'No more risks for me.' Her face was dead-pan. 'Bed for me. We can plan your future tomorrow. I will ring up the soon-to-be Sir Piers and tell him I'm coming.'

'But –'

'We've had enough for one day.' Hugh watched her trail up the stairs. Folly stayed with him until he too climbed up the stairs and, while he took off his clothes, she turned several times around, pulling the duvet into a lump with her paws, waiting for him to get into bed. He held her close to his chest, stroking the silky ears while he tried not to think of Matilda's pain. The dog sighed, breathing warm air into his neck while he lay sleepless, listening to the summer night. He wondered whether Matilda considered God, as his mother professed to do, or whether Death was her only certainty where there would no longer be the possibility of love dying? And did she love Louise, Mark, Anabel and Claud? She had loved her husband. Her voice altered when she spoke the name Claud. He would study it if he had time perhaps. Blood relationships inclined to surprise when there was the inability to communicate.

12

When Hugh woke the sun was up. Below his window he could hear the gander talk, Matilda answer. The bird stood on the brick path watching Matilda hoeing along a line of spinach, her movements brisk, economical.

Hugh pulled on his trousers and shirt and opened the door into the passage. Matilda's door was open, the bed unmade. Hugh looked again at the cupboard, parting the dresses on the rail to see how large a space lay behind. Satisfied, he prowled round the room, glancing at her things; a silver mirror, a brush, few pots or bottles on the dressing-table. He opened a drawer full of bras and nylons. Remembering his mother's habits, he tried the bedside table, found what he sought, a pile of snapshots. Tom, tall, handsome, fine eyes, hawkish nose, something fanatical about the mouth, a mouth that had kissed wife and daughter. Other snaps jumbled up of children, dogs, Matilda with the children, Matilda holding a puppy, scrawled on the back 'Stub – three months'. She held the animal with more care than she did the children. Another snapshot – Tom with Louise. The photograph had been crumpled, then smoothed out. Hearing Matilda come into the house he shut the drawer, went down to the kitchen.

'Sleep well?' She looked fresh, healthy.

'Very well thanks. I was prowling round upstairs. I saw you in the garden.'

'It's the best time to do chores. I'll get breakfast.'

'Have you any photos of your family?'

Matilda looked up. 'Try the dresser drawer. There's an envelope on the left, taken before they all flew.'

'Flew?'

'Birds leave the nest. It's the best thing.'

Hugh opened the drawer, found an envelope. 'Is this it?'

'Yes. I don't much care for snaps. It's other things which bring them to mind – smells, sounds, materials.'

'Claud's dresses?'

She laughed. 'Of course, his dresses. That's me. Younger.'

A younger Matilda stared at the camera, her hair blown across one eye. 'That's Louise with Pa.' The voice was dry. Louise, tall, exquisite, standing close, too close to her father. 'Anabel.'

'Oh, Anabel. It's a bit blurry.'

'It's very good of Stub and Prissy.'

Anabel lay by the dog and cat who stared from eternity with enigmatic eyes. Another of Anabel, a better one – one wouldn't get much change out of her. He put the snap down and picked up the last. Two exquisite girls in jeans, long fair hair, laughing eyes, long narrow legs, the one on the left so beautiful she leapt from the snapshot, so desirable she moved him.

'That's Claud – he's still like that.'

'I'm bowled over.'

'Everyone is.'

'No wonder he made trouble for the girls.'

'There's always trouble,' Matilda said.

'You love him the best.'

'I do.' Matilda picked up the snapshots and put them away. 'Yes I do.'

Outside the house Gus honked. Matilda motioned Hugh out of the room.

'You in, Mrs Pollyput?'

'Yes.'

Hugh slid into the hallway.

'Post.'

'Oh, George, thank you. Only bills I bet.'

Hugh saw a man's shadow, heard steps.

'Looks like Claud's writing.'

'George, you are unethical. Like a cup of tea? Postmen shouldn't pry.'

'Wouldn't say no.' A chair scraped on the stone floor. Hugh risked a quick glance and stifled a laugh. This Claud's postman? Large head, massive shoulders, ginger hair getting thin, a heavy brutish face.

'How is Rosie?'

'In whelp again.'

'George, don't be crude.'

'She's a bloody bitch, Mrs Pollyput.'

'George, shut up! You love her. You are very happy.'

'If you say so.' George sounded sulky.

'I do say so. It's no use pretending anything else.'

'It's just this, Mrs Pollyput. Things might have been different. I feel trapped married, like every other fellow. Now it'll be three kids. I might – well, when I see his writing, I just think, that's all.'

'When you see Claud's writing you should thank your lucky stars that Claud left you. God knows what would have happened. Get on with your job, George. You had a sniff of sulphur – be thankful for Rosie.'

'You are right. I daresay it was the glamour.'

'He's not really glamorous, he's a clown. He says here on this postcard he is hard up. Did you read it? I bet you did. Hard up means he's been chucked out of another job or has quarrelled with his feller.'

'Oh, Mrs Pollyput.'

'Still owes you, does he? How much?'

'Never mind, Mrs Pollyput. I'm sorry I read the card. It set me remembering.'

'Push off, George. Give my love to Rosie.' Footsteps faded, Gus honked, Matilda sighed.

'Claud's postman?' She glanced at Hugh. 'Rather unlovely.'

'He picks them for contrast. Dreadful boy.'

'Don't pay his debts.'

'Goodness no!' Matilda sighed again. 'Now. Let us be clever, make lists and timetables so that you know when to make yourself scarce, where to hide and when you are safe. You must keep out of sight until you have your money and the hunt has died down. Then if you want to move on you can.'

'If you really mean it. Tell me your daily routine. I can memorize. For the unexpected I can improvise but I am worried about any consequences for you.'

'I've told you,' Matilda snapped, 'I'm enjoying it. Don't you see, you've given me something to do. A bit of life, for Christ's sake. I was bored stiff.'

'Okay, okay, let's make a list then. What happens from morning till night.'

Matilda made a list, starting with the postman at the same time each day as she was finishing breakfast so that he could be fairly sure of an offer of tea. 'I owe it to him. Claud behaved very badly.'

'Was it first love?'

'It was for George. Claud's first love is Claud. He can only hurt himself.'

'And your first love was Tom?'

'Yes.'

'Are you sure?'

'Of course I am.' Matilda was overemphatic.

'There must have been others before him. When you

were a child were you not in love?'

'No.' Again the emphasis. Hugh waited.

'There is a rota of postmen. When it's not George's turn they come before I am up. I never see them so you won't have to bother about them.'

'Okay.'

'The milk comes Mondays, Wednesdays and Fridays. You hear the van, Gus honks, you can keep out of sight. The dustbin men come round Thursdays. You hear them miles away. That's about all. I do my shopping in the village or the town.'

'Where we met.'

'Yes.'

'Anyone else?'

'Mr Jones. He gives a shout when he's some way off. He's nervous of Gus. If I don't answer he goes away.'

'Sure?'

'Yes. Quite often I don't answer. He can be a bit of a bore.'

'Made a pass at you?'

Matilda blushed. 'I'm too old.' She caught Hugh's eye. 'Well, he did, but I took evasive action. One must be kind. He's got the male menopause, Claud says. Louise said the same thing.'

'What other neighbours?'

'Few. They wave as they go by, shout "How are you?" or "It's a fine day." Gus keeps them away. Nobody cares to get nipped. Gus will warn you.'

'What about exercise for me?'

'I hadn't thought.'

'I'll walk at night.'

'That would never do. Everyone would know. Dogs would bark. You'd be seen.'

'I can't stay cooped up. I'll go mad.'

'You'd be cooped up in prison.'

Hugh did not rise to this bait. 'I'll play it by ear,' he said.

'All right.' Matilda agreed, then, remembering another danger, said: 'Never ever answer the telephone. That would be fatal.'

'Do many people ring up?'

'No, but if I go to London and collect your money and you answered the telephone it would be known there was someone in the house.'

Hugh was bored by this meticulous planning.

'Suppose you carry on exactly as though I were not here – let me keep out of sight. If someone does come in say I'm a friend of Claud's or something.'

'You are not his type. I'd say Mark, a friend of Mark's.'

'He has catholic tastes?' Hugh was pleased not to be suitable fry for Claud.

'Mark is straight hetero.' Matilda smiled. 'No problem there.'

'I thought this Mr Jones fed Gus for you when you go away –'

'He thinks I've given him away.'

'Won't he find out?'

'Damn! Of course he will. When I go you'll have to avoid him.'

'I expect I shall manage. What would you be doing if I were not here?'

Matilda glanced at the kitchen clock. 'I'd go to the village, do a little shopping, come home, have a snack, work in the garden, snooze in the sun, go to the sea if it's fine.'

'Then why don't you do just that?'

'There's you.'

'Don't bother about me. Let me manage. I'm not half-witted. If you go to London I will be deeply grateful. I swear I won't be seen. Why not go and do your shopping – carry on as usual?'

Matilda looked doubtful, then agreed. Hugh watched her drive down the lane with relief, glad to have the house to himself. The fuss she was making was tedious, all the more irritating since he felt he should be grateful.

He sighed and set about exploring the house. He felt it impossible to believe Matilda had really swept herself away. There must be clues to her character that she was unconscious of leaving. He remembered exploring his home as a child, his discoveries among his parents' possessions. The thought of his mother, lovely, young, made him pause. She had been old looking up from the sofa, really old. The recollection of her sitting there, eyes full of terror, rid him of any wish to pry on Matilda. He would do it later, in a better mood. He wandered back to the stream in the copse, Folly at his heels. If he stared long enough at the running water he would stop seeing his mother's hands, rings loose on old fingers. The rings, in his childhood, had fitted tight. She had pulled hard to get them off. 'Try them on your thumb, my love,' she had said. 'Try them on your thumb.' He looked at his hands. None of those rings would fit now. He sat watching the water flow past, the dog beside him, companionable, alert, quizzing a black and green dragonfly zipping up and down the water.

Presently Gus floated past, proudly paddling.

'Goose murderer,' Hugh called to the bird. 'Goose assassin.' Gus barely turned his head, floating on to land further down to crop grass on the bank.

'Thinks he's human,' Hugh said to the dog. 'Thinks himself like us, free to take life.' The dog looked up at him briefly, then lay in a ball against his thigh, her nose under her tail, the warmth of her body consolatory.

Gus finished cropping grass, crossed the stream and waddled back to the cottage past Hugh who heard him honk as a car passed along the lane.

The gander set up a different honking when Matilda returned. Hugh heard her voice raised in greeting. Followed by the dog, he went to meet her.

'I've bought stocks of food for you for when you're alone. Tins and dry stuff. You won't have to shop. I won't be away long. D'you think you can manage with cold food?'

'Oh yes.'

'If you have the fire the village will see smoke and if I'm away someone may come and look.'

'I'll be all right.'

'It's rather drear but –'

'Less drear than the nick.'

'There's that. Oh, by the way, Mr Jones – he sees UFOs.'

'What?'

'UFOs. He's given up telling the police because they laugh but he still tells me. It's just possible that he may appear suddenly then –'

'What do you do about it?'

'I pretend to take an interest. Tom did. He always took note; it's a neighbourly act.'

'Do I hide?'

'He can appear silently on bare feet. It's awkward. Even Gus has missed him on occasion.'

'It's a hazard I must take.'

'Yes.'

Gus honked. 'Telephone.' Matilda ran to answer it.

'Hullo? Oh darling!' – a cry of joyful greeting. 'How lovely to hear your voice. Where are you? In England ... how long for? Oh... shall I see you? Oh, I see ... yes, of course, too busy ... no, no, of course you must ... yes ... no ...

93

no, of course not ... yes, I'm well, of course I am ... yes ... no ... really? ... well, best of luck, it sounds a brilliant idea, quite honest too ... what? ... I said quite honest too ... must rush ... goodbye.' He heard the telephone ping as she rang off. Several minutes passed before she came outside.

'That was Claud.'

'Too busy to see you?'

'Yes. He has a new venture. So like Claud. It's brilliant. I hope it makes him lots of lolly.'

'I talked to my mother like that.' Hugh watched her.

'Me too, but I hated mine and she me, whereas Claud –'

'Is too busy.'

'I had to be quick to be the first to ring off.'

'I noticed.'

'I used to drag on until he said, "I must go now, Mama." I've learned. I've learned to be the first to ring off.' She looked side-long at Hugh for approval. 'It's hard learning not to be a bore. I damn near invited him to my funeral but –' She began to laugh.

'What's the joke?'

'His new venture. He's buying up old gravestones with beautiful inscriptions to sell to Americans. He's going up to Yorkshire where they are turning several graveyards into car parks.'

'Who sells them?'

'Oh, I wouldn't ask!' Matilda broke into cheerful giggles. 'An impoverished curate perhaps? The Church of England doesn't pay well, so –'

'If you found some round here?'

'I'd see him then of course. He might even stay the night and charge up the County Hotel to an expense account.'

Hugh said nothing.

'It does prove it's time to be off.' Matilda sounded

almost pleased as she reversed disappointment to hope.

'To London?'

'To the next world.'

'Will he phone again?' Hugh found himself hating Claud.

'No, no, that's my ration.'

13

Two days passed. The weather stayed hot. Her feeling of trepidation subsided; Matilda grew calm. Hugh gave no trouble. He ate sparingly, slept a lot, spent hours out of sight in the copse with the dog. In a conscious effort to act normally Matilda worked in the garden, shopped in the village, read the papers, watched television, went to bed, got up at her usual time, cleaned the house in a desultory manner and cooked meals for herself and Hugh. She decided on action.

'I must ring up John/Piers, he always gives me a bed in London. Tom and I always stayed with him. He was my friend but became more Tom's. I'll telephone tonight and fix it. It's a very comfortable house. Perhaps you know him? John seems to know everybody, he's very social.'

'No, never heard of him.'

On the line from London John was warmly welcoming. Of course she must come. When? Soon? 'Come soon, I'm going away, come before I go. I'm very busy but we can have the evenings together.'

'That would be nice.'

'How long can you stay?'

'Oh, not long, a night or two.'

'Nonsense, you must stay at least ten days, get back into your London ways. Mrs Green will give you breakfast in bed. We will cosset you.'

'Would Monday be all right?'

'Of course. I shall expect you in time for dinner. You'll

take the usual train?'

'I expect so.'

'Monday evening then.' John rang off.

Matilda looked at Hugh. 'Did you hear him? He has a very loud voice, always has had.'

'Every word. What does he do?'

'Some branch of the Treasury. He wanted the Foreign Service. He was disappointed. We met when we were young. His aunt was a friend of my mother's. He's rich, rather an old woman, likes his comforts, won't ever come here, it's not grand enough. He likes birds and fishing. Tom and I could never decide whether he liked girls or boys or neither. That side of him is non-existent, he's sexless.'

'Or it's carefully hidden.'

'That's what Tom said – carefully hidden. He always pretends he is something to do with Intelligence, it's his sort of snobbery.'

'What form does it take?'

'He talks as though he knew about spies, defectors to and from Russia, the C.I.A., French Intelligence, even Chinese. To hear him talk he might be all the M.I.s rolled up in one umbrella. He carries an umbrella, wears a bowler.' Matilda laughed. Hugh liked to see her laugh; she had small teeth, unhorsey.

'He's an odd man,' Matilda went on, 'good-looking in a way. He always talks as though he knows me better than I know myself. He also knows the children better. He knew Tom better, too.'

'Differently, perhaps?'

'Perhaps that's it. Another side to the side which was mine? People are so much more difficult than animals.'

'You love animals best?'

'Oh yes,' she said quickly. 'I trust animals.'

'Not Tom? You didn't trust Tom?'

Matilda flushed.

'I'm sorry,' High said quickly. 'I'd forgotten.'

'I didn't trust Tom before I found him in bed with Louise. There was a part of Tom I never knew and John, in an odd way, knew it. He knows more about Mark, Claud, Anabel and Louise than I ever shall.'

'Why does John want to be called Piers? Does he hate his name?'

'No.' She shook her head. 'He wants to be Sir Piers, it's more elegant.'

'Are you afraid of him?'

'He is a bit creepy. Claud says he's creepy. When the children were small he pretended he knew all about Burgess, Maclean and Philby. The children called him "Beclean filthy". A silly joke.'

'How well does he know you?' Hugh wondered whether Matilda would tell this man about himself.

'We've known each other since we were tots. I don't tell him things, not since I killed Felicity. I've been very careful since that episode.'

'Maybe there's some other thing?'

'What could there be?' Hugh watched her puzzled face and a minute breeze of fear flickered in her eyes. She also seemed puzzled. I'm getting to know this woman, he thought then. 'Let me tell you where the money is.'

'Yes, do.'

'If I give you my latchkey could you get me a pair of my own shoes?'

'Of course.'

'What else shall you do?'

'Get my hair done, shop.'

'Don't let them spoil it!'

'If I go looking like this John won't take me to good

restaurants. He'll say nothing and take me to cheap, pokey places, hide me.'

'Nasty man.'

'Just vain. He likes to be seen with presentable women.'

'Not Polish Fowls.'

'Certainly not.'

'He doesn't like animals best.'

'I don't think he likes animals at all, or people. He is the sort of person who likes power. Poor old boy, it would be nice for him to be Sir Piers. That would give him a certain power. Sir Piers first, then after a few years Sir Piers will shift into another gear. Who knows – KCMG? I think he would like that.'

She is being malicious, Hugh thought and wondered whether Matilda knew she did not like this man or whether she had buried her feelings too deep to germinate.

'Shall you see friends?'

'I have so few left in London.'

'That's no answer.'

'We, or I, have changed. There isn't much left in common.'

'Your other children?'

'Neither Anabel nor Mark are in London.' She straightened her back. 'I wouldn't know if they were.'

'Surely?'

Matilda grinned. 'Did you keep your mother posted?'

'No,' he said. 'I did not bother.'

'She had her cat.' Matilda's unkindness was intentional.

'You need not invite me to your funeral either,' he said.

'Love all.' She pursed her lips.

14

When Matilda set off, respectable in her London clothes, Hugh sighed with relief. He intended a voyage of exploration. He was still sure that he would find some clues about to amuse him during her absence.

In the dressing-table drawers were the photographs – Louise, Mark, Anabel and Claud from babyhood to adolescence. He turned them over. Sometimes something was written on the back – 'Mark in Berlin' or 'Picnic near Helston'. In a good-looking family Claud's beauty was outstanding. He was like Matilda, but beautiful. He put the photographs aside, feeling that he knew Claud, would not care for Louise, would like to fuck Anabel, be bored by Tom and really dislike Mark who had a priggish expression. He searched for letters but was not rewarded. He put the snapshots back. There was a space in the drawer where probably Tom's letters had lain – now destroyed? No sign of any in Matilda's writing. At the back of the drawer a yellowed postcard of Trafalgar Square. 'Come at the same time. I'll take you on to the party. It's in Guildford Street.' No signature, but Hugh was reminded of the voice on the telephone which he had, 'You will take the usual train.' The postcard was in an authoritative script. He put it back.

Hugh prowled, felt the bed, a deep mattress. He examined her books. There had been a poetry phase. Then, rather surprisingly, the Russians: Chekov, Dostoevsky, Tolstoy. Then Camus and Sartre. The flyleaf of each book was initialled and dated. She had tried Bertrand Russell but not got far, had read Thomas Mann, left Jane Austen untouched but managed Shaw. Graham Greene and Muriel Spark were read and reread. In Ivy Compton-Burnett she had written on a flyleaf, 'needs more concentration than Dostoevsky.' In Margaret Drabble's first novel, in Claud's hand, 'Darling Mama, try this, she knows about your kind of despair.'

Hugh opened Matilda's drawers. The clothes were not the clothes of a woman who felt the need of sexy knickers. She wore Indian cotton shirts as nightdresses, Jaeger wool tights in winter. The clothes were rather worn, unglamorous. In the middle dressing-table drawer a note: 'Have put jewels in the bank, listed for each of you. Don't quarrel – take what's given. I flogged the pearls.' That wouldn't make much difference with Matilda dead, Hugh felt. There was an envelope with a bent corner as though it had been stuck in the corner of the mirror. Hugh tried it. The crease fitted. He went downstairs and put the kettle on to steam the envelope open. Inside on a plain sheet of paper dated the day he had met her was a note:

Darling Louise, Mark, Anabel and Claud. I have had enough. Please have me cremated and scatter my ashes over the stream. I love you all. I am in full possession of my faculties. My Will is at the bank. Goodbye. I love you. Don't feel guilty. Your loving Mother.'

Hugh wondered why she had said twice that she loved them. It tinged of doubt. He stuck down the envelope and went back to the room to replace it. He closed the drawer and lay down on Matilda's bed. Folly, who had kept silent company, got up and lay sighing, pressing her nose against his neck, her breath warm and damp.

'She must be about fifty.' Hugh put his arm round the dog. 'She hasn't quite swept herself out of the house,' he whispered to the dog. 'She left her anxieties about their subsequent behaviour. Poor fare.' Hugh sighed and repeated 'poor fare' which made him feel hungry. Matilda would be arriving in London about now. 'Let's get some food and then get out.' He stroked the dog who was making a draught with her tail.

Downstairs he fed her, made tea and ate a tin of tuna fish with pepper and raw onion, then lay again on Matilda's bed until it grew dark.

He let himself out of the back door, locked it and set off across the fields, desperately in need of exercise.

He walked up the valley, taking his bearings by the stars. The air was clear, the country very still. Walking across the fields, trying not to disturb sheep and cattle, he zigzagged to find gates, kept on uphill. Cars drove occasionally along the lane but he kept below the skyline, gaining confidence as he walked, feeling his unused muscles working easily. Near the top of the valley he came to the village – a post office, one pub, a church, scattered houses, two farms in the village itself. He debated whether to try and skirt round but decided to walk through. It was September, there would still be holiday people about, he would not be conspicuous. The pub was surrounded by parked cars, a cheerful hubbub came out of open windows. Dogs barked as he passed the farmyards. Folly closed in on his heels. From the houses came the sound of television, music and loud laughter. Beyond the village a stretch of road, then a wood, a stile, a path sign-posted. He climbed the stile and followed the path, disturbing a pair of lovers. It led through the wood, over a stretch of moor to the top of a hill, turning left downhill. He stopped to get his bearings. Below and behind him lights from scattered houses and farms, the headlights of cars probing along the main road, far off the red glow of the town. To his right, away from the patch and below it was a long reservoir, silver from the rising moon slicing the black water. He jogged down-hill to the water's edge. Folly drank. Hugh felt the temperature of the water. He listened. There was no sound other than faint rustling in the reeds.

His mother, he remembered, as he crouched with his hand in the water, had told him that in her youth, sent to Germany to learn the language, she had swum at night in the lakes. He remembered her voice.

'We swam naked, darling. If we rode we took off the saddles and swam the horses. We held on to their manes and they drew us along. It was poetry.'

Hugh had been delightedly shocked, unable to imagine his mother so.

'Naked?'

'Yes, darling, naked boys and girls. Of course our parents thought we were all in bed.'

'Together?' Hugh had asked. His mother had said:

'Don't be improper. Of course not.'

'Wasn't the swimming improper then?'

'It didn't feel it. They were all young Nazis, strength through joy and so on, handsome creatures. Their father was a Graf – very pro-Hitler for a while.'

'But Grandfather!'

'Your grandfather sent me there to get a good accent. When I wrote to him about the Strength through Joy he came at once and fetched me home. He'd never bothered about the quarter of Jewish blood in my mother before, never thought about it.'

'Poor mother.'

'Well, the swimming was lovely, you should try it some time in a lake at night.'

He took off his clothes and waded into the water, trying not to make a splash. Folly followed. They swam out together. The dog came too close and scratched his shoulders. Hugh swam out to the middle of the reservoir, thinking of his mother, trying to visualize her swimming in Germany, but it was Matilda he thought of who, having had enough, had been about to swim out to sea. He turned back to find his clothes. He dressed while Folly shook herself and rolled in the rough grass by the water's edge.

He walked back slowly, astonished at the distance he had covered on his walk. His mother was right, the swimming was good. He decided to do it again. There was no need to tell Matilda, who would worry and push her hair up in a crest. What had she had enough of, he wondered? Loneliness? People adjusted to being alone. Was she bored? Certainly not ill. She appeared to have the wherewithal to live without undue worry. Guilt? Not guilt – she barely remembered killing that woman – he was half inclined not to believe it. What then? What? He was very tired when he got near the cottage, anxious for food and sleep. In his scullery Gus honked loudly. Hugh stopped. Gus could not have heard him yet. Folly pricked her ears. Hugh stood at the edge of the copse. A figure was creeping round the cottage, a short thickset man with a beard. He peeped in at the windows, funnelling his eyes with both hands to look in, moving from window to window, trying the back door. Gus honked.

'All right, all right, I hear you. She out or something? Not like her to be going out.' The voice was faintly Welsh. 'She can't be away or she would have asked me to look after you.' He was now peering in at the scullery window, standing on an upturned bucket to look in. Gus flapped his wings.

'All right then, all right. I'll be round again tomorrow, eh?' The visitor stepped off the bucket and set it right way up. Hugh watched him walk away, waited for him to be well out of sight before letting himself into the house. Gus throttled in his throat in greeting.

'Mr Jones, was it? Seen a UFO or something? I'd forgotten about him.'

Not daring to put on a light in case the man came back, Hugh felt his way about the kitchen, finding the bread, butter, a bottle of beer in the larder, cheese.

He sat at the table munching, still thinking of Matilda. Despair? Self-hate? Maybe. Hugh shrugged his shoulders, climbed the stairs. He went into Matilda's room, got into her bed with Folly. She had not changed the sheets, they were rumpled, the pillow smelled of her hair. He felt comforted. It was on this pillow she snored open-mouthed.

15

The ringing telephone woke Hugh. He had overslept; it was late, nearly ten.

He let the thing ring. He had promised Matilda not to answer it. They had arranged a code. If it rang three times and stopped it would be Matilda. She would do this twice. The third time he would answer, otherwise he would let it ring unanswered.

When the phone stopped Hugh went down to let Folly out and feed Gus his mush by the back door, which he propped open with the bootscraper. He made toast and tea, got out marmalade and butter. He stood eating, watching Gus guzzle his food then move slowly across the grass, cropping.

Hearing a car in the lane he hurried into the hall. Folly joined him. The car stopped by the gate; he heard voices. He looked out cautiously. The man he had seen prowling round the cottage was getting out of a police car. He slammed the door.

'Well, thanks, Constable. Thanks for listening anyway.'

'That's all right, Mr Jones. Any time.'

'I'll just tell Mrs Poliport.'

'You do that. You tell her. She and Mr Poliport were always interested I understand.'

'Oh yes, he was particularly.'

'A nice gentleman. Goodbye, Mr Jones. See you.'

'Goodbye.' The car drove off, footsteps came up the path. Hugh retreated up the stairs to the landing.

Gus honked.

'Hey, Gus, where's Matilda then?' The man came to the kitchen door, calling.

'Matilda, hey Matilda, where are you?' He thumped the back door, walked into the kitchen. Hugh slipped back into Matilda's room, caught up Folly into his arms and dived into her hanging cupboard, bending down, pushing between the coats and dresses to the back where he sat down on a heap of cushions.

Mr Jones moved noisily about downstairs, talking to himself and the gander.

'Where is she, then? I came early this morning. She wasn't here, boyo, not here to see Jones. There, there, don't honk so. You know me. You honked this morning but she's fed you since. Ah, kettle's hot. She's had her breakfast, not put away the butter nor the marmalade. Don't come in boy and make a mess, you know what she's like.'

There was a listening pause. 'Matilda? You ill or something, Matilda?' Then steps on the stairs. Mr Jones was coming up. Hugh held Folly's nose lightly.

'Matilda, you in there?' Steps in the room. 'Not made her bed. Funny. Gone out in a hurry.' The springs of the bed were bounced. 'My, what a comfortable bed she has.' Hugh held his breath. The cupboard door opened suddenly, letting in light. 'Not in there either. Hardly be hiding in her cupboard. Must look in the garage.' Then a loud shout as the footsteps retreated down the stairs. 'Matilda! I know I bore you woman, but there's no need to hide. I told you I won't do it again, I told you!' There was anger and pain in the voice, frustration. Mr Jones in the kitchen called for the last time.

'Matilda?'

Hugh crept out of the cupboard, keeping well out of sight, looked down on Mr Jones. Short, thickset, a forest of a beard, thin strands of hair trained over a large head from ear to ear. From Hugh's view-point the top of Mr Jones' head looked like spaghetti junction. He stood looking about him with one hand stroking the strands into place. Presently he moved off to the garage, his feet slapping on the stone path. Hugh heard him say, 'Gone out then. Where's she gone, Gus? Ah me, poor Jones, I should have known better. I should never have tried.' The gander honked and flapped dismissing wings. Mr Jones reached the gate. 'You tell her, boyo, I'll be back.' The gander resumed his cropping, unmoved by the rather affected Welsh voice. Hugh swore. Damn the man, when would he be coming back? Obviously he'd got a lech for Matilda. He tidied Matilda's bed. Fine thing if Jones had come in to find him in it. He sat on the edge of the bed considering what to do, idly thumbing through the book she must be reading at the moment. Rosamund Lehmann's *The Ballad and the Source* – notes in pencil on the flyleaf in Matilda's hand, but shaky:

I think only people like me do this. I get heightened perception. I'm insecure. I'm pissed on pot, Claud darling. I found it in his overcoat, him of all people! He made me safe. This perception is awful. I found it last night, I wonder if – no not last night – last year *Claud, it's made me remember* – it was at a party –

The writing straggled and stopped. Hugh sniffed the book. I'm not a trained Labrador, he thought. Then he remembered the overcoat at the back of Matilda's cupboard, crawled back in.

In the pockets of an overcoat he found a sizeable amount of cannabis and a packet of heroin. He flushed the heroin down the lavatory and pocketed the cannabis. It would be interesting to know why Matilda had left evidence of Tom while sweeping herself out of the house before her picnic. And the note to Claud? Perhaps Claud was the only one she could talk to. Hugh walked thoughtfully downstairs.

Mr Jones was standing in the kitchen.

'I thought there must be someone here,' he said. 'Who are you?'

'My name is Hugh Warner.'

'The Matricide, eh?'

'Yes.'

'Mine is Jones.'

'How d'you do.'

'Matilda usually asks me to care for Gus when she goes away.'

'I'm doing it.'

'Good.' Mr Jones looked hesitant. 'Do you know when she will be back?'

'No.'

'Oh.'

'I've just flushed the heroin down the loo –'

'Oh de-arr!'

'I suppose it comes in the UFOs.'

'Clever you are.'

'Matilda seems to have found out.'

'Oh de-arr.'

'Shall we ring the police separately or together?'

'Whatever for?'

'You can tell them about me and I can tell them about you.'

'No.'

'No?'

'Too upsetting for Matilda. When did she find out about Tom, then?'

'I don't know.'

'I bet she's strangled the knowledge.' Mr Jones teased his hair carefully. 'She does that, it's her gift. She won't remember anything she wishes to forget, if you catch the drift.'

'I've caught it.'

Mr Jones laughed.

'How much heroin was there?'

'One packet.'

'Good, that's what I missed. Ah well, not to worry. Since Tom's untimely heart attack all that's over.'

'But you reported a UFO this morning.'

'So you were listening? They don't come any more, not since Tom's demise. I just go on occasionally reporting one. You should never stop anything suddenly, it makes the police suspicious.' The Welsh accent had returned. Hugh began to laugh.

'Do you play chess?' asked Mr Jones. 'Tom was a very good player. I miss it.'

Hugh nodded.

'Good. Did you sleep in her bed last night? It was warm when I felt it.'

'Yes.'

'In the cupboard were you?'

'Yes.'

'It would be nice to sleep in that bed with Matilda.'

'I hadn't thought of it.'

'But I have.' Mr Jones sighed. 'I suggested it. Fatal. She was offended. Took offence.'

'Poor Mr Jones.'

'Yes, poor Jones, poor Jones.'

'I suppose,' Mr Jones said later as he took his leave, 'you were missing your mother.'

Hugh made no reply.

'I was referring to your sleeping in Matilda's bed, obliquely of course. It is Freudian.'

'Of course.'

'And what do you know about UFOs?'

'Nothing.'

110

'Hah! Nothing he says. They came up the creek, a little sea-plane it is, was, I should say.'

'Where?'

'On the river. They cut out the engine and landed on the water. So easy it was.'

'Your idea?'

'No, no, man, Tom. Tom's idea, his organization, a sideline.'

'Well, I flushed it down the loo.'

'Couldn't flush your mother. Had to leave her on the sofa. That was messy.'

'Heroin's worse.'

'A point there. Do you mind the pot?'

'No, I'm not averse. I think it's harmless.'

'So is death. The newspaper said she could not have known much. It is you that do the knowing.'

'Oh, bugger off.'

'All right I will, but presently we can play chess and share a joint while Matilda's away?'

'All right.' Hugh felt inclined to like Matilda's suitor. Heavily bearded, paunchy, squat, he had beautiful liquid black eyes.

Mr Jones walked crabwise along the path. 'I will bring my chessboard. It is nicer than Tom's. It was my Da's. The feel of the ivory is good to the fingers, engenders thought.'

'Goodoh.' Hugh was amused.

'And yesterday's paper. You were seen in Rome at the airport changing planes, it says. It says in the *Daily Mirror*, look you.'

'Jolly good, Dai Jones.'

'My name is not David, it is also Huw, but HUW not HUGH.' Mr Jones paused to let this sink in, then, 'Not to worry, it is the disappearing bride from the beach they are on about. The poor husband is frantic, naked she is, wandering.'

'Ah yes, I'd forgotten I had competition. What about the man who ate his wife's dog?'

'Ah that!' Mr Jones paused, one foot slightly airborne. 'That woman is clever, oh she is. She said the dog had rabies. The poor husband is in an isolation hospital having painful injections in his greedy stomach. He is under observation, look you, daren't take the risk.'

'Are you really Welsh?'

Mr Jones laughed. 'Never been there. Born in Tooting. It's the fashion, that's all. Gives me class.'

'Of course.'

'Not like Winchester and Oxbridge but it's cheaper to obtain.' Mr Jones reached the gate. 'See you for chess then.' The gate clicked shut and he was gone.

16

Matilda arrived in London in the early evening, taking a taxi to Chelsea. She put the window down so that she could hear and smell London, the roar of the traffic, heels clicking on pavements, engines revving as they waited for lights to change. The constant chat on the taxi radio, blare of musak from open shops, exclamations in foreign languages, people of many nations hurrying across before the lights changed. Just as she thought she could bear no more the taxi turned into John's cul-de-sac on the border of Chelsea and Fulham.

John came out to meet her, paid the taxi, took her case, bent to kiss her.

'Lovely to see you, Matty, absolutely great. Come in and have a drink.' He was using a new shaving lotion she noticed and was glad. Up to now he had used the same as Tom. She wondered whether this was tact or chance. He led her into his sitting-room. 'Sit down, Matty, you must be tired. What will you drink? Whisky? Vodka? Sherry? Gin? I'm drinking vodka, suits the weather. Vodka and tonic?'

'Yes please.' How like John to offer a choice but do the choosing.

'You've altered the room.' She accepted her vodka with a slice of lemon. He must have had that lemon sliced, she thought, doesn't want it wasted.

'Yes, do you like it? I've got this new sofa. I sold the old chairs. They fetched a very good price.'

'They were a bit rickety.' Matilda felt the need for

assertion. This was London she had just sniffed, one must be sharp.

'Yes, need a bit spending on them. They've gone to America.'

'So much does.'

'So much does, yes. I've changed the house round a bit, hope you will like it. I sleep at the back now. The spare room is at the front.'

'Oh good, how clever of you. It must be almost like a new house.' Matilda sipped. 'What frightfully strong vodka. Might I have a little more tonic?'

John took her glass. There would be no memories of Tom in the new spare room, she thought, looking at John's back, so young for his age, such a good figure. She knew he did exercises. John poured in a little tonic. He wondered how much she still grieved for Tom.

'I thought we'd dine at home tonight and go out tomorrow, unless you have plans.' He handed back her glass.

'No plans. Dinner here will be lovely. I'd rather not be seen until I've had my hair done.'

'You look very nice, as always.'

'My hair looks like a chicken.' She could not say "Polish Fowl" and, as she withheld it, wondered why not.

'A ruffled hen.' John smiled. Goodness! Matilda thought, he is bland.

'You *know* you like your women well dressed. I shall have my hair done and wear a decent dress. I have a new one.' He wouldn't know she would be wearing a cast-off of Anabel's and shoes that had been Louise's.

'What are your plans?' John, sitting opposite, quizzed her. She wore well, he thought. He hoped the dress would be Anabel's as he didn't care for Louise's taste. The elder of Matilda's daughters dressed rather loudly. Anabel,

114

whose very appearance was a call to bed, had the quieter dress sense.

'What are your plans?' he repeated.

'My hair, some shopping, any exhibitions I may fancy, nothing much, just a sniff of London.' As though searching for a handkerchief, Matilda felt in her bag for Hugh's key.

'I'll give you a latchkey. You must come and go as you please. Another drink?'

The man's got sixth sense, Matilda thought. Christ! I must be careful. 'No, no more. May I have a bath before dinner?'

'Of course. The supper is cold. Take your time. There's no hurry.'

Matilda looked at him. 'Dear John, it is good to see you and you look so well, such a marvellous figure.'

'Piers. I play squash. Try and remember Piers. And I garden –'

She went upstairs. He followed, carrying her case. 'I hope you will be comfortable.'

'I'm sure I shall.'

How stilted we are. He behaves as if he's being careful too. I must be crazy. Matilda turned on the bath, began unpacking, hanging Anabel's dress in the cupboard, throwing her nightdress on the bed, putting her few clothes away in the chest of drawers. She lay in the bath. I must be very careful, she thought. When I've used that key I'll post it back to myself at home. It was silly to be afraid of John but it would be sillier to risk anything. Better to humour him, call him Piers if that's what he wants.

At dinner John gave her a run-down of new books, plays, films, exhibitions, current affairs. The fishing season good on the Test in spite of the long dry spell, birds at Minsmere, mutual friends. Matilda listened, saying 'Yes?', 'No!', 'Oh really?', 'How extraordinary and how very interesting!', while she ate delicious iced cucumber soup, salmon mousse with a ratatouille, which she herself would not have served together, and mountain strawberries with Kirsch. She would have preferred them plain but exclaimed with delight over them. John's choice of wine was impeccable – a Niersteiner. She refused brandy, accepted coffee.

Without asking whether she minded, John turned on the radio to listen to a concert he wished to hear. She's not musical, she can put up with it, he thought. Matilda, who happened to know and like the particular symphony being played, listened until the end and, when he switched it off, remarked:

'I love that one, so much prefer it to the sixth, don't you?'

'Oh yes, the sixth is played far too often.' The bloody bitch, John thought, looking at Matilda's chin, slight and undecided. 'More coffee? A brandy now before bed?'

'No, Piers, no thank you. Have you been away?'

When she smiled the chin altered, stopped being weak. He wondered why, as he often had before, liking to know people exactly.

'I was going but then this Warner affair blew up. I shall go next week, it's a small delay that's all.'

'Where are you going?' Matilda kept her voice steady by refusing to hear the name Warner.

'Czechoslovakia.'

'Fishing?'

'No, no, this is work. The fellow is, it seems, in Prague, which complicates things slightly.'

'What fellow?' Her voice steady, lifting up her coffee cup, looking across at John/Piers the future knight.

'Hugh Warner, the man they call the Matricide. You must have read the papers. Killed his mother, smashed in

116

her skull with a tea-tray.'

'Oh, of course.' Matilda hoped her heart could not be seen thundering against her ribcage. 'Of course I've read about him. I'm more amused though by the man who ate his wife's dog. He must be some sort of pervert, don't you think?' She put her cup down on the table beside her, triumphant when it did not rattle.

'He's not a pervert.'

'Oh John – to eat a dog!'

'I'm talking about Warner. The "ate wife's dog" man must have done it for publicity. No, I'm talking about Warner.'

'What's he to do with you?'

'The office is interested. The assassination of his mother was just a cover.'

'It must be very serious to have such a desperate cover.' Matilda affected eager interest. 'Tell me more – what's it about?'

'I can't, Matty.' She hated him calling her Matty. 'You should know by now I don't talk.'

'Another Burgess and Maclean? A Philby? They didn't murder their mothers, did they? Goodness me, reading the papers one would never guess.'

'Don't be silly, Matty. It's a sort of – let's call it a parallel.'

'Call it anything you like, Johnnie. How do you know he's in Prague?'

'I can't tell you that but he is. Why d'you call me Johnnie suddenly? You never have before. Call me Piers.'

'You call me Matty and I hate it. Are you going to Prague to see him?'

'I can't tell you that either. Don't pry, Matty. I shall call you Matty. I want to, I always have. It would be difficult to change now.'

'I'm sure I asked you not to. I must have.'

'No, no never.' John well remembered the occasion when she had, the intonation of her voice. It was all a long time ago but clear.

'It must have been someone else, then. What a fascinating life you lead. Off to Prague to meet the Matricide. Will you say "Boo" or will he?'

John laughed. 'Keep it under your hat.'

'Of course I shall.' What a comical old bugger he is, thought Matilda. This is a real Beclean filthy. 'The papers keep saying he's been seen in a new place every day but they haven't mentioned Prague yet. Why d'you think he went there?'

'I can't discuss it any more, Matilda. You know me.'

'I wonder whether I do. What did he do? What's his profession? The man who ate the dog is a builder.'

'I don't think there's any connection.' John got up and poured himself another brandy. How these London people put it away. Matilda shook her head when John made a mute offer.

'Just the Silly Season.' Matilda smiled. 'What was his profession?'

'He was in publishing, lived not far from here.' John mentioned the address Matilda had memorized, the house whose key lay in her bag.

'Oh really? Not a bad area now. It's grown quite smart. Our mothers thought it beyond the pale, poor old snobs. Have you been there?'

'Of course not. The police let my people have a look. Nothing to see, naturally.'

Matilda yawned, putting her hand up to her mouth. 'What an interesting job you have, absorbing,' repeating herself.

'Not bad.' John looked at her hand. Hands showed age

more than faces. She was six months younger than he, or was it a year?

'I must go to bed.' Matilda stood up. 'A long day tomorrow.'

'Shall we meet here, then, for dinner?'

'Yes please.'

'Would you like to dine at Wheelers? They have oysters. I have rung them up.'

'Dear John, I should love it. Sorry – Piers.' Matilda held up her cheek to be kissed. 'Goodnight, bless you.'

John kissed the proffered cheek – quite hard, not flabby. 'Goodnight, bless you.'

'How easily we say "bless you". Do we mean it?'

'Of course we do, Matilda. What can you mean? One always blesses an old friend.'

'I was joking, Piers, joking.' Matilda went steadily up to bed, determined not to hurry. In her room she pulled the ribbon off the top of her nightdress and, stringing Hugh's key on it, wore it round her neck, pulling the duvet up to her chin. It was like John to have the most expensive duvet from Harrods. She missed the weight of sheets and blankets and, with a sudden pang, missed the pressure of a dog in the small of her back. She must not think of Stub, it was weakening.

Sleep did not come easily. She listened to John moving about downstairs, locking and double-locking the front door, bolting the windows. If there were a fire, she thought, we'd never get out. The key lay heavy between her breasts. Hearing John's footsteps on the stairs, she held it tight in her hand.

'You all right, old girl? Got everything you want?' he called from the landing.

'Yes, thank you. Lovely new duvet.'

'Harrods. Sleep well.'

'Thanks, same to you.' She turned on her side, away from the window, disturbed by the light from the street lamp. For what seemed hours she lay wakeful, worrying. Would Hugh be careful – keep out of sight? Would Gus be safe? The dog? Had she forgotten anything? The unaccustomed rich food was taking its time settling in her stomach. She got up and tiptoed to the window. It only opened a little way, not enough for even a thin burglar to climb through. She knelt down and breathed the street air, listening to the roar of the city which never quietened.

In childhood she had listened from her grandparents' house, heard trains shrieking in the distance, tugs tooting on the river, taxi doors slamming, the creak of cowls on chimney pots as they whirled in the wind, turning this way and that like the heads of armoured knights. The Clean Air Act had put paid to them. She remembered, too, how once when she was very small she had heard sheep and seen a flock driven through her grandparents' square to Hyde Park. She wanted to remember that dawn, was comforted that she did. I will get his money tomorrow, she thought, and then forget all about him while I am here. She fell asleep, holding the latchkey in her hand, her mouth open, snoring.

Across the landing John, roused by his bladder, stood in his bathroom. He thought crossly that in youth he would have lasted the night. Then he cocked his head. God almighty, how she snores. Nothing wrong with my hearing anyway. How could Tom have put up with it all those years? A bit uppity calling him 'Johnnie'. Menopausal cheek, must make allowances. She'd seemed a bit edgy somehow, something on her mind. Probably still missing Tom. It had been a pity, that heart attack.

17

In the morning Matilda sat in bed eating breakfast
brought up by John's housekeeper. Mrs Green was a
woman who while modern in appearance could create a
Mrs Tiggywinkle atmosphere if she so wished. The tray
placed across Matilda's knees held coffee, boiled eggs,
toast, butter, marmalade and a linen napkin.

'It's lovely to see you. It's ages, isn't it? You are spoiling
me.'

'Far too long, Madam.' Matilda knew well that the
'Madam' bit was a joke, that she was referred to by her
Christian name behind her back.

'This is delicious. Dinner last night was a dream.'

'I'm glad you liked it.' Mrs Green smoothed Matilda's
duvet. 'He would have the ratatouille with the mousse,
said it had to be eaten up. Getting a trifle mean, our Mr
Leach, doesn't like anything wasted.'

'It was a very good ratatouille.'

'I just thought I'd mention it. I wouldn't like you to
think it was my idea.'

Matilda crunched her toast, poured coffee, topped her
eggs. There was more to come.

'It's his age, Madam.'

Matilda raised an eyebrow, glanced at Mrs Green.

'The male menopause, Madam.'

'Go on –'

'True, Madam, Mr Green has it too.'

'Wow!'

'Of course Mr Poliport wouldn't have –'

'Didn't live to have it, Mrs Green.'

'Oh, Madam.'

'Don't let's think about it.'

'No, Madam, of course not. But I just thought I'd mention it in case Mr Leach seemed a bit funny.'

'No funnier than usual.'

'Oh good. Of course I took Mr Green to the doctor. He takes pills now. That settles him.'

'Female hormones?'

'Oh, you know about them.' Mrs Green was disappointed.

'I don't really think Mr Leach needs pills, not yet anyway. But he's got you to keep an eye on him, lucky fellow.' She could see that Mrs Green also considered John fortunate.

'Would Madam like the telephone? I can plug it in for you.'

'Oh, I would. I've got to do something about my hair.'

'I took a chance. I made an appointment for you at Paul's for eleven.'

'Mrs Green, I could kiss you.'

'Also your friends Lalage and Anne are in London, but Mrs Lucas and Mrs Stern are away, Madam.'

'You've been spying for me!'

'Anticipating your desires, Madam.'

'Stop the "Madam", Mrs Green. You know you call me Matilda to your husband and everyone else.'

Mrs Green laughed. 'I'll get the telephone. D'you want your dress for tonight pressed?'

'No, it's that black thing of Anabel's. D'you think I shall look all right in it?'

'If Anabel does, you will. You are the same size.'

'Have you seen Anabel lately?'

'No,' said Mrs Green, who had, and thought Anabel a

122

selfish good-for-nothing tart to neglect her mother so.

'Nor have I. She seems to like living in Germany.'

Mrs Green made a non-committal noise and went to fetch the telephone. 'Don't be late for your appointment. You know that Paul –'

'All right, I won't.' Matilda telephoned Lalage.

'Lalage? It's me. Lunch tomorrow?'

'La Green warned me,' shrieked the telephone voice. 'Of course, sweetie, lunch tomorrow. Come here. Anne left a message. Lunch with her the day after tomorrow. La Green rang her up. All right?'

'Sure.'

'See you tomorrow, must rush. I'm having my face done, late already, 'bye.'

'She's having her face done, Mrs Green.'

'Wait till you see it.' Mrs Green showed her teeth.

'Oh, Mrs Green, up again? Really?'

'Yes. Cost a thousand, I believe. Her husband's made of money – diamonds – a new car too.'

'None of that envy now. I must get up. I have to see to my hair. Just look at it.'

'Her hair is blonde now.'

'Thank you for warning me. What's Anne's?'

'Same old red.'

'Ah.'

'You keep yours as it is.'

'I shall, I shall. Can't do anything else in the country even if I wanted to.'

Matilda put on her frock, several years old but dateless. She had bought it with Anabel's help for Tom's funeral. She had barely looked at the garment when Anabel had taken her to buy it, her mind had been full of the horror of meeting the plane carrying Tom's coffin. The coffin had lain in the sitting-room for the time it had taken to arrange

the cremation, buy the dress, wait for Louise, Mark and
Claud to arrive. Louise had said:

'Why here, for God's sake, Mother? Why can't it be in
the crematorium chapel?'

'I want it here. He would be lonely in the chapel, out of
place. He had no beliefs.' Then Claud had said, 'Shut up,'
to Louise, and Mark, who agreed with her, had shut up
too. Matilda zipped up the dress.

'Do I look respectable?' she asked Mrs Green.

'Very chick.' Mrs Green pronounced her 'chic' as in
Chicago. She had heard Matilda say this when younger,
happier.

'It's not new. I'm mean about clothes. I live in jeans in
the country.'

'You look fine.' Mrs Green watched Matilda go out into
the street. 'Don't let that Paul ruin your hair.'

'I won't.'

Matilda caught a bus, rocked and roared along the
King's Road, up Sloane Street, lurching round into
Knightsbridge, grinding up to Piccadilly. She walked
through side streets to Paul's.

The silence as she went into the hairdresser's was a relief
after the racket in the street. Paul met her.

'Hullo, Paul.'

'I've got a job ahead of me I see. Evie, shampoo Mrs
Poliport then bring her to me. Just got to cut a slice off a
Frog visitor then I'll be with you.'

'She'll hear you, Paul.'

'What if she does? These Frogs and Krauts only come
once or twice. It doesn't pay to bother, I haven't the time.'

'He doesn't change, does he?'

Matilda submitted to a brisk shampoo, feeling relief
when Evie finished and turbanned her head in a towel.

'Now what have we got here?' In disgust Paul flicked

124

Matilda's wet hair upwards. 'Who cut it last? Been nibbled by a mouse?'

'You cut it.'

'Never.'

'You did, when you came to do that demonstration at the Grand Hotel.'

'Oh, I remember. It wasn't my day. Robert and I had had a row.'

'Be more careful this time. I hope you haven't had a row lately.'

'We split up. I'm ever so peaceful now, living with a gloomy Dane.'

'Good news.'

'Wouldn't you like a rinse?'

'No, I wouldn't.'

'All your friends have them. Needn't be red, you know. Just a bit of gold in with the silver. It would suit you.'

'No thanks.'

'Honestly? Why not tart you up a bit?'

'Honestly, Paul, leave it alone.'

'How right you are. All the old Fraus look years older than you, your hair looks terribly distinguished with your skin. How do you do it?'

'Come on, Paul. Concentrate. Snip, snip, but don't get carried away.'

'Very well.' Paul's tired eyes met Matilda's in the glass. 'I'll take great care. You don't come often but I'm glad when you do.'

'What a nice thing to say.' Paul snipped, concentrating, combing her hair this way and that, snipping off tiny bits, the scissors, razor sharp, flickering between his fingers.

'Have you seen Anabel or Louise lately?'

'No, Paul. I think they have their hair done abroad. They haven't been over for ages.'

'No.' Paul, who had cut Anabel's hair a few days before, agreed. 'They've got lovely hair like you, though I don't think either of them will go your colour.'

'Why not?'

'All those rinses. Girls forget the colour they were born with. Very few white heads these days. There, how's that? Suits your head.' He held a mirror so that she could see. 'Janey, blow Mrs Poliport then bring her back to me.'

Janey led Matilda away and brushed and blew.

'That's better.' Paul gave a final snip or two. 'Be all right now.'

'Thank you. I feel ready to face the world.'

'See you soon?'

'I don't know when I shall be in London again, if ever.'

'Goodbye then –' Paul was already hurrying to another customer. Matilda was forgotten. She paid the astronomical sum asked, tipped the girls, walked downstairs into the street, strolling slowly along to Green Park Tube.

As she went down the steps the hot air blowing up from below lifted her new hair and blew it every which way. She bought a ticket to Gloucester Road and went down into the bowels of London. It was time to find Hugh's money. She wanted the job over, behind her, so that she could forget it.

Sitting in the train, which was bursting with young foreigners carrying parcels, shouting to one another above the noise of the train, Matilda breathed deeply to calm her nerves and repeated Hugh's instructions to herself to be sure she had them right. She got out at Gloucester Road and walked to Hugh's flat. Long before she rounded the corner into the Gardens she had his keys in her hand, one for the street door, the other for the flat.

The police would no longer be watching the flat but John's fantasies of the night before made her nervous. If there were suspicious-looking people in the street she would walk past the house. But who was or was not suspicious? The few people about looked ordinary enough. When she reached the house she fitted the key in the door, opened the door and walked in.

The hall was dark and drab, the stairs steep and badly carpeted. She counted them as she made a slow ascent – eighty-five, eighty-six, eighty-seven. Eighty-seven brought her to the small landing and the door which still had a card by the bell which said 'Hugh Warner'.

Matilda listened.

No sound. Nobody coming up or going down. Hugh had said that nearly everyone in the house went out to work all day every day. She ran her finger under the left hand edge of the landing carpet and found the string. He didn't lie about this, she thought. She pulled. From under the carpet came the envelope. She put it in her bag. Two steps down in the fold of carpet over the step another string brought a second envelope. Two steps more, another tweak and she had the rest of the money. She was breathing hard. Should she or should she not go into the flat? It was not really necessary; he could manage without shoes. Curiosity won. She let herself in quickly, closing the door behind her. The flat looked undisturbed though there had been a search by the police. She did not believe in John's Beclean filthy people.

She looked curiously round Hugh's home. Books. He was considerably more erudite than he appeared. Some good pictures. A stack of records, a very nice record player. A bathroom she envied. She looked wistfully at a Greek sponge, decided to leave it. Clothes she must leave too. The bedroom was comfortable. She felt the big bed gingerly. The flat was friendly. A snapshot of a woman smiling at the camera from a garden chair, a black cat in her arms – unmistakably his mother, the nose feminine but large. 'Well, Mother.' Matilda looked at this version of Hugh. 'You were not afraid that day.' In the street a car door slammed. She heard voices, the insertion of a key in the front door. She looked around for a hiding place, moving out of sight of the door. Footsteps pounding up the stairs, a man and a girl talking.

'My God, what stairs! How much further? My legs ache.'

'Top floor, I'm afraid.'

'Ooh!' in a squeak. 'You didn't say the Matricide lived here.'

'I did, stupid, you were too pissed to hear. Come on.'

'It's scary.'

'Don't be stupid. He isn't in there.'

The footsteps went on up the stairs. Matilda let out her breath. She snatched up a pair of shoes from the rack, let herself out of the flat and ran down to the street. In Gloucester Road she bought a carrier bag and put the shoes in it. The shop girl looked at her briefly, then away to the next customer while she held out her hand with the change.

She asked in a fruit shop where the nearest post office would be and walked steadily along the pavement towards it. She was sweating with retrospective fear. Her feet hurt in their thin soles on the London pavements. She hoped she looked unobtrusive among the throng of foreigners pushing and barging towards the tube.

'*Qu'est qu'elle fait ces jours, Madeleine?*'

'*On dit q'elle fait le trottoir.*'

'*Pas vrai, elle s'est bien installée avec un Suisse?*'

'*Elle doit s'ennuyer!*'

Perhaps Madeleine's feet had hurt on the *trottoir*? Matilda pushed into the post office, joined a queue edging slowly towards the counter. Her feet swelling unbearably, she waited, holding Hugh's keys in her hand. As she moved slowly up the queue she took the keys off her nightdress ribbon, putting the ribbon back in her bag. When at last she reached the counter she found herself face to face with an Indian, whose sad eyes looked through her.

'A registered envelope please, medium size.'

Delicate fingers pushed the envelope towards her. She paid. He would not know her again, this man imprisoned behind the counter, so infinitely more dignified than nose-picking Mr Hicks. Mr Hicks feeling superior with his itchy nose and putty-coloured skin would call him a nig-nog or coon.

'Next please.' The Indian waved three fingers just a trifle. She was holding up the queue staring.

'Sorry.' Matilda blushed, hurried to a counter and addressed the envelope to herself, put in the keys, first wrapping them in a telegraph form, licked up the envelope, closed it firmly, pressing hard, then posted it. Overwhelmed with relief she went out to the street and waited to take a taxi which was disgorging some Arab ladies outside an hotel. After giving John's address she sat back, easing her feet from their tight shoes.

That evening at Wheelers she greedily ate a dozen oysters and a sole and listened with pleasure to John's description of a day's fishing on the Test, conscious that with her hair properly cut she looked more than presentable in Anabel's dress and glad that Louise took shoes a size larger than she did.

'London pavements are death to my feet, John dear, does it show in my face – Piers, I mean.'

'You look younger than I've seen you look since Tom died, if I may say so. You look splendid, Matty. What are you doing these days?'

'Just living, John – Piers.'

'It's been very hard for you, you two were so close.'

'Dreadfully. I wished for a long time to be dead, in fact I wish it still.'

'The children should be considered.'

'Louise, Mark, Anabel and Claud have their own lives.'

'They come and see you.'

'No. One visit each after the funeral, then away they went.'

'I should have thought –'

'None of them lives in England. They are all busy people.'

'Do you go to see them?'

'I haven't so far.'

'Really? It's three years since Tom died. I should have thought –'

'I don't particularly want to go. The States are so far. I hate Paris. I don't like Frankfurt either.'

'Tom liked Paris.'

'I never went with him.'

'Yes, I know that.'

'How?' Matilda asked sharply. 'How did you know? We were pretty well inseparable.'

'I suppose he told me. Yes, yes that must have been it.' John looked slyly at Matilda. 'There's no harm in telling you now. I knew you never went with him. He told me so, naturally.'

'What do you mean, naturally?'

'Tom used to do little jobs for my department. They paid for his trips.'

Matilda flushed. 'John, you go too far with your fantasies. Don't start telling me Tom was a spy. It's too bad of you.'

130

'My dear girl –'

'I'm not a girl, yours or anybody else's. I'm too old to play silly spy games with you. It used to be funny, but bringing Tom in like this isn't. It's indecent, it's worse than rotten taste.'

'I'm sorry if I –'

'I should hope so. We laughed at you over Burgess and Maclean, and Philby and you made me laugh last night over your date in Prague with the man who murdered his mother.' Matilda prevented herself from saying 'Hugh'. 'But I tell you, John, it's not funny when you insinuate Tom was a sort of agent; it's revolting.'

'Sorry, my dear. It's a foible. Forgive me.' John signalled to the waiter to bring his bill, looking away from Matilda, pleased to find she knew nothing, suspected nothing. He had not been sure these three years that Matilda believed in Tom's heart attack. It had been unfortunate. Nice to make sure of Matilda's ignorance. They had been close, those two.

Matilda watched John pay the bill and thought, the cost of this meal would keep ten third world families going for months. She was still angry.

'It's a dangerous foible, John, and hurtful.'

'I apologize, Matty, I am truly sorry. How can I make amends? Tell you I am not going to Prague to meet this mother-murderer, that I'm only going for the fishing?'

Matilda looked at him doubtfully. She had enjoyed the Prague fantasy; it had made her feel safe.

'I don't think you know truth from fiction and it doesn't matter but you should be more careful. You hurt me.'

'Matty, I am sorry. Shall we go? Finish the apologies.'

'Let's walk a little. I'll tell you a secret. I'm wearing a pair of Louise's shoes. My feet swell on these pavements.'

John took her arm and said cheerfully, 'And I will tell you one too. I sleep with a revolver under my pillow – always have.'

Matilda burst out laughing. John laughed too, though he was still a little annoyed with what he considered her prissy reaction over Tom. 'I showed it to Tom on one occasion and he said, "Never tell Matty, it would scare the pants off her."'

'He never called me Matty.'

'No, of course he didn't.'

'And I don't believe in the revolver.'

'There is no need for you to.'

Matilda thought this answer ambiguous and decided to cut short her visit. London suddenly seemed too large, too noisy, too much for her altogether. Too much for her feet.

'I shall have to go home very soon.'

'You've only just arrived.'

'There's nothing for me in London, John, not any more. Piers, if you like.'

'It's lovely to see you. Don't hurry away now you're here.'

'It's such a pity there's no fishing near me. Wouldn't it be nice if there were?'

She's taken offence, thought John. No matter, she's saved herself a heart attack which would be boring for me to arrange. I don't want to stay with her anyway.

'When must you go?'

'In a couple of days, if I may stay that long.'

'You know you may. I'm not going to Prague until Saturday. Today is Tuesday.'

'I shall go on Thursday then.'

'Why don't you ring up?'

'There is nobody to ring up. I live solo.'

'Yes, of course.'

132

'Don't advise me to marry again.'

'I wouldn't dream of it.'

'Louise, Mark, Anabel and Claud have.'

'Fools.'

'And you're an angel.'

'With foibles.' They had reached John's house and he reached for his key. 'A nightcap? Brandy?'

'No. Bed for me. Thank you, I've had a lovely evening.' Matilda left him and later in bed wondered whether he did or did not sleep with a revolver under his pillow. She felt anxious and disturbed, wishing she were at home.

In his room John read for a while, checked that his revolver was correctly placed before turning off the bedside lamp. He lay smiling. Matilda was splendidly naïve. He thought and wondered, without being more than mildly amused, what sort of fellow she was shacked up with and why she should be toting his shoes around in a carrier bag. Larger feet than Tom's, not Mark's or Claud's style. It was probably somebody quite unpresentable. He switched his mind to his trip to Prague. There were various conundrums which might be clearer after a night's sleep. It was aggravating that he had to do so many little jobs himself. Tom Poliport had proved irreplaceable, small cog though he had been.

Restless and unable to sleep, Matilda remembered Hugh's shoes. She had left the carrier bag in the hall. My Christ! What stupidity, she thought, tiptoeing down to fetch them. What a daft thing to do, though Mrs Green would not be in until morning.

18

Matilda was in good spirits at breakfast. John put his head round the door.

'Dinner tonight?'

'Yes, looking forward to it, Piers.'

'What are you doing today?'

'Lunching with Lalage. Some shopping. We won't lunch till late, knowing her.'

'Give her my regards.'

'I will.'

Later she set off, taking a quick look round Habitat and Peter Jones before taking a bus to Piccadilly. She crossed the street, looked in at Hatchard's on her way to what Tom called 'St Fortnum's, Piccadilly'. They had bought one another presents there when courting but today the memory did not bother her. She had discarded yesterday's high-heeled shoes and strode along in espadrilles. She bought a paté for Claud, arranging to have it sent to his New York apartment. The salesman gave her a card on which she wrote: *Eat this in memory of me. Mama.* He would eat it with his lover if it had not gone bad, which she rather hoped it would. She paid by cheque.

A short step into Jermyn Street, the careful choosing of a shirt for Louise at Turnbull and Asser. Louise would prefer something else and lend it to her husband whose colouring would be better suited to the shirt than Louise's. Matilda knew Louise would wonder whether her mother had chosen the shirt with this in view and tell herself her mother was not sophisticated enough to do anything so mean. She paid by cheque and had it sent to Paris.

She walked briskly to Liberty's where she chose two scarves for Anabel to match her most frequent moods, lust and satiation. Anabel would know what was meant. Here too she paid by cheque. A taxi to Foyle's where she bought the latest Russian poet in translation who had defected to the West and had it sent to Mark who would put it on his coffee table. She paid by cheque.

The shopping elevated her spirits to the necessary pitch to meet Lalage with a fair degree of calm, arriving for lunch a calculated ten minutes late.

'Darling, you are late! What on earth have you got on your feet?' Lalage kissed the side of Matilda's face, managing to look her over from head to foot. 'Darling, come in. I see you've been to Paul's. His prices are getting more astronomical every week.'

'Pretty steep,' Matilda agreed. 'How does it feel to be blonde then?'

'Oh sweetie, it's my natural colour. You must remember that. Your father used to call me Blondie.'

'That 'thirties cartoon?'

'Don't be naughty. Come in and tell all.'

Over lunch Matilda listened. Lalage chattered, her mouth full, about herself. In the time spent on drinks and the first course she told Matilda in immense detail about her face lift, each stitch, each pleat, and the price.

'I thought after the last lot you would not need to have it done again. That's what you said.'

'It didn't work out that way. I had a gallop. Swear you won't tell? It got damaged.'

'Who should I tell?'

'You might tell John, you're staying with him.'

'I won't if you don't want me to.'

'I don't mind really. It's just who I had the gallop with.

135

After what he did my face fell so I had to have it pulled up again.'

'Who was the galloping Major then?'

'Not the Major, sweetie, the brother. The one who killed his mother. You must know him – Warner.'

Matilda swallowed her soup and laughed.

'Lalage, come off it. He murdered his mother four weeks ago. You can't have been sleeping with him, had your face done and recovered in that short time.'

'You've got your dates mixed. How do you know, anyway?' Lalage, her expression limited by the amount of slack taken in, managed to look cross.

'I read the papers, watch the box, listen to the radio.'

Lalage, not put out, grinned. 'I'll use that one in a few months. All right, it was someone else. I did meet Hugh Warner once. I thought him very dishy. The huge nose is so sexy. Have you ever met him? His brother's a bit of a bore.'

'I don't think so.'

'I fear he's dead, must be or he would have been caught.'

'They don't catch them all.' Matilda was pleased by the steadiness of her voice. 'They never caught Jack the Ripper.'

'Well, he went for tarts, that was different. I don't suppose they really bothered. One's mother is different.'

Matilda grunted. 'Who were you galloping with then?'

'Ah, he's at the German embassy. He knows Anabel.' Lalage's glance was barbed.

'Lots of people know Anabel. She hasn't necessarily slept with them. She isn't a tart.'

'Steady on, love, I never said she was.'

'You implied by voice.'

'No, darling, no. Anabel's lovely. She gets around a lot.

She's so pretty people are bound to talk about her. It's a pity about her hair.'

'She's young, it doesn't matter what she does to her hair.' How fast, Matilda thought sadly, one catches the breeze. What am I doing here talking to this spiteful old bag, she isn't my friend at all.

'I always loved Tom's hair, the way it flopped forward.' Lalage was removing their plates, fetching the next course. 'The same colour as Anabel's exactly, wasn't it?'

Lalage had her back to Matilda who sat forcing herself to be quiet, forcing herself not to get up and hit that freshly lifted face that knew that Tom's hair only flopped forward when he bent over making love. Then it flopped, but at no other time. She was surprised how mild her feelings were at having what had been a suspicion verified. So what? If he had slept with Lalage it didn't matter. Once she would have tried to kill Lalage; now she would not even slap her.

They finished the meal to the tune of Lalage's other affairs, her new fur coat, her new car, a hoped for diamond. As she combed her hair in Lalage's bedroom Matilda, her feet comfortable in their espadrilles, was able to say with easy laughter:

'Everything new, darling, face, clothes, car, lovers, everything except old moneybags. You are so clever to hang on to him.'

'My husband's not just an old moneybags, Matilda. You are a bitch.'

'Yes, I know. Thanks for the lunch. Take care of yourself. Give him my love. I suppose he's a veritable Kojak by now, poor Bertie.'

Matilda crossed Oxford Street and walked down to the Curzon cinema where there was an erotic German film showing. As she settled in her seat she thought idly, Tom must have been sloshed to sleep with Lalage. There

137

was no doubt in her mind that he had. She was surprised she did not care. She dozed off after the first half of the film, took a taxi back to John's house, soaked agreeably in a boiling bath before dressing to go out. If Tom had slept with her friends then life was a little diminished. Time to go, time for the picnic.

'Would you like to have dinner at the Mirabelle or The Connaught?' John's voice called from the landing.

'You choose John, Piers I mean.'

'The Mirabelle then, and The Connaught tomorrow.'

'You spoil me.' Matilda ran more water in the bath. Staying with John was like having a rich, undemanding husband, though perhaps as a husband he might have demanded more? Somewhere at the back of her mind Matilda knew what he would demand. She decided to entertain him during dinner with a spiced up version of lunch at Lalage's.

John surprised her by taking her to a concert at the Festival Hall before dinner.

'You can rest your tootsies while I listen to music.'

'I do like music too you know –'

'You never used to.' He drove well, nosing his car easily through the traffic.

'Since Tom's death I've listened a lot to the radio. One can't help getting to know, recognize, love music.'

'Very bad for your ear unless you have a really good radio.'

'I haven't. All the same I've learned some music and a lot about current affairs. Sometimes I listen all day, it helps me.'

'Helps what?' John was parking the car, hoping Matilda wouldn't drop off during the concert.

'Helps me keep alive while I must.'

'Of course you must. You are not a suicidal character.'

That's what he thinks, poor old sod. Matilda was glad

138

the concert was to be Mozart, a great cheerer-upper. Beethoven, John's favourite, was inclined to depress. She did not wish to drip tears onto Anabel's frock. She annoyed John by sitting alert and upright through the concert without nodding her head or toe-tapping, making several knowledgeable and intuitive remarks about the conductor. When at the end she turned and gave him a huge smile of thanks he was astonished to find how touchingly like she was to the Matilda he had known before her marriage. Driving her to the restaurant he felt kind and indulgent. She wasn't bad company; certainly tonight she looked presentable.

Eating dinner Matilda told John what Lalage had said or hinted about Anabel.

'She's like that, I shouldn't pay any attention. She's jealous of you, that's all.'

'Jealous of *me*?'

'Yes. Poor Bertie is the dreariest of bores. No wonder her face falls and has to be lifted.'

'But so rich.'

'I grant you that. He's disgustingly rich, does nothing interesting with it, just makes more money for Lalage to spend.'

'No need for her to pick on Anabel. How could she be sleeping with this German when he's in London and she's in Frankfurt?'

'There's that modern invention the aeroplane.'

'So it's true, then?'

'What if it was?' John, having seen Anabel with the German quite frequently, was not prepared to deny.

'I shouldn't mind.' Matilda looked around the restaurant. 'She's a beautiful girl. For aught I know she sleeps around a lot. She should be here, not me, it's a good setting for her. I don't belong anymore. The pavements

139

are a disaster to my feet and I feel out of place. Anabel belongs, I don't.'

'Did Lalage suggest she had slept with Tom?'

'No,' said Matilda, too quickly, reinforcing John's knowledge.

'Have a brandy?'

'No, thank you, it would keep me awake.'

'Did you sleep well last night?'

Matilda wondered whether he had heard her creeping down for Hugh's shoes. 'Oh, I always use Claud's cure if I can't sleep.'

'What's that?'

'Composing letters to *The Times* about the Queen's hats. You have to write a letter which is not derogatory to the Monarchy but expresses your distaste for her headgear. Without appearing unpatriotic it's not possible. In despair you drop off and snore.' Matilda laughed as John grinned at her.

'Sure you won't have a brandy? D'you mind if I do?'

'Of course not. A brandy will suit you sitting there in your super pin-stripe. The onslaught of years has made you very distinguished, Piers.' Matilda liked serving the occasional flattery.

'You are looking very pretty yourself.'

'It's the brief whiff of London you are treating me to.'

'Stay longer. Aren't you lonely in your cottage all on your own?'

'I've got a dog and a gander. I am a country bumpkin.'

'But not a lonely one?' She's being very secretive about this chap, John thought as he ordered brandy. I expect he's good in bed but drops his aitches.

'Not lonely at all. I won't mind going home on Thursday.'

He must be good, thought John. When I have the time I

must find out who he is.

What a boring conversation this is. I prefer Gus any day. Matilda swallowed a yawn. It was long past her bedtime.

'You used to have a cat.'

'She died.'

'I'm sorry.'

'No use being sorry. Death is death. Tom's dead and our cat's dead. It won't be long before I'm dead too. Most of me died when Tom died. We had planned to die together.'

'Death control.'

'Yes. Did Tom tell you?'

'He must have. He wanted to go while the going was good. He got his wish.' John sniffed his brandy. If Tom had wished to die young the heart attack in the rue Jacob was really of little consequence. If I felt guilty which I don't, thought John, I should have no need to.

'Well, it was our wish. I got left. It's bloody hell,' Matilda snapped, anger making her look rather beautiful.

Whoever fits those shoes is lucky, if you like that sort of thing, which I happen to know she does. John watched her colour rise, pleased that Matilda believed in the heart attack, that there was no need to arrange one for her.

'You and Anabel are very alike.' He swallowed the brandy.

'Anabel and I? Goodness no.'

'Not in looks perhaps. Sexually.'

'What an extraordinary –' Matilda paused.

'Accusation?'

'Yes. I never slept around.'

'You might very easily have gone that way if Tom had let you out of his sight.'

Matilda let that pass, relieved that John was about to pay the bill.

'I'm lunching with Anne tomorrow. I wonder what she

141

will have to say.'

'She will pick on Louise, you had Anabel today. Louise is also very beautiful, though not as sexy.'

'I shall try and be ready for her.'

'I'd let the girls protect themselves if they were mine.'

But they are not, thought Matilda, feeling sorry for John, unmarried, childless, sexless. What did he do on long winter evenings?

'You are an enigma,' she said later when she kissed his cheek goodnight. John felt complimented but not pleased and before going to bed checked his engagement diary and was annoyed to find there was no way of getting down to see Matilda until November. Big Feet must wait, he thought, switching off the light, feeling for his revolver.

In her room Matilda was not composing letters to *The Times* but congratulating herself on the fact that by the time the cheques she had written that day had bounced she would be dead. Let Mark worry. It would do him good to feel he had always been right in his opinion of his parents as unworldly, feckless people. As for her host John, if he had thought earlier of calling himself Piers a feast of confusion and derision would have been lost to anyone interested in her entourage, such as Claud. Matilda liked the words 'interested in her entourage' and mulled them over gently before snoring.

Listening to the snores, John lay thinking about Matilda, remembering their youth. It had been too late to hold her, even if he had wanted to, when she had come running to him after killing Felicity. He had been glad she had killed Felicity, who was a nuisance. Desperate Matilda, so upset so long ago. 'I was so frightened I peed in the snow. It was so cold –' She had minded the cold more than killing. He had made her drink brandy, taken her along to Tom. And now, he thought, she's past fifty and snores like the devil.

142

19

On her way to lunch with Anne, Matilda strolled from Chelsea to Harrods. It had occurred to her to surprise Anabel by leaving a really beautiful dress worn only once. She would choose a dress which would suit both Anabel and Louise. They would find it, be aware of its cost, both want it. They would quarrel over who should have it. Anabel, the more ruthless and determined, would get it. Adrenaline would flow, brisk up the funeral. Later Louise would make her husband buy her an even more expensive dress and the anger would spread to him while Mark, who by this time would have visited the bank manager, would be furious. Only Claud would be delighted. Of all my children I love Claud the best, Matilda thought, as she walked into Harrods by the Hans Place entrance and strolled through the men's department to the lifts.

She enjoyed trying on and making up her mind. She was helped by an assistant who was not yet unkind to middle-aged ladies. Matilda confided that the dress was to be for Anabel after she had worn it once.

'I shall wear it tonight, then my daughter can have it.'

Matilda decided against white or black, havered a bit over a lime green which would suit Anabel but looked distressing with her white hair.

'There is a deep rose which would suit you.'

'Let me see it.'

The rose dress did suit. 'I shall have it. Anabel will look marvellous in it.'

'What about the length?' Matilda was wearing her

espadrilles. 'It will be rather short with heels.'

'I loathe heels, they hurt. I'm wearing these things to save pain. What shall I do?' She was distressed. She wanted the dress. With heels it would look ridiculous, too short.

'If you tried in the shoe department you might find a pair of dancing shoes. They are quite flat. I wear them often after a long day at work. My feet swell.'

'Do they at your age?'

'Yes.'

'Shall I go at once and find out, then come back if successful and pay for the dress?'

'Of course, Madam.'

'Will you take a cheque?'

'Of course.'

Successful with the dancing shoes, Matilda left Harrods carrying the dress and shoes, light in heart and lighter by one cheque for several hundred pounds. She walked through Montpelier Square to the park on her way to Anne in Mayfair.

Strolling along by the Serpentine she passed the spot where long ago she had biffed Felicity out onto the ice to her death without even the vaguest recollection of the event. She was filled with the euphoria of spending money she had not got. She enjoyed the crowds of young people walking, sitting, lying on the grass, in one case openly copulating. She liked the boats, ducks, prams, small children running. She enjoyed the shouting and screaming from the Lido, the flying of kites, orange, blue, red and green kites soaring and swooping in the late summer sky, reminding her for a moment of the blue sail she had seen on the sea during her abortive picnic. Next time she would surely be alone.

Anne lived in Mayfair; not for her Chelsea or Kensington. It was known that if she had consented to move to one of these areas her husband would have taken her on more holidays, given her a cottage in the country.

'I can only live in Mayfair, nowhere else,' had been her cry. 'It's so near the shops.' It was said she could be seen shopping in street markets as far away as Lambeth, wearing black glasses and a headscarf – a rumour unconfirmed.

'Lovely to see you, darling.' Anne kissed Matilda. 'What have you got on your feet, for heaven's sake?'

'Espadrilles.'

'Darling, you can't be seen like that, people will laugh.'

'Suppose they do?'

'Oh, you've been *shopping*! Let's have a peep.' Anne's voice was the tone of a daily communicant who has caught a lapsed friend coming out of Mass. It combined surprise with forgiveness. Matilda showed her the dress and dancing slippers.

'It's not you, you know, is it the new mode? Those baby shoes?'

'Yes. I lunched with Lalage yesterday.'

'Darling, she mostly talks about her face you know.'

'I noticed. How is the family?'

'All right. Peter's in Greece, Humphrey is sailing. So boring, and death to one's hair. He always asks me to go too but it's not on, is it?'

'Why not?'

'Well, one feels sick, one gets bored, one's hair goes the most dreadful carrot, you know, and it's difficult to get back to normal, you know.'

'How would I know?'

'Well, love, you can wear it white but at this moment in time one can't, you know.'

'How is Vanessa?'

'Vanessa has some dreadful man in your part of the world. You probably know him, Bobby something. She's been on the bed thing with him, someone said she even does it on the beach. She wants to marry him. You know what girls are like, you've got two.'

'Oh yes, the penny's dropped. I saw her on the beach. They were going to have a barbecue. She swam naked and kept saying everything was super, super.' Matilda accepted an offered sherry.

'"Super" is her latest word. How one hates these expressions! At this moment in time its "super". One never had these verbal tricks oneself, one was prevented by one's parents.'

'Have you been seeing a lot of Princess Anne?'

'Why should I? We don't move in those circles, though one's not far off you know. How is Claud?'

'I thought you might ask after Louise.'

'Why? One's more interested in Claud. So like Tom isn't he – his manners, habits, you know.'

'What habits?'

'One supposes it's the genes, you know. Claud has inherited Tom's – you must have noticed – it's all genes.' Matilda listened for an unspoken 'you know' hovering at the end of the unspoken sentence. What am I doing here? Who is this dreadful woman? Where is the Anne who was once young, pretty, full of life. Who is this bore?

'Claud lives in the States. I never see him.'

'One couldn't very well go and see him, could one? One sees that.'

'Sees what?'

'One sees in Claud what you never seemed to notice in Tom. You carried it off marvellously. We all thought so, you know.'

'Are you implying Tom was a bugger?'

'Matilda!'

'Well, Claud is, "one" knows that. You seem to imply Tom was too.'

'Didn't you know?'

Matilda grinned. 'No, and nor did you. I bet you tried to get Tom into bed and he refused, so now you say he was a bugger.'

'If you weren't one of one's oldest friends –'

'How old are you, Annie?'

'Well –'

'Same age as me.'

'A good deal younger. I married when I was sixteen.'

'Anne *don't*! Not with me. Please. We are old, nearer death than birth, time to get ready. You can't go on dyeing your hair, using silly expressions like "one" instead of "I" or "we" and mischief making.'

'I should think,' said Anne, her face clashing with her hair, 'that living as you do has softened your brain. You should come up to London oftener and keep up.'

'Keep up with what?'

'Life, of course. Life you know.'

'I am more interested in death, so should you be. You haven't much time left to be nice to poor old Humphrey. Why don't you tie up your hair and go sailing with him? Why don't you go to bed with him now and again? Have a good romp.'

'At this moment in time I don't want to.'

'Not during lunch but when he comes back from the Solent? Why not be like Vanessa? She has fun, I've seen her. Sexy.'

'You always had a vulgar streak, even at school.'

'That's like the old Anne. I'm going now. I can't take any more. I'm sorry. I don't belong any more. I'm off –'

'Leaving London?' Suddenly aware of Matilda, Anne caught her hand.

'London and life. Give my love to Humphrey.' Matilda picked up the dress in its Harrods bag.

'Don't get uptight, Matilda. You know you –'

Matilda kissed her quickly. 'I'm sorry, I must go, really sorry.'

Her lunch unfinished, Matilda got into the lift and down into the street conscious of behaving badly in her need to get away. Fool, I didn't go to the lavatory, she thought, walking quickly along the hot pavements to Piccadilly, into the Ritz where in the calm of the cloakroom she assuaged her need, washed her hands which were trembling and combed her hair. He may have slept with Lalage but he was not a bugger.

Matilda stood at a basin letting the cold tap run over her hands, wondering how to fill the afternoon until she could go back for dinner with John. The running water made her want to pee again. Sitting on the lavatory seat she remembered periods at parties when nobody had wanted to talk or dance with her and she had spent much time in cloakrooms. There had been one party which was different. She tried to remember why, in what way it had been different. Where was the party? When? What year? The memory escaped. I can't sit here the whole afternoon. This is ridiculous. She left the lavatory, washed her hands again then sat in the hall to collect herself. She felt angry that yesterday Lalage had sniped and hit and today Anne. They had attacked like birds when a member of the flock is wounded. They wanted to kill me, thought Matilda. How shocked they would be if they knew I mean to kill myself. I am already extinct, a Polish Fowl, a Tufted Hamburg. She smiled and caught the eye of an old man who was sitting near by. He winked infinitesimally. He was listening to his daughter. She must be his daughter since she addressed him as 'Papa', speaking French. Papa was to sit here and

rest while she did her shopping at Fortnum's and
Elizabeth Arden and Liberty's. He could rest, order tea,
she would be back in an hour. Meanwhile he must rest.
She went off with a cheerful wave, high heels trotting.

'Is being old very boring?' said Matilda in French.

'*Je m'emmerde, Madame.*'

Matilda moved to the chair beside him.

'May I tell you what I am going to do about it for
myself?'

'*Je vous prie,*' politely.

'I am not going to get old,' said Matilda. 'I am going to
kill myself.'

'You have cancer, perhaps?'

'No, no. I just refuse to suffer the horrors of age. I have
had all I want. I have decided to stop.'

'How will you stop?'

Matilda outlined her picnic.

'I wish I could accompany you,' said the old man, 'but I
have waited too long. I cannot walk without help, I can do
nothing without help. It is undignified. Only my cat
understands. I have a cat in Paris.'

Matilda told him about Gus.

'That presents a problem.'

Matilda agreed, thinking of Gus, his honking and his
feet slapping on the path. She had forgotten Folly as she
had forgotten Hugh.

'My daughter has gone to the shops. I must sit here and
wait. I can no longer go myself. I am a prisoner of age.'

To amuse him Matilda told him about her shopping,
her choice of presents for her children, of the dress she had
bought that morning for the girls to quarrel over.

'That does not sound like a death wish.'

'All my cheques will bounce.'

'And you will be gone when they do?'

'That's the idea.'

'*Quel révanche.*'

'It is my eldest son, he is such a respectable man - '

'Like his father, perhaps?'

'No, not a bit.'

'What is called "a sport"?'

'Yes, just that. Here comes your daughter. Thank you for listening to me. I should have liked to tell you about my two women friends.'

'The one who said she had slept with your husband, the other that he was homosexual?'

'How did you know?'

'That is an old trick. Have a happy death.'

'Goodbye.'

Matilda left him and, feeling cheered, took a taxi to the Hayward Gallery and thence, on her way back to John's house, to the Tate. She would have liked Claud to meet that old man. She made a quick little prayer for Claud, ejecting it from her mind like a cartoon bubble. If there was 'anybody' about to hear it, perhaps he would do something for Claud?

As she waited on the pavement outside John's house for the taxi driver to give her change she began to hum,

'There's a small hotel
By a wishing well
I wish that we were there, together.'

'My Mum and Dad used to sing that song.' The taxi driver counted the change into Matilda's palm. 'Said they danced to it.'

'I did too.' Matilda separated the change for the tip.

'Stood up hugging?'

'Yes, we hugged as we danced. We hung on to one another.'

150

'Shocking, you does that –'

'In bed?' Matilda laughed. 'We did a lot of hugging upright. I don't see the point of dancing separate from your partner.' She gave him her tip. He drove off laughing. 'Funny old girl.'

20

If Matilda had known that Hugh was spending the nights walking the countryside and swimming in the reservoir she might have worried.

He came in before dawn, slept until lunch when Mr Jones came to feed Gus, a task he had taken upon himself, and to chat. What Mr Jones wanted to chat about was Matilda.

'I love the woman.' Huw Jones sat at the kitchen table, resting his beard in his hands.

'Does she reciprocate?' Hugh was making a pot of tea.

'She does not. She was in love with Tom, that is what she thinks.'

'She wanted to die because she can no longer live without him.'

'That is the uppermost version.'

'Oh, what's underneath.?'

'Who knows? Does my Matilda know herself?' Mr Jones threw out a dramatic enquiring hand. 'She has a great talent for putting matters out of her mind.'

'Your Matilda?'

'Alas not. There was an attempt, a brief scuffle it was but –'

'But what?'

'She pushed me downstairs. I might have broken a bone. I tried to clasp her in my arms but she pushed.'

'What were you doing upstairs?'

'It was the ballcock of the loo. She had asked me to

mend it. I saw her great bed in her room, the bed you slept in, desecration that. I thought it would be lovely to roll on the bed with Matilda so I – but she pushed and down I went. She laughed! Laughed,' he groaned.

'When was this?'

'Several years ago. Since then I keep my place.'

'But you love her?'

'Yes. Silly, isn't it?'

'Depends.'

'Of course it's silly. She is mad. She wants to die. She does not want to grow old and clutter the earth. I love her. I would look after her.'

'You would be old too.'

'Ach! We would be old together but she hates old age, refuses it. She wants to push off. It is arrogant!'

'What about her children? Can't they stop her?'

'Her children!' Mr Jones held up a finger. 'Louise, beautiful, married, two pretty tots, husband with money, lives in Paris. Louise, she is grand, she is the cat's whiskers. She has a lover, all very discreet. Then there is Mark.' Mr Jones held up a second finger. 'A right bastard, a pompous pillar of the establishment, always at conferences. I read his name in the paper. Then there is Anabel. She is flighty, a tart, hard, beautiful of course.' He lifted a third finger. 'Ah, Anabel!' A fourth finger went up. 'Claud. The youngest, a cissy, a pouf. And none of them,' Mr Jones thumped the table so that Folly barked and Gus honked, 'none of them bothers to visit their mother.'

'Perhaps she does not encourage them.'

'True, but they should try. I visit my mother in Tooting and very boring it is too.' Huw Jones laughed, tears leaping from his black eyes to flow into his beard. 'She is so boring,' he cried joyously, 'but I go. She whines, she cries, she is lonely.'

153

Hugh laughed with him, pouring the water into the teapot, putting the pot on the table.

'I constantly visited my mother.'

'But you murdered her.'

'I know, but she wasn't boring.'

'Tell old Jones about it.' The black eyes stopped twinkling, the laughter died.

'No thanks.'

'Okay. So now we have an embarrassed pause while we think of something else to talk about.' Mr Jones was huffed.

Making toast, Hugh asked, 'And Tom, what was he really like?'

'Matilda's Tom?'

'No, yours.'

'Mine? An amusing man. Loved Matilda as well as he was able. I only knew the UFO side of him.'

'And what was that?'

'He had experience in the war, see? Brought people over from France in boats to the estuary here and in a little seaplane. So later he started smuggling, not very often, just now and then. He was a mysterious man. I think he did some work for that chap Matilda is staying with, but I'm not sure.'

'Does she know?'

'Oh no, no, no. Tom also brought in pot. He liked to smoke it just as I do. But just before he died he was cheated. Whoever sent the pot sent heroin too. Tom said he'd been double-crossed, that someone wanted to incriminate him –'

'Why did he not destroy it?'

'He did, he destroyed it, flushed it down the loo just as you did. But he told me he was keeping one packet to confront –'

'Confront who?'

'I don't know, do I? Tom went off to Paris and never came back. There have been no more little boats or little seaplanes, nothing.'

'But you go on reporting UFOs?'

'Yes I do. The police think I am harmless, so I am safe.'

'Did Matilda know of this?'

'Nothing. I think she knows nothing.'

'So she is bored.'

'Matilda is lonely, she has cranky ideas. She is middle aged, has nothing to live for so she falls in love with death. There you are,' Huw Jones exclaimed. 'I am brilliant! Talking to you has discovered for me what Matilda wants. She wants death because she wants something she has never had, a splendid deduction.' Mr Jones looked enchanted.

'But we all get it. Death is the one certainty.'

'But we don't all love it, do we? It is love she wants.'

'I thought she'd had love.'

'I think,' Huw Jones said sadly, 'that she has discovered she never really had it.'

'That can't be true.'

'She could love me but she won't even try. I love her. I look after Gus when she goes away. I would die for her. I have never betrayed Tom to her. I lie at her feet and I don't get a sausage.'

Hugh gathered up the tea things, took them to the sink.

'That woman loves Gus, she does not love poor Jones.'

'Shall we play chess?' Hugh hoped that playing chess would distract his visitor. He found this talk of Matilda painful.

'Okay.' Mr Jones set up the board. 'We will play chess, stop talking about Matilda who thinks old poeple should not be encouraged to live, that weak babies should not be

155

put into incubators. I think she secretly thinks it's a good thing when a lot of old people are suffocated in a fire in an old people's home, when faulty brakes fail on the buses on old people's outings, when they catch the 'flu and die by the score. She is a horrible women, just like Hitler, and I love her and I hate her and her Death. I want to hold her in my arms and roll about in that bed.' With tears coursing down his cheeks Huw Jones set up the board. 'Your move.' His voice was desolate.

Hugh moved his Queen's pawn. I could not comfort this man, he thought, he loves his grief.

When the telephone pealed, which it did occasionally, they watched one another, counting the rings then waiting for it to stop.

'The machine is broken.'

'I taped it up for her. Stub knocked it over, he hated its noise, poor old dog.'

'She could have a new one. It looks untidy.'

Ruminating over his next move Huw Jones muttered, 'She is not a tidy woman. The house is usually a mess. She feels a mess, so death is logical, tidy.'

Thinking of his mother, Hugh exclaimed harshly, 'I don't find it tidy.'

Aware of Hugh's thought, Huw moved a threatening Bishop.

They did not hear the lorry roll to a stop in the lane, though Folly pricked her ears and Gus honked.

'Hullo,' said Claud. 'Where's Mama?'

'In London.' Hugh looked up.

'I telephoned.' Claud looked from one man to the other. 'An hour ago. I thought she must be out. She never goes away.'

'She is.' Hugh took in the full beauty of Claud in tattered jeans, worn suede jacket, Gucci shoes, dark brown eyes in sunburned face, improbable yellow hair, Matilda's mouth.

'She is away, she's staying –' began Mr Jones.

'With loverboy Sir Piers to be.'

'He's not her lover.' Mr Jones spoke crossly, jealously.

'No? Why didn't you answer the phone? Were you here?' Claud looked from one to the other. 'Oh, I *see*!' he exclaimed. 'The Matricide. Is Mama hiding you? Rather brave of her, sporting, jolly sporting. When will she be back?'

'Day after tomorrow.' Mr Jones's voice did not disguise dislike. 'Why are you here?'

'I wanted to show her my find. I've a lorry of the *most* exquisite Delabole and Serpentine headstones. She'd like them. They were in a place I heard of in Cornwall.'

'Pinched?'

'No, Jonesy, not pinched. They were being – er – moved, lined up. Car parks now not graveyards. We move with the times, move to the New World.'

'She'll be back.'

'I can't wait, have to get them packed in the container. Pity. She would have liked them. She never goes away this time of year. Sorry to miss her. Must get them shipped.'

'She – '

'She hung up on me when I phoned, cut me off. I was about to say I might be around, couldn't be sure.' He looked Hugh over, grinning slightly, Matilda's mouth, Claud's expression. 'Well then, another time. Give her my love. This her new dog? She can't live without animals.' He stroked Folly's head as she stood on her hind legs, feet braced against his thigh, tail wagging. 'Taken old Stub's place, then?' Patting the dog, he looked from one man to the other, the question 'taking my father's place?' in his eyes. 'How's her terminal illness?'

'Her *what?*'

'How's her life? Bet you've cheered her up.' He looked at Hugh. 'I shan't tell. A good lech is what she needs; a lot better for her than her infatuation with –'

'Who with?' Mr Jones's voice betrayed fear.

'Death, chap with a scythe. That one – spells it D-E-A-T-H. 'Bye then.'

They listened to his quick step, the slam of the lorry door, the engine starting up, dying away.

'Bastard! He might have told her he was coming.'

'He expected her to be here.'

'Took it for granted.'

'He did telephone. We didn't answer.'

Mr Jones was furious. 'Young sod!'

'It will be better not to tell Matilda,' Hugh said quietly, putting the chessman away.

'Oh, much better,' Mr Jones agreed, 'much better, if better's the word.'

'Worse would be her disappointment. I've done the same –'

'Your mother wasn't like Matilda, you killed her.'

'Oh shut up about my mother you improbable fool.'

'One thinks another time will do, you are right, I do it too. But my mother's so boring, so lonely, she whines at me.'

'Sod your mother.' Hugh tipped the chess board onto the floor.

21

John liked the new dress, Matilda saw at once. He seldom commented on her clothes. Walking to The Connaught from Berkeley Square where he had parked the car, she noticed too that wearing flat shoes not only allowed her to walk comfortably but made John look taller, more distinguished. Tonight he wore a dark grey flannel suit, a cream shirt and black tie. He held her arm lightly, steering her towards the restaurant.

They sat at a corner table and had a drink before ordering. Matilda told John about her day. He laughed.

'You should not take Anne and Lalage seriously.'

'But I do. They make me suffer. It is a fine art with them.'

'Rubbish.'

'They have perfected the detection of the weak point.'

'You should be safe against pinpricks.'

'I am not. I used to be better at it when Tom was alive, better in London. Now it exhausts me. I have lost my vitality.'

'I would hardly say that.' John had been amazed by her itinerary. 'You never crammed so much into two days. You would have used up two weeks in the old days.'

'Old age is creeping in.'

This irritated John, who picked up the menu. 'What will you eat?'

Sensing his irritation, Matilda obediently studied her menu, flushing slightly at his tone. Immediately John was sorry. 'You look ten years younger than our age.' There was so little between them he could safely say this.

'Our age. Yes.' Matilda flashed him a grateful smile. 'I have always envied you your assurance.'

'I always thought Tom a very lucky man.'

Matilda stifled a yawn behind the menu. Why must they talk such balls? After a lifetime knowing each other, she thought, we might have at least one absorbing topic in common. She looked at the menu and longed to be home with Gus, eating a bowl of onion soup, reading a book propped up against the teapot.

'I shall eat mussels, then salmon. I never get decent fish living so near the sea.'

'Shall you be glad to get home? Aren't you lonely?'

'No.' Matilda looked John straight in the eye. 'Not a bit.' It occurred to her that John thought she had a lover. 'I like living alone, I am used to it now. You know what it's like. Of course I'm not lonely.'

John ordered grouse. 'Why don't you change your mind and have grouse? There are no grouse in your part of the world. Oysters first.'

'All right. I gather you want to drink red wine. All right, oysters first.'

'That's about it, you read my mind.'

They ordered grouse with matchstick potatoes. John ordered a second bottle of wine. Matilda drank more than she used to, he thought, watching the way she drank, not one mouthful at a time, but two, even three, emptying the glass frequently. The wine enhanced her looks. He told her about a very beautiful villa where he had stayed that spring.

'In France?'

'No, Italy. Marvellous wild flowers in April, one can still find so many different kinds of orchids.'

'I'd rather you didn't come to my funeral, John, Piers I mean.'

'What?'

'I said I'd rather you didn't come to my funeral.'

'I was telling you about Italy. Weren't you listening?'

'Only half. I'm obsessed by death.'

'All right, we'll talk about it. Why don't you want me to come?'

'You get too close. You think I have a lover.'

'It occurred to me.'

'Mr Jones made an advance.'

'That fellow with a beard, that fat bald chap? What cheek.'

'No it wasn't. He isn't fat, he is square. He can't help being bald. It was very sweet of him really.'

'Sweet!'

'You talk as though –' Matilda stopped, realizing the unwisdom of what she was about to say. I do not belong to John, she thought. He mustn't get that idea in his head. She drank more wine.

'I'm verging on tipsy.' But John was looking towards the entrance. Matilda followed his glance.

'Oh Christ!'

Strolling in, cool, young, exquisite, came Anabel, followed by a very tall black man with quite extraordinarily beautiful features. Anabel was laughing up at him, her teeth, larger than Matilda's, flashing, her face alight with the joy of conquest.

'What a wonderful young man. Who is he?' Matilda had jerked into sobriety.

'Quite a sizeable fish at the U.N.'

'Is his wife beautiful?'

'Yes, a very brilliant woman.'

'Poor Anabel.'

But Anabel had seen them. She came forward in a rush.

'Ma! How super to see you! No wonder I couldn't get you on the phone, you were up here with your beau all the time. How are you, Piers darling? This is Aron, Ma, isn't he exquisite?' Matilda shook a firm hand. 'Oh, Ma, what a dress! You do look wonderful, doesn't she look wonderful?' Her great eyes swivelled from John to her escort. 'Wonderful!'

'Won't you join us?'

'Oh, no, darling, we can't. We only came in for a drink. How is home? How is Stub? How is Prissy?'

'They have both been dead for a long time.' Matilda felt no anger.

'And Gus?'

'He's alive.'

'He'll be next then, won't he?' Anabel let out the words with a yelp of laughter.

When Anabel and her man had gone Matilda began to laugh. 'It's the surprise! The surprise I have every time I meet her that I in my belly created that girl.'

John grinned.

'How long has she been in London? You always know everything.'

'About three months.'

'Little bitch. Couldn't get me on the phone. I suppose the others have been over too?'

'Not Claud, I haven't seen him.'

'His teeth are better than Anabel's and he doesn't go about with his mouth open. He telephoned me, you needn't cover for him.'

'Don't be a cat, Matty. Anabel probably has adenoids. You're her mother, you should have seen to them. How long is he here for?'

'Girls with protruding teeth always get men, it makes

162

them look amiable. Oh, Claud – he went to Yorkshire.'

'Have another drink.'

'I see why people become alcoholics. They learn to accept. No thank you, no more.'

'You must learn to accept your children.'

'Why should I?' Matilda was suddenly extremely angry. 'Why? I don't like any of them except Claud. Let them come to my funeral. I don't want you but I do want them. How dare she not know about Stub and Prissy?'

'Perhaps you didn't tell her.'

'I'm sure I didn't.'

'Well then.'

'Well nothing. I want to go home.'

'We will.' John waved to the waiter. 'I'll take you home.'

'Not yours, mine. I must get back. It's nothing but stab, stab, stab in London.' In an unconscious gesture Matilda cupped her breasts in her hands, then folded them in front of her on the table.

'D'you know that someone somewhere put his hands over my breasts and said, "Chimborazo Catapaxi has stolen my heart –"'

'I should think lots of chaps did.' John was signing the bill and counting money for the tip. 'That was one of the poems our generation quoted like *A Shropshire Lad* and one or two particular sonnets we'd done at school.'

'How bracing you are.' Matilda stood up. John followed her out thinking that after all that wine she was wonderfully steady on her pins.

Arriving back in Chelsea, Matilda's mood changed. She hummed and sang snatches of Cole Porter. John joined in.

'A lovely evening, so educational.' She watched him lock the car, standing in her flat shoes on the pavement, still warm from the long hot summer. John opened the door and they went in.

'A nightcap?'

'An Alka-Seltzer more like.'

'I'll get you one.'

Matilda kicked off her shoes and spread her toes.

'You and your feet.' John stood in the doorway, holding the Alka-Seltzer, smiling indulgently.

'My country feet.' She pulled at the toes of her tights, easing the constriction.

'Have you seen my bedroom?'

'No.'

'You are wonderfully incurious, Matty. Come and look.' Matilda followed him across the landing.

'New curtains.'

'Very pretty. Where did you get that stuff?'

'Paris.'

'They are not like you somehow –' She was puzzled. 'More Tom's sort of thing.'

'He got it for me.'

Just one more prick in the heart, thought Matilda, keeping her face blank. Trust John.

Pulling the pink dress over her head she was dazzled by the momentary darkness. Whoops! I'm tipsy! Carefully she put the dress on a hanger, turning it this way and that to see whether she had spilled food on it. She took off her knickers and bra. Her head was singing, it was difficult to focus. In the bathroom she mixed Alka-Seltzer and drank the noxious mixture, sitting naked on the edge of the bath, expecting to throw up.

After a few minutes she put on her nightdress and got into bed. She kept the bedside light on. If she turned it off her head would whirl.

She said a little prayer asking for asleep.

No sleep.

She lay thinking about Anabel. So beautiful. A horrid girl on the whole. She had never been able to communicate with her, nor with Louise or Mark, only Claud, and even then only on occasion. It is my fault, she reproached herself. I cannot reach them any more than my mother could reach me. I am not wanted. What could I have said to Anabel? Something warm, loving, maternal. I felt none of those things. I felt resentful. She never comes near me. I should have made friends with that man, he would then be kinder to Anabel, dispose of her less lightly. I don't mind her going about with a black man. Why should I? Stub was black.

That's it. Matilda drunkenly saw her nature revealed. I can only get on with animals. I only trust animals. Stub, Prissy, Gus, all the animals in her past, as demanding as children but never nasty. Wow! Black, brown, multi-coloured animals. Ah! She loved them.

Gosh, she thought, I'm never going to sleep. She put on her dressing-gown, put out the light, opened the window and leant out. Somewhere in London lovely Anabel lay in that man's arms. I envy her. I hope he will not hurt her. It will make her take it out on someone else, some white dolt. Anabel, so self-assured, no great animal lover she. Matilda remembered Anabel drowning a rabbit in a bucket. Bloody child. In a way she was like Tom. This unforeseen thought caused Matilda to weep. She walked up and down the room weeping. 'Tom, Tom, oh poor Tom, did I love you?'

Matilda felt so uncertain she became distraught. I must walk, she thought, putting on her slippers. She wrapped the dressing-gown round her, took her latchkey, tiptoed downstairs, letting herself out into the street.

Roused by the slight sound, John looked out onto the landing, wondering what the hell Matilda was doing now.

'What on earth is going on? he called querulously.

'I'm going for a fucking walk.' Matilda slammed the street door.

'If anyone behaved like that to me.' Matilda said aloud in the empty street, 'I'd never have them in my house again.' She walked weeping along the pavements, composing nice things she should have said to Anabel, clever intelligent things she could have said to the beautiful black man. Aron – a splendid name – balanced, biblical, dignified. My word, she thought, he was sexy, no wonder Anabel – do hope she enjoys it, lucky girl.

She walked briskly, passing the Royal Hospital, far from John's house. The Alka-Seltzer was working. She turned left through Burton Court, into Smith Street, along the King's Road. A middle-aged widow, she saw herself walking down the King's Road in her dressing-gown, sober now. It was a pity that she liked animals best, but there it was. At some moment, she could not remember when, she had nearly loved human beings. It must have been a moment of passion. Passion was something so tremendously rare. Animals were better, safer, Now she was nearly back at the cul-de-sac. The latchkey? She had it in her hand. I couldn't bear to wake him again, she thought, letting herself in quietly. He may have owned Tom but he doesn't own me. She shut the door and crept up to bed.

22

In the train Matilda leafed through *Harper's*, a luxury bought for her by John with *The Times* and the *Guardian*. He had found her a seat, kissed her goodbye and left before the train started, putting her out of his mind before he reached his car.

Matilda, too, had forgotten John, it dawning on her that for four days in London she had not listened to the news or read a paper. This had happened to her before. Usually she found she had missed nothing and what news there was was fresh and interesting.

She had hardly thought of Hugh since visiting his flat. Now, skipping through the *Guardian*, it seemed silly to have bothered to snatch him a pair of shoes. Any man in his senses would have long since left and be far away. He had no real need of the money. A man ingenious enough to keep a cache under the communal carpet of a house full of flats would be clever enough to have moved on. The probability was there and as the train moved out into open country she hoped it was a certainty.

Matilda laid *Harper's* down. Its contents were a catalogue of the shops she had visited. The train, gathering speed, rocked along by the Kennet and Avon canal. Harrods, Fortnum's, Habitat and Liberty's seemed to her more like museums than places where persons like herself shopped. She was glad she had sent her children presents and that from a flower shop in Knightsbridge she had arranged for an exotic fern to be delivered to John with a note of thanks. She would write an apology too. A group of geese crossing a farmyard seen from the train made her feel intensely anxious. If Hugh had left would Gus be starving when she got back? Normally if she went away she would ask Mr Jones to keep an eye on Gus, but Hugh did not know Mr Jones and would have left Gus to his own devices. Nervously, as though the action would make the train go faster, she felt in her bag for the keys of her car. For the rest of the journey she held them in her hand.

Anxiety bunched her stomach. She shook her head when the attendant came down the corridor calling 'First Lunch,' then 'Second Lunch,' then 'Coffee, Tea, Ices.' All she could think of was Gus starving. She had shown Hugh the maize bin. Perhaps he would have gone off leaving a large basin of maize and a bucket of water. If he had let Gus out to fend for himself the neighbourhood fox would have killed him.

Then again perhaps Hugh was still there. He had food for some days. All he was short of was milk. She had made him promise to be careful, to keep quiet, to keep hidden. She wondered how she had got herself into this situation, it was lunatic. Obviously, she thought, clutching the car keys, by now something would have happened to alert the police. The dog would have barked, Hugh would have been seen, arrested after a chase, be 'helping the police with their enquiries'. Why had she not read the papers or listened to the news?

Of course John was joking when he said he was meeting the Matricide in Prague. He read the papers, would have taken it for granted she did too, would have made his joke. Oh God, thought Matilda, he must think I'm mad. Perhaps I am. It's high time I replanned my picnic or I shall end my days in a bin. Too boring for Louise, Mark, Anabel and Claud. I care for them enough not to inflict that on them. The car keys bit into her palm.

168

She made an effort towards calm and how to react to the police when they told her they had found Hugh. It would be best to be flustered, astonished, indignant. Then, remembering Hugh's shoes were in her suitcase, she thought, how incriminating, I must throw them out of the window, and stood up to reach for her case on the rack, when she noticed the train slowing down. She had reached her destination.

23

The car was where she had left it, exactly the same, just a bit more dusty. Somebody had written in the dirt on the back windows:

The driver of this car is a sex maniac.

Matilda put the key in the lock. The car was airless. She opened the windows, starting the engine, letting it idle. The palm of her hand felt sore from clutching the keys. As the engine livened she thought she would never know whether those hints dropped about Tom were true. As she drove out of the station yard she told herself she didn't care whether he had been a part-time spy, slept around or been a bugger. It made no difference now.

Driving through the town she saw faces light up with laughter as people read the message on the back window. It's great to look respectable, she thought. Then she thought it must even soften the hearts of the police who would be waiting for her. If Hugh has any gratitude he will have broken a window to make it look like a break-in, messed things up a bit, not too much, just enough.

She stopped to buy milk, then drove fast along the road bordered by bristly cornfields waiting for the plough, pheasants gleaming in the stubble. She felt hot and sticky after the train, looked forward to changing into old clothes. It felt warm enough to swim, make a trip to the sea. As soon as she had dealt with the police she would go.

In the three miles of lanes from the main road to her cottage, late holidaymakers were sticking firmly to the middle of the road, determined not to scratch their paint against the tall banks of this alien countryside. Their care was alarming to Matilda, used to judging the width by a whisker.

She opened the gate, drove into the garage. She switched off the engine. Silence, then a loud honk and the slap of Gus's feet as he came to meet her.

'So you are all right my handsome, my gorgeous brute.' Gus flapped his wings, excreted.

'All alone?' She stroked his neck. Gus honked louder, walked slightly ahead towards the back door. Matilda listened. Not a soul about, no Panda car, no surprises. She felt a sense of loss. Hugh had gone just as she had thought he would, as she had hoped he would.

My Christ, Matilda said to herself, what a fake I am. I am sadly disappointed. What shall I do with his shoes and his money? He might have waited, might have trusted me.

Crossly she felt for the key under the scraper and opened the door. The house was orderly and empty, as empty as when she had closed the door and set off for her picnic.

'Damn, blast and to hell with that barbecue,' she said to Gus, who craned his neck in at the door, blue eyes meeting hers. 'That bloody girl Vanessa and her Bobby.'

'I wasn't expecting you back so soon' Hugh, followed by Folly, walked in past Gus. 'Hullo there.' He bent and kissed her cheek. Matilda burst into tears.

'What's up?' Hugh stood back while Folly leapt up, wagging her tail in ecstasy, scratching Matilda's London clothes. 'What are the tears for?'

'I was expecting the police to be waiting for me. I was all ready.'

'All keyed up?'

'Yes.'

'No police, sorry. Were you hoping?'

'I thought you'd gone.'

'Sorry, I haven't.'

'I brought your money and a pair of shoes.'

'Oh good, I need shoes. Well done.'

'But I absolutely felt you'd be gone or that they would have caught you. I saw it all in my mind.'

'So you're disappointed.'

'God, no, I'm –' Matilda pretended to herself she did not know what she was feeling.

'Don't tell me you're pleased.'

'Very,' Matilda whispered. 'Very pleased.'

'Ah.' Hugh took her face in his hands and gently kissed her mouth. 'Nice to see you back, sex maniac.'

Matilda giggled. 'Some naughty child.'

'Did you have a good time?' Hugh was filling the kettle, putting out cups while Matilda, in her London clothes, watched him.

'Not really. No. I had good meals, went round the shops, saw people –'

'Friends?'

'They used to be friends.'

'Not any more?'

'One suggested Tom was a bugger, another that she'd slept with him and the friend I was staying with had the nerve to hint that Tom was a spy.'

Hugh laughed. 'Strong or weak? India or China?' He held a tea-spoon in one hand, a caddy in the other.

'Strong Indian.'

Hugh made the tea.

'It's been pretty boring here without you. If it hadn't been for Mr Jones I might have left.'

'Have you met him? Oh my!'

'Yes. Day after you left. He came to tell you he'd seen a UFO. He and I play chess.'

Matilda kicked off her shoes, sat at the kitchen table.

172

'He used to play with Tom.'

'So he says.'

'Has he told anybody you are here? Who does he think you are?'

'He says he never sees anybody except you as they think he is barmy. I like him. He plays a very odd game.'

'Tom said he cheated.'

Matilda took from her bag the envelopes, handing them to Hugh. 'What made you think of hiding it in such a public place?'

'My brother and I used to dream up places, have competitions between ourselves when we were children.'

'The Major with the nose?'

'Yes. Life was simpler then. We trusted each other. It was like Mr Jones. He trusts me. I trust him.'

'When did he see the UFO?'

'Day you left. He's coming presently for a game and supper.'

'It's not safe.'

'I can't tell him not to come. It would upset him.'

'A secret between two people is a secret, but not between three. More than three, I daresay. He's really crazy.'

'No, no,' said Hugh comfortably. 'He is eccentric. He likes to talk, he's lonely.'

Matilda groaned, put down her cup and went up to have a bath, running the water very deep, almost hotter than she could bear, to wash away insinuations about Tom. She came down to find Hugh and Mr Jones lying on the grass, chatting in the dark.

'Mr Jones, Huw, how nice.'

Mr Jones scrambled to his feet, short, square with his beard grey on the chin, brown at the sides, his black eyes observant and bright.

'I brought a bottle with me.' Mr Jones held Matilda's

hand between both of his, squeezing it reassuringly before letting it go.

'Oh, how kind.' She tried to enthuse.

'Not dandelion, whisky.' Mr Jones smiled shyly. 'From the pub.'

'I'll fetch some glasses.' Hugh went into the house.

'How was London?' Mr Jones asked politely.

'So, so.'

'Nice to get home then?'

'Yes.'

'I was delighted to find Hugh here when I came to see you. I would have been disappointed to find the house empty.'

Hugh came out carrying a tray with water and glasses. Mr Jones ignored him. 'It is important to help Hugh.'

'Help? In what way?'

'Oh, give him a lift.' Mr Jones reached out to take a glass from Hugh and passed it to Matilda. 'I am interested in the extreme.'

'What do you mean?'

Mr Jones took the glass Hugh offered. 'Just a little water. It's extreme to kill your mother.' He sipped his drink, eyes downcast.

Matilda couldn't see Hugh's face. She let out her breath. 'You sly old boots.'

Mr Jones swallowed a gulp of whisky. 'I am neither sly nor mad. I listen to the radio and read the papers. I mind my own business. You should know that, Matilda. Hugh knows it.'

'After all these years I certainly should.'

Mr Jones looked gravely at Hugh then at Matilda. 'It seemed to me no business of mine to inform on your visitor and Tom never informed on me so fair dos, I thought, finding Hugh Warner here, fair dos.'

174

'We, I mean I, never believed –' Matilda hesitated.

'Never believed in the UFOs?'

'Well, not really.'

'Just as well, nobody else does, so in return I do not believe in the Matricide. You *cannot*,' Mr Jones leaned forward to put a hand on Matilda's knee, 'you cannot believe all you read in the papers or hear on the radio, that's a fact.'

'It is.'

'Mind you,' Mr Jones laughed, 'I don't suppose he ever told you.'

'He didn't. I only found out after his death.'

'Well then, you know now. Sorry.'

'For the last few days almost everyone I've met has been hinting at a Tom I didn't know. I thought that was spiteful London but now you do it too.' Matilda paused. 'He hid things from me.'

'Not telling is not necessarily hiding. He knew and I knew if he upset me about the UFOs I'd take umbrage. I would have stopped him, so he said nothing, that's all'. Mr Jones finished his whisky, put his glass down on the grass and sprang to his feet without using his hands.

'We'll play chess another day,' he said to Hugh, shook Matilda's hand and walked off jauntily.

'Well!' Matilda sat back on the grass, stretching her legs, 'I'm blowed! What a simpleton I've been. It never dawned on me he and Tom were partners.'

'You look shocked.' Hugh gathered Folly into his arms. 'You must have had an inkling.'

'None. It was after Tom's death I found –' She hesitated.

'Evidence.' Hugh was smiling, his teeth foxy. 'Pot and heroin.'

'You've been prying.'

'Surely you didn't expect me not to?'

'Rather ungentlemanly.' Matilda's voice was tart. Then she giggled. 'What did you find?'

'Heroin. I flushed it away. What did you do with the pot?'

'Smoked it.'

'All of it?'

'No.'

'Where is it?'

'In the bank.'

'And you say under a stair carpet is imaginative.'

'I didn't have much left. I packed it into a silver cigarette box of my grandfather's and left it for Claud. He likes it.'

'How much did you use?'

'Don't know. It lasted some months after Tom –' She sat up suddenly. 'D'you think Tom really had his heart attack in the rue Jacob or d'you think it was in Louise's bed? She lives just round the corner, she could have pushed him out.'

'Don't be vile,' Hugh shouted at her. 'Don't imagine worse than you need. He was probably on his way to see her.' He was very angry.

'Yes, I expect you are right. One thinks such dreadful thoughts. That's why I smoked pot. The hallucinations are mostly nice.'

Hugh refilled her glass, put it in her hand. 'Tell me about Louise.'

Matilda did not look at him. She sat, the glass in one hand and with the other hand stroking Gus, who had come to stand beside her.

'She was our first child, a love child. Tom was crazy about her. I was pregnant when we married. I don't like babies much. I prefer animals.' Gus sank down beside her, his neck twisted, blue eye looking up at her. 'Tom looked

176

after the baby better than I did. He changed her nappies, washed her, fed her, had her in bed when she cried, cuddled her, was marvellous really. She adored him. It was always Tom she loved, not me. I suppose in the event they were so close nappy changing evolved into fucking. I should not have been surprised.'

Hugh said nothing, watching her face, as did the gander.

'I loved Tom,' she said quietly. 'They didn't see me when I found them in my bed, well, our bed I suppose. I went for a walk and had a think. I couldn't stop loving Tom. I loved Louise, not as much as Claud but I did love her, so I decided half Tom was better than no Tom. I never told him I knew.'

'Go on.'

'I thought when Louise married it would stop.'

'Did it?'

'No it did not.' She flushed. 'It became more so. Tom brought home lots of new bedtime tricks. I pretended I didn't notice.' She glanced at Hugh. 'I enjoyed them. I felt a bit funny learning new aspects of sex from my daughter but it's true, I liked it.' She grinned at Hugh. 'I tell you everything, don't I?'

Hugh felt he had had enough of Louise, that it was better to leave Louise while she was tasting good. 'Tell me about Jones. Have you slept with him?'

'Does he say I have?'

'No, but I wasn't sure.'

'I haven't. He wanted to and there was a time when I might have. He is such a contrast to Tom, all that hair and short legs, but Anabel – oh!' Matilda gave a shriek of laughter which she tried to stifle, putting her hand across her mouth.

'Anabel?' Hugh probed.

Tears of laughter oozing from the corners of her eyes, Matilda gasped. 'It's so unkind to laugh. Anabel had come. It was after Tom had been dead some time, a year perhaps. Mr Jones was being helpful, so kind, weeding the garden. I'd let it go dreadfully. Anabel was with me in the kitchen. She'd just said in an arrogant, bossy voice, "Ma, you should brace up. What you need is sex. It's very bad to stop suddenly and give it up altogether. You've tried pot," she said – I don't know how she knew –"you've tried pot and it doesn't do anything for you, you must have sex. Why not," said Anabel, fixing me with those great brown eyes, "have old Jones? Do him a favour. You know he pines for you." ' Matilda wiped the tears with her finger. 'We looked at him. He was crouching there wearing wide khaki shorts and his balls were hanging down over the carrot leaves. Oh!' Matilda's eyes filled again. 'I've never been so close to that girl. She said, "They look like nut bags you hang out for the tits. Sorry I spoke." Poor girl. She laughed until she threw up and Mr Jones came in and made us a resuscitating cuppa. He thought we were crying over Tom. That was the last time she came here. I saw her in London. She came into The Connaught looking lovely with the most beautiful man. John, Sir Piers to be, knew him. She wasn't expecting to see me. She carried it off rather well.'

'You didn't know she was in London?'

'No. She had not wanted to see me. I might have asked her to visit me. It's a risk.' Matilda shook her head. 'Poor Mr Jones.' Hugh felt it safer to leave Anabel sick with laughter.

'So Mr Jones's UFOs?'

'Why are you changing the subject?'

'That's the art of conversation – edge. Did you know about the UFOs, what they were?'

178

'Not until I found the drugs after Tom's death. While he was alive it all went on under my nose so. . .' She seemed unwilling even now to say more.

'So?' Hugh pressed.

'So if he was a smuggler and I didn't know, it may well be true that he slept with Lalage as well as Louise and that he was one of the next-honours-list Sir Piers's spies. But I cannot see him as a bugger, as Anne suggests.'

'Would you have loved him less?'

'No. I loved him. If you need proof there's Louise. No divorce.'

'You couldn't cite your own daughter.'

'I don't see why not. I thought of doing it but it wouldn't have altered anything. Louise is married to a man I like, it would have broken him, whereas you –'

'Whereas I, who have killed my mother, can understand, is that it?'

'I suppose so.'

'Tom and Louise didn't kill anything or anybody.'

'How d'you know?'

'What are you suggesting now?'

'Louise's second child is abnormally like Tom.'

'You repellent woman! It's well known children take after their grandparents. Louise would never have let herself –'

'Conceive her father's child?'

'That's what I mean.'

'You don't know Louise.'

'She sounds very like you.' Hugh's voice expressed disgust.

'She's very like me, very like indeed. Tom always said so.' Matilda laughed. Hugh joined in the infection.

'The Egyptians, the Pharoahs.' Matilda grinned at Hugh. 'If they did it, why not Tom and Louise?'

Hugh left the question unanswered, setting himself to opening the envelopes and counting the money.

'How much?' Matilda watched him.

'Quite a lot. Enough to get away. When my brother gets back, if he ever does, he will find the cache gone. He'll know.'

'But he won't tell.'

'Money is funny stuff, it does things to people. If he is needing a couple of thousand and it's gone, he may well be irked. So –'

'So you'd better go.'

'Yes,'

'How?'

'Like everyone else – train and plane on a busy day. Passport Control are very pushed, all those faces just become a blur.'

'Why not a boat? One of the UFOs?'

'That has stopped. I wouldn't involve him anyway. I like him.'

'What about me? I'm involved.'

'Like you say, you're a dead woman.'

'And you don't like me. Repellent, you said. Evil.'

'Truthful. Truth may be a laughing matter but it is quite refreshing. Shall you miss me?'

'I shall plan my picnic.' She would not answer directly. 'You can stay as long as you like,' she added quickly.

'What about Gus.'

'I love him.'

'That's true, an uncomplex love to you, easy, but the poor bird's so twisted he kills a goose when put with one.'

Matilda wasn't listening to him. She tapped her teeth with her empty glass.

'John, Sir Piers to be, was in this somewhere. I believe he was in on the smuggling thing. I think he and Tom worked together or Tom worked for him. I had the impression in London that he was trying to find out if I knew. No, that's not right; I have the impression now. He said he was meeting you in Prague.'

'What did you say?'

'I pretended to believe him, played along. I didn't exactly want to tell him you were here. He's sinister.'

'Maybe my brother is one of his minions infiltrating the Guerillas or some ploy of that kind. They train in Prague.'

Matilda stood up suddenly, startling Folly. 'All I really mind,' she said bitterly, 'is being left out. I feel such a fool left out of the *fun*.'

'Hurt pride.'

'Of course my pride's hurt, battered.'

Hugh said nothing, finding no word of comfort.

Matilda lay in bed that night hugging the bedclothes, full of suspicions. The annihilation of her pride was complete.

24

Equally perturbed, for he had no reason to hurt her, Hugh woke Mr Jones in his bungalow, inviting himself in for a drink. Pleased to be needed, the lonely man arose, wrapped an old kimono round his hairy person, took the whisky from its cupboard, found glasses and set up the chessboard.

'Your mind is not on the game,' he presently said, checkmating Hugh too easily.

'I have hurt Matilda.'

'She is vulnerable.'

'How did her husband manage?'

'He had the knack. She is not all that bright.'

'Bright?'

'That is what I said. She is young for her age, she believes what she wishes to, always deludes herself.'

'I think she is getting over it.'

'A pity for her.'

'Why?'

'Well,' Mr Jones looked uneasy, 'it is far better for her to remember Tom as she liked to have him.'

'You are ambiguous.'

'Tom had her caged where he wanted her. She never knew he was a rogue, dishonest you might say, but there you are, she loved him.'

'She loves that goose.'

'It's the same thing. Her gander is a fantasy, so was her husband, but she was satisfied, thought they'd live and die together. It was tommy rot, romantic. Tom would not have killed himself before he got old to save people trouble. My God, he would not. No, no, he would have had Louise, Mark, Anabel and Claud belting round waiting on him in his invalid chair.'

'And Matilda?'

'He would have let her die first, worked her to death and made her enjoy it.'

'It sounds just as well for Matilda he died in Paris.'

'I don't think so.' Mr Jones yawned and scratched his hairy chest. 'She is finding out more about him, liking him less, getting disillusioned, it is a pity.'

'She will find a modus vivendi.'

'Not Matilda. Whatever anyone does she will remain what she is. She and the gander are well suited.'

'I think she will kill herself. She should have some fun first though, take a lover, go abroad –'

'She has no wish to go abroad. She has the goose.'

'Gander.'

'Okay. Now what did you wake me up for in truth?'

Hugh laughed.

'Can you, if I give you the money, get me some foreign currency?'

'Sure, of course I can.' Mr Jones did not add that he had a trunkful of German marks and Swiss francs as he did not think Hugh would believe him. 'How much have you got?'

'A thousand.'

'Bring it to me tomorrow. Do you want to go over in the UFO? Nice boat. It's in the harbour.'

'No. I shall go from London Airport, it's the most crowded.'

'Very good, you do that. That is how your murdered mother would travel.'

Hugh answered shortly, 'There is no need to harp.'

'Takes all sorts. Louise, Mark, Anabel and Claud would

not kill their mother, only want to.'

'Poor Matilda.'

'She has the goose.' Mr Jones had began to look sleepy. Hugh got up.

'I will bring the money tomorrow in cash.'

'I will have the currency ready for you in a few days.'

I bet he has it stashed around the bungalow thought Hugh. He said goodnight and walked back to the cottage.

Gus, recognizing his step, gave a token honk from the scullery. As he climbed the stairs Hugh heard Matilda's snores. By morning, he thought, she will have forgotten her unease, have buried the discoveries about Tom in her unconscious.

He stood in the dark, looking out of his window at the moonlit countryside, thinking of his mother, remembering her face looking up at him in terror and hearing her voice – 'Oh Hugh, quick, *please*.' Her eyes large, stone grey, fringed with, for an old woman, ridiculously long lashes, haunted him. He recollected how, as a boy at school, homesick, unable to sleep, he had tried to bring her face and voice to mind for comfort in the alien enviroment of his dormitory. He had had trouble in those days to see her clearly; now he both saw her and heard her voice. 'Oh Hugh, quick, *please*.' She would travel with him whether he willed it or not.

25

Hugh made his arrangements without consulting Matilda. While she was shopping he tried on Tom's clothes, looking at himself in the glass, wearing various garments. Tom's taste in dress was unlike his own. He felt unnatural in most of the clothes. From a store of trousers, jeans, suits, shirts, jerseys, he made a final choice of pale corduroy trousers, a tweed jacket, red socks. He hesitated whether to wear a polo neck jersey or a shirt, settling for the shirt as more respectable. He put aside, for packing, jeans, T-shirts, spare pants, a shirt or two, swimming trunks and sweaters. Ranging round the house he found several pairs of black glasses.

He dressed himself and waited for Matilda, listening for her car, standing out of sight in the hall. When the car drew up Gus honked from the back door and slapped his feet as he ran to meet her. Listening to her voice greeting the bird Hugh thought she sounded younger, happier, altogether more cheerful and full of confidence.

She dumped her parcels on the kitchen table. 'Wait, Gus, wait,' she said to the bird. 'I'll get you some maize.' She kicked off her espadrilles. Her feet were barely audible on the stone floor. 'Here,' she said, 'here, Gus, my love, eat this.' She put the bowl on the step and straightened up. Catching sight of Hugh in the doorway she gasped.

'Hullo,' she said, 'were you looking for me?' Hugh came forward a step. 'Or my husband?' Matilda's voice tightened. 'He's around somewhere, I'll call him.' She raised her voice and called loudly, 'Tom. Darling? There's a man here to see you –' She edged towards the telephone.

'Matilda.' Hugh stepped forward. 'It's me, don't be frightened.'

'Oh!' Matilda whispered. 'My God, you scared me. I nearly wet my knickers. How d' you do it? You've changed yourself completely. I thought you were the police.' She sat down abruptly.

'It's good, isn't it?' Hugh turned around so that she could see him. 'What do you think?'

'Those trousers were Mark's.'

'Not Tom's?'

'No, and the jacket was Claud's until he took to wearing suede. Where did you find the glasses?'

'In the hall cupboard.'

'Those were Anabel's when enormous lenses were in fashion. They make your nose quite small. What's this in aid of?'

'I want to get out. I'm getting claustrophobia. I feel like taking you out to lunch and a swim. What do you say?'

'Risky.'

'I have to start some time. Come on, it will give me confidence if I'm with you.'

'We can't start off together, nobody knows you are here.'

'Very well. I'll go through the copse and meet you at the bus stop.'

'I must change my clothes, get my bathing things. I don't think you should risk it.'

'Come on, Matilda, try.'

'Wait a minute then.'

Matilda went upstairs and snatched up a cardigan, put on a clean shirt, combed her hair, excited.

'Okay, I'm ready.'

'Give me ten minutes' start.' Hugh left the house.

Ten minutes gives me time to ring the police. Ten

minutes gives me time to make a plan with them. She watched the clock jerk its minute hand. 'Ten minutes is a life,' she said to Gus as she filled his bowl with maize. 'Why does he tempt me with ten minutes?' She locked the back door, put the key under the scraper, went to the car and sat with her eyes on her watch until the ten minutes had passed.

Hugh sat on a stile by the bus stop, Folly beside him. He got in beside Matilda. Folly sat behind.

'First mistake was to bring Folly. She's been seen with me. People think she's mine. You mustn't do that again.'

'Right, I won't.'

'You shouldn't have given me ten minutes. I might have phoned the police.'

'But you didn't?'

'No, but please don't do it again. I thought of doing it.'

Hugh laughed. 'There are two Matildas, one who phones the police and one who is kind and loves Gus. For all I know there are many more; those are just the two I've met.'

'How many of you?'

'Count.'

'There's you hunted, about to go out with the tide. There's you with Folly. There's you with Gus. There's you with me. There's you –'

'Killing my mother.'

'I wasn't going to say that.'

'You were. Be honest, stay honest. We are near death, both of us.'

'All right, there's you killing your mother. End of conversation.'

Angrily, Matilda trod on the accelerator and drove fast on the main road.

'Don't drive so fast, there's a Panda car behind you.'

Matilda slowed, letting the police car overtake them. 'I'm frightened every time I see them. I was brought up to like them.'

'So was I.' Hugh looked at her profile. 'Where's the best place to eat?'

'We'd better go somewhere quiet.'

'No, I want a busy place. I don't want a quiet place, as though I were hiding.'

'All right. The best place is the Crab Inn if we can get a table.'

'Does it have a bar?'

'Yes.'

'Right. Take us there.'

Matilda parked the car. They made their way to the restaurant along the crowded street. Hugh held Matilda's arm, liking the feel of her skin, glancing about him at the people.

The Crab Inn was crowded. They agreed to wait for a table.

'Let's sit outside. Can we eat out, it's pleasant.'

They were told they could. Hugh ordered drinks, sat facing Matilda who, with the sun in her eyes, screwed up her nose and sneezed.

'I forgot my dark glasses.'

'Stay here. I'll get you some. Sit in my place.' He did not offer Anabel's glasses.

'I'll come too.'

'Wait here. If there's a free table, take it, start ordering. I shan't be long.' Hugh loped off up the street. He bought a plain pair of dark glasses for Matilda, guessing at the fit, then went to a travel agency. He enquired the times of trains to London before strolling back to Matilda.

'They are just getting us a table overlooking the harbour.'

'Nice.' He handed her the dark glasses.

'Thank you.' She put them on.

A waiter brought the menu. Hugh asked for the wine list.

'What's good here?'

'They do a delicious smoked trout paté. The crab's always good. Sometimes they do a lovely goat cheese with garlic, blows your head off.'

'We could finish with that. I shall have the trout paté. What's the steak like today, waiter?'

'Well – sir –'

'Okay, not steak then. I'll have the gigot of lamb, the paté first and the goat's cheese. What will you have Matilda?'

'Just the gigot, the cheese and salad.'

'And a bottle of No. 17 please.' The waiter scribbled on his pad.

'It's a nice place and Folly can sit with us.' Hugh smiled across at Matilda who looked at him anxiously. She made a tiny sideways gesture with her thumb. Behind his dark glasses Hugh let his eyes swivel without moving his head. A rather vacuous girl sat at a table with her parents who were stolidly eating their pudding. The girl had finished eating and was idly flipping through the *Express*.

'It says the police have a line on the Matricide, Mummy, and they are charging the dog-eater.'

'The what, dear?'

'The Matricide, Mummy, he's been seen in Paris on a barge on the Seine.'

'Can't think why they haven't caught the fellow.'

'Oh, Daddy, he's clever, grown a beard, it says here, a red beard.'

'Have they arrested him, dear?'

'No, Mummy, it says here one of his best friends recognized him.'

'Can't be his best friends if he tells the police.'

'Oh, Daddy, he'd have to! He did murder his mother after all.'

'Bribed I expect.'

'Who's bribed?'

'Someone's bribed the police. What the hell do I pay my taxes for, I'd like to know, if they can't catch a simple murderer. Waiter, my bill.'

'I don't think he's so simple.'

'Don't contradict your father, dear.'

'I wish you wouldn't call me "dear", Mummy. My name is Inez.'

'I know, dear, we chose it for you.'

'There you go again, *dear*! It's common to say "dear" all the time. Why can't you call me Inez or "darling". "Darling" is all right.'

'So you call your mother common do you? You'll be murdering her next.'

'Oh Daddy, I'd never.'

'Call me Dad. Dad's common. This is a bloody expensive lunch.'

'Poor man, I expect he regrets it now. Such a large nose. Rather an attractive man from the photograph.'

'Mummy! Your taste, really!'

'Well, dear, you can be both, dear, attractive *and* a murderer. D'you want to powder your nose before we go to the car?'

'I want to piss.' The girl got up, dropping the paper.

'Who's being common now?' Her father tipped the waiter and roared with laughter, his stomach joggling as though it had a life apart. Matilda let out a sigh as the party left. Hugh was choking with laughter.

'How can you laugh?' Then she joined him, enjoying the food and the wine, the pleasure of being taken out to lunch, sitting in the sun.

'I'd never thought of you as attractive to stout matrons.' Matilda looked across at Hugh. The sun had caught his nose, turning it red. 'If you go on sitting in the sun your nose will peel.'

'Mustn't have that. Have you got any sun stuff? I can't afford to draw attention to it.'

Matilda fished in her bag, found a tube of Ambre Solaire. 'Try that.'

Hugh squeezed a blob onto his finger and applied it to his nose. 'Thanks.' He gestured to the waiter for the bill. 'Let's go and swim. Will you take me to your death beach?'

'It's a long walk.'

'Our lunches can settle before we swim, then we won't get cramp.'

Driving to the cliff, walking down the steep path to the beach, Matilda felt a surge of happiness. She called cheerfully to Folly who raced up and down the path, passing so close to their feet that she nearly tripped them.

'It's a golden afternoon.'

Hugh nodded, enjoying the moment, the pretty dog, the sun, the sea. Matilda ran barefoot on the sand at the cliff bottom, racing along to the flat rock she considered hers. They sat in the sun before undressing and Matilda, remembering the young people's barbecue, told Hugh about it.

'There was a girl who kept saying "super", everything was "super". They wanted me to go away so that they could use this rock. If it hadn't been for them I shouldn't have met you. I had my picnic with me, I was going to swim out.'

'From here?'

'Yes. See that smooth bit of water? That's the current. It carries you out past the lighthouse. Tom was caught in it once. He was lucky, he was picked up by a boat.'

'What was the plan? You've never told me.'

'To eat my Brie and rolls, swallow my pills, wash them down with Beaujolais, then I reckon I could just make the water. The current would have done the rest. The tide has to be exactly right.'

'Drowned people look disgusting.'

'Not like Ophelia?'

'Not one bit. The body bloats.'

'I shall be picked up long before I swell up. One of the fishing boats will find me.'

'Horrible for them.'

'Oh rubbish,' said Matilda. 'They'll enjoy it, tell their friends about it in the pub. I reckon my carcass is worth lots of rounds of drinks.'

'Have you ever seen a dead body?'

'I don't think I have. Let's swim.' Hugh ran down the beach into the water and swam.

'Put my foot in it,' Matilda said to Folly. 'He's seen his mother's. Sit by our clothes, there's a good dog.'

Folly wagged humbly and stayed watching anxiously as Matilda walked down to the water.

Matilda swam, watching Hugh's head moving away from her. 'Dear God,' she said aloud. 'I've put ideas into his head, he won't come back, he's gone.' She called loudly and waved her arm. 'Hugh, come back!' He swam on, his head growing smaller on her horizon. A small wind sprang up, flipping the sea into waves. 'Hugh!' Matilda called. 'Hugh!' A wave filled her mouth, making her gag.

Matilda was further from the beach than she thought. She swam back, her arms and legs tiring. She could see Folly down by the water's edge, advancing, then retreating from the waves, giving small anxious barks.

'Damn him, damn him, damn him!' Matilda cursed

192

Hugh as she pushed her arms through the water. 'Damn him, oh damn him!'

'The wind's getting up.' Hugh swam alongside. 'Sea's getting quite choppy.'

Matilda did not answer. When her feet touched bottom she waded ashore, spitting out the taste of salt, pushing her hair away from her face with wet hands.

'Now what's she on about?' Hugh greeted Folly who jumped and cavorted in the shallows. 'Think we'd get drowned, did you, you foolish little creature.' He watched Matilda walking up to the rock, reach for her towel, rub her face with it, pressing it against her eyes.

'Lovely that was.' He joined her. 'This rock's quite hot.' He sat down and let the water run down him. Matilda, angry with herself, did not speak rubbing herself dry. 'Look the other way. I want to strip,' she said tersely.

Hugh, leaning back on his arms, looked out to sea. He could hear her pulling down the bathing dress and the rubbing of the towel. He glanced along the beach.

'Here come our lunchtime neighbours.' He looked round at Matilda standing naked beside him, rubbing her hair with the towel. With her arms raised her breasts looked quite girlish. She had a flat stomach.

'Oh Christ! Not them again!' Matilda grabbed her knickers. 'I'm used to having this beach to myself. Nobody ever used to come here.'

'I bet fat Dad saw your bush, it's very pretty.'

'Don't be common.' Matilda imitated the girl's voice. 'It's common to talk about bushes. I have grey hairs in it.'

'Distinguished. I didn't note your wrinkled bottom.'

'I'm wrinkled all over. Neck, face, hands, bottom, all wrinkled through to my soul.'

'I must be short-sighted.'

Matilda struggled into her shirt and jeans. 'Put your

glasses on, for God's sake. That woman thinks you're attractive in your photographs, she'll recognize you.'

'Does it matter?'

'Don't let's give her the pleasure.'

'The father and mother are sitting down. The girl's going to swim.'

'Let's go. Do get dressed.'

'All right.' He stood up.

'D'you think they heard me calling?' Matilda was suddenly anxious.

'Did you call?'

'Yes. Didn't you hear? I thought you were going out too far.'

'I didn't hear. What did you say?'

'I shouted, "Hugh, Hugh, come back." They could have heard.'

'Suppose they did?'

'That woman knows you are called Hugh. Do hurry.'

'Hurrying would be the stupidest thing. You go ahead if you're nervous.'

'All right.' Carrying her towel and bathing dress in one hand, her shoes in the other, she started along the beach, taking a line which would bring her close to the family party.

The father lay back, his head on his arms, eyes closed, his stomach a mound above skinny legs. The mother sat upright, glancing about her. The girl carefully oiled her arms and legs. She had rather bony knees.

Matilda, walking silently, strained her ears.

'No, dear, I don't suppose so. I only said it's funny he should be called Hugh, that's what she was calling, dear, she was calling "Hugh". I told you. Hush, here she comes.'

'Oh Mummy, don't keep saying "dear", can't you say "darling" or Inez?'

194

'That Dereck you are going to marry is supposed to be so democratic. Why should he mind if I talk common? If I want to call you "dear" I shall. "Darling" doesn't come naturally to me, you know that. You used to say it was the thing to be common.'

'Oh Mummy, that was in Nigel's day.'

'I only said it was a funny thing that that man over there who looks like the Matricide should be called Hugh, dear. That's all. It's his name, Hugh Warner, it's been in all the papers.'

'Hardly likely he'd be using his own name, is it?' Dad looked up at the sky.

'The *Express* says he's in Paris and has grown a beard.' The girl had turned sulky.

'You can't believe all you read in the papers, dear.'

'Oh Mummy,' the girl almost screamed in desperation. 'Must you say "dear" all the time?'

'Now then, Inez, don't you be rude to your Ma.' Dad sat up and glared at his daughter. 'We've been "dear" to each other all our lives and "dear" we shall stay. We may be common but we are dear to one another and you are dear to us. Eh, Ma, how's that?'

As she pulled on her espadrilles, Matilda listened anxiously.

'It's a very common name.' The girl poured oil into her palm and massaged her throat upwards. 'Think of all the radio and TV Hughs, Hugh and Huw.'

'You contradict everything I say, dear. It's becoming a habit.'

'I wasn't contradicting, I just said –'

'Did your paper say what the chap who ate his wife's doggy-woggy is being charged with?' Dad spoke with his eyes shut. Matilda blessed him.

'Eating dogs isn't a chargeable offence. I asked Dereck.'

'Your Dereck knows it all.'

'Dereck says that bride who vanished from the beach had probably been murdered. That's what Dereck says.'

'Beaches aren't all that safe then. Better be careful when you honeymoon on the Costa what's it, Inez girl.'

'Oh, Daddy.'

'Call me "Dad" like you always have. I don't like this "Daddy" bit, it stinks.'

'Yes, dear, call your Dad "Dad". No need to change all of a sudden now you are engaged to Dereck. Call him "Dad" like always, dear.'

'Oh, Mummy,' the girl whined in exasperation.

'Just because he works in a solicitor's office and talks posh doesn't mean he knows it all. Call your Dad "Dad", dear.'

Matilda, moving away, detected hurt in the mother's voice, then suddenly aggression. 'I'm not saying anything against your Dereck, but we all know people can take elocution lessons.' Matilda risked a backward glance at Inez's angry mother. 'You call us Mum and Dad like you always have. Dear.'

Matilda moved on, her heart thumping. She started up the cliff, daring to look back. She was appalled to see Hugh talking to the family party.

'Is he quite crazy?'

Presently they all laughed and Hugh walked on towards her, followed by Folly.

'Are you quite mad?'

'No. The mother accosted me, said I looked like the Matricide, was I often mistaken for him.'

'Christ! What did you say?'

'I asked, in my best German accent, who was the Matricide? They told me. I made a joke and we all laughed. That's all.'

'They must have heard you talking English at lunch.'

'I doubt it. We never raised our voices. I was on the far side of the table. We listened to them, not they to us.'

'I pray you are right.'

'Don't be so panicky and spoil the afternoon.'

'Sorry. It's been lovely.' Hugh stood looking down at the beach.

'My mother would have loved this beach. She adored places like this.'

'Your *mother*?'

'Just because I killed my mother doesn't mean I don't know what she liked,' Hugh said coldy, looking at Matilda with dislike. 'I know very well what gave her pleasure – pain, fear.'

'Let's get back to the car.' Matilda shivered. 'I'm afraid. That woman heard me call "Hugh". I'm afraid.'

'Yes, she mentioned that. I said "Hugo" was my name. Sounds much the same when shouted. My mother used to call "Hugh-o"? A sort of yodel.'

'You loved your mother?'

'Of course I did.'

'I'm afraid.'

'That's life. All your claptrap about death is rubbish.'

'No, no, it isn't, wasn't.'

Hugh walked ahead to the car. His back view expressed annoyance. Matilda cheered up on the way home, and sang as she drove.

> 'I paid a shilling to see
> A tatooed Lady
> Ta ta-ta ta-ta ta

I can't remember the words. D'you know them?'

'No.'

'I remember, it ends like this –
> On her hips were battleships

Oh my, but they were fine,'

Matilda sang, 'and

> Right down her spine
> Were the King's own guard in line.

Oh, I have it all wrong. I wish I could remember. Joyce Grenfell sang it at a troops' concert in 1939. I don't suppose you were born.'

'Not quite. Go on singing.'

'I'll try and remember the words. My Pa was in the Territorials. Ma took me to their concert.'

'It sounds Edwardian. Go on singing. I like it.'

'I forget the words, just as I forget my life, huge chunks of it.'

'It will all flash before your eyes out by the lighthouse.'

'Maybe. That's something I hadn't thought of. Surely I shall think of something more profound than tattooed ladies?'

'You will think of your lovers, perhaps.' Hugh, lolling beside her, thought of her standing naked, arms raised, on the beach. 'You must have had plenty.'

'No, I didn't. Vague experiments, then I married Tom.'

'But surely –'

'I was faithful.'

'Prig.' Hugh teased. Matilda frowned.

'I was, I promise. No chance of anything else. Tom was a jealous man, he chased other men away. We lived like swans. They mate for life,' she said, knowing she lied.

'Swans,' Hugh jeered.

'I know, I've found out haven't I? But I don't suppose I would have been any different if I had known it all.'

'But since his death?'

'I'm too old. No one. Well, a glint in Mr Jones's eyes soon doused.'

'Well I never.' Hugh thought of the tussling Mr Jones in bed. 'I daresay he'd put up a creditable performance. Maybe you're not keen though.'

'Keen on what?'

'Bed.'

'I adore fucking,' Matilda said intensely. Hugh raised his eyebrows, looking at her sidelong, full mouth, small chin. She opened the mouth and sang, repeating the words she could remember.

'I paid a shilling to see
A tattooed lady,'

then, breaking into a piercing whistle she turned the car off the main road and drove through the lanes to the cottage.

'It's been a lovely day. Thanks.'

'I enjoyed it.'

'Here we are. Where's Gus?'

'Can't see him.' Hugh gathered up their bathing things. 'I'll hang these up.'

'Okay. Gus, Gus, where are you? Gus? Sometimes he goes down the river. He always comes back.'

'You sure?'

'Yes.'

'I have to see Mr Jones. I won't be long.'

'Don't let anyone see you.'

'Of course not.' Hugh went up to his room, took his money from the dressing-table drawer. He counted a hundred pounds in notes, put them in his wallet, then counted the rest. Matilda was in the garden picking vegetables. From time to time she called, 'Gus, Gus, come on boy,' in a high voice.

'He'll come, he does this sometimes. It's his way of asserting his independence.'

'You sure?'

'Yes, quite. Don't be long. I'm hungry.'

'Not long –' Hugh walked along the stream, through the copse, followed by Folly, to Mr Jones's bungalow. Mr Jones was sitting in his porch smoking.

'I didn't know you smoked.'

'Pot.' Mr Jones offered the cigarette to Hugh who drew on it deeply. 'Improves the view', Mr Jones said, 'makes things twice as clear, if you want clarification.'

'I've brought the money.' Hugh gave back the cigarette, handed over the envelopes. Mr Jones counted, then said,

'Okay, fine. I have francs, dollars, deutchmarks, that do you?'

'Yes, thank you.'

'Hold this.' He gave Hugh the joint. 'Won't be long.' He went into the bungalow. Hugh smoked quietly until Mr Jones came back.

'Here you are.' He handed Hugh an envelope. 'That should keep you going for a while. When are you off?'

'Soon.'

'Right. No need to tell me. Does she know?'

'Matilda?'

'Yes.'

'I haven't told her. I'm just going to be there one minute, gone the next.'

'That's the best way.' Mr Jones nodded. 'The *Express* says you've been seen in Paris, the *Mirror* says East Berlin, they're always keen on East Berlin, it's not easy to check.'

'I shall leave the dog.'

'Sure. Something to remember you by.'

'She won't want to remember me. It's her husband she remembers.'

'That's an illusion.' Mr Jones spat, drew on the last dregs of pot. 'She's conned herself all her life, that woman.'

200

'She doesn't seem to have had much life. I must go.'
Hugh stood up quickly. 'She's cooking supper. It's getting dark.'

'Autumn's here –'

'Yes, nearly.'

'Where shall you go?'

'East Berlin.'

Mr Jones waved as Hugh left. As he walked away he could hear him chuckling.

The cottage was strangely still. Hugh paused, smelling danger. Matilda was silent. There was no car by the gate but something had gone wrong. Hugh gestured to Folly to run ahead. The dog trotted along the brick path and in at the kitchen door.

Inside the house Matilda made a noise, just a noise barely human. He ran into the house. Matilda looked up at him. 'The police –'

Hugh felt his heart constrict, sweat break out, pins and needles in his fingers. 'Where? When?'

'They saw him from their car, they tried, one of them went into the water and got wet. There was nothing they could do. His head was bitten off.'

'What are you talking about?'

'Gus. He's dead. A fox, they said. A struggle by the river. His body was in the water. Feathers on the bank, they said. He must have put up a fight.'

Hugh let out his breath. 'Where is he?'

'They took him away. I wouldn't want to see him like that, they said. He pecked one of them once. I thought they were coming for you, but it was Gus. What shall I do?'

Hugh moved, picked up Matilda in his arms and held her close.

'Shut up. Don't speak.' He carried her upstairs. She was lighter than she looked. He pulled off her clothes, snapping buttons, yanking her arms out, unzipped her jeans, pulled them off.

'What are you doing?'

'Undressing you.'

'Why?'

'Shut up.' He kicked off his shoes, tore off his trousers, 'Come here, hold on, open your legs – '

'I –'

'You like fucking, you said so, shut up.' He put his hand over her mouth. There, be quiet, just move a bit – there.'

Matilda came alive, gasping, struggling, fighting, joining in, holding him, her response sudden, silent. Then she sighed.

'It hurt, it hurt, you raped me.'

'I didn't mean to rape you. I meant to console.'

'Like your mother,' Matilda murmured.

'What?'

'Nothing. It hurt nicely.'

'You haven't for so long. It will be better next time.' He held her, stroking her back. Outside the room Folly yawned and stretched then, with a sigh, fell asleep. They would remember her dinner in time. She wasn't all that hungry though it was late.

Owls on their silent hunting zoomed over the fields. Holiday makers drove along the main road, making for the motorway and urban life.

Matilda lay in Hugh's arms. 'You will flash before my eyes,' she murmured.

'Hush.' He kissed her mouth gently.

'I am old enough to be your mother.' He kissed her, running his tongue along her teeth as a child rattles railings with a stick. 'A good joke. Sleep now, it's not the moment to say so.'

'Would I have liked your mother?'

202

'I think so. Sleep.' He kissed her.

He slid out of bed, dressed, crept downstairs. His wallet was on the kitchen table. He crept up again for his passport and small bag of clothes, stood by Matilda's door listening.

Matilda snored.

Downstairs Hugh fed Folly, scooping dog meat from a tin, watching her wolf it.

'Quick now, have a run.' He let her into the garden to pee. 'Hurry up.' She came in. 'Stay now. Take good care of her. Be a good dog. Go to your basket.' He pointed to the basket. The dog went to it, sat uneasily, watching as he swallowed a quick sandwich and drank milk. He patted her once. 'Lie down, be good. Take care of her.'

He let himself out by the kitchen door, closing it gently. If he walked fast he could catch the 11.30 to London. Then who knows, he thought. Who knows where my dollars, deutchmarks and francs will take me. From London I can take the tube to Heathrow, into the world, back to life. Walking fast across country, Hugh thought bitterly of his mother and of Matilda. She always hoped I'd find a woman I could love. Now, he thought, pausing by a gate, leaning his head in his arms, thinking of Matilda, now I can't have her. They shan't find me, not now, not ever, for her sake they must not. He hurried on, across the main road, down a side road to the town, to the station. He was engrossed by Matilda, her body and his joined, smelling her, hearing her, feeling her. He did not hear the squeak of brakes or the yelp as a car driving fast clipped Folly on the head and killed her, tossing her body to the curb. He was so absorbed by Matilda that it had not occurred to him that Folly would leap out of the kitchen window and follow.

I will write from wherever I may be, he thought, thinking aloud as people do under stress. I will tell her everything and she will laugh. It will be good for her to remember me with laughter. She needs laughter.

At the station he bought a ticket to Paddington and fell asleep as the train drew out of the station.

Folly's body was hit by two more cars before she was found by the police, squashed flat. 'Poor Mrs Pollyput,' said the constable. 'First that gander, now this. She isn't in luck exactly.'

26

Waking, hearing the birds, Matilda stretched, then curled up again. She wanted to prolong her sense of ease. She felt as though each bit of her body was free from the tension which had been there so long. She felt the bed beside her. Hugh had gone. It didn't matter. A wren sang loudly in the garden. He would come back. There would be more. She tried to remember whether it had ever been like that with Tom. It hadn't. Good but not perfect. Hugh was so much younger than she, it couldn't last. He would go away, indeed he must go away otherwise sooner rather than later he would be in prison. She slept a little then woke, thinking of Gus.

No more honking, no more slap of feet, no more throttling noises, no more messes. She felt calm now, her horror and grief over his death had raised her emotions to the pitch which had allowed love. By Gus's death I am complete, she thought. It was pleasant to stretch her legs without disturbing a dog. Since Stub's death she had slept alone. Folly had slept lately with Hugh, she was his dog. Matilda hoped Hugh had fed her during the night. She remembered him leaving. He would have fed her surely. The police had been kind about Gus, nice of them to come and tell her, they might easily have telephoned or done nothing. It was lucky they had not run into Hugh, that he was out when they came.

Matilda remembered the two policemen. She had guessed that Gus lay headless in their Panda car. She had guessed too that one of the policemen would give the body to his wife and that Gus would be roasted and eaten. She was not shocked or angry about this, it seemed natural. She thought again of Hugh and, turning away from the light, thought he must be sleeping deeply after so much – she searched for the right word – expenditure. Yes, a great night of spending. She smiled, pulling the sheet up over her eyes, dozing, conscious of happiness. She must guard it.

At the police station the two constables from the Panda car made their report. The sergeant made notes.

'Okay, just an ordinary night.'

'Do we still keep an eye open for the fellow who killed his old mother?'

'Nothing come through to the contrary. That missing bride is more urgent.'

'Seems a waste of time.'

'Putting the public's back up. Every man with a large nose is feeling awkward,' said the younger constable.

'You've got a large nose, Sergeant,' ventured his mate.

'I know that. That's why the public has my sympathy for once. The moment I'm in civvies I feel awkward. My wife says people stare.'

'They stare because you're such a fine upstanding man, Sergeant, not because of your hooter.'

'Enough of that.'

'Okay, Sarge, what about the dog, then? What do we do?'

'The goose was last night, wasn't it?'

'Yes.'

'You passing her way as you go off duty?'

'No, we aren't.'

'Well pass her way, take her the dog, tell her before you go off duty.'

'That's overtime.'

206

'No it isn't.' The sergeant wrote up a note. 'That's paying for the goose. It's my guess one of you is going to eat it.'

'Very well, Sergeant.' The two policemen went out.

'Crafty bastard. My Annie says with an old bird, boil it first, then roast it slow and it will taste like a young one. She knows a thing or two. She was brought up on a farm.'

'Lot to be said for country lore.' The second policeman, who was courting a secretary in the Council Offices, slipped the car into the gear. 'Seems stupid though to me.'

'What does?'

'We keep the bird and you eat it but the dog, which is much more of a mess, we return.'

'You don't licence a goose and you can't eat dog.'

'They do in China.'

'I know that. Let's get it over with. I hate this kind of job. Who is this Mrs Pollyput anyway?'

'They've lived here a long time. He died a few years back. She doesn't mix much. Got grown children. They never come to see her. He ran some sort of travel business from home. Never been any trouble there apart from the odd motoring offence. She doesn't belong to the W.I. or go to church. She's not above the occasional coarse expression. Talks to herself and sings too. It's her time of life, I suppose.'

'My Mum's having hot flushes.'

'There you are then.'

'And here we are. You carry the dog and I'll do the talking.'

'That isn't fair.'

'Isn't it? Afraid of messing your uniform? It's in a sack isn't it? Hold it well away from you so it won't drip. You carry the dog, you're eating the goose.'

'We could share it.'

'Oh belt up. I don't fancy it.'

Matilda heard a car door slam and, shortly after, a knock on the door. She got out of bed and looked from her window.

'You again? I'm asleep, can't you bugger off?' Her voice rose high.

'Sorry, Mrs Pollyput, but –'

'Wait a minute, I'll come down.' She withdrew her head.

'You're right, she is coarse.'

'Told you so.' They stood patiently.

Matilda's knees trembled as she pulled on Anabel's dressing-gown, ran a comb through her hair. She looked at the clock.

'Christ, it's late. What an oversleeping.'

She took a deep breath, put the comb down, pulled the sash of the dessing-gown tight and left the room. Before coming down she looked into Hugh's room, her finger on her lips. It was empty, the bed made.

'Taken Folly out. Please God keep him away while they are here.' She ran downstairs and opened the door.

'What is it?'

'Mrs Pollyput, it's –'

'What is it?'

'Is this your dog, Mrs Pollyput? Found her on the main road. Can't have known what hit her.'

Matilda said nothing.

'Must have been following somebody, she was nearly in the town.'

'Following somebody?'

'That's what the sergeant thinks.'

'Who?'

'Who what, Mrs Pollyput?'

'My name is Mrs Poliport.'

'Yes, Mrs Poliport.'

'Was she seen following somebody? Who would she follow?'

'It was just his idea. We only found her.'

'When?'

'Coming off duty we –'

'You were coming on duty when you found my gander.'

'Yes Mrs Pollyput, Poliport.'

'Yes, she's my dog.' Matilda put out a hand to touch the mangled body. 'She's cold.'

'Er, yes.'

'This is an idiot conversation. Where did you say you found her?'

'On the main road by the turning to the station.'

'The turning to the station. I see.' Matilda was quite still. The policemen stood embarrassed.

'You all right, Mrs Poliport?'

'Would you be?' Matilda started at him. 'Give her to me.' The younger policeman made a protesting noise.

'Give her to me.' Matilda took hold of the body in the sack, holding it close.

'Following somebody.'

'Or running away. She may have been frightened, Dogs get scared on roads, Mrs Poliport.'

'Yes.'

'You all right, Mrs Poliport? Would you like us to make you some tea?'

'No thank you. I must buy some Brie and a bottle of Beaujolais.'

'What, Mrs Poliport?'

'Cheese and wine –' Matilda stood staring at them, her face white, 'not tea.'

'Oh. You sure you're all right? We could –'

'You couldn't do anything. Just bugger off.' She turned into the house, shutting the door in their faces. The two men exchanged glances, one of them took off his hat, resettled it on his head. The other straightened his tunic. They turned to go. Matilda opened the door and shouted, 'He'll make very tough eating,' and slammed it again. They heard her scream '*Cannibals*!'

'Phew!'

'Holy Cow!' They drove off.

'Hot flush or no hot flush, she's put me off my dinner. Bugger off, is it? The sergeant can go himself another time.'

'Funny her being in bed this time of the morning. She's usually up at dawn, everybody knows that.'

'Perhaps she had some fella for the night.'

'Don't be daft – at her age?'

'Daresay it was just shock. She hasn't had that dog long, only bought it a licence the other day, she told me. I told her it wasn't yet six months and not to worry.'

'Wasted her lolly then.'

27

When her arms began to ache, Matilda put the sack down
on the kitchen table. The clock said midday. She went
across the room and wound it. She felt dizzy and put out
her hand to steady herself against the Rayburn. It was
cold. She looked in the firebox. The draught she made
opening the stove stirred the embers. As she straightened
up she saw the mess on her dressing-gown. She took it off
and wrapped it round Folly's body. The rather tarty
chiffon and lace garment which had once belonged to
Anabel made a neat wrapping. Realizing she was naked
she went upstairs and ran the bath very deep and hot. She
washed thoroughly and shampooed her hair, ducking
under the water to rinse it.

She dressed in the jeans and shirt she found on her
bedroom floor. There was only the top button left, the
others twinkled up from the carpet. She pulled on a
sweater, combed her wet hair, put on espadrilles,went
back to the bathroom to clean her teeth. As she brushed
them she noticed that Hugh's shaving things were gone
from the shelf, that his sponge was gone and his
toothbrush.

She looked at her reflection in the mirror without
recognition.

From the garden shed she fetched fork and spade and
dug a deep hole by the rhubarb bed where the ground was
soft and free of stones. When it was deep enough she
fetched Folly and laid her in the hole, covered it with earth
and trod it flat. Her espadrilles were full of grit and she had

hurt the sole of her foot, digging. She took off the espadrilles, shook out the grit, then walked awkwardly to the tool shed, carrying the shoes in one hand, the fork and spade in the other. Her hand was not large enough to hold the tools; she dropped the spade with a clatter, bruising her foot. She hung the tools on their hooks and closed the shed door.

'Matilda. I heard. I came to see whether I could help.' Mr Jones stood a few yards off.

'Excuse me, I've just had a bath. My hair is wet.'

'I heard about Gus and Folly. I wondered –'

'Yes?'

'Is there anything I can do?'

'Do you have a large flat stone?'

'I can bring you a slab from my path, one of the paving stones.'

'Could you bring it at once?'

'Yes, of course. You look strange. Shall I make you some tea?'

'Not tea!' Matilda exclaimed harshly.

'I'll get the stone at once.'

'Please do.'

'I'm sorry.'

'Sorry to be rude. It's just –'

'I know. I'll go and get it.'

Mr Jones broke into a trot, running towards his bungalow. Matilda thought he looked ridiculous from behind. Short, fat, middle-aged men should not run.

She went back to the house to wash her hands at the sink, cleaning the earth from under her nails with an orange stick. There was a stain on the kitchen table. She wiped it with a wet cloth.

Waiting for Mr Jones, Matilda wandered round the house. Everything was in its place. The spiders were back

212

slung across ceiling corners. She left them alone.

In her room she made the bed, smoothing the stained sheets, pulling up the blankets, puffing up the pillows. She held her breath so that she would not smell what was there, covered the whole with the patchwork bedspread Claud had sent from America. 'Pretty.' She stroked it. 'Sweet Claud.'

Hugh's room was empty. She inspected for traces of his occupancy. There were none.

Mr Jones came with a stone slab in his arms.

'Will this do? It's Delabole slate.'

'Yes, it will. Thank you.'

Together they went to the dog's grave.

'Where shall I put it?'

'Here, across here.' Matilda pointed.

Mr Jones laid the stone, rocking it to level the earth.

'Thank you,' she said again.

'It's nothing. Can I do anything else?'

'No thank you. I have to go out and shop.'

'Could I not do it for you? You should rest.'

'No thank you. I'm going for a swim.'

Mr Jones stood looking miserably at Matilda.

'I know Hugh has gone.'

'Yes.'

'He meant you to keep Folly.'

'She was his dog. She followed him – naturally.'

'He wouldn't have wanted her to.'

'I daresay not. I don't think it matters now what he wanted, not any more, not now.'

'He would have wanted to leave you happy.'

'Don't talk drivel.'

'I'm sorry. I – I wanted.'

'You *what*?'

'I wanted to tell you I love you, Matilda. I always have.

213

I want to comfort you. I'd like to begin by making you some tea.'

'I don't want tea, Mr Jones. It's very kind of you but I don't need comforting. I don't think you do love me, it's just an idea, all in the mind.'

'It's not only in my mind, it's in my balls.' Mr Jones found himself shouting at Matilda, longing to hit her.

'It makes no odds to me whether your love is up or down, Mr Jones. I'm sorry, I have to go out.' Matilda moved towards the house.

'I chose the wrong moment. I thought we could live here in your house or in my bungalow –'

'Oh, fuck your bungalow!'

'All right. I'm sorry. I'll go.'

Mr Jones turned and went. Matilda watched him out of sight, fetched her towel and bathing dress from the line, noting that Hugh had even remembered to take his swimming trunks, which had belonged, she thought resentfully, to Tom.

She looked in her bag to see if she had any money. Hugh might have taken that too, but her purse was full. She put it in the beach bag with the towel and the bathing dress, went out, locked the door, put the key under the doorstop, got into the car and drove off to the town.

It was market day so she had trouble finding a place to park the car, finally leaving it on a double yellow line.

She made for the wine shop where she bought a bottle of Beaujolais, then to the baker where she bought rolls. At the delicatessen she persuaded the girl behind the counter who was more than usually busy to butter the rolls while she chose some Brie.

'What d'you want to do that for? A whole crowd of people are waiting,' the man who owned the shop hissed at his assistant as she buttered the rolls.

'She had a funny look in her eye. I didn't like to say no.'

'Don't let me catch you at it again. Here you are, Madam.' He handed the Brie in its paper bag to Matilda. 'Glad to be of assistance.'

'I don't suppose she'll ask me again, she never has before.' The girl watched Matilda leave the shop.

'Did she pay for the butter?'

'Paid for half a pound and only wanted what I used on the rolls. I think she's a nutter.'

There was a ticket under the windscreen wiper of the car. Matilda handed it to a passer-by, who examined it, puzzled, then shouted, 'Hey!' as she drove away without looking back.

Parking the car at the usual place, she sauntered along the cliff path, looking down at the sea, which was calm but grey. The beach was empty, the season over. She was glad she had her sweater, wished she was wearing socks. It was chilly and her foot bruised where she had dropped the spade. She sang softly going down the cliff path:

> 'I paid a shilling to see
> A tattooed La-a-dy.'

Reaching the sand, she kicked off her espadrilles, leaving them to lie, hurrying barefoot to the far end of the beach to the flat rock.

> 'And right down her spine
> Were the King's Own Guard in line.'

The rock was cold when she sat on it. She shivered, unpacking the rolls and Brie, standing the Beaujolais carefully so that it would not topple over. She felt in the bag for the corkscrew.

'Oh God! I've left it behind.' She began to weep. 'It's got to be there –' She tipped the bag over, shaking it. No corkscrew. A sheet of paper slid to her feet.

Darling Matilda. Hugh's writing, a little blurred by the damp towel. *I love you. I can't impose my life on yours. I must go away. I love you. You are the kind of woman my mother would have loved. You are what I have wanted, what she wanted for me. I thought she knew nothing of love, was old, naïve. Christ, this is an impossible letter to write. Forgive me. Folly will look after you, hook on to her. She belongs to us both, just hook on. Killing my mother was an accident. She was terrified of mice. Don't laugh. There was a mouse on the sofa. She cried to me for help. I smashed at it with the tray as she moved. I've been too embarrassed to tell anyone. Please don't laugh, though I love your laughter. Hugh.*

Matilda tore the letter, letting the breeze scatter the pieces. She undressed, pulling on her swimsuit, goose pimples on her legs. Sitting on the rock she reached in her bag for the pills, spilled them into her hand. She knocked the neck of the bottle against the rock, crammed her mouth full of pills, choking them down with the wine. The jagged glass cut her mouth. She poured in more pills, more wine.

The tide was just right, on the turn, the sea waiting. Matilda stood up.

'Folly?' she called, feeling dizzy, 'belongs to us both?' She fell on her knees, crawling down the beach on all fours. 'Gus?' She retched, keeping the pills down with an effort. 'We all belong to you,' she whispered, reaching the water. 'I'm coming.'

A gull swooped down to snatch a roll from the rock, followed by others, screaming, fighting, white wings beating, yellow eyes glinting, beaks snatching.

The sea caught Matilda as she began to swim out. She

216

did not wish to get her hair wet.

It's late in the year for swimming. She pushed her arms out mechanically, turning the grey water pink with the blood from her mouth. A memory came tentatively. She had read or heard that people shit as they die. In distress she pulled off her swimsuit, getting her hair wet as she did so. She let the thing drift away.

At least I shall die with my body clean. She swam more slowly now. I should see my past life flash before my eyes. Her wounded mouth smiled. A memory which had so long eluded her came uselessly back. John/Piers in Trafalgar Square, his bowler, his umbrella. Whose party had he taken her to? Some place in Bloomsbury. I got drunk, she remembered, swimming very slowly now, never been drunk before. He had taken her into a bedroom. She had smelled his hair oil from Trumpers.

She had pushed it out of her mind. 'Hugh,' she called in the cold tide, 'Hugh, I want to tell you –' John/Piers next honours list had pushed her onto a bed, pulled up her skirt, hadn't even pulled off her knickers.

'This will be a new sensation.' That voice of his.

'Death you are new too,' she said to the tide.

The fishing boat found the body floating by the lighthouse.

'Looks as though she's laughing,' the younger man said.

'Cut her mouth on the rocks,' said his father. 'Haul it in. Cover it with a bit of tarpaulin, 'tisn't decent, not as though she were young.'

'Buggered up a day's fishing, this.'

"Tidy, swift entertainment. . . . [Rei Shimura] stands out as one of the most appealing characters in an ongoing series."
—*Richmond Times-Dispatch*

"As usual, Massey is masterful at contrasting American and Japanese cultures and customs, but Rei remains the glue that holds this delightful series together."
—*Booklist*

"Massey is at her witty best in this latest caper, with surprising and charming takes on everyone from Asian culture to the high-stakes world of looted antiques. . . . Massey is truly a master of her craft."
—*Asian Journal*

"Massey gleefully contrasts the young, bizarrely garbed generation, including Rei's own cousin, Chika, and Takeo's fiancée, Emi, with traditional Japanese society. Rei winds up with a badly bruised heart, but the ending hints at intriguing future possiblities."
—*Publishers Weekly*

"Most enjoyable."
—*Baltimore Sun*

"Massey makes good use of the clash between American and Japanese cultures as a backdrop for an enjoyable story. . . . Entertaining."
—*Chicago Sun-Times*

"Sujata Massey's latest whodunit has it all—great plot, exotic settings, and a mature protagonist."
—*India Abroad* magazine

"The Japanese-American antiques dealer who can't stay out of trouble has just celebrated her thirtieth birthday and is ready to raise some more hell."
—*Chicago Tribune*

"A pleasure. Massey's skills as a writer give us palpable settings and deliver an intricate story. . . . Holds the reader captive from the first page."
—*Crime Spree* magazine

Jim Burger

About the Author

SUJATA MASSEY was a reporter for the *Baltimore Evening Sun*, and spent several years in Japan teaching English and studying Japanese. She is the author of *The Salaryman's Wife, Zen Attitude, The Flower Master, The Floating Girl, The Bride's Kimono, The Samurai's Daughter,* and *The Pearl Diver.*

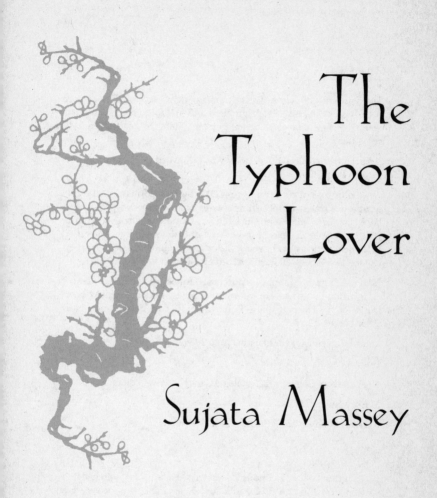

The
Typhoon
Lover

Sujata Massey

HARPER

NEW YORK • LONDON • TORONTO • SYDNEY

HARPER

A hardcover edition of this book was published in 2005 by Harper-Collins Publishers.

FIRST HARPER PAPERBACK PUBLISHED 2006.

Designed by Nancy B. Field

The Library of Congress has catalogued the hardcover edition as follows:

Massey, Sujata.

   The typhoon lover / Sujata Massey.—1st ed.
     p. cm.
   ISBN-10: 0-06-076512-7
   ISBN-13: 978-0-06-076512-5
   1. Shimura, Rei (Fictitious character)—Fiction. 2. Women detectives—Washington (D.C.)—Fiction. 3. Japanese Americans—Fiction. 4. Washington (D.C.)—Fiction. 5. Antique dealers—Fiction. 6. Tokyo (Japan)—Fiction. I. Title.
   PS3563.A79965T97 2005
   813'.54—dc22   2005046374

ISBN-10: 0-06-076513-5 (pbk.)
ISBN-13: 978-0-06-076513-2 (pbk.)

06 07 08 09 10 ❖/RRD 10 9 8 7 6 5 4 3 2 1

Acknowledgments

The Typhoon Lover owes its existence to many helpful people on both sides of the Pacific. The things that I've done right are because of them; all mistakes are my own.

I am indebted to my Sisters in Crime writers' group of nine years: Marcia Talley, John Mann, Karen Diegmuller, and Janice McLane. The staff at the Smithsonian Institution's Sackler Museum was amazing, especially the curators Louise Cort and Ann Gunter, its former public relations director Barbara Kramm, and Sarah Rodman of the Air and Space Museum. And with regard to the realities of modern espionage, I am grateful to the retired CIA analyst Rob Krespi for vetting the manuscript. I also salute the people who keep my spirits up with excellent coffee and conversation: Mike Sproge, Glen Breining, and the entire crew at the Evergreen coffeehouse, and the Baltimore intelligentsia who inhabit it (you know who you are).

In Japan, I give my deepest bows to Satoshi Mizushima, an English teacher at the Japanese Self Defense Forces School in Taura who carefully checked my Japanese; Chris Belton, an established Japan hand and great writer, for details of geography; Hidetomo Hirayama for the music; and my former neighbor Mihoko Morikawa, for the walk along the Hayama beach road. To William Morgan, Peter Vanburen, and Gentry Smith at the United States Embassy in Tokyo, thank you for welcoming me at a time of increased tension and for answering my many questions about how things are done to help Americans in trouble abroad. I also raise a glass to my dear friend and mentor, John Adair, Jr., owner of Kurofune Antiques in Roppongi, who continues to teach me about Japanese antiques. At the Grand Hyatt Tokyo, I thank Mark Kobayashi and Chisato Yagi for the tour. Yohei Omori, Waseda University alumnus, was a great tour guide to the campus and so helpful in many other ways.

This book was written during the year that my husband, Tony Massey, was mobilized by the Navy Reserve and left our home to serve with the Navy's Medical Corps. Despite the stress of his new job and cramped living quarters, Tony took charge of our children so I could return for a while to do research in Tokyo. I couldn't have done it without him—whether in uniform or not, Tony will always be my Navy hero.

Finally, there are the many good souls at HarperCollins who ferried this book from manuscript to print, and I thank you all. I remain in awe of my longtime editor and friend, Carolyn Marino; her able assistant, Jennifer Civiletto; and the publicity, art, and marketing departments. At Inkwell Management, the encouragement of my agent Kim Witherspoon and David Forrer made writing this book almost easy. *Arigato gozaimasu*, everyone!

Cast of Characters

REI SHIMURA: Japanese-American antiques dealer and woman-about-town.

HUGH GLENDINNING: a lawyer from Scotland currently working for a firm in Washington, D.C.

KENDALL HOWARD JOHNSON: Rei's socially and politically connected cousin.

GLASWEGIAN HANGOVER: a British band with buzz, featuring Hugh's brother, Angus Glendinning, and Angus's friends Sridhar, Keiffer, and Nate.

CHIKA SHIMURA: Rei's footloose first cousin, the daughter of Rei's aunt Norie and uncle Hiroshi Shimura, who live in Yokohama. Chika's older brother, Tom "Tsutomu" Shimura, works at St. Luke's Hospital in Tokyo.

MICHAEL HENDRICKS: rising star at the State Department's Japan desk.

YUKIO WATANABE, code name ITO: the consul of the Japanese embassy in Washington, D.C.

BRENDA MARTIN: colonel in the U.S. Army.

HARP SNOWDEN: a senator from California.

RICHARD RANDALL: Rei's former roommate, a Canadian teacher of English.

SIMONE: a friend of Rei's living in Tokyo who teaches French.

TAKEO KAYAMA, code name FLOWERS: Rei's former boyfriend, now head of the Kayama School of Ikebana.

EMI HARADA, code name THE BRIDE: eighteen-year-old daughter of Kenichi Harada, minister for the environment (alias Harmony), and his wife, Yasuko.

FUMIKO NAGASA: Emi's friend.

KAZU SAKURAI: celebrated potter; a Living National Treasure, who is married to Nobuko.

ALI and OSMAN BIRAND, code names BROTHER A and BROTHER B: brothers and partners in an antiques business based in Istanbul. Ali is single. Osman is the father of a son, Ramzi, code name Robert.

Plus a motley crew of students, fishmongers, cops, cabbies, club kids, and others who make a trip to Tokyo the ultimate experience.

The Typhoon Lover

I've never thought of myself as the blindfold type.

Not on planes, not in beds, and certainly not in restaurants. Especially not a place like DC Coast, where I was sitting on the evening of my thirtieth birthday, listening to my dinner companion trying his best to be persuasive.

"What happens next will be very special." Hugh said, picking up the small black mask that he'd placed next to our shared dessert. "You don't have to put the blindfold on inside here. Just a little later."

"You promised no party," I reminded him, but not sharply. My stomach was filled with a pleasant mélange of tuna tartare and crawfish risotto and crispy fried bass. It had been an orgy of seafood and good wine, just my kind of night.

"Hmm," Hugh said, studying the restaurant bill.

"If it's not a surprise party, where are you taking me?" I prodded.

"Let's just say I've got two tickets to paradise."

I rolled my eyes, thinking Hugh was showing his age, when I'd rather keep mine confidential. I didn't mind having a delicious, leisurely dinner, but he'd practically rushed me through cappuccino and crème brûlée. Hugh was frantic to leave, making me think he definitely had something planned.

As we waited for the car to be brought to us on the busy corner of Fourteenth and K streets, Hugh folded the tiny black blindfold into my hand. "It's never been used, if that makes you more comfortable. I saved it from my last trip to Zurich."

"I thought you didn't believe in regifting?" I asked lightly.

"Well, you didn't want a ring. What else can I offer you?" The undercurrent of irritation in Hugh's voice was clear. I'd worn his beautiful two-carat emerald for a short while, but ultimately returned it, because engagement rings scared me just as much as turning thirty did. Hugh was thirty-two; he'd been ready for the last three years. I wondered if I'd ever be.

The valet pulled up with the car and jumped out to open the passenger side for me. I got in, feeling a mixture of excitement and fear about what lay ahead. As we pulled off into traffic, I reclined my seat as far as it would go, hoping that this way, nobody would notice the woman with short black hair and a matching mask over her eyes. Anyone who caught a glimpse might think I'd just come out of plastic surgery or something like that—though most Washington women who went in for that flew to Latin America, where the plastic surgeons were good and there were no neighbors to bump into.

"Are we headed for the airport?" I asked, with a sudden rush of hope.

"No chance." Hugh sounded regretful. "It would have been fun to get away, but I can't risk any absences when the partner-track decisions are forthcoming."

Hugh was a lawyer at a high-pressure international firm a few blocks away. He'd been working for the last year on a class action suit that still wasn't ready to roll. His work involved frequent travel back to Japan, the country of my heritage, where we'd met a few years earlier. I would have loved to travel with him, but I couldn't, because I was banned from Japan. It was a complicated story that I didn't want to revisit on a night when I was supposed to be happy.

"Don't think about it," I muttered to myself. It was my habit to talk to myself sometimes, to try to shut out the bad thoughts that threatened what was a perfectly pleasant life.

"What don't you want to think about?"

"I'm getting nauseated from wearing a blindfold in a moving car," I said. "Not to mention that my nerves are shot because you won't tell me what's going to happen next."

"Oh, I'm sorry. Just hang on, I'll open the window." Hugh pressed the control that slid down the passenger-side window next to me. "We're just going around the corner to park. Will you survive another two minutes?"

I nodded, glad for a chance to listen to the sounds of the road. I could tell this wasn't our neighborhood, Adams-Morgan, with its mix of pulsating salsa music, honking horns, and shouting truck drivers. All I heard was a slow, steady purr of cars caught in traffic. After a while, the car moved again and turned a corner. Then it stopped. Hugh's window slid down.

"Paradise, sir?" A strange man's voice asked.

"That's right. Were staying till the wee morning hours," Hugh said. "Will this cover it?"

Before the parking valet could answer, I had a few words of my own. "Hugh, you *know* that I have a nine-thirty meeting at the Sackler Gallery tomorrow. You can very well stay until the wee hours, but I can't."

"Job interviews come and go. Thirtieth birthdays are only once!" He sounded positively gleeful.

My door was opened, and I unbuckled my seat belt. Then I felt a hand on my wrist, helping me out.

"You must be the girl getting the big birthday surprise." The valet's voice came from somewhere to the left.

I was busy working through the situation—was this a boutique hotel, maybe?—when Hugh tugged my hand. "There's going to be a downward flight of steps in a moment. Just take it slowly."

"What kind of a hotel has subterranean rooms?" I demanded.

"You'll know soon enough." Ten steps, and then a flat surface. "I'm going to hold the door open. Just step through."

I had no sight, but my other senses were bombarded. First, the sounds—"Japanese Girls," an Eels song pounding ominously, and lots of voices: talking, laughing, shrieking. Then there were the smells—smoke from cigarettes and sandalwood incense.

Someone took my other hand and pressed briefly down on the area over my knuckles. I guessed that I was getting a hand-stamp, the way bouncers did at bars.

"Hugh, this is so silly," I complained. "I want to see where I am.

If this is the S and M club we read about in *City Paper* I'm not going any farther."

Hugh sighed and said, "I'd hoped you'd stay blindfolded until the magic moment, but if you're that anxious, you may as well take it off. Go ahead."

Had I known of the series of events about to unfold—not this night, but in the crazy, dangerous days that rolled out, right after my birthday—I might have just kept the blindfold on. I would have remained in Hugh's thrall, powerless to make my own choices, but secure—still twenty-nine and safe as houses.

But I'm not the kind of girl who stays in one place for long, whether it's a city or a nightclub vestibule.

I slid off the blindfold, and opened my eyes.

2

The club was packed as tightly as Tokyo's Cube 326 on a good night—impressive for a live venue rather than a DJ club. I had never been inside a place in Washington this crowded and smoky. Wasn't there a no-smoking law in Washington clubs now? I wondered about it as I scanned the crowd, looking for familiar faces.

"Is that Kendall?" I asked Hugh, pointing to a slender redhead in a black leather jacket who looked like my married cousin from Potomac, but who was embracing a handsome younger man with a goatee.

"Yes, I gather she brought a toyboy from her office. But there's an even better spectacle right ahead." Hugh touched my shoulders and turned me so that I was facing the other side of the room. A stage was set up with a drum set and keyboards and microphones. Above it was a banner that said in glittering silver letters, HAPPY DIRTY THIRTY, REI!

I looked from it to Hugh. "You promised you wouldn't throw a surprise party."

He raised his eyebrows. "But I told you I was taking you to Paradise."

Suddenly I got it. This unfamiliar nightclub was probably a hot new music venue on U Street. I was amazed Hugh had been able to book it on a Friday night for something as inconsequential as my thirtieth birthday party.

I asked, "Is this Club Paradise?"

"Yes, isn't it brilliant?" He squeezed my hand back. "I had to keep the newspaper away from you all week so you wouldn't catch wind of what was going on." Hugh looked very pleased with himself.

"But I must know only a fraction of the people here."

"Andrea, Kendall, and I shared the invites. There are about a hundred fifty of our crowd here. The others, well, they've all paid to get in and that helps make up the cost of booking the space. I'm sure they'll be your friends by night's end—" As he spoke, he was putting a small glittering tiara on my head.

"People would pay to come to my birthday?" I was becoming even more confused as Andrea, a beautiful but moody restaurant hostess who'd become a good friend recently, came over to deliver some air kisses.

"Happy birthday, Rei," she said. "I'm going to handle the door and make sure nobody gets in on the guest list who should be paying."

Kendall bounced up and gave me a kiss on the lips that tasted like a Cosmopolitan. "Happy dirty thirty, dear. You know, I tried to talk Hugh into staving your thirtieth off for a few more years, but he wouldn't listen. Men!"

"What do you mean? She's thirty tomorrow." Andrea looked at Kendall as if she thought my cousin, who loved to brag about her M.B.A., couldn't count.

"A lot of girls don't publicly celebrate thirty until they're a little bit older, like thirty-five. Some of my friends from boarding school are going to do that, and I'm trying to decide whether I can carry it off. What do you think?" As Kendall spoke, she was twinkling at the young man she'd draped herself over before.

"It looks like some of your friends are here," I said, not wanting to answer her question. "You'll have to introduce me."

"Hugh let me bring about seventy-five of my nearest and dearest. They're so excited about the show, just thrilled once I explained about—"

"Watch it, Kendall," Hugh said warningly.

"Hugh, I never! George is just my intern, okay?"

"I'm sure he meant about the show, Kendall, not your toyboy—"

I bit my lip. The Viognier I'd had at the restaurant had made me too loose.

"Let's get some drinks," Hugh suggested. "Then I've got to dash up there, get the emcee thing started. We're half an hour behind schedule."

As Hugh brought each of us a drink and then wound his way through the crowd to the stage, I watched Kendall's pretty girl-friends in their preppy prints and Hugh's lawyer friends in suits begin to circle each other. Around them were many more young people in black leather and heavy metal, as well as fashionable young men with shaved heads and guayabera shirts, and girls with ironed hair and thigh-high boots. Now I understood why Hugh had been so obstinate about my clothes for the evening.

I was wearing a favorite pair of black shorts with a vintage Adolfo jacket in purple and black bouclé. Underneath the jacket was a purple camisole that barely grazed my navel, which glinted with a couple of pearls—a recent body alteration about which I had mixed feelings. Because I didn't want to be taken for a hooker, I'd insisted on mid-heel sandals rather than the Manolo Blahnik stilet-tos Hugh had given me that morning. Now I was sorry I hadn't worn the Blahniks, but overall, I was well dressed for the setting.

"Come on." Kendall took my hand in hers. "Let's get close to the stage so you'll be right there for everyone to see when Hugh makes a personal tribute."

"Kendall, I don't know anyone! I hardly want to be embarrassed in front of hundreds." I was being so Japanese, I thought while Kendall resolutely dragged me close to the stage. She was from my American side—my mother's old Maryland family. I couldn't be-lieve she was so enthusiastic about Club Paradise. She was no stranger to the bars at Zola or Zaytinya, but this place was consid-erably more downscale than her usual party haunts.

Hugh placed his whisky glass on a speaker and picked up a mi-crophone. The raggedy buzz of noise faded as he greeted everyone in the suave Edinburgh-goes-to-London-and-next-flies-to-America accent that made Americans swoon. What was it about the British accent that made everything sound smarter? It was similar to the effect of a Japanese accent, which made everything sound sweeter.

Hugh said how pleased he was at the turnout for the birthday celebration for someone known to readers of the *City Paper* as the current "Most Notorious Woman under Thirty."

"Rei's the first girl who's made the listing without sleeping with a politician, and for that, I'm enormously grateful," he said as a spotlight suddenly found me in the crowd. I waved reluctantly, because to hide behind Kendall would be pathetic. The people in the crowd were grinning at me now. A cocktail waitress with a nose ring pressed a *mojito* into my hand, and—ignoring all the warnings I'd heard about taking drinks from strangers—I sipped it, glad for something to do while the roasting continued.

"Now, when Rei and I met, she thought we had nothing in common until I lured her into my car to listen to my collection of eighties and nineties tunes. To make her birthday really special, I wanted to bring her that music she loves."

If a band was the focus, the spotlight would move from me. Great!

"Knowing Rei's taste, I aimed my sights at the European bands. I tried for Echo and the Bunnymen, but unfortunately, that lot are playing a show in London tonight." A chorus of groans. Apparently Echo wasn't a big favorite here. "Next I went for Bjork, but she's undergoing a crisis of fashion confidence and won't leave the house." There was some light laughter. "Massive Attack are recording the score for the next Lexus car commercial, and Garbage said they have to put out their recycling tonight."

There were more groans and a call from the back of the room, "Get on with it!" Hugh refused to be rushed. He took a sip of whisky and said, "I began to think there was some kind of bad star hanging over the night that Rei was born, but in the end, the answer was right before my nose. It's a mystery band, an up-and-coming British group that had its video premiere on VH1 last month, and made it into the British equivalent of Billboard's listings. They're touring the country, and this is their only stop in Washington. They turned down the bloody 9:30 Club to be here with us tonight!"

There was sharp applause at that, and I began to feel the hairs on my arm prickle. There was only one band that I knew Hugh was close to, and that was his brother Angus's group, Glaswegian Hangover, which was making a ragtag tour on the west coast at present.

"So, without further ado, let me introduce a band with true grit and originality. Yes, the band you've been waiting for . . . Angus Glendinning and the Glaswegian Hangover!"

The lights started flashing, and the band took the stage. I screamed with the others because I hadn't seen Hugh's younger, guitar-strumming brother in three years. The twenty-year-old who'd slouched around Tokyo with auburn dreadlocks had shaved them off so only a thin auburn halo edged his head. He wore a black T-shirt studded with rivets and tight blue jeans tucked into motorcycle boots.

The crowd howled as Angus picked up his guitar and lashed into an old Beatles song, "Happy Birthday," with a few new lyrics that made me blush. He followed it with a song that I'd heard him working on in Japan, all discordant clanging, but with new lyrics about being dragged into a war by an older brother he'd once loved but now hated with every ounce of his being. I would have liked Hugh's take on the lyrics, but he was back at the bar, grooving to the music while he waited for another drink.

I checked out the rest of the band. On bagpipes was a mournful-looking blond wearing a denim jacket and kilt with combat boots. An Indian-looking guy in a Manchester United football jersey was lost in the rhythms of the drums. There was a black bass player dressed in a battered leather jacket and jeans. All they needed was a Japanese to complete their United Nations, but I wasn't volunteering.

The band finished the song with a defiant upward-climbing riff and then Angus took a sip from a bottle that a fan thrust up at him. "Thanks, love. And thanks to Shug for organizing the venue and, what's that, a free round of McEwan's for all? Brilliant!"

Half the crowd surged toward the bar, wanting to take advantage of the beer. The die-hards who stayed at the stage started screaming names of songs they wanted to hear. "Methadone Morning!" "On the Train!" "Bleeding Heart Liberal!" I realized that the band's CD must have aired on more than a few college stations. The Glaswegian Hangover were semifamous.

"We'd love to get the jam going with a few songs off our new disc, *Liberal Elitist*. This song's called 'Pudding' 'cause it's unhealthy, which is the way we like it." Angus's accent was affected Glasgow working-class, which probably was crucial if your band was called Glaswegian Hangover. "We'll be playing our new songs mixed in with Rei's birthday track. Oh, and Shug—that's me brother, right?—wants me to let everybody know that our celebrity guest has arrived and will be appearing onstage shortly."

"Who is it?" I called out.

Angus shook his head. "Don't know exactly, but it's supposed to be a Japanese celeb. So don't go awaaayyy!" He launched into "Pudding" with a crash of guitar strings.

I wondered who the musician might be as I started dancing with Hugh, who had suddenly showed up and grabbed me around the waist. I had trouble keeping my balance, given the two *mojitos* I'd downed in the last half hour. Hugh moved behind me as the band slowly segued from its song about a Scottish school dinner gone wrong into the Grandmaster Flash classic, "White Lines." I was quickly wrapped up in the beat and the feeling of Hugh's body behind mine—finally, Hugh had to physically direct my attention to the stage, where I saw the Japanese guest: a young woman in a gold leather skirt, white go-go boots, and a white halter top. A curtain of perfectly streaked hair—gold and black—hung before her face, and when the hair flashed back, I saw my twenty-two-year-old cousin Chika's face.

"Chika!" I screamed in delight.

"I gave her my frequent-flier miles!" Hugh shouted in my ear. "She didn't want to miss your birthday!"

I turned and hugged him. "So she's staying with us!"

"Yes, she'll come back with us tonight. And I hope you don't mind, but the, ah, band will be with staying over, too."

"But where?" I knew I should be accommodating, but I felt a frisson of annoyance. Every week, it seemed, Hugh invited at least one or two overnight guests. Whether they were lawyers from his office having wife trouble, rugby players who'd been served eviction notices, or drinking buddies from Adams-Morgan who'd had one too many, Hugh unfailingly brought them home. He liked company. Hell, he'd been keeping me in his apartment, on and off, for years.

"Any free bit of floor," Hugh shouted again to make himself

heard over the din. "The lads are accustomed to bunking in bus stations and bathtubs. And they'll only be here a couple of days. It's not going to be like when Angus stayed for months in Tokyo."

"Hope not." I winked at Hugh, because I was actually fond of his hard-living brother. I turned back to the stage to admire my cousin Chika dancing in her high-heeled boots. Almost mechanically, she moved her arms and turned her hips, a robot-like contrast to the wild and woolly band, and the flailing bodies in the mosh pit in front of the stage.

"Chika's too cute," Kendall shouted in my ear as she danced by me. "Find out where she bought those boots."

"I'll ask!" I was overflowing with so much happiness that I wasn't shy anymore. My head felt light and my body full of rhythm as I jogged up onstage to join my cousin. We embraced, and before I knew it, Angus had grabbed us both in a pelvis-grinding hug. Chika pulled away, obviously startled by the bald white boy, and the audience roared.

Angus launched into my favorite 1980s classic, "Lips Like Sugar." As Chika and I started to dance together, I gazed over the mosh pit and into the crowd. All the way from the bar, I saw Hugh smile at me and raise a McEwan's in salute.

Kendall had commandeered some male friends to boost her from the mosh pit to the stage, and the next instant she was dancing alongside Chika and me. I wasn't surprised; Kendall was the most competitive woman I knew. She wasn't one to stay out of the limelight for long.

I danced between my cousins, thinking about my Japanese past on one side, and the American future on the other. I was shot through with joy, not caring that my Lycra top was inching upward, revealing the navel ring glinting in the spotlight. Chika was performing a careful series of steps, and Kendall was unzipping her black leather jacket and, now, pulling off her T-shirt.

Her T-shirt? I took a second look. Kendall, seemingly delighted by the catcalls of the audience, was wearing only a red lace bra and jeans. I glanced at Chika, who looked unimpressed, probably because girls in Japan had been disrobing on nightclub stages for years. Now I glanced back over the bobbing heads on the dance floor, looking for Hugh. He wasn't at the bar. He was probably close to the stage, getting a bird's-eye view of Kendall's cosmetic enhancements. That's what they had to be. We'd shared an outdoor shower during a beach vacation in college, and she'd been much smaller. Although maybe I was being unfair—could the breasts be a result of childbirth?

The crowd was screaming for me and Chika to take it off, too, and I felt a twinge of nervousness. I'd brought it on myself, I knew, but suddenly I felt that my navel ring was more than I wished anyone had seen.

"I'm stepping down!" I shouted to Chika as "Lips Like Sugar" drew to a close.

"Okay, I'll come along," she shouted back. "That girl is crazy!"

After we made it offstage, Chika asked me where we could get water. I was parched, too. I glanced back and saw that Kendall had started working on the top button of her jeans.

"Where's Hugh-san? I'd like to say hello to him—he was so kind to give me the ticket. Business class, even!" Chika's happy chatter brought me back to the reality that I was with her, and life wasn't as out of control as I'd feared.

"The last place I saw Hugh was the bar," I said, leading my cousin along. But he wasn't there. After Chika and I each bought a bottle of water, we threaded through the crowd to the back, where Andrea was standing at the door, checking names against a guest list. She was being very hard-hearted with a group of Georgetown students who were claiming they should be on the guest list.

"But I know Rei," one of them was saying. "She's, like, my best friend."

"Do you know this girl?" Andrea, her arms folded over a skintight "Power to the People" T-shirt, appeared ready to grind the girl under the her six-inch boot heels.

"Sure. Let them all in. Hey, have you seen Hugh?"

"Last time I saw him he was buying drinks for all his rugby friends. Are you loving your party?"

"Very much so," I said, and gave Andrea a quick hug before going back into the depths of the club.

"Is that Hugh-san?" Chika tugged my hand and I followed her

down a hall lit only by a sign for an emergency exit. There, one of the suits was vomiting over a trash can.

"Oh, no!" I said, because I recognized the suit. It was Hugh's.

"What did he eat for dinner?" Chika asked in a horrified voice.

"I don't think it was the dinner." I'd tried everything Hugh had eaten, and the restaurant had an impeccable reputation. Hugh must have been done in by the bottle of wine chased by whisky followed by the lager. It wasn't really his fault—he'd once been able to drink like that and hold his ground, but now he was thirty-two. Perhaps his metabolism had changed—as mine would, too.

I sent Chika into the ladies' room to bring back both wet and dry paper towels, while I helped Hugh through the end of his agony.

"Sorry," he said, sounding weaker than I'd ever heard.

"Don't be." I stroked back his hair, examining him. The charming Scot who'd toasted me with champagne a few hours earlier had been replaced by a red-eyed stand-in who had almost lost his accent. It was getting exhausting, living like this. Just two nights before that he'd gotten sick after a dinner party in Kalorama. I reminded myself that this was the same man who'd loved me enough to let me live in his apartment, who hauled antiques without complaint, who made a pot of tea for me every morning.

"I'm missing a great show, aren't I?" he asked, sounding pitiful.

"Angus and the band are amazing," I said. "But you'll hear them again."

"Yes. He's coming home with us." Hugh sat down on the floor, his back against the wall for support.

"That's right, but a little later on. I'll figure everything out. We'll have to take a taxi home, because I can't drive either."

"Don't take me home," he said. "You're having a—grand time— a birthday time—"

I shook my head. "Staying here doesn't matter. I'm as trashed as you are, practically. I'm beat."

It was true. Three years earlier, I would have stayed the whole night. But now I just felt exhausted.

My twenties were over. Thirty had already taken a very dirty toll.

3

The claim I'd made about a morning meeting had been all too true. I woke up at eight-fifteen with a pounding headache, knowing that I had to be at the Smithsonian within seventy-five minutes.

I dragged myself into the bathroom, where Hugh was sleeping in the tub. I pulled the shower curtain to give myself privacy while I used the facilities. I would have loved a shower, but it wasn't worth drowning Hugh.

I felt bad that he'd slept there. But he'd been sleepy enough to drop anywhere, and the spare bedroom and living room were filled not only with Angus's bandmates but with two roadies as well. In the bedroom I usually shared with Hugh, I'd placed Chika, who was still sleeping facedown in her tiny chemise. Before I'd gone into the bathroom, I pulled the sheet over her, just in case anyone stumbled into the room. I also wrote DO NOT DISTURB! on a Glaswegian Hangover flyer and taped it to the door.

How my head hurt! I would never drink like that again. I'd recklessly chased one glass of wine with another at dinner, then spent the rest of the night slamming down hard liquor. The evidence was all over the place—red pupils, triple creases under the eyes, and a greenish tint to my skin.

After gulping down two Aleve tablets and patting on a bit of makeup, I dressed in dark blue Donna Karan suit handed down from my mother, which I'd laid out the day before. I had a bit of panic when I couldn't find my panty hose, but they turned out to be on my dresser, coiled underneath a potted bonsai tree—yet another birthday gift that had appeared in the foyer the night before. I lifted the pot up and gingerly pulled out the stockings, praying they hadn't been torn. They were fine. I took this as a good omen—the only thing, maybe, that I had going for me on such a challenging morning.

I wasn't quite sure how the Sackler had located me, because I hadn't applied for any job there except for a college internship that never happened. Of course, I sent out résumés all the time, so when a brisk-sounding woman had called the week before, asking me to come to discuss a potential consulting job, I'd immediately said yes. Any offer of steady employment would be fantastic, given that I'd finished a big restaurant decorating project and was at loose ends.

I stepped into the Bally alligator pumps I'd gotten at the San Francisco Opera thrift shop the last time I'd been home, visiting my parents. Then I returned to the bathroom to bring Hugh clothes for his own workday.

"Who bashed in my head?" he muttered.

"You did it to yourself," I said, then relented. "You must feel awful. And I'm sorry we put you in the tub last night to sleep, but I needed a bed for Chika—she's sleeping in our room right now, so I brought you some clothes."

"Oh." He yawned. "Where are you going so early in the morning?"

"It's already eight-forty and I have that meeting at the Smithsonian in less than an hour."

"Sorry about last night." He sighed. "And I—lost it, didn't I? You saw me at my worst."

"You've seen me sick, too." But compared with him, I was the picture of blooming health. "It was a wild night. Parts of it were wonderful."

"I swear that I just had a whisky and a lager or two—"

"You also had a half-bottle of wine and a glass of champagne at the restaurant." I began brushing my teeth at the bathroom sink.

"Right. We drove from there— My car! Where is it?"

"I'm sure it's still wherever the valets put it yesterday evening. I can swing by after my meeting to retrieve it."

"No, no, I'll do it. I'll take care of it today. That shall be my penance," Hugh said darkly.

It was a twenty-minute walk to Dupont Circle, plenty of time to get the blood moving. I had a skim latte with four sugars in hand that I'd carried out from Urban Grounds. I'd have to finish drinking it before I entered the Metro, which had a strict prohibition against food and drink. As I sipped, I considered the situation ahead of me. I'd have to present myself to strangers, without knowing what they were after. But they had thought enough of me to seek me out. That was something I could cling to, with hope.

I regretfully tossed my half-full coffee and boarded the train. I held my bag closely against me, protecting it from the crush of people. Inside the bag were two different résumés. The first one presented my work as an antiques buyer; it focused on freelance work I'd done for a restaurant in Washington and private clients in Tokyo. The second résumé made me look more like a scholar—citing a sale that I'd made years ago to a folk craft museum and the writing I'd published about a historic collection of Japanese flower-arranging vessels. There were a few flamboyant successes on both résumés, but sadly, no evidence of a real job anywhere. The longest job that I'd had since getting my master's degree was working as an English teacher in Japan, and that, I sensed, was totally unrelated to anything the Smithsonian might want me for.

I hopped out at Gallery Place–Chinatown, but instead of turning toward the restaurant district as I did for my last job, I walked the few long blocks to the Mall. The sun had broken out at last. It was a day on which, if I hadn't had a headache, I might have jogged to the gym where Hugh and I shared a membership. I'd become addicted to gym classes, especially the ones that featured weight lifting, yoga, and ballet. It sounded like over-the-top fusion cooking, but I was happy with the new, sinewy muscles that had emerged in my arms and shoulders. Hugh said the best part of it was that I could now move heavy furniture without his help.

Well, today wasn't a weight-lifting day, but at least my posture was better than it used to be. I sucked in my abdominals a touch as

I passed the majestic, redbrick Gothic castle that housed the Smithsonian's administrative offices, and kept them in place as I entered the circular glass atrium entrance of the Freer Museum's Ripley Center, which led in turn to the Sackler Gallery, a few flights down.

I'd sworn I wasn't going to look around, but I had to pause for a second glance at an impressive art installation right inside the entrance. A modern Chinese artist had dredged up the hull of an old wooden Japanese fishing boat and perched it atop thousands of pieces of broken white porcelain cups and saucers. A boat afloat on china; I loved the metaphor, but cringed at the thought of all the pottery smashing that had gone on.

"Ma'am? The museum doesn't open until ten."

The security guard who'd been at the desk was suddenly at my side. I'd gotten too close to the artwork. I apologized and told the guard that I was a few minutes early for my appointment in the administrative offices with Michael Hendricks.

"We have nobody working in our museum with that name," she said, frowning at me again. "Are you sure he isn't a part-time volunteer?"

"I don't think so." I scrambled through my bag for the paper where I'd written down the few details I'd been given. "A woman called me back as well. Her name is Elizabeth Cameron—"

"She's the ancient Near Eastern curator." The receptionist flipped through some papers. "She left a message about someone coming to a nine o'clock meeting."

"That might be me. My name is Rei Shimura." I felt uneasy, because I didn't think ancient Near Eastern art was anything I could take a stab at. Also, the timing of the meeting was off. Michael Hendricks had said nine-thirty, or so I'd thought.

But it turned out that the security guard's message had my name on it, so she called another guard to escort me through the labyrinth of dimly lit galleries to the administrative section.

Not an auspicious start, I thought as we rode down the elevator to the second floor, where the administrative offices lay. I was stupid to have arrived late and without knowing more about why I was being interviewed. Perhaps they'd made a mistake calling me in. I knew about the art of the Far East, not the Near East or

Mesopotamia, as it used to be called. I would make that clear right away, I decided, and I'd be out the door fast—before nine-fifteen, probably. I would be able to make a ten o'clock Pilates class at the gym, if I hustled enough.

Huge double doors to the administrative section were locked, but the guard unlocked them for me. Right behind them there was someone waiting, a tall, slender African-American woman in her fifties. The green skirted uniform that she wore had silver oak leaves on the shoulders; her black name tag read simply "Martin."

"Are you Rei Shimura?" the woman officer asked.

I nodded, surprised that she not only knew my name but had pronounced it correctly. Rei rhymes with X-ray—which was what she seemed to be doing as she surveyed me all the way from my conservative pumps up to my bed-head hairstyle and bloodshot eyes. It seemed, from the tightness of her expression, that she could guess the kind of night I'd been through.

"You may come in, Miss Shimura. We're all here."

The guard departed and I followed the woman along a wide, carpeted hall and into a large room where a few people were sitting. The woman locked the door behind her, and I gulped.

I surveyed what lay before me: a windowless room decorated with a few framed posters from past exhibitions at the Sackler, and a huge film screen similar to the ones I remembered from college lecture halls. The room was filled with a long, teak table, a much larger table than was needed for the one woman and two men sitting at it. One of the men was a distinguished-looking, older Japanese; the other an athletically built man with hair cropped as closely as a soldier's. He was wearing what seemed to be the official D.C. uniform: a Brooks Brothers suit, the all-American label that Hugh, who wore only European designer suits, abhorred.

"Coffee?" The woman who had been seated at the table spoke to me gently, as if she realized I needed special handling. I nodded gratefully, even though I'd already had a huge dose of caffeine. As she moved to a coffeemaker set up on a side table, I checked her out—brunette pageboy hairstyle and a hip-length, hand-knit olive green sweater over a calf-length black skirt. Very artsy; perhaps she was the curator?

"Sugar? Cream? I'm Elizabeth Cameron, the one who called you." The woman confirmed my thoughts. "I'm so glad you could join us."

"I'll take both," I said. "And I'm glad to be here too." The last was a slight exaggeration, given the locked doors and serious faces. I knew that this was going to be like no interview I'd ever had before.

"I'm Michael Hendricks, from the Japan desk at State. Senator Snowden gave me your name." The guy in Brooks had taken the coffee from Elizabeth Cameron and handed it to me. He had an accent that I couldn't place, as clipped and correct as his military haircut. On second glance I realized that his hair, which I'd first thought was brown, was actually a salt-and-pepper mix of brown and silver. Men could gray prematurely and look fabulous, I thought sourly. At least, I thought it was premature graying. I couldn't guess his age at all, just as I couldn't make out the details of where he worked on the ID tag that hung from a chain around his neck. My eyes were simply too tired.

I turned from him to the Japanese-looking man, who was wearing a conservative dark blue suit. He was a guest here, too, I thought. I wasn't sure what to do until he bowed to me slightly; I bowed back more deeply. He smiled, and in that moment I knew I'd seen him somewhere. But my brain was too frazzled to make the connection.

I hesitated, holding my coffee, not wanting to be too presumptuous about my next movement—or any movement at all.

Michael Hendricks said, "We have a place set up for you on the other side." I tripped slightly in my awkwardness to get around the table.

"*Kiotsukute kudasai,*" the Japanese man said. *Be careful, please.*

"*Gomen nasai,*" I apologized back to him, then said in English to the others, "I'm a little uncoordinated," as I sat down gingerly on an unholstered chair.

"Oh, I don't think so. You danced pretty well last night." Michael Hendricks smiled easily. "I apologize for not introducing myself, but it was hard to get through the throng."

Could this be some game of Hugh's—a faux interview on the tail of a wild night? Was the military officer going to slide out of her uniform, any minute? Confusion washed over me. Carefully, I said, "I'm afraid I don't understand what this meeting's about."

"I'll start by introducing the remaining people. Now, you've spoken with Elizabeth on the phone already, I understand, and you just met Colonel Martin, who came in from Baghdad a few days ago to join us."

Brenda Martin nodded at me and sat down next to Hendricks as he continued his introductions.

"I'm grateful that Mr. Yukio Watanabe, the Japanese consul general, was able to take time away from his responsibilities at the embassy to join us." Michael paused. "Everything that we say must be kept confidential, Miss Shimura. Are you comfortable with that?"

Feeling flabbergasted by both the power of Mr. Watanabe and the demand being put on me, I said, "I could give you an answer if I knew what this was about."

"It's about considering you for a job," Michael Hendricks said.

"In that case, of course I'll maintain confidentiality. And I've brought my résumé." I extracted the résumé with the scholarly focus and slid it onto the table. Nobody picked it up. Feeling awkward again, I asked, "Does the job relate to Japanese art or antiques?"

"Not exactly." Michael Hendricks leaned back in his chair, studying me with eyes the color of a cold fall sky. "This mission involves ancient Near Eastern art. Even though this isn't an area you've worked in during the past, we believe you are qualified to handle this assignment."

"Dancing and all?" I thought I'd make a joke to relieve my nerves, but nobody smiled.

"I think we can all safely agree that dancing doesn't hurt anyone or anything. And now, we're running a few minutes late, so I'll get right to the presentation." As he spoke, I finally placed Michael's accent: eastern-educated—absent of slang and regional influences. He'd probably attended Andover, Exeter, or a similar northeastern boarding school.

The lights went out, and slowly the film screen at the end of the room lit up with the glow from a projector. REI SHIMURA BACK-

GROUND, the screen said. The words vanished and there was a photograph of me, a reproduced photo clipped from the Japanese newspaper *Asahi Shinbum.* I straightened up a little, because I'd always liked this shot, in which I appeared stunningly slender in an Azzedine Alaia dress a girlfriend had lent me to wear to a party at the Tokyo American Club. The Japanese paparazzi had snapped me because of a murder investigation I was peripherally involved in— something that had fortunately come out all right in the end.

"Rei Shimura lived in Japan from the age of twenty-four. Here she is outside the Tokyo American Club, a place where she once socialized with prominent expatriates like Joseph Roncolotta, who still runs a consulting business in Tokyo."

Next came a shot taken from the *Tokyo Weekender* party page: a picture of Joe Roncolotta lifting a beer at one of Tokyo's several German beer gardens, surrounded by Japanese businessmen. After that, the screen showed a picture of my antique-dealing mentor, Ishida-san, and then a picture of my Aunt Norie with a prizewinning flower arrangement that had appeared in the Kayama School of Ikebana newsletter. There was even a picture of me with Hugh, back in his days as a lawyer in Tokyo, leaving his old apartment building in Roppongi.

"May I say something?" I interjected. "My personal life really shouldn't be taken into account if this is about a job. It may even be illegal."

"Your personal life is what's *perfect.*" Michael Hendricks's voice sounded almost reverent. "But don't worry, Hugh Glendinning is not of particular significance."

Hugh's image faded and was replaced by a new man's. It was another media snap, this one of Takeo Kayama emerging from the doorway of the Kayama School. Takeo, who had been my boyfriend a very long time ago, looked different. He still had the same knife-edge, elegant features, but the long, floppy, rock star hair was gone, cropped to a length perfect for business. He was wearing a long black trench coat open, flapping behind him, giving him the look of a bat. The coat, in fact, cut off half the face of the woman trailing behind him—a young woman, probably his sister.

"Now, here we have Takeo Kayama, the recently appointed

iemoto—that means headmaster, right, Mr. Watanabe?—of the Kayama School of Ikebana in Tokyo."

The outside details on the picture blurred as I focused on Takeo's expression, which seemed harder than I remembered. When I'd decided to return to Hugh, Takeo had been unpleasantly surprised—but I'd heard on the trans-Pacific grapevine that he'd quickly bounced back. Well, men always did, didn't they?

I listened as Mr. Watanabe, in careful English, described Takeo's life: the lonely childhood in a luxury apartment, his schooling at Tokyo University, and then the University of California at Davis, the building passion for environmentalism, and his brief passion for me. Or, as Mr. Watanabe put it politely, "the pleasant friendship with Shimura-san."

A shot of Takeo's country house flashed on the screen, and I felt a pang. I had spent a whole summer helping Takeo brighten old, stained walls to the colors of sea, sky, and garden. I loved that house, which had been built in the 1920s; it was one of the places I missed most in Japan. Takeo and I had been together at the house, ostensibly restoring it, but in truth spending almost as much time at the beach, or in bed. My friends had harangued me to invite them for a country weekend, but we'd never wanted company. Takeo and I had no need for anyone that summer.

"The friendship with Miss Shimura kindled Mr. Kayama's interest in antiques. Under her guidance, he began a study of Japanese antiques." As Mr. Watanabe spoke, the image on the screen changed to a photo that a paparazzo with a long lens had taken of us behind Takeo's beach house in Hayama. The two of us were lying close together, poring over a comic book. Now I looked at the image of my younger self and felt dismayed by how pin-thin my arms had been. Takeo hadn't minded, of course—one of his hands rested lightly on my Speedo bikini bottom. With a sudden rush, I remembered the things that Takeo and I had done, within the walls of that ancient, always empty house.

I tried to focus my attention back where it belonged. "That's a comic book we're reading, actually. I never taught him anything about antiques. He has no interest."

"Then why did he spend just over eighty thousand pounds on

Asian ceramics at Christies in London last year?" Michael Hendricks said, flipping to a photograph of a sales slip from Christies. "And just before that, ten million yen at Meiwashima Auction House in Tokyo."

"Really? I'd like to know what he bought." Ten million yen was about $100,000, and Meiwashima was a high-end auction house, a far cry from the country auctions I usually frequented. It had been a major effort for me to get a membership at Meiwashima, and once I was in, I realized I couldn't afford anything.

"Vessels," said Michael.

"Do you mean—like the boat upstairs in the atrium?" My eyes widened.

Michael shook his head, and looked as if he was trying not to laugh. "Containers. Mr. Kayama is after historic containers of all kinds—urns, bowls, vases, anything that could hold water and plant material."

"Oh, for *ikebana* purposes. Well, I'm glad he has a new hobby. Everyone should have a hobby." I felt embarrassed to have made the mistake. Of course I knew that ceramics with openings were called vessels—why hadn't I understood Michael the first time around?

"The problem is that the young headmaster's hobby may be illegal." Michael Hendricks cleared his throat. "Colonel, maybe it's time to give Rei the background on the situation with the National Museum in Iraq."

"I'm sure Miss Shimura has read accounts of the looting at the museum during the early stages of the war," Colonel Martin said. "Hundreds of civilians stormed the museum, grabbing whatever was nearby and looked valuable—mostly gold items from the closest open galleries. At the same time, many priceless treasures were actually hidden by the curators, who had anticipated the looting. But there was a third class of museum items that were probably taken by a few insiders who knew their worth. Within this category of missing items is a group of Mesopotamian vessels dating from approximately three thousand years ago." A grainy black-and-white slide flashed on the screen, showing a rustic pottery vessel shaped like a goat. Its long, curved horn made a handle, and there was room to pour something in at the tail, and then out at the goat's mouth.

"Our Iraqi colleagues at the museum called this the ibex ewer, because it's made in the form of an ibex—a wild goat native to the Mesopotamian area, which includes modern countries like Iraq, Iran, and Syria. The ewer vanished during the looting along with about three hundred other objects from the museum."

"What a shame," I said. For a country to lose its art was to lose its soul. Legend had it that the Americans had chosen not to bomb Kyoto during World War II because it was the center of Japan's high culture. But they'd bombed Tokyo plenty.

Next, a photo flashed on the screen of a round-faced man with thinning black hair. He was trudging toward an airplane with an oversize briefcase in one hand, looking every bit like a lawyer going to court.

"This is Osman Birand," Colonel Martin said. "A millionaire Turkish antiques dealer with a business in Istanbul. He's suspected to have dealt in antiquities stolen from mosques and museums throughout the Middle East. We believe that he may have been involved in brokering antiques stolen from the Royal Museum, but we have yet to find the evidence, and a buyer who'll testify, in order to charge him with anything."

The next picture: Osman Birand, without his briefcase and looking considerably more relaxed with a wineglass in hand, standing on a yacht with a taller, slimmer companion. The photo had been shot at dusk, so I couldn't see the details very well.

"Osman Birand had a party on his yacht in Hong Kong, just a few months ago. Takeo Kayama, pictured here, was one of his guests," Colonel Martin said.

I wasn't at all convinced that the fellow onboard was Takeo, and the situation didn't make sense. "Why was Takeo there?"

"Fund-raising for an organic flower-farming cooperative." The colonel raised her thin, arched brows. "He says he wants to apply the kibbutz prototype to help poor Arabs help themselves. Birand contributed the equivalent of twenty thousand dollars."

Organic flower farming did sound like Takeo, I admitted to myself as the image on the screen changed again, back to the country house. The headline over the magazine spread said "Seaside Beauty!" in the phonetic *katakana* script used for foreign words like these. It was true that the room was beautiful, and one could see the sea through the new, floor-to-ceiling glass windows that formed one wall of the old living room I remembered. When I'd last been in the house, it had been under renovation, so there was no furniture; now I saw it in its restored glory, filled with eclectic Japanese pieces from the early twentieth century, and other things that couldn't have come from Takeo's family: a carved dark wood Indian colonial *almirah* cabinet and a low, midnight blue couch that curved with a feeling of art deco. In front of the couch sat a gorgeous lacquered tea table decorated with an animal-shaped vessel with a sinewy hawthorn branch arching up from it.

"When this picture in the Japanese magazine *Lovely Home* was brought to our attention, we ran a computer-enhanced analysis of the ceramics in the cabinet," Colonel Martin said. "And then we brought it to Elizabeth, at the Sackler, for further analysis."

The next image was a split screen—a color shot of the vessel in Takeo's cabinet, and then the black-and-white image of the ibex ewer from the museum in Iraq.

"It's too bad that you don't know the color of the urn from Iraq," I said.

"It has that same distinctive reddish slip," Elizabeth Cameron said. "It's an ancient slip technique that not many use today."

"This vessel is believed to be one of the oldest original ceramics in Iraq," Colonel Martin added. "The ibex ewer has been visited by every schoolchild who ever went to the museum and ranks among the nation's most beloved treasures."

"So this is why you brought me in. It's not about my being so brilliant with ceramics, but about my connection to Takeo!"

Michael Hendricks cleared his throat and said, "Both ceramics and the knowledge of our suspect are items in your favor, but there are other factors as well. We know about your activities here and abroad. You've demonstrated an ability to think on your feet. You've always been remarkably successful—when you want to get something."

"But I don't want to get Takeo," I said. Takeo was toxic, I knew from my experience. I couldn't risk being around him, now that I was semisettled with Hugh, couldn't risk it for a second—

"Takeo Kayama may have bought this on the black market, but he is not the suspected thief," Colonel Martin said. "If we can get back this vessel and find out whether your old friend acquired it from Birand, we will finally have the piece of information we need to apply pressure."

I pressed my lips together, then spoke. "I still don't believe that I can do anything for you."

"As Colonel Martin has been explaining, the American forces are in a bind. We have, of course, military police and some investigators present in Japan, but the scope of their powers is extremely limited. Without permission from the Japanese government, they can't force a search of a Japanese citizen's home."

"I've told Mr. Hendricks that we can't do anything, either," Mr. Watanabe said in his soft voice. "There is not enough evidence for our national police agency to obtain a warrant."

"Why not just ask Takeo to submit his piece of pottery voluntarily to an inspection? Have you even tried to seek out a peaceful resolution?" I asked.

"We cannot risk creating a situation in which he might alert Osman Birand." Michael Hendricks pushed a thick manila envelope toward me. "In here, you'll find a new passport and an itinerary."

I didn't touch it. "What do you mean?"

"We'd like you to take a short trip back to Tokyo. You'll have a cover story—that you're buying antiques—and a new passport with an official visa that shows your affiliation with our embassy. During that time, we'll expect you to visit with your old friend Takeo Kayama at his family home. Without making it obvious, you'll find a way to examine the vessel closely and tell us if it's the item stolen from the museum."

"He'll never let me do that! After the way things ended, he won't ever want to see me, not in his beach house or anywhere that I can think of—"

The screen flashed another picture that had once run in a Japanese tabloid. It was taken on a gray afternoon in Roppongi, when Takeo and I were saying good-bye to each other as I was getting into a taxi. You could tell from the way our bodies leaned into each other that we had not wanted to part.

I felt something clutch deep inside me, and I began to sweat.

"He'll let you in," Michael Hendricks said, a hint of amusement in his voice. "Who wouldn't?"

4

Up-two-three-four.

Hold!

The eighteen-pound bar felt more like eighty during this third, most excruciating set of repetitions. I pressed upward, trying to keep the bar level, while at the same time gluing my lower back to the bench.

I had been insane to undertake a power-lifting class with a hangover, but after my ordeal at the Smithsonian, I couldn't imagine going home soon. I'd lightened the load I usually lifted, because this time I had a different kind of weight to bear.

It was my duty to go, each one of them had said. Colonel Martin said it was a chance to serve my country. Michael Hendricks argued that it was important to stand up against international art criminals who robbed the people of all nations. The Japanese consul believed that it was a special privilege to solve a serious international problem. But Takeo—I couldn't get near Takeo. If I did, I would wind up hurting him, hurting Hugh, hurting myself.

"Rei! Come on, don't forget the powerhouse!" Jane, the blond, outrageously muscular teacher, barked at me.

This powerhouse was not a sandwich, though I could have used one. Jane was referring to the abdominal muscles. I hardened my belly as I pushed up the bar, struggling to keep the left side in balance with the right.

I couldn't undertake a classified project that was actually governmental spying, though no one had used the word. When I'd suggested that this might be a job more appropriate for a CIA operative, everyone had reacted as if I'd passed wind. It was as if nobody in government used that acronym, just as nobody in Japan said the word *yakuza*. And Michael had asked me, completely straight-faced, to work for them for no pay. They'd give me my expenses, but that was it.

Not quite it, I thought, as I sat up and rubbed away the ache on the back of my arms, still brooding. At the end they'd revealed the carrot, the only reason that the mission really would appeal to me. If I went, I'd get to keep my new passport, with its clean pages and embassy stamp. I now had a legal method of entry back into the country that had ordered me deported because I'd once unlawfully entered a room to find evidence. I'd been caught by the Japanese police, and that was the end of me; greater good to society be damned.

Since that nightmare a year earlier, returning to Japan seemed akin to penetrating a high-security vault. Now I was being offered the passkey. The question was whether I could live with myself if I spied.

Hendricks and Martin had hammered into me the classified nature of the operation: nobody, not even Hugh, could know that I was working as an informant. Michael Hendricks had explained the story I'd give people: I'd been hired as a consultant to the Sackler, to shop for some antique Japanese ceramics at a major Tokyo auction taking place in two weeks' time. I'd spend a week or two in Japan, ostensibly visiting auction houses and catching up with old friends, among them Takeo Kayama, whom I was to refer to by the code name Flowers, Flowers-san, or Mr. Flowers. The code word for the ibex vessel that I was hunting down was Momoyama Period Vase, so it would sound to anyone listening as if I really were after seventeenth-century Japanese ceramics.

Feeling sick, I dragged myself into the locker room, stripped, and went to the showers. The water pounded down on my hurting head. I knew that my shoulders and arms would be throbbing with new pains the next morning. I didn't usually do straight weight lifting, just as I didn't usually go to espionage planning sessions or contemplate lying to Hugh.

Several women were waiting for showers now, women whose voices were slightly raised in irritation. I turned off the water and grabbed a towel, stepping out of the shower so fast that I slipped. Down I went on the ceramic tile floor, so fast that the women gasped but couldn't reach out in time to catch me.

The truth was that nobody could save me. As I struggled to my feet and wrapped the skimpy gym towel around myself, I knew that it was up to me, entirely, to save myself.

"Good timing," Angus Glendinning said when I walked back into the apartment an hour later. He was sprawled on Hugh's leather sofa, an unfolded map covering his chest like a blanket. Around him were scattered the remnants of breakfast: a five-liter bottle of Mountain Dew and some half-eaten bagels.

"What's doing?" I asked dully. I was too upset about my own situation to care about the mess.

"Do you know the way to Baltimore?" Angus sang in a dreamy voice. "We're supposed to be playing a live bit on a radio program in an hour and a half—"

"An hour and a half?" I repeated, looking at him, shirtless and shoeless and wearing trendy thigh-length gray underpants. "And you need to get through the DC traffic and out to the freeway and then to downtown Baltimore?"

"It's not downtown. The station's in an area called Tozen."

"What?" I took his creased itinerary and discovered that he was supposed to go to the campus radio station at Towson University. Towson was just north of the city, so the trip would be longer than he'd thought. "You're looking at a good hour and a quarter, if you hurry."

"Sridhar went out to pick up our van. The parking in this neighborhood's wretched. We had to park a bloody mile away last night."

Sridhar had to be the Indian tabla player, I guessed, because he was the only one of the band I couldn't physically place. The Caribbean bassist was at the dining table, smoking a cigarette and reading Hugh's copy of the *Wall Street Journal*. Through the open door to the powder room in the hallway, I could see the blond bagpiper working on his hairstyle. He was wearing a very nice terrycloth bathrobe—mine, I realized.

"You'll need to hurry to get there," I said sotto voce to the *Journal* reader, deciding he had to be the brains of the bunch. "I'm Rei Shimura, by the way. I hope you were comfortable. I'm sorry I wasn't here in the morning—"

"You're Hugh's chick. I recall from last night," he answered in a broad accent that Hugh had taught me was North London. "I'm Nate. And the digs are great, yah? Love the wooden chest over there—is it from Japan?"

As I answered Nate in the affirmative, Angus interrupted me. "We don't have to rush anywhere, Rei. People anticipate our arrival. They schedule around us."

I couldn't help smiling. "Is that so?"

"Yah. In fact, when we go to Japan next month, the promoters told us just to get ourselves there, and then they'd arrange the shows. They already arranged our visas—it's bloody brilliant."

"You'll be going to Japan?" It struck me as ironic that Angus had free access to the country, his visas arranged by Japanese music promoters, while I had to creep in through the back door.

"Of course! You know we've been signed to a label there, don't you?"

"I didn't!" This was major news. I wondered if Hugh had heard.

"We've got an Asian tour in the works," said Nate, who'd stood up and was starting to get dressed, pulling on black jeans. "Taiwan and also Singapore."

"Angus, I'm embarrassed I didn't know all this! You'll have to tell me more after you get back from Towson. I don't want you to be late."

"Right, well, we'll be talking about this on the radio show. Do you think you'll be able to hear and tape it?"

"It might be too far—"

"You can listen on the web," Keiffer said, emerging from the bathroom. I noticed that the blond drummer's hair, which he'd apparently been working on so hard, still looked as if he'd just rolled out of bed.

"Keiffer, if you'd like a private place to dress, try Hugh's and my room," I suggested quickly, when I saw him pick up a pair of red bikini briefs from the dining area. The boys' underwear styles appeared to be as diverse as their onstage attire.

"Shug's still there, in a rather bad way." Keiffer made a face.

"What?" I shot a glance at the bedroom door with the DO NOT DISTURB sign I'd tacked up when I'd left Chika there, sleeping, a few hours earlier.

"Relax, Rei, he's there by himself," Angus cackled, as if he'd read my mind. "Chika got up a while ago, woke us all with cups of green tea, actually. Totally gorgeous, that cousin of yours. Why didn't you introduce me when I was in Japan before?"

"Chika was away at school," I said, even though it had been summer when Angus was around. I had done everything to keep my Japanese relatives from learning about the decadent young troublemaker in my apartment. "So where is Chika, then?"

"She wanted to see the neighborhood, so she went with Sridhar to get the van. She's attending our gig as well."

"Sounds like a good time." The apartment would be empty for a few key hours, hours that I would use to broach the subject of my return to Japan with Hugh.

They left thirty minutes later, fully dressed and teeth brushed, after I gave out spare toothbrushes to the ones who'd forgotten. I should be a mother, I thought wistfully, as I watched out the window as they recklessly crossed Mintwood Place, oblivious of the delivery truck that had to brake for their passage. Who did they think they were, the Beatles crossing Abbey Road? They'd kill themselves before the end of the day.

Only Chika waited demurely in her pink pleather coat at the curb, and looked both ways as she crossed. I found myself hoping that she would be the driver.

I turned away from the living room window and cracked open the bedroom door to check on Hugh. The room was dark, the curtains were drawn, and a foul smell lingered in the air.

"Still feeling awful?" I asked as I came to sit down next to him.

"I've been sick all morning," Hugh said. "I set off for work, but had to return. It could be a virus, I suppose."

I looked at him. "I don't know. Binge drinking is pretty hard on the system."

"Oh, don't be so damn American," Hugh grumbled.

"What do you mean?"

"You go to a pub with Americans, and if you have more than two drinks, they think you're a lush."

"I didn't keep count of myself last night. That was the problem." Thank God that I was slowly and steadily feeling better. The exercise had done me good.

Hugh sighed heavily. "I'm just sorry the band's landed on us at this point. I'd expected that you'd give them breakfast, but since you were gone, I had to send them to the bagel shop. D'you think they minded?"

"They seemed to bear no resentment." Though I did, for his expectations. "Hugh, I had a job interview this morning! I told you last night, and every day for the last week. You knew I had to be out early in the morning."

"So, d'you get the job?" he said sarcastically. "And what's the salary, high five figures or did you push them to six?"

I shifted uncomfortably atop the duvet. The fact that I made about as much as a salesclerk—despite my education and ambitions—was something we didn't talk about. Nor did we address the fact that Hugh paid the rent, the car insurance, the grocery bills. I knew there were plenty of married women who lived this way without question or worry, but to me, unmarried and not even engaged, it was an embarrassment. And maybe that was why he expected me to be a short-order cook, at moment's notice.

"God, my head hurts," Hugh muttered.

"I'll bring you some Motrin," I said, picking up the bonsai plant, which wouldn't thrive in the closed-curtains gloom of the bedroom. I was not a doormat. I was just helping my boyfriend, who was not his usual self. "And then, I think I'll make some brunch for both of us. Would scrambled eggs suit you?"

"That's sweet, but I don't think I could bear it."

"At least try some toast fingers!" I implored.

"No, no. I could sip some tea, though."

Of course, tea healed all Asians and Brits. "Your favorite Darjeeling?"

"Too sweet; it'll make me sick again." He sounded woeful. "I'd better go with green. Chika made a large pot of it earlier, maybe there's some left to warm up."

No proper Japanese believes in warming over old tea, so I put on a fresh kettle of water to boil as I set about reorganizing the apartment. It was a wonder Nate had been able to notice the fine old pieces of Japanese furniture, buried as everything was by opened magazines and newspapers and discarded clothes. I picked up a can of Mountain Dew that had sweated a ring onto my hundred-year-old *tansu* and tried in vain to buff its finish back. Then I threw away more old newspapers and cans and put in their place the bonsai plant that I'd carried in from the bedroom. The gift-giver's card had been lost, so I'd have to guess who had sent the sweet little dwarf pomegranate tree with dark green leaves and reddish orange trumpet-shaped flowers. Whoever had sent it couldn't have known me too well, because I typically killed house plants through neglect.

Now I was thirty, I'd have to be more responsible. I pulled out the care instructions printed on a little plastic stick buried in the potting soil. The pomegranate bonsai needed occasional fertilizing, regular watering, and full sun. The card went on to promise ornamental fruit in the fall. Hmm, it was already October. Where was the fruit? As I gently explored the plant's thick foliage, my fingers touched something inorganic. I drew back the glossy leaves to see a tiny black plastic disk. I'd seen enough spy movies to recognize it as a miniature microphone.

Happy birthday, indeed. I'd been bugged.

5

After I'd put the bonsai straight out of the apartment, I sank down on the sofa and considered the situation. Covert wiretapping had once been illegal, but probably wasn't anymore, because of the sweeping changes in civil liberties that had arrived with the new century. Someone had clipped the microphone to a plant that I'd brought in myself from the foyer of the apartment building. This was shrewd, a way to get the bug inside without physically entering the apartment. Now I wondered if there was a wiretap on the apartment telephone as well.

I shivered, because I'd almost persuaded myself to take the job. Despite the creepiness of the work, I was desperate to be in Japan. I could practically inhale the incense at the Yanaka Shrine, and my tongue curled at the memory of the smoky-sweet yams from the best potato-roasting cart. Autumn was the perfect time of year to visit Japan, when the persimmon trees along the train tracks hung heavy with red-orange fruit.

The thought of fruit returned me to my problem. The plant was outside the apartment now, but was that the right place for it?

I retrieved the bonsai tree and brought it into the study, where I found a place for it on a bookcase for the time being. This was the perfect act of revenge, I decided; the government team would now have the pleasure of listening to the Glaswegian Hangover for as long as they were in town. After that, I'd have to come up with something even more obnoxious.

The kettle whistled, reminding me of my original plan to make Hugh some tea. I poured the steaming water over the fragrant green tea leaves—tea leaves my aunt had brought on her last visit from Japan, a stash that was almost gone, but that I could replenish if I went on the mission.

I watched the tea brew to the right color, poured a cup, and took it to Hugh's bedside, but he was asleep again. I lay down next to him, intent on bringing up the potential trip to Japan the moment he woke up.

The afternoon stretched into evening, and still Hugh slept. Eventually, I did too. I was in the midst of a dream that I was climbing the moss-covered steps up to the fox shrine in my old neighborhood when I awoke suddenly. The little fox statue had been tumbling over and over, down toward me—I heard it shatter as it hit each step. No, what really was happening was that the telephone was ringing.

I grabbed the receiver and said a sleepy hello.

"Rei-chan, help me!" It was Chika.

"What's happened?" I asked, the panic in her voice spreading to me.

"It's a fight. I was just trying to park the van, you see—"

"Where are you?" If they were still in Maryland, I couldn't do much to help. The clock said that it was two in the morning.

"We're just around the corner in your neighborhood, on that street with the church. I didn't know the other car wanted to park in the same space. But some boys came out of their car and started shouting. Before I could do anything, Angus and his friends jumped from the van and started shouting back. Now they are hitting each other!"

"Does anyone have a gun?" I asked immediately. The content of my question finally roused Hugh on the other side of me.

Chika told me no. I shook my head at Hugh, who had staggered out of bed, and I continued talking with my cousin. "Chika, listen to me carefully. Can you get the band to return to the van?"

"No, no! I have tried. The boys told me just to lock myself in and keep safe."

Next idea. "Okay, I want you to roll down the window and tell everyone that the police are coming. That should slow down the fight. And we'll be there in a minute."

I put the cordless phone back in its cradle and explained the situation. Hugh nodded and began hunting around for his shoes.

"I don't know if you should go out."

"I won't let you go by yourself." Hugh grimaced as he spoke.

"I think we should call the police after all," I said, taking another look at Hugh. He appeared ill enough to be knocked over by the slightest blow. He'd be no asset to me on the street.

"The neighbors may have done that already," Hugh said. "We've got to get there first. If the police book them, my brother's tour is as good as over. Not to mention the threat of deportation."

I scrambled into my Asics. Hugh was having trouble of his own, coming up with only one running shoe and one Italian loafer—paired with his old University of London sweatshirt and flannel pajama bottoms, they looked pretty odd, but there was no time to be fashionable. I gave up on finding shoes and went out in my slippers, throwing a raincoat over my pajamas.

"How two exhausted people over thirty are going to break up a fight, I don't know," I muttered as we sped along the dark street. The old, bumpy sidewalks in Mintwood Place had charmed me at the beginning, but were a liability in the dark. Right around the corner, Chika had said. Oh, God, there they were. I could see a police car double-parked in the center of Octavia Street.

"We're too late," I said.

"Christ. I'll have to be their attorney," Hugh said grimly.

Something strange was happening. A Ford Explorer with an American University decal on its back window was reversing down the street toward us. The driver was a policeman, who pulled it into the no-parking spot in front of the church. He stepped out of the car and rejoined the police cruiser, which moved off slowly in the opposite direction.

Hugh had somehow gotten half a block ahead of me, so I hurried to catch up. The band's van was parked in a legal spot—I hadn't seen it before, but I recognized it by the "Scotland Forever" sticker on the back. Now Angus, Sridhar, Nate, and Keiffer were spilling out, their voices high and excited.

"They took 'em away, just like that!" Sridhar said.

"First time a bloody copper told me to take care. Great city!" Angus said admiringly.

Chika emerged from the driver's-side door and fell into my arms. She was trembling.

"What happened?" I asked.

"The cops came," Angus said. "They asked us if we wanted to press charges, but we said no, and they took those college prats off anyway, to issue some kind of citation for—what was it?"

"Disturbing the peace," Sridhar finished.

"That's right. The police dinna touch us at all, just told us to go home. Never got such gentle treatment before, not in the brawls we've been in!" Angus said, a note of wonder in his voice.

"They just let you go?" Hugh seemed as shocked as I was.

"Wait a minute." A suspicion was growing. "Angus, are you saying that the police specifically asked which ones were the college students?"

"That's right. It's like they could tell the whole story, that Chika was parking, and the others started the whole bloody mess. We dinna have to say a thing."

"What else did they say to you?" Now I knew for certain that our phone had been tapped. Angus and his friends were off the hook, and the others in trouble.

"Rei, let's not stand outside any longer," Hugh said in a low voice. "We'll get everyone home, that's the best thing."

But as we all made it through the apartment door, and it was locked behind us securely, I felt myself still spilling over with questions, which nobody but Michael Hendricks and his friends could answer. The government people listening in had to be behind the bugs, and thus behind this too-quick cleanup of a street brawl. Hugh seemed dazed by it all, and once inside, he turned down the boys' offer of an impromptu drinks party in favor of going back to bed.

"I'm very sleepy, too," Chika said, yawning. "But please, Hugh-san, don't give up your bed again to me. I really don't need it."

Now I had the bed problem all over again. "Maybe we can come up with some arrangement of pillows on the floor. But which room?"

"The study," Chika said. "Already, the boys have offered the futon."

"I'll bet," I said. "You saw how they"—I broke off, wishing I could come up with the Japanese translation for testosterone-driven—"how rude they could be on the street. I hate to think of what kind of misunderstanding might develop, if you slept in that room." At present, I knew, the boys were mixing drinks in the kitchen, just getting started on their party.

"Rei-chan, you are my cousin, not my aunt." There was a hint of annoyance in Chika's soft voice. "But please not to worry. I will share the futon with Sridhar, because his religion forbids him to touch women before marriage. It is the perfect arrangement, I think."

I bit back any further protests. She was twenty-two. But still, I couldn't help imagining her mother—my Aunt Norie—shaking her head in horror at the idea of Chika in bed with a tabla player, with the rest of the band crashed out around them, and the pomegranate recording whatever might be said—or sighed—during the night.

"It's up to you," I said at last. "But please remember, Chika, the walls are very thin. It's quite easy to hear things."

"Oh, yes," she said. "Mother mentioned that about the time she visited here."

That could mean Aunt Norie had overheard me with Hugh. I felt myself start to blush.

"Don't worry," Chika continued cheerily, "I shall tell the boys not to practice their songs tonight. We won't disturb you anymore."

6

Senator Harp Snowden had a weakness for good food—good Asian food, especially. His scheduler had said she could squeeze me in during the late morning, so I decided to bring him something to make up for any delays that I might cause. A new specialty bakery had opened near the zoo, and it sold quirky Japanese baked goods like puff pastry packets with curried vegetables inside, and croissants filled with chestnut puree. This seemed perfect for late morning, when the thought of lunch was on the horizon, but not yet a possibility.

Around eleven I carried the beribboned pastry box carefully into the Hart Senate Office Building. After a quick trip through a metal detector and a brisk walk past a huge, inscrutable Calder sculpture, I rode a crowded elevator up to the senator's office.

A new woman sat at the reception desk. She looked Asian but had features I couldn't quite place. She also had the same northern California accent as mine, but she mutilated the pronunciation of my name when she announced me over the phone to the senator. "It's like a ray of sun," I said to her after she'd hung up. "And Shimura sounds almost like Timor—"

"You can go back there now," she said, clearly not interested. "But Marianna said to remember he's got to get over to the Senate in half an hour."

I nodded and went through the door. Senator Snowden's office suite was huge, a charmless warren of cubicles and rooms where young people sat with their ears glued to phones and their fingers hovering over keyboards. Nobody looked up as I turned a corner and knocked on the half-open door that led to the senator's inner sanctum. He was at his antique partners desk, ankles up, with stacks of periodicals around him; he waved me in. I glanced around the room, seeing that a new artistic find—a Hmong quilt—had gone up between an old portrait of him with Bill Clinton and another with Nelson Mandela. Harp was a few years older now than the senator in the pictures, but he was still very handsome, with his patrician features and thick, silver hair. He was what every woman hoped her boyfriend would age into, I thought, as he swung his legs down from the desk and walked over to give me a quick embrace. He walked with a very slight limp that betrayed the loss of one of his feet, many years ago in Vietnam.

"How nice to hear from you, Rei. It's been too long!" Harp said, smiling at me.

"Well, you were really kind to see me on such short notice," I said.

"It's an important reason for us to talk. Michael told me you might be calling," he said, motioning for me to sit down on one of a pair of chintz-covered love seats near a large window overlooking Constitution Avenue.

"When he dropped your name, I had to follow up," I said.

"Of course. Actually, I've known Michael Hendricks for years. His father's Owen Hendricks," Harp said, settling down on the love seat across from me.

"Who's that?"

"A retired four-star admiral who was once in line to be secretary of the Navy. Shame it didn't work out. Anyway, our families each have camps on the same lake in Maine. Michael skippered my boat for years. I guess I could describe him as the son I never had."

"He's too old to be your son," I pointed out.

"You flatter me," Harp said. "He's in his late thirties, mature enough to have earned a Bronze Star in the first Gulf War, but restless enough to have left the Navy for civilian government service. It turned out to be a good fit for him, with his background in Asia and the Middle East. He's a rising star over there, Rei. I think you'll like working for him."

"How can you say that when you don't know what the work involves?"

Harp leaned forward and asked, "Has Michael asked you to perform an action that's illegal?"

"Not exactly," I admitted. "But it's—classified, so I'm not allowed to tell anyone about it. And since our meeting, my whole existence seems to have changed. My personal freedoms and even my living space aren't secure anymore."

"You mean that someone broke in?" Harp's eyebrows rose.

I shook my head.

"Aha. So you must mean . . . they're monitoring it for sound?"

I paused, not knowing whether I should answer. Maybe I'd said too much already. If he was so close to Michael Hendricks, he might pick up the phone and report that I was too talkative.

"Of course, while you're on a mission, that's par for the course. It's for your own protection, as well as theirs. I can assure you this room is secure, and so is any conversation that we have. We have some serious shared history, Rei. I won't betray that trust."

"I just don't know what I should do. Ever since the restaurant closed, I've barely worked. So this would be good, not to mention that it could improve another—situation—in my life." I was thinking about my visa status.

"How are things with Hugh?" Harp asked.

I sighed, thinking about Hugh's slow, tortured-looking exit from the apartment that morning. "Hugh's been under the weather since my thirtieth birthday party the other night."

"Really? If the party was too wild for him, it's probably a good thing I had to send my regrets." Despite his passionate liberalism, Harp was cautious about his image. I'd grown to respect this caution as a sign of real intelligence.

"Hmm. Well, you missed a few spectacular sights, but probably it's for the best." I thought about Kendall and her striptease. "But to get back to Hugh, despite his being a little ill, things between us are fine. His brother and the band are here for the moment, as is my cousin Chika from Japan—"

"A full house." He looked at me sympathetically. "Not that you could talk with him about it, anyway."

"That's something I wanted to ask you," I said. "When people undertake special jobs like the one Michael wants me to take on, why can't they tell a significant other?"

"Because they love the other person enough to want to spare him or her the worry, and in the long term, it's for the person's safety. When I was in Vietnam, things happened that I never told my wife. But now, the dangerous time has passed, and I can be open."

Maybe—when the ibex vessel was safely back in Iraq—I could tell Hugh. And he might actually be proud, rather than anxious or angry.

"By the way, Rei, I've been wondering what's in that box you brought. That is, if it isn't classified information."

"A few thousand calories worth of Japanese pastries from the new shop on Connecticut Avenue. I don't suppose you'd care to try one?" I pushed it toward him.

"Only if you join me. Delicious!" he said enthusiastically, after the first chew. "You have unerring taste."

"You're kind to say that." I reached for a curry puff.

"Well, my dear, I'm already anticipating the other delicacies you'll bring me after you get back."

Harp knew something, I decided as I said good-bye to him, left the building, and walked down Constitution Avenue. He knew that I was supposed to be going on a trip, or he wouldn't have mentioned delicacies. Michael had told him something, but probably not everything.

And I knew now that I was ready to go. I'd been running hot and cold on the issue for the last twenty-four hours, and there were some things I needed to sort out with Hugh first. But I was going. If I didn't go, I'd regret it forever.

I dragged myself over to the Washington Mall, past the tourists and joggers, and found a solitary bench. I was just getting out my cell phone to call Hugh, to arrange some sort of outdoor meeting where I could talk, in a limited way, about the situation that lay before me, when the phone itself rang. "Private caller" appeared in the display. I clicked "talk" and heard Michael Hendricks's voice.

"How did you get this number?" And how, I wondered, did he

anticipate that I was on the verge of arranging a meeting to break it to Hugh?

"The résumé you left with us yesterday included this telephone number. I gather that I've reached you on your cell?"

"Why even ask? I'm sure your colleagues could clarify the type of phone it is."

"Oh. So you're concerned about—privacy?" He sounded cautious.

"I should say so! The little thing that happened last night with the police and the guys in the band. And what about the bonsai you sent me with a strange plastic growth?"

"Oh, I see." He paused. "You discovered both bugs."

"I did."

"You're good," he said. "That is exactly the level of observation I expect you to use in Japan."

"But you're violating my civil rights! And Hugh's!"

"Rei, for operational security reasons, we need to know that we can trust you." He paused. "Come on, didn't it work out for the best last night? The police were alerted that Angus and his friends all were European citizens to be let go without incident. If that directive hadn't been issued, the band might have wound up in jail overnight with common DC criminals—a situation that would surely test their fake grit."

"I'm relieved that they weren't incarcerated," I said stiffly. "But let's return to my point. You bugged a place that isn't even my apartment. Hugh is the one you're going to have to answer to if and when he finds out."

"Once he gets up from his illness, that is," Hendricks said. "What the hell did he drink at your birthday party, anyway?"

"None of your business, and you're not presenting a winning case for my joining forces with you—"

"Let me try again, in person. Where are you?"

"Oh, come on now, I'm sure you know where I am," I answered tetchily.

"No, I really don't know. What's the location?"

"I'm on the Mall."

"Can you be more specific?"

I wondered if he was testing me again. "I'm on a bench near the National Gallery. Tell whoever has the binoculars to focus on the bench near the one with the wino stretched out."

"Rei, my office is not on the Mall, it's in Foggy Bottom. I'm going to go out and grab a taxi. I'll see you in ten minutes."

"That's ridiculous, I'm not staying here in the cold—" The temperature was fifty degrees, but weather was the first excuse that popped into my head.

"Then why don't you go inside the Freer? Let's meet by the coat-check area so that we don't miss each other."

It wasn't likely that we could miss each other, I thought, as I leaned against the entrance to the coat-check room, which was no longer operational—perhaps because of renovations, or maybe because of fears that a checked coat might hold a bomb. I didn't know.

Now I waited, sweating in my new fall coat, a pumpkin-colored wool melton, thinking about the good old days when a woman could hang a coat in a museum and not worry about the motives of the person she was meeting.

Michael Hendricks came through the door a few minutes later, dressed in a navy-and-black pinstripe suit, without a tie or an overcoat. He had taken a taxi, I guessed.

"You look irritated," Hendricks said. "Am I that late?"

"No. It's just that it's so hot in here, and the checkroom's closed."

"I'll take your coat. There's a place we'll leave it, deeper into the museum." He held out his hands for the coat, but just as I was about to hand it to him, I changed my mind and kept it draped over my arm. No chance that I'd allow him any opportunities to slide a bug into its lining.

The Sackler's galleries were subterranean, so we walked down a flight of stairs and were buzzed through the same locked doors to administration. Directly off the hall was a room with a buzzer, which Michael pressed.

"This is storage," Michael said while we waited. "They're paranoid about damage, so I'm sure they're going to ask me to leave my pen. Will you keep it at the bottom of your purse for me, and give it back when we leave?"

The pen looked like Mark Cross, but who knew what kind of pen it really was, I thought as I dropped it into the recesses of my bag and the door was opened to us by Elizabeth Cameron. Behind her stretched a series of tall steel cabinets, which I quickly figured out held all the goodies that weren't on display. I felt my interest rise, in spite of everything.

"Hello, you two. I can be with you in just a few minutes—I'm in the process of finishing assembling things for the lesson." Elizabeth inclined her head to the right, and I saw that there was a tall man with glasses doing something with one of the cabinets. Obviously, she didn't want to work with us in front of him.

"Sure. We wanted to look at the Islamic exhibit, anyway. May I leave Rei's coat somewhere around here?" Michael asked.

"No, that's all right. I'll carry it." Already, it seemed my impromptu meeting with Michael and Elizabeth had been planned. I was determined not to take any more risks with my privacy.

Michael wanted to go straight to the show's masterwork, a 600-year-old ceramic platter painted with images of men carrying spears, but I cut him short. I'd been to the show a few months earlier, and it was a piece that I thought attracted more attention than was seemly.

"I've seen it," I said. "And what I find bizarre is that the museum label says that it was owned by a warlord. Warriors traveled a lot, so why would they carry such a huge ceramic item? Brass or gold or silver would be travel-worthy, but this just is unbelievable."

"Are you saying you think it's fake?" he said, drawing closer to the glass.

"Because of the cracks and the type of pigments used, I'm sure it's very old, though not being an expert in Islamic pottery, I can't tell you how old. In any case, the plate probably was crafted to look as if it had a noble, war-going heritage—as if those two words can be used in the same breath," I added.

"Given my years at Annapolis, I'd like to think so," Michael said easily.

"Oh, so you went to the Naval Academy." I was determined to give him a taste of having his own life on trial, just as he'd done to me the day before.

"Yes, I was there. Harp wrote the recommendation for my application. I believe it was the only time our infamous antiwar senator helped someone join the military." He smiled easily. "I graduated a few years before you started at Hopkins. It's a shame, because you certainly would have, ah, enlivened our mixers."

"Hopkins girls don't usually socialize with Annapolis boys," I said briskly. "But getting back to you, before the academy, you must have been at boarding school: Andover, Exeter, somewhere like that—"

"Exeter." He looked at me a bit more warily. "And I know about myself already, thank you very much. What else can you tell me about the ceramic?"

"I think it was used in a home. A wealthy private home, where the people who owned it liked to encourage an illusion of a link to the ruling class."

"Well, that's a good inference."

I turned to see that the speaker was Elizabeth Cameron herself.

"Rei, I'm glad you came back. It sounds as if you have a pretty good base of knowledge already."

I shrugged off her compliment. "It just doesn't seem plausible that traveling warriors would have carried breakable ceramics. If you think so, too, why does the label say what it does?"

"Its history is all information this museum's staff received from the Victoria and Albert." She paused. "Well, now that you're here, Rei, I was hoping you might like to look at some things that are usually in storage, that the staff's brought out for our study. My colleague has gone to lunch, so we'll be able to make ourselves comfortable there."

"All right," I said. "I always welcome the chance for a behind-the-scenes tour at a museum."

"I'm glad to hear that," Elizabeth said. "I reviewed your master's thesis on Japanese ceramics. I think you'll find this new arena of scholarship a natural fit."

"Rei, you're turning out to be a jack-of-all-trades," Michael said. "Kimono, pottery, furniture . . ."

"Conversant in many things, but fluent in none," I replied lightly.

"Now, that is unbelievable." Michael gave me one last speculative look with his icy blue eyes before saying good-bye.

7

I was glad to have eaten the curry puffs with Senator Snowden, because it turned out that I never ate lunch. I spent the whole afternoon with Elizabeth Cameron, examining a table laden with dozens of fabulous ancient ceramics. As I pondered a 2,000-year-old urn, marveling at the history between my hands, I asked her whether it had been exhibited before.

"Ten years ago," she said. "We have so many holdings that it is a challenge to give everything a chance at the spotlight. And the truth is that the public prefers colorful items to earthenware."

"I haven't seen anything like—what we saw on-screen yesterday," I finished carefully.

"The ibex ewer? Yes, that was a unique piece. This museum at least doesn't have anything in the same form. I think the important thing happening today is that you're getting used to the texture of these ceramics, the color of the clay—look at that distinct ashy whitish interior on the chip. It is very different from the red clay that's more common."

"So this particular, lighter clay . . . it's from a certain region?" I asked.

"It's from Babylon. Later on, pottery making took place in other areas, where the clay had a different mineral content."

"And where the aesthetic was more lavish," I added longingly. These pieces really weren't my taste at all.

"Later pieces are usually more highly valued by collectors, though I myself tend to appreciate the simple beginnings."

So that was one of the differences between someone like myself who sold antiques to people who wanted stunning home decorations—and someone like her who wanted to keep them safely behind glass for all to see, free of charge. As I left the museum late that afternoon, I felt I had mastered some basics, but I needed to keep learning. If I was going to look at Takeo's vessel with any confidence, I would have to examine many more examples from the period.

I rode the Metro back to Dupont Circle, and as I walked toward Adams-Morgan, I dialed Michael Hendricks at his office.

"You forgot your pen," I said after he picked up.

"Really? Hang on to it until I see you again, will you?"

"I left it at the security desk in a bag with your name on it." There was no way I would trust that pen anywhere in my household. It could be a camera or another bug or even a weapon.

"Well, then, thank you very much." Michael sounded almost amused. "By the way, Elizabeth told me you had a very productive time."

"It was productive, but not quite enough."

"What do you mean?"

I explained that I wanted to examine more ceramics from that time period, at other museums. In each place, I'd need hands-on access, and a curator to help me.

He paused after I'd told him what I wanted. Then he said, "Do you have a few museums in mind?"

I told him the Walters Art Museum in Baltimore, the Metropolitan in New York, and the Philadelphia Museum of Art. I'd done research at these museums before, and they were all within a few hours of Washington.

"All right," Michael said when I was done, "I'll fund your travel to those places. But first, let me contact each museum with a plausible story, and we'll have some business cards made up for you. But it's got to be done quickly, since our goal is to have you out to Tokyo by the end of next week."

"I still don't know if I can take the job," I said. "Aside from learning more about ceramics, I have to be sure that Hugh is comfortable with my going."

"What, you have to ask his permission?" Michael sounded impatient.

"I didn't say I needed permission. But he's never taken a job that I didn't want him to do—"

"What about Edinburgh?" Michael Hendricks said. "He went back there, supposedly to help draft the new Scottish constitution, and he wound up with Lady Fiona."

"It was a brief engagement, which he terminated," I finished. "So, it seems like you examined news clippings from the *Tatler* party page. Why didn't you include them in the slide show for everyone's amusement?"

"It wasn't pertinent, just as I think the exact nature of your work for your government isn't pertinent knowledge for Hugh. It's enough for him to know that the Smithsonian is sending you to look into buying some Japanese ceramics."

I hung up, thinking that Michael didn't know about Hugh's instinct for sensing trouble. Even though Hugh was sick, he was still sharp.

"What's the crisis?" Hugh asked when I called him at work—something I very rarely did.

"I wanted to see if you're feeling better," I said.

"I'm hanging in," Hugh said. "But I'm swamped with work. I don't think I'll make it home till late tonight. Sorry."

"Don't apologize to me," I said. "It's more of a shame for you, trying to recover, and your brother in town for just a few more days—"

"Angus and I already said our good-byes. He's heading off for Philadelphia today, remember?"

"Oh. I'd forgotten. Well, anyway, when you get home, maybe we can go out for a quick bite. There's something we need to talk about."

"Over food? Have you forgotten the state I'm in?" Hugh laughed weakly.

"No, it's just that . . . I would rather get out of the apartment to talk to you, that's all. It doesn't have to be a restaurant, it could be a coffee bar—"

"That place around the corner closes by six, and I doubt I'll be through till ten. I'd rather just see you at home."

"What are you doing for dinner, if you're staying so late at work?"

"I thought I'd pick up a takeaway soup, if I can find a delicatessen that's open after six. Downtown is pretty dead at that hour, so it might not be worth the walk."

"Let me bring you food," I said. "It'll save you time."

I must have worn Hugh down, because he reluctantly agreed. We made plans for my arrival bearing tom yum goong in three hours' time. In the meantime, I went home and told Chika that we were going out to eat at my favorite Thai restaurant and that afterward, while she packed her suitcase for her next stop at my parents' home in San Francisco, I would head to Hugh's office to take him something to eat.

"So, he has to go to work when he's still sick. It's a shame," Chika said gravely.

"That's right. And I don't know if he's going to be sick again, so I think it's probably better if I'm just there."

"Of course. I'd like to be home this evening, in case the boys call between sets. Sridhar promised."

I looked sideways at my cousin. "How was last night on the futon?"

She beamed radiantly. "Very fun. Liberating, really. I never spent so much time with foreign men before."

"All the men I know are foreigners," I mused. Hugh was so profoundly Celtic, and Takeo came from centuries of Japanese inbreeding. Come to think of it, the boyfriends I'd chosen in college had all been bilingual and of international ancestry. My roommate used to call the motley parade of beaux that crossed our doorway Rei's United Nations. I'd never dated anyone all-American like Michael Hendricks.

I shook myself. Why had that thought popped into my head? Probably, it was because I had turned thirty and felt a need to evaluate all the men I met, whether I liked them or not.

"Foreigners," Chika continued, interrupting my distressed thoughts. "They are more intense. The differences . . . it's exciting at first. But it cannot last for eternity, as my mother says."

"Oh, does she."

"She's not watching me that closely right now. She's working on an *o-miai* for my brother, though."

"Tsutomu-kun is going to have an arranged marriage?" I felt faint at the thought of her older brother, my beloved cousin Tom, so attractive, lively, and caring. Why did his mother think he needed help finding a partner?

Chika answered my unspoken question. "My brother is so old— thirty-three already. Japanese girls are becoming choosy. They won't want him in two more years. Now is the time he can still have any hope of selection."

"All he needs is some time off from work! Time to socialize, meet people on his own," I said. "How could a matchmaker find a better woman for him than we could?"

"I have no interest in fixing up my brother. But if you do . . ." She waved an elegant hand studded with heavy rings. "*Onegai-shimasu!*"

I request of you, she'd said in formal Japanese.

In a week's time, I would have the chance to see her brother and ask him how he felt about arranged marriages. But first, I had to get to Japan—and that meant working things out with Hugh.

8

"No!" Hugh said.

We were sitting on the carpet in his office with the Thai food spread out like a picnic between us. I had spent the last ten minutes explaining my situation: a onetime contract job for the government to bid for antique Japanese pottery, a special passport back to Japan. An opportunity to jump out of my diplomatic black hole—an opportunity that might never come again.

He'd listened carefully the whole time I'd spoken, not eating a bite. And now, the verdict was negative.

"You mean you don't think I should go?"

"No, no, no!"

"But why—"

"I mean no, as in no kidding! I can hardly believe it. What brilliant luck." Hugh's serious expression had turned into a radiant grin.

I could breathe again. "So you think I should take it? I haven't told them yet—"

"Of course you should bloody take it! Rei, thank God you came to Washington. Because of all that publicity you gathered in the last few months, someone high up must have twigged that you're the right person for the job. When you return here with whatever Momoyama vase you buy, I want to throw a party. Do you think, if you ask nicely, they'll let you have it at the Smithsonian?"

"I doubt it. Hugh, you must be on the way to recovery if you're thinking of parties again."

"Yes, watch me eat rice and soup without losing it." He did so, and when he spoke again, his voice was slightly hoarse from the chili-laden soup. "I'm not ready to open a bottle of champers yet, but if you'll do the honors of pouring us each a glass of water, we can toast to your legal reentry in Japan, which I'll be thrilled to witness."

I went to organize the lead crystal tumblers he kept in a cabinet, along with a bottle of mineral water, and various spirits. I asked, "Does this mean you'll actually drive me to Dulles Airport in rush hour? You don't have to, really. I can take the Metro."

"Better than that. I'll fly with you, babe. We can hunker down under the blankets and get into the kind of trouble that we used to on all those night flights."

"Hold on." I thought quickly. "You—you didn't even have time to fly anywhere for a three-day weekend for my birthday. How can you get the time off to go with me to Japan? And I'm in a situation where I have to go in a real rush—next week, in fact."

"Have you forgotten that I'm supposed to visit Tokyo every three or four months for trial preparation?" Hugh raised the glass that I'd handed him in a toasting gesture. "I haven't been in a while. It would be a cinch to convince the managing partner that it's high time for me to return and get the Tokyo office in high gear."

"Hugh, I'm sorry," I said. "This job for the federal government— you know that it's my first, and I don't think I would come off as a professional if I travel with my boyfriend in tow."

He studied my face for a moment. "Okay. We'll fly separately and meet up at my company flat. No one shall be the wiser."

I took a deep drink of water, then put my glass down. "I can't explain all the details, but believe me, they'll know. I must go alone."

"What do you mean, they'll know?" Hugh sounded impatient. "And who the hell cares, anyhow? Rei, I want to go to Japan with you. You're the one who made me fall in love with the country, and it's just not been the same going on business there without you. You know how to read street signs and order theater tickets and all the—" he stopped, as if he'd finally noticed how grave my expression had become.

"I must go alone," I repeated. "It will only be for a week, two weeks at the most. And if all goes well, I'll get my visa status changed so I can return again, as much as I like and with you. We're used to separations, sweetheart. I think we can manage."

"I wish you'd let me go with you, but if it means that much to you that you go alone . . . I understand. Yes," he said, his voice growing stronger, "I'll keep the home fires burning. I'll take a break from gadding about and put some extra energy into researching the case, which you know is greatly overdue."

I looked at him, blinking back the tears that I felt. He was really hurt. I said, "You're being very tolerant of the situation. Thank you."

He snorted and said, "Well, the bosses you've got sound just the opposite, if they've made you this agitated and uptight about the trip. I certainly hope they're paying you a living wage."

"They're sparing no expense, flying me over business class. You'll have to give me tips, so I can fully take advantage of the situation—"

Hugh frowned. "The government doesn't usually fly its employees business class."

"Well, this is a special branch of the government. I mean," I amended hastily, "because I'm a consultant from the outside, and not a federal employee, I get some perks."

"Ask them to put you on one of the planes that have the seats that recline back like beds. If there's fresh-squeezed orange juice, drink it. And don't forget to bring home the comfort kit."

The comfort kit. It would probably contain a little black eye mask like the one I'd been given on my birthday, a mask designed to help a person get some sleep—or to block out the truth about what she would have to do.

The next few days passed in a blur of travel and talk. I saw Chika off to visit my parents, and that very afternoon I took the Delta shuttle to New York, where I stayed overnight in the apartment of an old college friend before my big day at the Met.

There, I was able to look at and touch more Mesopotamian pottery, and I received an in-depth tutorial on the hand-shaping of vessels before I boarded the Metroliner to continue my journey. At the

Philadelphia Museum of Art, the curator turned out to know all about color, and we had a delightful two hours going through the museum's exquisite collections. By the time I showed up at the Walters Art Museum in Baltimore the next day, I was thrilled to examine an ibex pitcher that was a little bit younger than one missing from the museum in Iraq. Everywhere, people seemed surprised that they'd never heard of my being at the Sackler, but grudgingly came to accept that I was a new employee preparing to work on a forthcoming exhibition.

My time had gone so well that I was bolstered with enough confidence to spontaneously telephone my grandmother Howard, who lived in Baltimore, to say hello, and tell her I'd just been in town at the Walters. Grandmother Howard—Grand, as she wanted me to call her—was not easily impressed, but she was on the museum board, so I guessed that my visit there would please her. She was surprised but cordial when I called, and commanded me to meet her for lunch within the hour.

It was the first time I'd seen my grandmother in almost a year, I realized as I entered her favorite luncheon place, which was located in a pretty nineteenth-century town house just two blocks south of the museum on Charles Street. Grand looked just the same, with her fluffy white hair and a violet wool bouclé St. John suit. I hadn't known that we'd be dining together, so I'd worn pants—but very nice pants, part of a fawn-colored Jil Sander suit that my mother had passed on to me.

My sharp-eyed grandmother immediately recognized the pants as my mother's castoffs. After she had let me kiss her cool, powdered cheek she'd said, "I'd take you shopping for some new clothes, Rei, but the problem is that all the department stores have deserted downtown. Supposedly our new city government is putting on a renaissance, but how can you talk about renaissance when you can't buy a decent pair of shoes or a skirt in a city?"

I smiled, thinking how like my mother she was at that moment—and also, how like me. I'd been frustrated with the shopping in Washington until a branch of the European retailer H&M had opened downtown. Aside from a Thomas Pink boutique in the Mayflower Hotel, there wasn't much shopping for Hugh, either.

"Well, downtown Baltimore doesn't look too bad, aside from the streets being torn up. This restaurant, for example, seems greatly improved," I said, looking around at the restaurant, which still had its original black-and-white checkerboard floor, but repainted walls and an upgraded menu—a shift to mixed baby green salads with goat cheese from the molded chicken salad and tomato aspic platters that I recalled from childhood.

"I miss the aspic," my grandmother said. "At least we have some of the same waitresses who've been here since the late fifties, which is a comfort. Now, tell me about your browse through the Walters. I hope you caught the Renoir exhibition because it's only here another week."

"It was my first time there since they opened the Asian wing, so I spent all my time there," I said.

"The Asian wing. Yes, I suppose you would like that best." Grand sounded disappointed in me, as always.

"I'd love to hear about what you've been doing at the museum, and your other civic involvements." I wanted to change a loaded topic.

"Fund-raising and more fund-raising! It's supposed to be fun to give money away, but the situation's gotten bad in the last few years. Museums, theaters, all the places devoted to culture are falling by the wayside." She sighed. "So you said to me on the telephone your visit here was because of your new position at the Smithsonian?"

"Technically I'm a consultant," I said, "not a regular staffer. If this first assignment goes well, perhaps they'll ask me to do more."

"It's good for a woman to have a flexible kind of job, especially after marriage," Grand said. "And that wedding of yours, it was supposed to happen a few months ago, wasn't it? Your mother told me that something came up, but I'm afraid I never understood the real reason."

"We both got cold feet."

"So, has Hugh returned to his home in Scotland?" Grand raised the thin, silver shadows that were her eyebrows.

"No. Despite the canceled wedding, we're still together."

"Still together? But the engagement's broken, you said. I'm afraid that I don't understand." My grandmother pressed her thin, peach-glossed lips together.

"There's no more to understand than that. We choose to live together, in Washington, for the time being." I was trying to remain
patient, but I had an urge to flee.

Grand shot me a look over the menu and said, "It's a question of
morals, don't you think?"

"My morals are fine. In fact, I'm feeling so moral today that I
think I'll start with the morel mushroom soup. What are you having, Grand?"

Later that evening, when I was telling Hugh about my experience
over a quick supper of scrambled eggs, he was more charitable toward my grandmother than I'd been.

"Just think of the disappointments in life she's suffered, Rei. Her
only daughter went on to move so far away, and now her grand-
daughter's showed up so terribly briefly—and cheated her of the
fun of a wedding where half the gents would be wearing kilts."

"I haven't seen you in your kilt for a long time," I said, looking at
him.

"Perhaps I'll break it out of the mothballs while you're away and
go dancing," Hugh said, picking up our used plates and putting them
in the sink.

"Sure. I'll get it for you when I'm in the storage closet hunting for
my suitcase."

"A suitcase? Can't you do with a carry-on if the trip's just a week?"

"There's never enough room for shoes and clothes in a carry-on,"
I said. Actually, my carry-on would be jammed with all the important things related to the job—a tiny handheld computer capable of
wirelessly connecting to the Internet, a miniature digital camera, an
entire dossier of papers and pictures related to the ibex vessel, and
the itinerary for my stay. I also was carrying reference books and
the Meiwashima auction catalog, because I'd be attending the auction to evaluate Japanese antiques for sale as part of my cover.

"I'll lend you my new carry-on, then. I managed to cram it with
three suits, a pair of wingtips, and my trainers on my last trip to
Asia. I'm an expert at packing."

"Yes, you are," I answered, knowing that I could not let him any-where near my luggage. Subterfuge was difficult, I decided as I brought over to the sink the last few dishes from the table. "Speaking of travel, have you heard from Angus?"

"Yes. He's added another week of shows before flying on to Asia," Hugh said. "All things considered, he's had a good experience in the states. Thank God he wasn't arrested that night. I still can't believe the cops let them off."

"Justice works oddly in our nation's capital." I yawned, thinking that I'd finally found the right place for the bugged bonsai: the fire escape, where it would have good sun and could pick up the sounds of burglars, not us. Michael had agreed to take the bug off Hugh's phone once I'd left for Japan. I was pleased at how readily he'd agreed to that until I realized there were almost certainly listening privileges attached to the cellular phone he'd given me.

"I'm worn out from my travels. I think I'm going to bed," I said.

"How tired, exactly? Shall I draw us a bath?" Hugh turned off the sink and put his arms around me. I lay with my head against his chest for a minute, enjoying the feeling of warmth and strength. It was nice to rest quietly for a minute, knowing nobody else was in the apartment. I could have easily just gone to sleep, but I had a sense Hugh had different plans.

Hugh slipped into the bath after me, and made it clear quickly that he intended to turn it into an outpost of a Japanese soapland. But it was easy to be seduced this way: pretty soon we'd tumbled out and had utterly soaked the sheets of the bed. I closed my eyes as his mouth began a familiar southward trek. In the span of a few minutes, all the city-to-city rushing and the long plane flight ahead of me were no longer things I was worrying about.

I twisted away from his mouth and climbed on top, the perfect position to take what I wanted. And Hugh loved it, too—I caught him watching me intently as I moved through the paces of pleasure.

"I'm memorizing you," he said, his hands tracing my breasts. "I don't ever want to forget this."

"Don't, then," I whispered just before I came, the pleasure radiating outward like a stone dropped from tremendous heights into a quiet lake. Afterward, I lay with one leg crooked over him, thinking about going to the bathroom to clean up, but feeling too weary and relaxed to move. "That was different."

"How so?" Hugh stroked my hair.

"You never talked about memorizing me before."

I felt his body stiffen against me, slightly, although his voice remained as warm as ever. "I'm sorry, darling. It's just that I have a rather melancholy feeling tonight."

"I'm sorry. I thought it was good for you, too." As I spoke, a chill settled across my skin, raising goose bumps. Could he have seen through my half-lies and figured out the truth about the creepy job I was going to perform?

Hugh took a deep breath and said, "I have a feeling that you might not—return to me."

"But of course I'm coming back! I have a round-trip ticket, open return, but you can imagine what the museum would do if I just went over there and blew them off."

"Right," Hugh said absently.

I hadn't understood his fear, obviously. "Do you mean—you have a fear that my plane's going to crash?"

"No, no, no! I'm sorry to be such a fool about it." Hugh slipped his hands over my buttocks, pressing me closer to him. "I suppose I'm anxious because this is new for me, being left behind. I don't want to stop you from going."

"I will come back to you," I said firmly. "And you'd better believe that this was not the last time for us in bed or I'll—have to put you through the drill again, right now."

"Heaven help me," Hugh said, sounding happier. "Give me a break, Rei. There are four more nights."

Four more nights.

We used them all.

9

The situation at Dulles Airport was chaotic, with my navel ring setting off the metal detector. This, in turn, inspired a pat-down body search and the unpacking of my luggage. I was very glad that I hadn't packed the Gorgonzola cheese that my aunt had wanted me to bring to her, because I could only imagine what the Japanese authorities would think when I arrived, eighteen hours later, smelling like it. Michael had cautioned me that an official passport was not a diplomatic passport; I was subject to search just like anyone else.

By the time I reached the departure gate, I found out that they'd given my business class seat to a salesman cashing in his frequent-flier upgrade. I started arguing with the flight attendant about the loss of my originally designated seat, not understanding that they'd put me in first class.

"Listen to me, Miss Shimura," the flight attendant said, as slowly as if she were talking to a child. "You go two rows up front, you get the ice cream sundae. You get the champagne. You get any damn thing you want, practically, but you do not have the right to yell at me."

I looked at her, a blond woman about ten years my senior, but made up to look twenty years younger. *Was this my future?* I thought bleakly as she waved dramatically at the first-class cabin where a few Japanese and American businessmen sat in solitary splendor. So, it was a perk; maybe because there was something special about my ticket, or maybe because I had come off like a cranky old lady.

As I settled in, the Japanese businessman who'd had a newspaper on the empty seat next to him looked disappointed to be losing the space.

How much did a seat like this cost? I wondered if there was some kind of State Department code in my passenger profile. The seat had been booked by an agency called S.A.T.O., which sounded Japanese, but turned out to have something to do with the government. Well, it was an agency I'd have to try to use again—if I had the chance.

I took a long, full sip of Veuve Cliquot and watched Virginia drop away below me. The sky was deep pink, darkening to purple. By the time we got to Tokyo, it would be eighteen hours later, and then, I was sure, the luxury would end—I would strap my suitcase onto the wheeled carry-on and hazard my way into Tokyo on a rush hour train. I'd be exhausted, but I'd be in the country I loved most. That was something to drink to any day.

I slept, surprising myself. When I awoke, the businessman was staring at me. He looked away quickly, then returned his gaze.

"Did you take a good rest?"

I nodded. I didn't usually talk to people on planes, given the trouble talking had caused me in the past. This man—round-faced; sleepy-eyed; wearing an expensive, conservative business suit—didn't seem like my cup of tea, especially since he reeked of whisky. I looked away, but still he persisted. "You sleep six hours, I think. We are only two hours from Tokyo, now."

"Isn't that nice," I said in Japanese and opened my Meiwashima catalog.

His eyelashes fluttered. "You speak Japanese?"

Welcome to the land of lost identity, I said to myself. In the United States, if people didn't think I was from Japan, it was because they knew for sure I was from China or Korea. To Americans, my identity was clearly Asian, never mind the half of me that was as WASP as Grand's favorite tomato aspic. It was the same in Japan; even after I'd spoken, I was always pegged a foreigner.

"A little," I replied, because I realized that now he really might not let me alone. I stuck my face back in the Meiwashima catalog, which of course was in Japanese, with only about ten percent of its written material comprehensible to me. My aim had been to study the catalog with a *kanji* dictionary at my side, decoding the information on the artworks that looked sufficiently superb to consider bidding on. But now I realized I'd have a helper hovering nearby who would wind up making me feel embarrassed about what I didn't know.

"Ara, Meiwashima. That's a fancy sale," he said. "But everything is—old! Do you like old Japanese things?"

"A little," I repeated, but this time in English—increasing my distance. "Excuse me, please. I would like to get up for a minute."

He got up with a creak and let me past, but when I came back from the spotless first-class lavatory, he made me step over his legs. I knew the trick—a chance to fully evaluate, and perhaps bump into, a woman's nether parts—so I made a point of going in face forward, and turning around in my seat.

"Can you read those *kanji*? Most foreigners cannot read," he said when I picked up the catalog again.

"The truth is, not very much. I may just put it away and sleep some more."

I slapped my CD player headphones on my ears and turned on my Rilo Kiley CD. Then I closed my eyes and listened to "Portions for Foxes" over and over until I fell asleep. When I finally opened my eyes again, the music was over and a bell was dinging overhead. The Japanese businessman and the nine other male passengers in first class were rising up into the aisle, collecting briefcases from overhead. I looked out the window into the grayness of Tokyo. It was late afternoon, the same time as when I'd left, but it was a new day.

Everywhere, the customs lines were long, except for the one that I was going to—an almost empty channel reserved for diplomats, or people like me who were lucky enough to have passports with a visa inside detailing an attachment to the American Embassy in Tokyo.

The man standing ahead of me in the diplomatic line was finishing up, so now my thoughts turned from global politics to anxiety. What if, somehow, the cover didn't work? I wasn't a diplomat. It was implausible that a museum employee would be in the line with a diplomatic passport. I'd be found out and humiliated by the customs officer, perhaps taken to a private room for interrogation by the National Police . . . my old friends, the ones who would remember my name.

I was thinking about the dark blue handcuffs I'd worn during my deportation a little over a year before, so I almost didn't notice the customs agent waving me forward. I tripped slightly and caught myself on the edge of the carry-on. Great. I looked like a diplomatic klutz.

The customs agent asked me in English for the passport. He opened the page to the picture, looked at it, then looked at me.

He turned the page. "American Embassy," he said, nodding to himself.

"*Hai*," I said in Japanese. I figured that if I spoke simple Japanese badly, it might eliminate a more complicated discussion.

I smiled at him, hoping that this might be the end of it, but he turned to the computer and typed in something, and my stomach started churning.

The agent returned his gaze to me and asked where I'd be staying.

I glumly gave the name of the Grand Hyatt in Roppongi Hills. I'd argued for a Japanese *ryokan*, but Michael said the government insisted on using American businesses as much as possible.

My passport was stamped, and I was waved through. Free, in the land I loved, and the job was about to begin.

I'd expected to take a train, but it turned out that right outside the customs exit, there was an American with a shaved head and a sign with my entire name spelled correctly. I went to him reluctantly, thinking if they wanted me to travel incognito, having an American soldier meet me wasn't the way to go. The businessman who'd sat next to me, in fact, emerged just as the soldier-chauffeur was taking my carry-on, and looked at me reproachfully, as if he'd expected the two of us to share a limo into town together.

I fluttered my fingers at him and went off with my escort to a distinctly unglamorous van, which was already half-full with other government-sponsored arrivals: two military families with young children. I made funny faces at their babies as we rode away from Chiba prefecture and toward Kanto, where Tokyo waited. Outside, the sky was even grayer than I'd remembered; it looked as if rain clouds were hovering. Hugh had reminded me to check the weather reports before packing, but I'd forgotten. As a result I had no umbrella or raincoat, just a 1970s tweed coat that was hardly waterproof.

Shopping for waterproof gear would be easy, I decided as we pulled up to my hotel two hours later. The Grand Hyatt was a glass-and-steel tower located on the corner of a street of designer boutiques that never existed in my previous Tokyo life. This was Roppongi Hills, an area that city planners had experimented with greatly, as evidenced by a curvy pink chair set out on the street as an example of modern art. I gaped at teenagers in blue jeans lounging on it, and then, a moment later, a cluster of young women dressed in short, frilly gingham-check dresses, frilled bonnets, and black patent Mary Janes, taking photos of each other.

What was this, the land of Cabbage Patch dolls?

The Roppongi I remembered was the stomping ground of girls in eighteen-inch platform sandals. I used to feel like a baby because I couldn't handle those shoes—but now I realized that being a baby was cool. I jumped off the bus and tried to give the soldier a tip for hefting my luggage to the hotel door, but he politely refused.

"That's okay, ma'am. Have a good stay."

Once I'd entered the insulated, expensive world of the Grand Hyatt, I saw no more young women posing as children. Half the people in the ultramodern limestone lobby appeared to be stylish Japanese. The rest looked like foreign businesspeople on expense accounts. The desk clerks, all Japanese and gorgeous, spoke perfect English with the foreigners, so I was privately thrilled when I came up and was immediately addressed in Japanese. It had been so long since this had happened that I wanted to cry. And, I reminded myself, it was going to keep happening every day, as long as I was here to work on the mission.

I was eager to see my room, which, when the bellman took me up, proved as starkly modern as the lobby. The room had a king-size bed—a radical departure from the usual twin beds in Western-style hotel rooms in Japan. The bed was a low mahogany wood platform covered with a crisp white sheet. There was an asymmetrical desk of the same wood, topped by a small, flat-screen TV. The bathroom was luxurious marble, with everything you could want: electric toilet seat with built-in bidet and yet another flat-screen television. I peeled my eyes away from the tub to the bellman, who was still in the bedroom, demonstrating how to use a remote control by the bed to raise and lower two different screens over the huge windows.

I supposed Michael Hendricks would have wanted me to have both shades drawn down all the time, but at the moment I couldn't bring myself to block out Tokyo. I was so excited to be back in town. The moment I was alone, I dropped my coat and headed for the telephone with a blinking message light.

The voice mail was from Mr. Watanabe, who wanted me to call him immediately upon arrival. He'd left a number with a Tokyo area code. There was a second call from Hugh, asking me to let him know when I got in.

So Mr. Watanabe was in the city along with me. That was good, I decided as I started to dial. Of all the people I'd met at the meeting, he seemed the most palatable.

"Was Shimura-san's travel comfortable? Are you safely arrived?" he asked after I'd given my name. There had been no secretary answering the phone; this meant, probably, that he was at home. I heard the sound of someone, probably a child, playing "Chopsticks" in the background.

"Yes, thank you very much, Watanabe-sensei," I answered, using the extreme honorific rather than the more prosaic *san*. Mr. Watanabe wasn't technically a teacher, but he was such a senior diplomat that calling him *sensei* was in perfect order. I wanted to butter him up, because I expected to call on him for advice in the next week.

I continued, "I didn't expect you to be here in Tokyo, too."

"Well, my wife and daughters live here, so when I return here on government business, I enjoy a chance to see them." He paused. "Just as I'm sure you will enjoy the chance to see your relatives."

"Oh, yes." I hadn't thought of calling Aunt Norie and Uncle Hiroshi and my cousin Tom tonight because I'd been so eager to get in touch with my friends Richard and Simone, and whoever else they could dredge up after they were done with their evening shifts as English and French teachers.

"Have you seen the auction catalog yet?"

"I studied it on the plane." I paused, because I was unable to come up with more.

"*Ah, so desu ka.* I'm actually telephoning about the sale. My assistant stopped by the gallery yesterday and learned that Flowers-san already expressed interest."

I understood the code word for Takeo, but not the rest of what Mr. Watanabe was trying to say. "Has he registered as a buyer?"

"Yes, that's the case. He may not be there, though. I hear he sometimes bids by telephone."

That made sense. Takeo was such a hermit that he'd much rather lounge around his house in Hayama with a pizza than dress up and make pleasantries with the important buyers in the Tokyo art scene.

"I'll do my best to find out what he's interested in," I said. "One of the auction assistants is bound to know."

"I will be at the auction, although of course we must not acknowledge each other's presence. We can meet outside later on."

"Of course," I agreed.

"I do suggest that you arrive a little early to the auction, although of course you'll be very tired on your first full day here. Will you ask the hotel to book you a wake-up call that gives you plenty of time to get there by four?"

"I don't usually nap on the first day. I've made this transition many times, Watanabe-sensei. I'll show up early and do my best." The fact was that I had a lot of things planned for the next day— things like picking up the new Eastern Youth compact disc for Hugh, and shopping for bras for myself in the only country where A-cups ruled. But that was too much information for Mr. Watanabe.

After we'd wished each other a good evening, I hung up the phone and pondered my little telephone-address book. I thought I'd want to go out for drinks, but I was beat.

I telephoned Richard's cell phone and left a message that I

wanted to meet him the next day, after I'd rested. Then I swallowed a Melatonin along with two glasses of tap water. I ran a bath and sank into it with the antiques catalog held carefully aloft. I would use my last hour to try to guess what had caught Takeo's discerning eye—and how I could do the same kind of thing myself.

10

To sleep a full first night in Japan, followed by an awakening at a normal morning hour, is an impossible dream.

My normal wake-up hour, the day after I arrive, is three o'clock in the morning—or four, if I'm extremely tired the night before. Unfortunately, these hours are still too wee for Japanese hotel operators to consider turning on the hot water heater or serve breakfast.

But hot water wasn't an issue in this hotel, nor was heat or room service. I took a long, luxurious shower. I debated which telephone to use to call Hugh. Michael Hendricks had given me a sleek, high-tech cell that could receive and make international calls, take digital photographs, surf the web, and serve as a receptacle for ingoing and outgoing e-mail. Still, the frugal traveler inside me wondered whether I would get into trouble for using it for personal reasons.

I put off the decision and dressed in the yoga pants and sweatshirt at the top of my luggage and moved through a half hour of stretches. My back and hips were stiff after the long flight. I needed to get out of my room and get breakfast somewhere.

Tokyo's wholesale fish market lay six kilometers due east. As I jogged the route I knew so well, I found myself running directly toward the rising sun—or the place where the sun would have risen, if there hadn't been so many gray storm clouds. I didn't mind. I was elated to run through Roppongi Crossing, passing my old favorite dance haunts like Gas Panic, Wall Street, and MoTown House. In the evening, you could barely walk a straight line through the crowds, but now it was uncrowded, and the only things I needed to dodge were the disgusting asphalt flowers that drunken salarymen had spewed along the sidewalk the night before. From Gaien Higashi-Dori I passed the Lamborghini dealer where Hugh had spent many wistful hours, and then the International Clinic, where many foreigners went for discreet treatment of venereal diseases contracted at the nightclubs I'd passed a few kilometers back.

In my pleasant reverie, with U2 blaring into my ears from the Walkman I wore, I sped along the uncrowded sidewalks, giving the wide gray streets to the first delivery trucks, bicycles, and motorcycles, none of which speeded—this despite the open path, and the lack of police.

I was tiring by the time I passed Tokyo Tower, but I knew the best part of the run was coming: Shiba Park, where I slowed down as I passed the graveyard of the Tokugawa clan of shoguns, and took a brief stop to drink some water at Zojo-ji Temple. I resumed my run again and emerged under a giant *tori* gate into the Hibiya business district, then Shimbashi, with all its wonderful little eating and drinking places still closed. Finally I ran through Ginza, the luxury shopping district where people said that if you stacked ten ten-thousand-yen notes anywhere on the sidewalk, the tiny portion of land underneath the bills would still be worth more. Then it was a right on Harumi Dori past the grand old Kabuki Theater and straight into Tsukijii, where I was delighted to slow to a walk to avoid running into the huge, glistening fish laid out directly on concrete sidewalks. The fishmongers with their thigh-high rubber boots and shrewd expressions glanced at me, but didn't bother beckoning—it must have seemed obvious that a sweaty young woman in Asics was not a major restaurateur.

I was a glutton, I thought, as I ran my eyes over the glistening sea creatures lying so ingloriously on concrete. A sleek blue-gray fish that looked as if it weighed only about ten pounds—big enough for a feast with my friends, though the price scrawled on its side made that fantasy unaffordable—gave me pause.

"Excuse me, but what's that called?" I asked the bored-looking fellow standing in a wool sweater and rubber wader overalls behind the beauty. The fish had a number scrawled on it, but that was its only identifying feature.

"It's a kind of *shusseuo*."

"Really! What kind, exactly?" *Shusse* literally meant "career progress," and *uo* meant fish. Mothers gave children *shusseuo* before school examinations. It was interesting, and perhaps apt, that I'd gotten to see this fish this morning.

He glanced around, then lowered his voice as if he were going to tell me a secret. "*Wakashi*. It's very, very fresh."

"Oh, I bet it will make wonderful sushi." He was talking about young yellowtail. If yellowtail was good, a younger version had to be heavenly.

"Ah, yes, it will be gone within a half hour, I'm sure."

"Where was it caught, in Japanese waters or—"

"What about some service for a real customer?" a sharp voice barked behind me and I stepped aside.

I'd gone too far, asked too much. And the fact was, I couldn't take the fish. I bowed to the fishmonger and the man who had interrupted me and slipped off. It was six-thirty, so some breakfast spots around the market had to be open. I began searching for a little hole-in-the-wall place where Tom had taken me for an incredible seafood stew a few years earlier. After a minute's walk, I recognized its sign—a smiling octopus—but the door was locked. However, two doors down a long blue curtain fluttered in another doorway.

A red-faced man with a kerchief tied around his head bellowed out a welcome as I stepped inside the tiny restaurant. It couldn't have been more than ten feet long and five feet wide, with a blond wood counter and five stools. Every stool was filled, but the chef motioned for me to stand behind the chair of a fishmonger, who was finishing up a plate of squid roe sushi. I took the time to look around and decide what I'd order. The man next to him was eating *tai,* one of my favorite fishes. Soon, the fishmonger had departed and I took his spot. I asked for *tai* and *wakashi hammachi.*

The chef shook his finger at me. "We don't carry *wakashi* fish. It's because the little ones are caught too early that we have fish shortages, *neh?*"

"You're right. I'm sorry." My cheeks warmed with shame. Why hadn't I thought of this myself, when I'd been joking with the fishmonger outside? Ever since sushi had exploded in global popularity in the 1990s, Japan's once teaming tuna and yellowtail population had dwindled. Fishermen who caught baby fish like the one I'd seen, rather than waiting for the babies to mature and lay eggs for a future generation, were thinking of quick profits and disregarding the environment. But the whole reason they chose to be unscrupulous profiteers was the existence of greedy gourmets like myself.

The chef suggested *inada,* which was a slightly more mature form of *hammachi,* and I agreed readily. I sipped a tiny cup of hot green tea while I watched the chef deftly slice the fish and layer it on fresh sticky rice. Then, it was my turn. I swirled each piece of sushi through a mixture of soy and wasabi in a little blue bowl at my side. I was in a state of bliss. The only problem was that I knew another person was behind me, subtly but hostilely waiting for the seat. A few years ago, I would have turned around to acknowledge him and apologize, but today, I was bent on enjoying myself. I didn't turn. I kept eating steadily, at a pace that suited me.

"Okusama, another honorable customer is waiting," the chef said, scooping my plate away from me after I picked up the final piece of *tai* with my chopsticks.

I cringed. Why had the man addressed me as "honorable housewife," the kind of honorific men used only with female customers of a certain age? I'd gone through my previous life in Japan with restaurant and shop owners calling me *oneesan,* which meant "big sister."

The *tai* in my mouth suddenly tasted metallic, but I dutifully chewed and swallowed. Then I picked up the hand-scrawled bill and squeezed through the standing-room-only crowd to the cashier. The sumptuous sushi breakfast had cost about $8.50, a bargain compared with what breakfast would have cost in the hotel. I got a receipt for business purposes and tucked it safely away in my pocket, confident that so far, I was handling expenses in a way that my government would approve.

My worries about not knowing how to behave correctly continued when I reached the Meiwashima Auction House in late afternoon. The young woman behind Gucci sunglasses who was guarding the door didn't recognize me. In fact, she attempted to stop me from entering.

"I believe I am preregistered. Shimura Rei?"

"Oh, I'm sorry." The girl looked at her clipboard and nodded. "Yes, yes, I see your name is on the list. You may pick up paddle number fifty-three at the main office."

I remembered her from half a dozen sales past, but apparently she hadn't remembered me. Well, there were a lot of people, I thought to myself, as I joined the long queue standing at a desk behind which a crew of women were issuing pine paddles approximately the size of fans. I looked around covertly at the well-dressed shop owners and private buyers who were nodding and smiling at each other as they waited. I spotted a few familiar faces, those belonging to the owners of some big, fancy shops in Roppongi, Omote-Sando, and the like. The ones who recognized me gave the correct half-bow, to which I bowed back at the same forty-five-degree angle. There was no need to chat. This was a chichi auction—a place to which it had taken me a couple of years to gain admittance.

It took a good twenty minutes to get to the head of the line, and when I did so, I asked, as innocently as I could, if Takeo Kayama was bidding.

"He has a number, yes! And here is your paddle!" the clerk answered brightly.

"Sorry to bother you, but what is his number?" I said, slowly taking the paddle numbered 53.

"It's not a problem for Kayama-san; he already knows the number. He already registered," the clerk answered.

"We are old friends, and I do not want to bid against him. For that reason I would like to know whether he's placed any absentee bids on any of the items in today's sale."

"Yes, he has. But it's against the rules of our auction house to give direct information on a particular customer's interests."

"Oh, is that so? I apologize. Well, then, if you don't mind, I'll take my paddle."

"You already have it, Shimura-san. And why don't I give you this brochure, which explains our company rules in detail."

I turned away, not wanting them to see the blood that had rushed to my face. I'd screwed up in front of gossipy antiques people. I'd come in looking so proper, wearing the claret-color St. John suit Grand had sent from Neiman's right before the trip; the suit was so grown-up it made me look over thirty, which actually was my goal. But now—I'd lost my advantage by behaving like a kid.

The setup for the auction was a high stage with multiple televisions suspended from the ceiling over it, for close-up views of the items to be auctioned. There was a table where small items would be placed for viewing, and a podium on which the auctioneer would stand. In front of the stage, tight rows of small gilt chairs waited for the audience. Most of the seats were filled; I realized that because of the long time I'd spent in line, it was only twenty minutes until the auction started.

Mr. Watanabe walked along the side of the room, as if unaware of my presence, though I knew, from a cell phone call I'd gotten while waiting in line, that he'd seen me. I made a slow circle around the room's perimeter, seeking out the items that had the highest estimated values in the catalog. Takeo wouldn't bother with little things, and neither would someone who was supposedly buying for the Sackler.

One of the most confusing elements of the viewing—something I anticipated because of my past experience at Meiwashima—was that not all the items for sale were Japanese. For instance, there was a huge, fantastically carved four-poster bed—Chinese, I'd figured out from the catalog copy, although to me it looked like the stuff of fantasy in an Arabian Nights.

I moved on to ceramics. My interest was caught by a graceful

Momoyama period vase with a mottled gray finish. This was the kind of thing that I should be interested in.

I asked a young man wearing the severe black suit that was the auction house's uniform to open the case. He paused until I reminded him that the house rules stated that auction attendees were allowed close examinations of goods for sale before the actual event took place. Apparently not many of the shop owners bothered.

The young man's eyes were wary as he placed the vase on the examination table in front of the case. I sank into a deep squat, a posture of which my fitness instructor would have approved, and took out the tiny digital camera-phone, but before I could use it, the man stopped me. Apparently, I was breaking another one of the rules.

I put away the camera, feeling irritated and deciding that I wasn't certain the piece in front of me was as old as estimated. Although the Tokyo antiques-dealing community had an overall good reputation for honesty, some Japanese potters were so traditional in their approach to hand-shaping and firing that it would be quite possible to pass off something newer as older. Only very subtle clues could tell me whether the vase was likely to be as old as the catalog said.

I stared at the vase, and in my long moment of indecision someone brushed past, causing me to lose balance and pitch forward.

My life flashed before my eyes as I struggled to keep myself from knocking against the vase. But the young man had it in his hands. All was saved, though I looked undignified on my hands and knees on the carpet.

"My God!" I exclaimed, so discombobulated that I accidentally lapsed into English. Immediately, I switched to a Japanese apology.

"It's okay," the young man said, his voice shaky. "That other customer was hurrying by very quickly. It was not your fault."

I slowly came up to a standing position. My dodgy right knee was going to trouble me for the next few days, after the way I'd smashed onto the floor. No more runs through the city for a while, but that was a small price to pay in exchange for not being responsible to Meiwashima Auction Gallery for $50,000 worth of damage.

"Do you still want to examine it?" the man asked, as if he'd noticed that I was backing away from the vase.

"No, thank you," I said faintly. I'd had enough excitement, and I planned on taking a seat, one close to the back of the room, to watch the proceedings. But as I headed toward my seat, I shot a glance toward the young woman who'd almost caused the accident. Too young to be a buyer, she was probably somebody's clueless child, I thought with irritation. She was tiny—barely five feet tall, I thought, and absolutely adorable in one of the new Pucci print dresses that I'd seen in magazines—far too expensive for me to ever contemplate buying. She must have had it altered to fit her tiny frame. I watched her raise an arm as long and thin as a Pocky Stick pretzel to wave.

I followed the direction of her wave but couldn't figure out to whom she was beckoning. But then my attention was suddenly drawn away, because among the people seating themselves in the audience, I'd caught a glimpse of a familiar profile.

I had already seated myself in one of the few single seats left—this one between an elderly couple there to see the sale of a prized family heirloom, and a flinty dealer from Kawasaki. For this reason, I was hesitant to leave my seat, but I strained for a better view of the man in question. Not until he turned his head, so that I could see his face in full, did I recognize Takeo pointing to the seat next to him.

Suddenly, I felt very hot. My sweat glands had gone into overdrive. Why would Takeo be coaxing me over? Had he learned that I was asking after him, and actually been pleased?

"Meiwashima Auction Number Fifty-seven is about to commence," a voice droned over the speaker system. "Our staff respectfully requests that you make sure that you bring your paddle with you and that your financial details are registered with the office before you sit down."

Takeo's expression was almost affectionate, a surprise to me given the way we'd parted. The warmth made him look even more handsome than he'd appeared at first glance. My job was going to be difficult indeed, with Takeo still shooting me such a sexy come-hither look.

I had just gathered up my bag when I noticed that the girl who'd tripped me had entered Takeo's row. Mouthing obvious apologies, the girl slowly proceeded along the line of patrons, all of whom stood up for her in a massive show of Japanese courtesy. At one point, she stumbled slightly against an older lady. Perhaps her collision with me had been not a matter of carelessness but a lack of coordination. But then all my theories vanished, replaced by shock as the girl settled happily into the place that I'd mistakenly thought Takeo was saving for me.

11

Takeo had a girl.

Friend?

No, I decided as I saw his arm slip around her shoulders.

Girlfriend!

I thanked God for the second time in ten minutes, but this time silently. Thank God I hadn't embarrassed myself by trying to take her seat. From my spot, I watched the girl tilt her face up to Takeo and giggle about something, to which he gave a gentle, reproving shake of the head.

The auction was starting, so I tried to concentrate on the point of the evening—making an appearance as a serious potential buyer. It was advantageous that Takeo would see me in this light, especially if Takeo wanted the vase. My interest in it—perhaps bidding for it at the start, then gracefully giving up—would be at least a conversation opener for the two of us.

Three hundred items were listed for sale, and the wait for item 159 was long. The auctioneer's pace was considerably slower, and more genteel, than what I was accustomed to in the American auction houses that I frequented. Still, it was a good thing I was there for the whole auction, because just thirty items in, Takeo's girlfriend started whispering to him, and he put his hand up for the Chinese bed.

I sucked in my breath. What was Takeo, who always had been happy with a basic futon, doing buying a bed? Was he—buying it for her? Various confusing scenarios ran through my mind as Takeo kept his hand up while the bed's price rose from 200,000 yen to 1 million. He was the only one left at that price, plus the auction house premium of ten percent. As the auctioneer called out that the item was sold at 1 million yen plus ten percent commission, Takeo's girlfriend bounced excitedly in her chair.

I'd thought I'd been through enough surprises, but five minutes later, a regal, blue-and-gold export Imari dinner service for twenty set off more tugging and whispering. Takeo's hand rose again. He got it for 500,000 —a steal, but then, not many Japanese gave big dinner parties. I didn't understand why Takeo, always so private, would want to buy a restaurant's worth of matching china. It had to be for the girl, not for him.

An intermission after the first 100 items gave me a chance to make my move. Takeo and his young friend had risen, too. She was tugging at his hand, as if she wanted him to go back to the display cases, so I headed that way, too. As I walked, I tried to look as if I were immersed in the catalog, so it seemed natural for me to almost, but not quite, bump into them.

"Pardon me—oh, hello!" I exclaimed, feigning surprise. "It's been a long time."

Instead of answering me, Takeo walked past, dragging his girlfriend along with him.

Maybe he hadn't realized I was speaking to him. I hurried after the couple, and tried again. "Takeo-san, I don't know if you, ah, recognized me—"

My use of his first name couldn't be ignored. The girl's mouth hung open in a little violet O while Takeo answered.

"Shimura-san, of course I recognize you. I'm a little busy right now, though. Will you excuse me?" He pulled a cell phone from his pocket.

"No telephone use allowed in the auction house except for employees," one of the auction helpers said, miraculously materializing. For the first time that evening, I thanked the powers behind the Meiwashima Auction Gallery for the rules.

Takeo snapped his phone shut. He looked from me to the girlfriend, and then back at me, obviously unhappy.

"I'm back from the United States." I'd decided to play the part of an old friend to the hilt. "It's so good to see you! I'd love to catch up on old times—"

"Circumstances make that difficult," Takeo said coldly.

"Really? What's going on with you these days, besides taking over your father's flower-arranging school?"

"I'm getting married. My fiancée and I are just picking out a few items for the house."

I was aware that Takeo was watching me closely for a reaction. I was determined not to look as pained as I felt. I unclenched my jaw and offered congratulations.

"I'm surprised you were allowed back into Japan so quickly," Takeo said, his words cutting. He knew what had happened, even though he and I hadn't seen each other at all during that last time in the city.

I shrugged, trying to seem casual. "Well, my client has some clout— the Sackler Gallery. Do you remember? It's part of our group of national museums that you visited when you were in Washington—"

Takeo interrupted me swiftly. "Unfortunately, we must excuse ourselves, Shimura-san. Good luck."

"What do you mean? The sale isn't over yet—" Takeo's fiancée began in a baby-pitched voice.

"Dinner with your parents, remember? I was just about to call them to find out where they are. Let's go outside to make the call."

The princess was digging her long, lavender-glossed nails into Takeo's arm. "But I want to stay longer. We need a few more things."

"Your father wants to pick us up early. He's anticipating traffic problems because of the rain." Takeo smiled at her in a way that made it seem like the sun breaking out over Mount Fuji. I looked away from that smile, just as I had looked away from the great, glaring diamond on the girl's tiny hand.

"But we at least have to pay for the bed and the china," she pointed out.

"I'll do it by telephone. Oh, I see your parents already." I followed his gaze to a couple in the doorway. The woman was stout for a Japanese woman, but elegantly dressed in a tweed suit, with a frozen-in-place, slightly bouffant shoulder-length hairdo that I'd noticed diplomatic wives seemed to favor. She bowed slightly as she approached us. The man at her side was about the same height—about five-six, a standard height for Japanese men of the older generation, and thin. He wore thick glasses and a dark suit. He didn't look glamorous at all, but he was obviously well known to the Meiwashima staff because the people who had checked my name against a list were bowing deeply and ushering him in.

I could have stayed and forced Takeo to introduce me, but I could imagine how awkward things would get. And the fact was that Mr. Watanabe was heading toward the parents, smiling and nodding.

Remembering what Mr. Watanabe had said about keeping away from each other, I took this as my cue to leave. I made my bows to the betrothed couple and quickly passed by the parents and went out of the auction.

I'd gone so hastily and in such a state of confusion that it wasn't until half a block later, when I was soaked in pouring rain, that I realized I needed an umbrella.

12

Mr. Watanabe caught up with me a few minutes later in the alley where we had arranged, over the phone the previous evening, to meet after the sale. He appeared under a large black umbrella, which he held over me as we spoke. He was being so gallant that I was ashamed to even begin to tell him about my breach of etiquette, but I did, sparing no details. When I was done, Mr. Watanabe didn't immediately comment, but instead told me about the girl and her family.

Takeo's fiancée was Emi Harada, daughter of Kenichi Harada, the recently appointed minister for the environment. He was also a former diplomat, so the two men had crossed paths before and had exchanged greetings at the sale. Yasuko Harada, Kenichi's wife, was an active flower arranger and the patron of many social welfare causes. *As her daughter would soon be,* I thought to myself. Takeo, despite his radical tendencies, had chosen for his bride what Japanese for centuries had wanted: the youngest, purest woman with the most elite pedigree. But I should have known all this. I asked Mr. Watanabe why I hadn't been warned about Takeo's engagement.

"Unfortunately, her name never appeared in any information I received," Watanabe said, his eyes wide. "And, when I was speaking with her father just now, he said nothing about the engagement to me. Are you sure it's the truth?"

"She was wearing a huge diamond ring on her left hand," I said. "Surely there must have been an announcement of it somewhere, in the newspapers or something—"

"I don't think so. Can you read Japanese newspapers?"

Of course I couldn't. I stood there, the rain hammering my umbrella, hammering me with the realization that I'd forgotten how everything worked in Japan, from buying fish to auction rules and relationships.

"I suppose you'll have to make a meeting with him again," Mr. Watanabe said.

I would have thrown up my hands if they hadn't been engaged with the umbrella and my backpack. "It seems impossible. I explained to you already that he was very unfriendly."

"Oh, I'm sure that's not the case. This was just a first meeting. I'm sure the next one will be more harmonious."

"It won't work. He's moved on, and I'm just a reminder of old times he'd rather forget."

Mr. Watanabe looked grave. "Do you feel that you cannot do the job that you said you would?"

I looked down at the pavement. How fast would he fly me out of Japan—on the next day's flight? It was entirely possible. I breathed deeply and said, "I'm sorry I wasn't effective tonight. I'll try again."

"*Gambatte!*" he commanded, then tapped the end of his umbrella on the concrete, and walked on.

Later, as I sat at the Brazilian mahogany bar in Salsa Salsa watching my old friend Enrique muddle together lime and rum to make a welcome-home *mojito*, I thought about the significance of Mr. Watanabe's parting command: *gambatte*, the imperative form of a uniquely Japanese word, *gambarimasu*, which meant "give it your all." People said *Gambatte* to you before a test or a sporting event. *Gambatte* was about responsibility to someone else, your parents or your teammates or your school. And, in this case, both the U.S. and Japanese governments.

I sighed and pulled the tiny telephone camera out of my purse.

First, I entered the password I'd come up with—TAKE0, in honor of the mission. The zero I'd used at the end instead of the letter *O* escaped my mind on the first try; but then I remembered it and entered the password again, and the screen flashed "ready."

Time to practice. I aimed the instrument at Enrique and punched buttons until I saw his smiling image appear on the tiny screen. After I'd taken the picture, I admired it for a while. I'd gotten him dead center, and with his eyes open. For me, this was a very good first photo, with a machine that had seemed unfathomably complex during the hour that Michael Hendricks had attempted to explain its use. I remained confused by the many buttons on the tiny camera. In fact, I wasn't sure if I'd just saved Enrique's photo or deleted it when it abruptly disappeared from the screen.

"That's a cool phone. Or is it a camera?" A strange accent on my left made me jump, and I turned to see one of the backpackers from a group that had been sitting together. I'd noticed them when I'd come in and made the mistake of smiling a brief hello.

"Both," I said, looking at the speaker, who was somewhere around twenty-five, though it was hard to tell from his face, which was either really tanned or really dirty.

"May I see it? Where did you get it, Akibarra or—" He rolled his *r*'s like someone from Germany or a nearby country.

"The electronics district is called Akihabara, and sorry, but I can't let you play around with this camera. I'm not the greatest technophile, so I don't want to take the risk of changing any settings."

"Hmm, I reckon you and I could have more fun playing around at something else! I'm Jürgen." He grinned suavely, and I cursed myself for the expression I'd used.

"Acually, Jürgen, I'm not the best of company because I need to make a phone call at the moment—"

"Ach so! You must be some kind of spy girl with a Chames Bond camera not for sale in the shops—"

Damn it, but his voice was loud. I looked at him stonily and said, "It's a gift from my boyfriend, who I was just about to phone."

"Don't you mean your husband?"

"What?" I looked at him warily.

"A woman your age would ordinarily be married, right?" He swung off with laughter and returned to his friends.

I'd had about enough of unruly men, but I really did want to speak to Hugh. And now it was early morning in Washington, time to catch him before he left for the office.

"Good morning, my sweet," I said brightly after he finally picked up.

"Rei. So what's, what time is it?" He sounded disjointed.

"I thought it was about eight-thirty in Washington. I'm sorry, you were probably up late last night painting the dining room." I had made sure he had all the paint and supplies he needed before I'd left.

"Not quite. Damn, I have a meeting in half an hour." He groaned. "I feel like hell."

"Oh! I can get off the line if you need. I just wanted to let you know I was here and safe—"

"Don't go," Hugh said. "I'll call my assistant to tell her to reschedule. She's come up with more than a few excuses since my brother came back. And today's the end of it. They're flying out of Dulles for Singapore and then Tokyo."

"But that sounds illogical, I mean, shouldn't they have flown from California and gone to Tokyo first?"

"Nothing my brother does is logical. Including drinking. We closed the 9:30 Club last night, Rei. I'm knackered."

"Aren't you getting a little old for that?" He was never going to make partner if he kept coming to work late with a hangover.

He groaned. "I didn't mean to. And now I'm so hungover I could kick myself. I must say, if you'd been here it probably wouldn't have happened—"

"As if I have any impact at all," I said, with heavy sarcasm. "Remember, I was there at Club Paradise when you were sick enough to lose it in a wastebasket."

"So do you think I have a drinking problem?" Hugh's voice crackled with anger.

"Not exactly. It's just that—you seem to be losing count of your drinks, when you go out. You can't blame me for being a little worried." I eyed the *mojito* in front of me. I'd thought it was two-thirds empty, and was on the verge of ordering another. Now I decided it was actually one-third full, and I was going to slow down.

Hugh began to rail at me, and I saw no point in becoming involved in an argument that the rest of the bar would find amusing, so I simply hung up. Almost immediately the telephone rang again, and I switched it on, still exasperated, but determined to at least give Hugh a chance to apologize and redeem himself.

"Darling?" I said.

"What a nice greeting," Michael Hendricks answered in his cool New England voice. "When I was in Japan before, it was just *moshi-moshi*. Perhaps times have changed."

"Hello, Michael." I paused to compose myself. "I apologize. I was expecting a call from someone else. Which reminds me—may I use this phone for personal calls?"

"You're obviously doing so already, but don't worry. Just remember to avoid saying things into the phone such as my name, and the names of others involved in our situation."

"Sorry." I took a swig of *mojito*.

"Can you explain who the man is in the picture you just sent? You didn't include a text message."

"He's not of any significance to you! I was just practicing—" I paused. "How the hell did you get that picture?"

"You must have pressed 'send.' As I explained to you last week, the camera is wired to send files straight to my Blackberry. "

"Oh. I suppose you're also interested in the bad news from Mr. Watanabe?"

Michael spoke rapidly, his anger practically flashing across the phone. "What bad news? I haven't heard any news, and I don't expect to get progress reports from him! You are the one I expect to hear from, and I wonder about the fact that you've been on location for over twenty-four hours and I haven't heard a peep, just a photo of this Hispanic-looking guy holding a silver device that looks like a grenade—"

"It's a cocktail shaker," I said. "And Enrique's a bartender, not anyone you need to worry about."

"I see. So you're in a bar again?"

"What do you mean by 'again'?"

"Is it a situation where you can talk?"

I glanced around. At their table, the backpackers were giving a drink order to Enrique, so I told Michael about the auction, how I'd met Takeo but quickly learned about his engagement to the daughter of the minister of the environment.

"Aha. I know that name. He was in Japan's diplomatic corps before. I ran into him once in the UAE." Michael sounded as if his annoyance had ceased.

"UAE?" I asked.

"United Arab Emirates. It was during the first Gulf War," Michael said. "And regarding this engagement, I'll have our guys check it out. He might not really be engaged, but just trying to pull your chain."

I snorted and said, "He declared the news right in front of Emi, and she certainly didn't protest."

"He spoke to you in Japanese?" Michael asked.

"No, he was speaking English, perhaps because he noticed that my Japanese isn't as good as it was," I said glumly. "But she seemed to understand completely. I also saw her ring and the way he looked at her."

"And how did you feel about that?"

There was something in Michael's tone that made me shiver, so I said briskly, "I'm upset because it greatly compromises my chances at succeeding. You know that I came here to do something, which I'll still try to do, but with this gorgeous young girl around, the situation's going to be little dicey—"

"On the contrary. Engaged men are easy marks."

"Excuse me?"

"Men on the verge of losing their freedom do last-gasp, risky things. Why do you think bachelor nights are such an institution?"

Michael seemed as if he wanted to rattle on, but I noticed that Richard and Simone had entered the bar and were heading toward me. "Ah, I can't really talk anymore."

"Okay. Keep going, then, and make sure the next picture you send off into cyberspace is of something other than a frigging bartender."

Very cranky. I clicked off while Richard and Simone took off their raincoats glittering with water and came at me for a group hug that smelled of perfume and smoke, a strange kind of smoke I couldn't identify.

"Rei, it's been so looong," Simone moaned in her pretty French accent and came in close to peck both sides of my cheeks. Then Richard rushed at me like a small blond whirlwind and kissed me long and hard on the lips.

"What was that about?" I pulled away, stunned by the unusual show of affection.

"Just trying to pull Enrique's chain," Richard said, smiling at his boyfriend, who was grinning at the three of us. "You're a good kisser, Rei. We should do it again."

"I'll take a rain check," I said uneasily, because Jürgen and his friends were watching with considerable interest.

"It's the crystal," Enrique said, coming in close and setting down a dubious-looking pink drink in front of Richard.

"Cristal? That doesn't look like champagne." I was confused by Enrique's offering.

"Happy pills," Richard said. "Also known as *shabu* or *yaba* around here. Enrique says I get wild when I pop one. But, ooh, is it fun. Teacher's little helper!"

"It's not an everyday thing, *chérie*," said Simone, seeing the shock on my face. "But you know how it is. One of Richard's students, he passed a tough English qualification exam, so he brought his sweet teacher a little *presento*."

"I thought we could go dancing after this!" Richard bobbed his head back and forth. "Rei, I've missed you so much that I could almost jump your bones."

"You're gay, Richard," I reminded my friend. Looking at him so ebullient and silly made me feel wretched. I'd missed Richard and longed many times for a heart-to-heart chat like those we'd once had as roommates in a shabby, cold apartment in Minami-Senju. Now, he had shown up for our reunion flying as high as a Boys' Day kite. There would be no way to talk with him about the confusing situation I'd gotten into with Hugh, let alone anything else.

"Will you come dancing, Rei?" Simone purred. "Bar Isn't It has a really good ladies' night."

"I just came in last evening. I don't think I could make it, but you know, in a few days Angus Glendinning and his band will be here. Why don't we go dancing that night?"

"Hugh has you by a ball and chain, huh?" Richard said. "I knew you should never have moved in with him."

"Don't be ridiculous. It's just I'm still going through jet lag and had hoped for a cozy night catching up."

"Oh, of course! We don't have to go dancing," Simone said, shooting Richard a reproving look. "I have longed to talk with you, Rei, so many times. I don't even understand what has brought you from Washington—"

"A very serious job, which is another one of the reasons I can't paint the town red tonight—I'll never cope tomorrow," I said.

"But you can't work here. Your visa's revoked," Richard said a bit too loudly.

"Not anymore," I said, shooting him a warning glance, which he blithely ignored.

"How? It's impossible to get visas these days. Immigration to Japan has been cut, like, in half, after 9-11. How did you get back in?"

Trying to seem casual, I shrugged. "I'm doing some consulting for a government museum. They wanted me over, so they were able to pull a few strings."

"That's surprising. Your country's reputation is in the gutter, worldwide." Richard, proudly Canadian, sounded almost gleeful.

"Let's not talk politeeks," Simone said. "It's very dull, don't you think? Rei, is something wrong with your drink? Shall Enrique bring you wine instead?"

I shook my head. All I wanted was to escape the manic gaze of two people whom I'd once been comfortable with, but who now seemed like strangers.

13

Despite Richard and Simone's protests, I left Salsa Salsa soon afterward. Finding a taxi in the rain in a fashionable part of town proved impossible. My Bally pumps were waterlogged, and Grand's beautiful wool suit smelled like a wet dog when I finally arrived back at the Hyatt.

"Oh, dear," said the desk clerk, looking at me.

Oh dear, indeed. The rain became even harder during the night, and it was mixed with rough, gusting winds that startled me awake at three. And given my jet lag and the two drinks I'd had, I couldn't fall back into slumber. I tossed through idea after idea of how to get to Takeo. By five in the morning I thought I had a possibility.

Eight o'clock was about the right time to telephone Aunt Norie, who would have already given breakfast to her family. The Shimuras usually breakfasted together, no matter what. My aunt was the kind of cook who made *miso* soup and rice fresh every morning, and would present enough pickled vegetables and fish alongside it to make you think you wouldn't need another meal that day.

"I'm back," I said when my aunt picked up the telephone.

"Your father told us you would be coming. This news is wonderful, that you're back in Japan. How did you manage it?"

"It's a long story. Could you come into Tokyo today? I'd love to take you to lunch somewhere to catch up. I'm staying in Roppongi Hills, but I'd love to get someplace more traditional—"

"But Roppongi Hills is extraordinary! Mrs. Morioka and I ate at the French Kitchen in the Grand Hyatt last week after *ikebana* class. There are so many restaurants in Roppongi Hills that we could easily choose something. And perhaps Chika can join us, because her office isn't too far away."

I agreed, thinking that I might as well take her somewhere nice, since for once in my life I was on an expense account. We settled on a spot called Kitsune, which Norie said served Japanese nouvelle cuisine.

After the meeting time had been set, I asked Norie if she'd have time to take me to the Kayama Kaikan, the headquarters of Takeo's family's flower arranging school. Norie was a master teacher at the school, and she had always enjoyed a close relationship with the Kayamas. Norie credited herself with getting Takeo and me together, and had mourned when the relationship ended. Still, the situation remained warm enough between her and Takeo that every fall, he came to her garden to cut back her hydrangeas with his own special technique.

"Do you wish to study *ikebana* again, Rei-chan? I assumed you would be too busy with this wonderful new job!" My aunt's excitement fairly crackled over the line.

"I am interested in *ikebana*." I paused, knowing that with my aunt, it paid to be direct. "However, I'd like to talk with Takeo Kayama about it. I thought you might be able to be our go-between and establish a meeting."

To my surprise, my aunt paused. At last she said, "I don't know if a go-between is a good idea. He's actually engaged to be married."

"You knew?" How ironic that my own aunt had the facts, while American and Japanese intelligence were clueless.

"Yes, her name is Emi Harada. She is a lovely young girl whose father is a government minister. She's started studying flower arranging at the school, of course."

"I see. Well, you're right that she's lovely and young. I saw Takeo and Emi last night at the auction, and I think he was embarrassed to talk to me in front of her. It's unfortunate because—because I really want to spend a little time with him, and this business trip of mine is so short. Does it seem too much to expect—that he would be civil and give me a few hours' time?"

"Perhaps it is," my aunt said gently. "Maybe it's an American custom for the ex-boyfriend and ex-girlfriend to remain friendly, but it's not often done here in Japan."

That's right, I thought bitterly to myself. Because in Japan, women and men had such prescribed roles that they rarely had pure friendships, once they'd left childhood. I said, "I thought Takeo was different. And after what we all went through in Washington—Hugh and Takeo and I—it seems a shame that I can't continue a friendship with Takeo."

"Well, knowing Kayama-san's personality, I'm still a bit doubtful, but I'll try to smooth things. I think the only way, though, is if it seems like a coincidence that you see each other, not planned."

That's what had happened the previous night, and had failed. However, my aunt was privy to resources I didn't have. She told me she needed to think a bit more, but she'd have a plan in place by the time we met for lunch. I thanked her and hung up the telephone, feeling hopeful for the first time since I'd touched ground in Tokyo.

Two hours later, the streets were a quarter inch underwater when I set off for Kitsune. The restaurant was only a five-minute walk from my hotel, so I shouldn't have gotten as wet as I did. However, I'd decided to go shopping for a raincoat, umbrella, and the pièce de résistance I'd been missing in my wardrobe ever since I'd moved away: rain shoes, the ankle-high rubber shoes that were, as far as I knew, unique to the practical Japanese. I knew I wasn't going to find them at Christian LaCroix or Louis Vuitton or any other of the luxury boutiques in Roppongi Hills, so I shot over on the subway to the Ginza and ducked into one of my favorite department stores, Matsuya, where I found rain shoes on the eighth floor, along with a zebra-patterned umbrella and a shiny black trench coat in young fashion on the third floor. I also couldn't resist picking up a pair of slim-fitting trousers made of pleather, the plastic form of leather that had looked so good on Chika. I paid with my own credit card for the pants, figuring they weren't a work expense that Michael would want to cover—although the raincoat, umbrella, and shoes might pass muster, so I put them on the card he'd issued me to use for the hotel and incidentals.

As cool as I felt leaving the Ginza, I realized when I arrived at Kitsune that I had gotten the fashion code wrong.

"Rain shoes—in Roppongi Hills!" Norie muttered in my ear as we'd embraced.

"But Obasan, it is raining." I broke the embrace, sat down quickly, and picked up a menu, so as not to attract any further inspection.

"Yes, but . . ." Her voice faltered. "Those are more for . . . the suburbs or country. Gardening and so on."

"You can't mean to say you think that I should have worn my Bally pumps today?" I glanced at her low-heeled leather pumps, which appeared strangely dry. "How did you get here, in a plastic bubble or something?"

"I came by train, of course. I wore different shoes until I arrived at Shibuya Station, where I changed them. I placed my wet walking shoes are in a plastic bag, which is in the coat check area, where you may leave your coat and umbrella." She sighed and picked up her menu. "This typhoon is going to be a terrible one. It's a good thing we're meeting today, because the trains might stop tomorrow."

"Typhoon?" I'd been so caught up in worries about the auction that I hadn't turned on the television in my hotel room, or taken the time to read a newspaper.

"Yes, Rei-chan. A big one." My aunt told me about Typhoon Nigo, the second typhoon of the fall, one that had originated in the waters off Thailand and had gained strength as it advanced northward to Japan. Schools and offices were open today, but scores of airline flights had been canceled. Right in my aunt's neighborhood, shopkeepers were hammering plywood sheets over their windows. "I worry about your hotel, Rei-chan. All that glass."

"Tokyo's a big city! I'm sure that the high winds will be broken by the presence of all the skyscrapers and big buildings. And that glass in the hotel windows must be industrial strength."

"It's true the city won't be as hard hit as the seaside areas. But you never can predict the outcome. You should come home with me this afternoon, just to make sure you are safe."

"But Yokohama is closer to the water." As I pointed this out, the thought came to me that there was a location at even greater risk: Hayama, the small seaside town where Takeo's summer house was.

"Yes, but we'll be together, taking care of each other. This hotel is nice, but who here cares about you? Who would answer if you called for help?"

"But it's such a nice hotel. They have an attendant on every floor—"

"Ha! I doubt your hotel will have many employees coming to work tomorrow, if the train companies halt operations."

It was time to get down to business. We ordered lunch sets, because they wouldn't take too long to arrive: mine a lacy burdock root crepe filled with sweet *kabocha* squash; my aunt's the fish platter featuring *kinmedai*, a strong-tasting fish similar to porgy. I kept my voice low, even though the nearest table was occupied by young American and Australian financial traders who looked completely uninterested in us, and weren't likely to understand much Japanese.

"I have the Kayama Kaikan's class schedule here." After the waitress had cleared away the lunch dishes, my aunt pulled a paper from her purse. "The master class ends at noon today. It might last longer, though, because the teachers are planning their arrangements for a show in the gallery space at Isetan next week. I'm on the operations committee for it, in fact."

"That's wonderful. Do you think Takeo will be at the class today?" Every now and then, I recalled, he dropped in on classes.

Norie shook her head, making her huge *mabe* pearl earrings shake slightly. "I doubt it. He has less interest in these—what does he call them?—commercial ventures. However, I have learned that he has an appointment with the school's accounts manager at twelve-thirty, so that means he's in the building right now."

"Do you think we should stop by?"

Norie held up a warning finger. "I will visit the Kaikan alone after lunch, and ask the receptionist to send word that I must speak to Takeo-san about the show at Isetan. I'll think of something important, maybe a problem with the location."

"That's a clever idea," I said.

"Yes, I could make him very concerned if he knows that Mrs. Okayama is thinking about using PVC pipes as a lining material in her flower arrangement. He doesn't like us to use material that can't be recycled." Her eyes gleamed mischievously, and I laughed. How well my aunt knew the flower master.

14

Half an hour later, the two of us had waded over to the Kayama Kaikan, the impressive modern tower building where the Kayama family housed the administrative offices and classrooms for its *ike-bana* school. The first floor was all glass, so I could see my aunt enter the dramatic sandstone lobby, shaking off her bright floral Hanae Mori umbrella. She caught sight of me and made a shooing gesture with her hand.

Where could I wait? The nearest building was the embassy of Canada. I was soon made aware of the fact that it wasn't a public waiting room, so I hurriedly asked for a visa form and began filling it out as slowly as I could. Americans didn't need visas for Canada, but I could always pretend later than I didn't know. And I might be a Japanese citizen, for all they knew.

If only my aunt would call. It was a long ten minutes until my mobile phone beeped. She told me that she was in the elevator, going up to the penthouse floor.

"Now remember, please ring my telephone in five minutes, because the fact is, once I get past the topic of the flower exhibition I won't have much to keep me in his presence."

I agreed, kept my eye on my watch, and dialed over to Norie at the exactly the prescribed moment.

"*Moshi-moshi*," she answered happily. "How nice to hear from

you! But the thing is, I'm sorry, I'm in a meeting at the school. . . .
Yes, I know you need to receive the key right away."

"May I get it from you now?" I asked, according to the script.

"The circumstances are a little bit difficult. I'm actually on the
ninth floor of the Kayama building, with the honorable headmaster . . . but if you come quickly, I think it would be all right."

"So, shall I do it?" I breathed into the receiver.

"Yes, yes, please come quickly." And she clicked off.

Phase two was under way, for better or worse. I left the Canadian embassy, sprinting the twenty or so yards to the Kayama
Kaikan. After I barged through the Kaikan's big glass doors, I had
to pause to have my backpack inspected by the doorman, who reminded me to put my umbrella in the stand. Once I was deemed
safe to enter, I walked past the jagged installation of sandstone
rocks—around which were placed flower arrangements that were
changed the minute a bloom started to wilt. It felt strange to enter
this dry, brightly lit facsimile of a garden, when the world outside
was so rough and stormy.

The receptionist, a beautiful young woman in a pink silk dress
who was raptly reading a magazine called *Gothic and Lolita Bible*,
didn't even look up when I told her I was going to the school's café,
which was open to the public.

"Third floor," she said dreamily.

"Thank you very much." I moved past, catching a glimpse of the
page she was studying, which showed a bonneted woman carrying
a teddy bear. The baby trend was driving me to distraction. I'd been
away, and gotten older, while everyone who stayed was getting
younger.

The elevator arrived and was disgorging a load of fifty-something women—who, because of their Japanese genes, appeared to
be somewhere in their thirties—carrying tall bundles of flowers.

I waited for them to pass, then got on by myself. Three, I pressed,
just in case anyone was watching. Then I hit nine, and all too soon,
the doors opened on the long, cinnabar-colored hallway that led to
the Kayama family's personal quarters. The first time I'd entered
the hallway, I'd been stunned by a Mark Rothko painting on the
wall. It wasn't there anymore. All the old, high-status paintings

were gone, in fact—replaced by framed photographs of wildflowers. A tiny penciled scrawl in the corner of each photograph told me that Takeo himself had been the photographer.

Takeo had taken over the reins of the flower school, and the details showed. He'd also moved offices. The old room, where Takeo had once lounged among decades' worth of *National Geographic* magazines, had its door slightly open, revealing not magazines but hanging racks of women's clothes. Natsumi, Takeo's twin sister, must have taken it for herself—unless the girlfriend had moved in, which wasn't likely. The next door over was the last in the hallway. It was the headmaster's study, once Takeo's father's room, and, I was guessing, now Takeo's own.

I knocked lightly, hoping that I'd guessed right. A few seconds later the door was opened by Takeo, wearing a gray cashmere sweatshirt and jeans. My gaze flickered from his tight expression to the welcoming room that lay behind him. Takeo had furnished his new office with what looked like Frank Lloyd Wright furniture from his Japanese period: elegant low chairs cushioned in persimmon velvet, with low tables between. There was a sofa in burnt orange laden with small, exquisite pillows made from old kimono silk. I breathed in happily at the sight of all my favorite colors, and my aunt seated in one of these chairs, her legs gracefully crossed at the ankle.

"What is this? You didn't tell me—" Takeo looked from me to my aunt with obvious shock.

"I'm sorry, I didn't want to interrupt the instruction you were giving me about the program by talking too much. But the fact is, Rei-chan has just come to town, and she has been so busy that today is the first time I've had a chance to see her! My dear, welcome home!" She rose to her feet, and beckoned for me to approach her for a hug.

"The key—I am—" I was forgetting how to construct a Japanese sentence, because Takeo was looking so irritated at my presence.

"Yes. Rei-chan came to receive our house key," my aunt said, taking it out and tucking it into my purse. "She will be leaving the Grand Hyatt to stay with us for safety during the typhoon."

"Isn't that a bit—overly careful?" Takeo looked out the window at the pouring gray sheet of water. "Even if a typhoon arose at sea, the likelihood that it would cause any trouble here in the Kanto area is very remote."

"But look at what happened in southeast Asia!" I decided to jump on my aunt's bandwagon. "Your country house in Hayama is quite vulnerable, to both typhoons and tsunamis—"

"It will be fine," he said stonily. "That building has gone through a war and more than a few typhoons. I'm not doing anything special."

"You must," I said. "At least pull out the shutters and make sure they're well latched. Do you still have that nice old retainer who can do that for you?" I'd forgotten the name of the Kayamas' manservant, who moved with them from home to home as the seasons changed.

My aunt interrupted before Takeo could answer the question. "I must rush off because I promised my son I would bring some food to him at the hospital—he'll never be released from duty, once the typhoon arrives. Anyway, Rei-chan, I hope that you can spare a few moments to say hello to Kayama-sensei. It has been a very long time," she added before stepping out into the hall.

"Well, she's right about that." I settled myself down in one of the chairs. "What beautiful furniture! It looks like Frank Lloyd Wright."

A flicker of something akin to pride passed across Takeo's face. He said, "I knew you'd recognize them."

"Wow." Did that mean he'd thought I'd pay him a call here? "I didn't know his furniture had gone into reproduction."

"It's not reproduction. They're originals," he said, sitting down across from me.

"Oh. So you really have become a serious collector," I said.

"Of course." He looked at me sternly. "Just as I'm serious about Emi. I won't jeopardize my engagement for any inappropriate interlude that you have in mind."

I willed myself not to blush, but it was impossible. "I can't believe you're saying that! I just sat down out of—courtesy—to finish the conversation we couldn't have last night."

"Well, this whole business of your aunt getting me alone, so you could arrive, was pretty obvious."

I looked out at the rain, steadying myself. Then I turned back to him. "Come on, let's be civil. We must talk, but you're right that this isn't the right place. I wish we could get away from it all, maybe drive out to Hayama and have lunch at the house."

"The weather's too bad for that," he said. "And Emi would hate it. She wouldn't stop asking me about you yesterday evening."

"Oh, really? What did you tell her?"

"I told a small lie. I said I knew you in college," Takeo said.

"Hmm. So she thought I was a classmate of yours at Keio?" I'd better get the cover right, in case I ran into her again.

"She believes you were, and still are, a professor. At UC Santa Cruz, where she knows I did my gardening certificate—"

"You mean—she thinks I'm old enough to be your professor?" I was horror-struck. I'd never wear that suit again.

"But you're American. She knows the rules are different there. She went to an American school when her family was in Turkey, you know."

"I didn't know. Another thing I'm wondering about is, how long have you been engaged?"

"Two months." Takeo smiled a bit unsteadily. "This is an *omiai*. There's no need for a long courtship."

"*Omiai!* Do you mean you're going to have an arranged marriage?"

He looked evenly back at me. "Why not?"

"But Takeo . . ." I paused, feeling helpless. "You're so . . . eligible. You don't need anyone to help you get married. And you're so . . . unconventional! From the looks of your fiancée, she's going to be more suited to attending fashion shows than Greenpeace rallies."

"I adore Emi," Takeo said softly. "She's beautiful and charming. We enjoy being together, and her father is most agreeable to hearing my ideas about wildlife preservation. Together, Emi and I can do quite a bit to help Japan."

So that was it. Takeo was marrying Emi because a close connection to the government minister would allow him to influence environmental policies. Feeling a chill run through me, I said, "You're awfully callous to marry someone just for her connections."

"Well, I've come to believe that we, the people who inhabit the earth, are not as important as the earth itself."

"But what about love?"

"With arranged marriages, we grow to love each other," Takeo said. "Whereas you Westerners, you love so passionately at first, and then there's nothing left for later on."

I was about to launch a counterargument when I realized that he might have a point. I'd been in love with Hugh for years, but we were nowhere near ready to get married. If only I were as certain about the future as Takeo seemed to be.

"I'd like to get to know her, too," I said stiffly.

"Why?"

"Well, I do still care about you as a friend. It's natural for me to want to become friends with my friend's wife, isn't it?" As I spoke, I looked out the window, because I felt too mortified to face him. "I don't know what Emi-san's work schedule is like, but maybe after the storm blows over, I could take her to lunch—"

"She doesn't have a job, because she just graduated this summer."

"Oh, which university?" I had already pegged her as the type who went to Gakushuin, the private university where the remnants of Japan's nobility still studied.

When Takeo mentioned Tokyo International Girls School, a private high school, I nearly choked. She wasn't even old enough to have started college. Talk about a Lolita complex; Takeo had it in spades.

"Well, Takeo, since Emi has some free time, perhaps we could all drive down to Hayama together," I suggested mildly.

"Rei, I'm tired of talking about this silly idea of a trip to the beach. It's not even summer."

"We could have lunch in the house, and then I'd really like to see what you've done with the rock garden. I'm thinking of doing something like that in Washington—" I cut myself off in mid-babble when I realized that Emi herself was standing in the doorway.

Emi was wearing a short, flared red dress that made me think of the baby-girl outfits I'd seen around town—but it looked about ten times more expensive. The front of the dress was obscured by an artwork she was holding, a colorful screen print of a Louis Vuitton handbag. Above it, her large eyes peered at me—really large, with big black pupils, like a girl character from anime.

She looked away from me and addressed Takeo in a soft, high, appropriately girlish voice. "Oh, excuse me! I didn't know you had an appointment with your *sensei*."

"Actually, I just dropped in. Takeo and I were talking about how his, ah, rock garden design could translate to one I am planning in the United States. Excuse me for not introducing myself last night! My name is Shimura Rei." I inverted my names, the proper way, and tried to elevate the pitch of my voice to sound like hers—girlish, proper, hopeful. What Takeo had said about her mistaking me for his teacher had gotten on my nerves.

Emi bowed back and gave her name in a bell-like tone. She smiled insincerely, then turned to her fiancé. "Takeo-kun, if it's not too much of an interruption, I would like you to consider this new painting. What do you think?"

"It's quite bright, isn't it?" Takeo said, after a moment's silence.

"It's Murakami Takashi," she said in a rush. "It will become even more valuable in another year, Father says."

Takashi Murakami's paintings of cartoonlike characters and status handbags were all the rage, but they seemed a little gimmicky to me, a materialistic new version of Andy Warhol, certainly not the kind of art an antimaterialist like Takeo would enjoy. But what did I know? He was now busy blowing thousands of dollars of the family fortune at auctions, on things like beds and china services.

"Sorry to be rude, but I shall be leaving now," I announced, wondering whether Emi's cheerful behavior was hiding the fact she'd overheard our bitter conversation. In any case, I didn't want to be suspected of trying to ruin their engagement, so I left, offering a second good-bye that neither of them acknowledged.

The door didn't close entirely behind me, and when I heard Emi's voice, I stepped into the doorway of the roomful of dresses. If she was going to rip into me, I wanted to hear exactly what she said.

"So . . . what about the painting? Do you like it or not? I only have it until Monday. The dealer wants to know."

"But I thought you bought it already?" Takeo sounded weary.

"I borrowed it. It's not sold until we decide we want it. I think it would really cheer up that musty old country house, don't you?"

"My house in Hayama?" Takeo sounded alarmed.

"Our house," Emi corrected him warmly. "You don't have many pretty things there, and I wanted to repaint anyway, to a nice bright yellow . . . kind of the Vuitton yellow, if you know what I mean."

I shut my eyes, trying to imagine a high school girl becoming chatelaine of that simple, elegant country villa. I couldn't fathom it.

"Perhaps we'd better see what it looks like there, first," Takeo said. "Actually, I was thinking about driving there tonight, because I should shutter the house."

So he'd taken my warning seriously—despite acting with me as if he weren't worried. This gave me a faint rush of pride.

"Why don't you get old Chiba-san to do it? That's his job, isn't it?" Emi's voice squeaked with irritation.

"Unfortunately, Chiba-san stays in Hayama only from spring to the end of summer. He's in Kyoto right now with my father and sister working on that installation at the Golden Pavilion."

"But you can't go to the country tonight. My parents expect us at the dinner for the French delegation."

"That's right. I'm sorry." Takeo sighed. "Well, then, you'll just have to tell the art dealer it's going to take a few more days to decide. He'll probably close up shop himself, because of the weather. If things are really so bad, I suppose we'll have to close the Kaikan."

"*Ah so desu ka*. With the Kaikan closed, will you be . . . less busy?" Emi sounded coquettish.

"Actually, I'll have lots of time. Now come here, Emi-chan. You haven't even kissed me hello yet." I heard a rustling and a laugh, and then the slow, unmistakable sound of someone's zipper going south.

Lolita in Humbert's lap. I tiptoed away, thoroughly disgusted with the two of them—and with myself, for the way I felt.

15

During the twenty minutes I'd been in the Kaikan, the rain seemed to have become harder. Torrents of water streamed out of the heavens, and when I stepped recklessly off a curb without looking, a swell of water rushed into the top of my rain shoes.

Miserably, I took shelter in the vestibule of an electronics shop to pull off the shoes and drain them. Through the store window, I caught a glimpse of television sets, small to large, all displaying the Japanese weather channel. After I'd gotten my shoes back on my feet, I went in to get a better view.

The screens displayed images of a swirling red circle moving across southwest Japan. The edge of the storm was now just seventy kilometers from Shikoku Island and predicted to arrive in full force by mid-evening. Several fishermen had been swept away and drowned in the swelling waves, and people living in small houses along the beach had been told to evacuate. Once the typhoon hit Shikoku, it might travel inland, wreaking havoc in Kobe and Osaka; or, if the wind changed, it might roll its way up the east coast, toward Yokohama and Tokyo. The government was urging that all possible safety precautions be taken in all towns along the coast.

The next shot showed Shikoku islanders preparing for the typhoon by boarding up windows and waiting in long lines for gasoline. There were film close-ups of grocery stores with bare shelves, and of housewives scrubbing their bathtubs with disinfectant before using them to store water.

Tokyo was inland, I reminded myself. No reason to panic. I returned to the rainy street, where I noticed, for the first time, how few people were around.

Well, it wasn't exactly a day for strolling. At mid-afternoon, the sky was as dark as if it were early evening; and the rain lashed relentlessly down. I wondered if my aunt's dire predictions about the storm would come true, since she'd been right about so much else.

Every taxi that passed had its "occupied" light on, and the unlucky pedestrians on the street all seemed to be running for shelter. My funky spotted umbrella blew inside out when I was still on Gaien-Higashi-Dori, a long five blocks from the Hyatt. I struggled in vain to fix it, but I was powerless against the wind. But at the end of the block, a lighted subway signpost showing six trees—the *kanji* symbol for Roppongi—had been knocked to the ground by the strong wind. But the signpost reminded me of another possible walking route. I could use the shelter of the subway to walk the rest of the way straight into Roppongi Hills.

The steep stairway leading down was slick with rain, so I had to tread carefully. A couple of times people bumped into me in their own haste to get out of the rain. I paid 160 yen to get down to the train platform, where I began my trek for exit 4, the way up to Roppongi Hills.

As I walked along, I listened to snatches of conversation. Two men were talking about how they were going to get to a business meeting, and then I overheard somebody else talking to a companion about hoping the line would be open again the next day. As I climbed the stairs up to the exit and passed through the turnstiles, I saw a hand-lettered sign in Japanese and English: HIBIYA LINE CLOSED EASTBOUND DUE TO FLOODING.

There was an attendant in the booth, so I stopped to ask him about it.

"Excuse me, but where's the flood?"

"Tsukijii. Twenty minutes ago, enough water rose to cause an electric short. The subway authority has closed the line until the storm passes."

He was talking about the fish market, where I'd gone the previous day. Of course, a station close to water would be vulnerable. How fortunate that Roppongi was farther inland.

I walked on and upward, out the Roppongi Hills exit. There were no teenagers congregating at the giant spider at the open-air Roku-Roku plaza; and while shops were open and glowing with light, nobody seemed to be inside. The escalators were turned off, for some reason, so I had to hustle up the stairs, then down a covered stretch until I'd made it to the Grand Hyatt.

At last, real shelter. As I kicked off the rain shoes just inside the entrance to my room, I saw that a folded note in a hotel envelope had been pushed under the door. I read the message that my aunt had left with reception. She hoped that I'd had a nice conversation with my friend, and she wanted me to remember to call her about when I'd be arriving in Yokohama. She'd decided to see her son at St. Luke's hospital first, but expected to be home by six.

Not likely, I thought, remembering what I'd learned about the flooding at Tsukijii, the stop closest to St. Luke's. I wondered if Norie had gotten there before the subway line closed down, or if she'd been trapped underground.

I kicked off the rain shoes, turned on the bath taps, and picked up the bathroom telephone receiver to dial my aunt's cell phone. A recording of a high-pitched woman's voice told me that all networks were busy; the call hadn't gone through.

It was rare for the Japanese phone system to have trouble, but at least I still had my American phone. I hadn't wanted to waste it on local calls, but this was a necessity.

I rummaged through all the wet clothes to get to my dripping black nylon backpack. Everything inside was damp: my hairbrush, my address book, my makeup case . . . I fished around for the phone, but it wasn't there.

No need to panic, I repeated for the second time in half an hour, as I began to work my way through every zippered pocket. When had I last used the phone? At the Canadian embassy, when I'd talked to

Norie. I'd placed it in the outside zippered pocket, so it would be handy in case my aunt called again. In that same space I found the visa application I'd started filling out to avoid suspicion. It was still there, along with my passport. But not the phone.

I used the hotel telephone to dial information, and I was quickly put through to the embassy. Nobody had found a cellular phone. Next, I tried the Kayama Kaikan. I recognized the voice of the fashion-loving receptionist and told her that I was missing a phone. She didn't have it either. I was too discreet to mention that I might have lost it in Takeo's office. I could only hope he'd contact me if he found it.

After I hung up, I looked out the window into the pouring rain, and wondered whether it was soaking my cell phone, somewhere or other. I could have lost the phone during my wild dash through the rain back to the hotel. Or maybe it had been taken out of my bag by someone. Now I thought about the people who'd seemed overly interested in me since the job had started. The man next to me on the plane, Jürgen in the bar, even the unseen person hovering behind me at the sushi bar. I'd just thought of them as annoyances, never imagining that they were a threat to my security. Any one of them could have been following me during the storm, when the rain had been so loud I couldn't possibly have heard someone run up behind me.

I leaned on the glass and shut my eyes against the avalanche of water outside. What a mess! I was stuck without my lifeline to Washington, Takeo was stuck with his ditzy fiancée, and my aunt was possibly stuck in a flooded subway tunnel. I'd almost forgotten the original reason I was looking for my cell phone.

I took out my little address book and dialed the Shimura family's number in Yokohama. Unlike my earlier attempt to reach Norie's cell phone, this call went through.

"I've been waiting to hear from you! Are you coming to us tonight?" my cousin Chika demanded.

"I don't think so, Chika. The train lines are flooded. That's why I'm calling, really, about Aunt—I mean, about your mother—"

"She's not here yet. She telephoned to say that she couldn't get back to Shibuya station, so she had to go a whole roundabout way using the Keikyu line. She's still traveling, I believe."

"I hope she gets home soon. You must let me know."

"Of course she will come home." Chika spoke with all the confidence of a Japanese child who was sure her mother would always be around to help. "But when are you coming to stay, Rei-chan? With this rain, I think you should travel tonight, before the floods tomorrow."

"I actually think it's safer to stay in place rather than travel." As I spoke, I flipped on the television, which was, unsurprisingly, showing a vista of heavy rain over rice paddies.

"Nobody's safe anywhere if there's flooding," Chika said darkly. "It's such a shame for you to be here now. And with this weather, I don't know when Angus-san and the band can arrive. They were supposed to fly in tomorrow, but I heard that all the airlines have stopped flying to Tokyo and Yokohama."

"When's the typhoon supposed to end?" I asked.

"Well, the worst of the winds and rain will be tomorrow, they think. Is the place you're staying safe?"

I looked around my room uneasily. I was so high up. I was sure the building was structurally sound and would not topple over, but I wasn't as sure about the safety of the windows as I'd made out to Aunt Norie. There was something spooky about being alone, in a tall hotel, with no one I knew nearby. And now I didn't even have a cell phone to use to call for help if the phone lines went dead.

I told Chika to please convey to Norie my gratitude for all her help, and to let her know that I'd lost my cell phone—so if she wanted to get in touch, the hotel line was best.

I hung up the telephone and crawled into bed. Then I remembered Hugh, and the bad way things had ended. This might be my last chance to talk to him, if, as it seemed, the phone connections would all go down. What time was it there, three or four in the morning? I always got confused about daylight saving time.

I dialed the apartment, and the phone rang eight times. Then the answering machine picked up in my voice. I left a message for Hugh apologizing for the hour of the call, but saying that I'd called early because of the typhoon—and if he didn't hear from me for days, not to worry.

It was a relief to have reached the answering machine, I thought after I'd hung up and settled down between the sheets. I could say exactly what I wanted and not worry about being interrupted and taken in other directions.

It was only when I was halfway to sleep that I thought about how strange it was that at three or four in the morning, Hugh hadn't been there to pick up the bedside phone.

I woke with a start while it was still dark and found that I'd soaked the thick cotton sheets with my sweat. In my dream, the moisture had been rain: I had been getting wetter and wetter, running through a downpour, with Michael Hendricks and Mr. Watanabe chasing after me. Ahead I could see a woman whose skin glowed gold; she had downturned eyes and a peaceful expression. Her right hand was lifted, with its palm toward me. In my dream, she seemed immensely comfortable, like someone I'd seen before, indeterminately Asian and of indefinable age.

I pulled myself up to a sitting position and turned on the television. The news showed smashed hotels and cottages throughout Shikoku. The electricity was gone, and hospitals were full of people who'd been hit with flying debris. The only blessing was that there hadn't been a tidal wave, because the storm had turned inland.

Inland. This meant it was heading up the Miura Peninsula toward Yokohama and Tokyo. What a time to be here, I thought, watching the footage of rain lashing the giant bronze Buddha in Kamakura. The newscaster droned on about how a storm of similar magnitude had swept the existing temple away from that Buddha some eight centuries earlier. I caught him saying something about how the electricity was gone in Kamakura and most of the Miura Peninsula, but then I stopped listening, because I'd clicked back to my dream.

Now I knew the identity of the golden woman: she was the goddess Kannon, the goddess of mercy revered by Buddhists. Kannon-sama was the savior of people in distress. Her image was a focal point in many Buddhist temples throughout Asia, but the Kannon I knew best was the thirty-foot-high gilded camphorwood image at the Hase Kannon temple in Kamakura, just a few miles from Takeo's summer house in Hayama.

She was calling me to go. And suddenly I realized that the typhoon itself would make the mission possible. Takeo was not going to be at the country house in Hayama, and his neighbors would be holed up in their tightly shuttered houses. Nobody would notice me borrowing the key that he kept under a potted hydrangea on the veranda or, if it was gone, gently lifting a window to get inside. I put my past conviction of breaking and entering firmly out of mind. Thanks to the power of the storm, and with Kannon-sama's protection, I'd be able to accomplish what needed to be done.

16

The 8:02 train out of Tokyo Station was still scheduled to run, although the government was urging people to stay inside. Only a few people boarded the train along with me in Tokyo, and it was easy to figure out who they were: workers who couldn't afford to upset their bosses. In short, people like myself.

I'd chosen Japan Railway's Yokosuka line, which was a slightly slower trip, because the JR rails were older and farther inland than its competitor, Keihin-Kyuko Railways. The only risky part of the trip was at the very end, the port of Yokosuka, but I'd be out six stops before that point. I was going to disembark at Kannon-sama's home—Kamakura—and take a taxi into Hayama, which didn't have its own station.

Japan Railway had upgraded the cars, which now had long inward-facing bench seats, rather than the cozy booth-style seating I remembered from my last time in Japan. You could pack more people into a train this way, but I hated sitting sideways on a train; not being able to look at the horizon made me nauseated. Sideways seats were another reason I had avoided the Keihin-Kyuko line. Now, I pulled out a little package of *sembei* crackers I had in my backpack and, despite the disapproving glances of people around me, began to munch. I couldn't afford to have an empty stomach in this situation. I also turned my head sharply to the left, intent on seeing what I could of the horizon. It was impossible to see build-ings or trees—just vague, hazy lights were visible. The route passed apartment buildings I remembered, an amusement park, a string of love hotels and small businesses. Everything looked so strange without the usual bright lights.

I checked my watch. The trip from Tokyo to Kamakura was usu-ally fifty-four minutes, but we'd already traveled ninety minutes and were only at the halfway mark, Yokohama. I was feeling pre-dictably queasy, so I took some deep breaths.

A new group of travelers had boarded in Yokohama: people who were leaving work, unusually for nine-thirty in the morning. Usu-ally, a commuter train was silent, but today, people were talking about the storm. Someone said that large sections of Shizuoka pre-fecture were flooded. Shizuoka was a little more than an hour's drive away. And at the pace at which the train was moving, it seemed possible that the storm's brunt would arrive in Kamakura before we did.

The train seemed to be moving more slowly, and it kept pausing, inexplicably, for varying lengths of time—sometimes two minutes, sometimes ten. I imagined that the conductor was getting informa-tion about flooded tracks ahead, and was waiting for the trains on those tracks to be diverted to other tracks.

The train lurched on, and finally we were approaching Kita-Kamakura: north Kamakura, the last station before Kamakura, where I would get out. But as we approached, there was a sliding sensation, as if the train were no longer connected to the track. Then the train jerked hard and stopped.

I'd shut my eyes when I'd thought the train was hydroplaning, but now I opened them and looked out the window. I could see nothing but rain.

A disembodied voice spoke from the public address system. "We have received word that there is flooding ahead at Kita-Kamakura Station, which makes it unsafe for the train to proceed. After we are granted permission, this train will return to Ofuna station, where our honored passengers may kindly disembark. Alternative trans-portation to points north and south will be provided for you as it becomes available. We apologize for any inconvenience."

I looked out the window again; through the rain I could see what looked like the Kita-Kamakura train station a short distance ahead. North Kamakura was almost within my reach, but the train wouldn't go there.

I stood up and turned to look at the bedraggled bunch of travelers in the car. I debated the danger of calling attention to myself, deciding it was a must in this situation, and waved a hand to get everyone's attention.

"Excuse me, but I was going to leave at this station. . . . Does anyone else live nearby and want to disembark as well? I think that perhaps we could . . . ask the conductor to open the door."

Nobody said yes. However, someone said, "But it's dangerous!" and another person, the man who'd given the weather report before, advised, "It's better to stay onboard for the return trip to Ofuna. There will surely be buses after a while."

After a while? That could be hours, maybe even the next day. I shook my head, gathered up my umbrella and backpack, and pushed on the door that opened down to the tracks.

As I'd anticipated, it didn't budge. I was going to have to get a conductor to let me out. I hurried out of the compartment and into the next one. I was in about the middle of the train, so I had quite a distance to travel to reach the engineer. As I ran through each compartment, heads turned in surprise at the sight of me. I tried more doors without luck. Two compartments later, I was met by a blue-uniformed conductor.

"Is there some trouble?" he asked.

"Yes, I'm sorry to bother you, but the thing is that I must get off this train now, rather than return to Ofuna. I noticed we're just a few feet from the Kita-Kamakura platform—"

The conductor pressed his lips together. "I'm sorry, but we can't go farther. We're waiting for another train to pass, and then we'll go backward."

"Would it be possible for you to release the control on the door and I'll just hop down?" It couldn't be more than four feet's distance to the ground.

"But there is no platform."

"I'll watch out."

The conductor looked distracted. "That is against rail policy—"

"This is an emergency!" I struggled to keep my voice controlled. "If the train were in danger, people would go out the windows to safety. Look, there are stickers demonstrating how to do it." I gestured to the window next to an elderly gentleman. "If I open a window, I'll get everyone wet. Please, if you just release the catch on the door for me, I'll be able to leave without causing anyone trouble."

The volume of my voice, and my growing histrionics, must have convinced him that I was more trouble onboard than off. Keeping his face grim, he lifted a handheld radio to his lips and spoke a jumble of quick commands and codes that I didn't understand, but that I gathered had something to do with alerting all other trains that a passenger was on the tracks. After he was finished, the conductor pressed a button that released the lock on the door.

Wetness rushed toward me as I carefully sat down on the edge of the train, letting my legs drop down into space. There were about three feet to the wooden railway ties below. The easiest thing to do was to slide down

"Please watch for danger!" he cried as I stepped carefully across the tracks, which were under six inches of water. When I reached the grassy bank on the western side, I turned and bowed my thanks. But the train had already started its backward course. Nobody was watching me anymore.

It was truly just a few minutes' slog to Kita-Kamakura station, which I found was in the process of closing when I walked in.

"No more trains," the ticket taker said. The usual courtesies—honorable customer and the like—seemed to be slipping away as the weather had worsened.

"I'm just going out to get a taxi," I said.

"Taxi? There are no taxis! No customer, no taxi!"

"Well, maybe I can call from the pay phone—" already I'd spotted a trusty lime-green NTT phone on the platform.

"Telephones don't work." The ticket taker seemed almost gleeful about the bad news. Maybe he had heard the "passenger on the tracks" signal my train's conductor had issued and was annoyed to have that passenger in his station. Or maybe things were just so bad outside that he was starting to crack.

"Are any buses running?" I ventured.

"Service suspended! Just as this station is closing, the bus system is closed, too."

I cleared my throat and attempted the girlish falsetto that Japanese women used to powerful effect. "I very badly need to go in the direction of Hayama. Is there any chance you will be driving home?"

"Not that way. And the beach road is already flooded in that section by the marina, I must warn you. The station manager is the one with a car here, and he's just about to drive to Zushi to gather some other employees who need transportation—"

"Please, could he let me out there, at Zushi station?" I asked quickly.

"But you are going to Hayama. Even from the turnoff, it's a four-kilometer walk. You cannot make it in this rain."

"I'm sure I can. I know it very well. I'm so close by," I said, running through the route in my mind. I'd taken it by bus before, past marine supply stores, antique shops, and restaurants. I was sure I would recognize these landmarks and know the turns.

He hesitated. "I can't let you stay in this station, because it's closing. Maybe I can ask."

"I'm willing to pay!" I cried again.

But it wasn't necessary. The station manager, a frazzled-looking man in his sixties, would not accept payment, even though he took me slightly past the station, to the main road that led into Hayama.

The roads didn't even look like roads anymore, I thought as we inched along. The rain lashed at a sideways angle because of the wind, a force so strong that it was making trees wave about. At some street corners, backed-up storm drains had created pools so deep that water stretched all the way up to the shop entrances. After we'd seen the second intersection like this, the station manager stopped his car.

"I'm sorry, but there's no point in going on," he said. "I will call the employees and tell them I can't continue on. I'm turning back. Perhaps you can take shelter at the nearest police box—"

The police were the last people I wanted to see. "Thanks, but I think I can get through on foot. I can get out here."

"But you can't! How will you cross the bridge ahead?"

"It's so short—I'm sure I'll make it," I said, sounding more confident than I felt. I knew the little half-moon-shaped bridge the station manager had mentioned. It was about twenty feet long. I could make it now, but there was no time to waste, if the flooding continued.

I said good-bye to the uneasy stationmaster and got out. The rain was being pushed hard by the wind, so hard that it seemed to be raining upward, over my rain shoes and onto my jeans, which within a few minutes were plastered to my legs. My breath came in gasps as I sloshed as quickly as I could through the water.

The bridge over the canal lay just past a deserted bus stop. It was a beautiful little upwardly curved bridge with short red handrailings—the kind immortalized in Japanese woodblock prints. I'd walked over this bridge before and taken photographs of the Zushi canal and the pretty antique shops and surf gear shops that lay along it.

I couldn't see the bridge today, because it was covered with water, but the handrails were still visible. I started across, clinging to the slippery wooden rail. Gusts of wind tore at me, and it felt as if the water was rising.

The water was up to my waist by the time I'd gotten over and was on land. I was shaking, but as I ran on, my pulse leveled out. I'd crossed the worst of Zushi's water, and now I was headed on the four-kilometer route into Hayama, running toward the mountain tunnels that would keep me dry for a few blessed minutes. I ran past restaurants, antique stores, and a post office and, finally, down to the beach road that led to Takeo's house.

From the left at the wall surrounding the emperor's palace, I still had two kilometers to go. I reminded myself about the seawall that would keep the sea from rushing inward, but in fact there was so much rain that the road was marked by deep pockets of water—flash floods like those I'd seen in Zushi.

As I ran, I held my head down because my eyes kept filling with rain. It was like crying in reverse. And the truth was that looking around was frightening. Things were clearly out of order everywhere; no cars drove along the road below me, although I did see some float by.

The back of my raincoat and jeans were as wet as if I'd been soaking in a bathtub. The front of me was a little less wet because I used my new umbrella like a shield, until it blew out about halfway down the hill that sloped down to what used to be the beach road. The road was now a fast-running river.

I stood at the edge of it, water up to my knees, wondering how deep it was in the middle. Merchandise from a beach souvenir shop—an array of life preservers, floating toys, and plastic buckets—bobbed past in the fast-flowing water. As a raft with the head of Doraemon, the magic cat from a popular children's television program, sailed by, I was hit by inspiration. I could travel the road on the raft.

Without giving myself a chance to change my mind, I reached out and grabbed for the rubber cat's head. I connected with the head, but found it harder than I'd expected to mount the small raft. My body swished through the water like a fish flailing on the end of a line, but I was able to keep hold of the raft with my arms. After a couple of failed lunges, I got my legs and the rest of me on top of the raft.

My weight was more than the child's raft was designed for, so it sank slightly in the water, but thankfully not all the way. We continued south past my old favorite restaurant, Chaya, then past the Morito Shrine, where I saw that the *tori* gateway was half-submerged. As we approached a big intersection, I realized that the stoplights were out, as in fact were lights everywhere. A power outage. Good thing there was no traffic at all.

Another two kilometers and I was drifting past the high wall of the emperor's summer palace. I wasn't sure of the palace's elevation—the grounds were landscaped in such a way that it was impossible to spy on the palace—but I had to imagine that it had been built, just like Takeo's family home, as high as possible. The gray police bus that always guarded the palace wall was gone. I imagined that the police had driven it somewhere safe for the duration of the storm. And surely none of the imperial family would be on the coast during this typhoon.

• • •

The street that led to Takeo's house was too small to have a name; it was really just a long, stone-covered driveway that led upward from a small group of cypress trees that marked the intersection. As the raft slowly sailed on, I saw the trees bent over like hunchbacked grandmothers—a situation caused by both the ruthless wind and the heavy wisteria vines on them, which were dragging in the water. Many people would have seen the vines as an overgrown weed, but Takeo had refused to let the city landscapers remove them. Now I was glad for it, because I reached out to the vines to help steer the raft to the trees. I grabbed hold and scrambled onto the bank. The raft sailed on.

As I scrambled up the path made of river stones, the water level dropped and my spirits rose. One kilometer to go. I scanned the few other old, great prewar villas on each side of the path. Heavy brown wooden shutters covered all their windows, and the luxury cars I remembered seeing in most of the carports were all shrouded in protective covers. I had made a fool of myself on the train and at Kita-Kamakura Station, but there was no chance that anyone in this area would notice me.

The long bamboo fence surrounding Takeo's house finally came into view. I could see rain cascading off its tiled roof, creating a small flood right outside the front doors. Some of the tiles were gone, smashed to bits on the ground amid dozens of knocked-over potted plants.

I unlatched the gate and hurried around to the back of the house. As I'd feared, there were plenty more smashed pots, and the potted hydrangea that was supposed to be on the veranda was nowhere in sight. It could have been blown away—or, I realized, it might have outgrown its pot and been planted somewhere. Takeo would have found another place for his spare key, or changed his habits and decided against leaving it outside.

The house key was nowhere on the veranda, but it could easily have been lost in the grass. I bent my head toward the grass and realized the impossibility of the situation. I really did not want to break and enter.

Was there an alarm system? There hadn't been in the old days, but given the value of what was in the house since Takeo's renovation, an alarm would seem like a smart thing to have. I pressed my face against the glass of the sliding windows that led to the living room. The paper *shoji* screens that normally would have shielded the room from the outside were not closed, so I could see into the darkened room, though not very well. It didn't look as if there were motion sensors.

Suddenly, I caught a blur of movement close to my face. To my shock, the sliding door was opening. As I tripped off the veranda in my haste to get away, the door was opened and a flashlight shone straight in my face.

Instinctively, I shut my eyes against the light. I knew I looked as gruesome and bedraggled as a mythical sea monster that had been thrown up out of the raging bay beyond the cliffs. And like a monster, I wanted to roar out my anguish at the trip I'd taken, only to be caught as a failure. But instead, all that came from me was a hoarse whimper.

The flashlight beam dropped, and I blinked my eyes to look at Takeo.

"Rei?" His voice was incredulous.

"Yes." I couldn't think of anything else to say.

Then Takeo said something I never expected to hear. "Come in."

17

Fifteen minutes later, I was in water again. But this time it was hot, surrounding me and still cascading out of a faucet. Takeo had sent me to his bathroom and had lit the candles, turned on the taps, thrown a towel and a robe at me, and left. I'd showered quickly, scrubbing off the dirt that had splashed over me outside, and entered the deep, hot bath. As I gazed at the candles on the bath's edge, illuminating the room like the Kannon's temple, I could admit to myself how foolhardy my journey had been. But I'd reached the end, I'd faced Takeo, and he'd let me inside.

I'd hoped to be alone, but if I played things carefully, I could still complete my mission. I was probably within a few rooms' distance of the vessel. Of course, the rooms all looked so different now, full of furniture and new things. Just like this bathroom, which had been redone with tiny tiles of amber, gold, and cream-colored glass that winked in the soft candlelight. There was a new sink that looked like a *raku* pottery bowl perched on a slate ledge. The bath's Grohe faucet was bronze and very modern, designed so that water tumbled out in a wide, flat sheet.

The sensual comfort of my bath made me feel guilty. The typhoon hadn't reached its apogee. The bathtub should be used as a collecting device for cold water, not for soaking myself.

After I'd toweled off and wrapped myself in the quilted winter *yukata* robe that Takeo had given me, I went out, following the banging noises to find Takeo outside on the thin ledge of veranda that ran around the house, pulling closed heavy wooden shutters. He waved at me, looking oddly happy, although he was now the bedraggled one, with wet clothes and leaves stuck in his hair.

"I'm almost done," he shouted, so I could hear him through the glass. "Just a few more rooms and all the shutters will be closed."

He came in a few minutes later, and I helped him get off his wet raincoat and boots in the flagstone entryway.

"You look like you need to warm up. I left the bath full," I said. It was Japanese custom to enter a bath clean, as I'd done, and reuse the same bathwater for the whole family. And if Takeo relaxed in a bath, I'd have the perfect opportunity for a quick look around the house.

"Okay, I'll go in. It could be the last hot bath for a while, if the town shuts off the gas supply," Takeo said, running a hand through his wet hair.

"I'd like to clean it out afterward and fill it with clean water," I said. "You'll want to have water stored, just in case."

"You're right. There was flooding here back in the seventies, when I was a child," Takeo said. "The house wasn't damaged, but we were without water and electricity for days. It was exciting for me then, but not so exciting for my father. I seem to remember we had houseguests who wound up stranded with us for a week."

"I don't want to do that to you," I said quickly. "But things are pretty bad outside—"

"You must stay overnight," Takeo said shortly. "You said the trains have stopped."

"Well, I'll do what I can to help you. I'm going to go through the rooms to make sure no delicate ceramics are near the windows, and so on. Would that be all right?"

Takeo smiled. "Thank you. You always remember the things I forget about."

"I hope Emi won't misinterpret my being here. Did she drive down with you?" My question was automatic, out of courtesy. I was certain that Emi wasn't around.

"No. She's back in Setagaya at her parents' house."

"Did she go there to stay during the storm?" I remembered how Norie had wanted me nearby.

"No, she's always there. It's her home until after the wedding, of course."

"Oh, of course." I was relieved to know she wouldn't be stumbling upon me in Takeo's robe. "But that's rough on the two of you, I suppose, all that parental control."

"We find our moments, here and there." Takeo winked at me and then went off to the bathroom.

After he left, I pondered what he'd said. This wasn't the way an arranged marriage was supposed to operate. But I'd caught a strong sexual current flowing between Emi and Takeo. It was a relief, really; I wouldn't have to worry about any unwelcome advances from him, though I hadn't understood why Takeo had winked at me. Was it because he now saw me as a buddy, an old friend with whom he'd share gossip about his girlfriend?

I reminded myself of what I really needed to be thinking about, and I got to work in the living room, going first to the sliding-door cabinet along an interior wall. I'd always admired this particular cabinet, which was covered in hand-painted paper that showed two girls, one in kimono and the other in a modish 1920s dress, sitting on a cliff overlooking water—a view similar to that of the east side of Takeo's garden. I thought, looking at it more carefully, it had to be the house's garden.

As I continued my flashlight tour of the various reception rooms, I found plenty of vases, small and large, but no ibex vessel. I was fortunate that I'd have the night hours to keep looking. If the vessel really were in the house, I'd definitely find it.

By the time I was done putting away the breakable items I'd mentioned to Takeo, the wind was at a nightmare pitch outside and there were frequent, ominous bangs against the closed shutters. Out of curiosity, I opened the front door a crack and felt myself stagger backward from the force of the sea wind.

There really was no chance of getting out tonight. After latching the door, I ventured into the kitchen to see what kind of provisions

Takeo had. He'd expected to be staying in his house alone, so I doubted he'd have stocked enough for two people to get through more than a day. I also knew he wasn't the kind who believed in canned and packaged foods. Not that he was someone who cooked from scratch; Takeo liked to order restaurant food at the last minute, but I doubted that the local pizza and ramen shops would be making deliveries.

I found uncooked rice and a few other basics in the cupboard, but the best prospect was the contents of a shopping bag from Matsuya's basement food arcade that I found sitting on the kitchen table.

It was better than I'd expected, and perfect for a vegetarian like myself: marinated tofu, pickled vegetables, roasted yams, spinach croquettes, and a petite apple tart. I put a saucepan of water on the stove to boil for the rice I'd make. Now there would be plenty for dinner and perhaps breakfast the next day.

I checked the refrigerator and found cans of energy drink and soy sauce, but nothing more. No bottled water. This was a new worry, so I went back to the crowded kitchen cabinet and took out the largest container, an old *miso* jar, and began filling it at the kitchen sink.

"I thought you were putting away the ceramics, not taking them out," Takeo said when he joined me a minute later.

"I didn't see any bottled water in your fridge, so I thought I should take a few preparations. And this was the largest container I could find."

"And one of the nicest," Takeo said. "You chose a two-hundred-year-old Kyushu piece."

"I didn't mean to use your oldest piece, but I didn't see anything more suitable. Sorry!"

"Oh, it's not the oldest ceramic in the house, but it has a great deal of sentimental value. It's been in our family a few generations, you know—"

"Do you want me to put it away?"

He shook his head. "Of course not. If it has held *miso* without accident for a couple of hundred years, it can hold water for a night or two. The fact is, I only have a half-case of bottled water in my car, which we'd better leave for emergencies. And I'll open sake tonight. Or would you prefer wine?" Takeo pried open the storage compartment that was built into the center of the kitchen floor. Where most Japanese would have stored root vegetables, he had squeezed in a wine rack and a wooden sake box.

"I—it doesn't really matter. I'll just have a glass of—whatever. Did you refill the bathtub with clean water?"

"Yes, indeed. And what do you mean, it doesn't matter? It's not like you to defer to anyone else about taste." Takeo's voice was teasing. Clearly, the bath had relaxed him.

"I'd say the same was true for you, too, except for your diplomatic reaction to the handbag painting." I smiled at him.

"The handbag painting—damn!" Takeo said. "After all of Emi's reminders, I still forgot to bring it. I was just thinking about the shutters."

"I hope Emi's not too upset." I didn't meet his eyes, but went instead to the stove, where I saw that the flame under the rice had gone out. "Hey, I can't get the burner back on."

Takeo went to the Tokyo Gas heater next to the kitchen counter and fiddled for a minute. "Well, I can tell you why. The gas has been turned off at the source."

"What does that mean?" Suddenly my thoughts were back to the storm outside. "Let's put the radio on."

There was no working radio in the house, so Takeo put a raincoat over himself and ran out to his car to listen to its radio. He came back ten minutes later with a report that the storm was at its peak, no great surprise to either of us.

"I wish there were better information than that," I fretted while Takeo shook off his wet coat for the second time in half an hour and laid it down in the entryway to dry.

"Well, if something really awful happens, we'll hear about it on the town loudspeaker. They broadcast from the police department, don't you remember?"

Any announcements of disaster would come after the fact, I thought grimly as I began arranging the takeout food on a blue-

and-white Imari platter. The Kayama villa, perched on a hill, would be a terrible place to be stranded or involved in a mudslide.

But I couldn't brood fatalistically, not when I'd been given such a succession of good luck: the miraculous passage to Hayama, unforced entry to Takeo's house, and food to sustain me. I was safe inside, and that was what counted.

18

Five minutes later, I had fixed the dinner tray and followed the sound of tinny, nostalgic music coming from the sitting room. Takeo had lit the room with hurricane lamps and candles. I set the food down on a low, lacquered art deco table and looked over at Takeo, who was hunched over a vintage windup gramophone I'd never seen opened before. Nearby there was a stack of old records, some of them just in paper sleeves and others in the original cardboard cases, their illustrations so faded that I could barely make them out.

"These are my grandfather's *enka* records," Takeo said, as if in answer to my inquiring glance.

I nodded, because I could have guessed as much. *Enka* was a kind of people's music, a songwriting tradition that combined current events with human feelings and flourished in Japan from the late nineteenth century into the early twentieth. I'd written a paper in college about the illustration of songbook covers, but I'd never actually heard a recorded *enka* song from this period. Listening to a wavering male voice barely audible against the wind outside, all the while standing in an almost dark house from the period, made me shiver.

I saw also that Takeo had filled a hibachi, a Japanese wooden table with a built-in brazier, with coal and lit it. A little screen sat above the glowing embers, and on it he'd placed a bowl of water, and within that, a flask of sake. I suggested that we finish cooking the rice on it. After I took the rice off to rest and finish its last ten minutes of steam-cooking, Takeo put the sake back on. It was time to eat.

The minute I'd sat down across from him and started to serve the food, a wrenching sound came from above.

"It sounds as if the roof's coming off!" I looked up in alarm.

"It's probably just some tiles. I remember, when I was having the roof replaced, you weren't pleased with the adhesive. Now I regret not following your advice," Takeo said.

"Well, I didn't push you very hard on it. You had a valid point about its toxicity, and whether it might get into the water supply." I couldn't put a finger on why Takeo was so mellow and gentle all of a sudden. I knew I should be grateful, but it made me a bit uneasy.

"Speaking of toxins, this is for you." Takeo handed me a brimming, gold-edged sake cup. "To what shall we toast?"

"How about to—just being here?" I offered. This was the way I felt. I'd thought getting into the villa was going to be impossible, and now I was in, having a cozy evening with an old friend. But now, of course, I found myself with a new problem. When I located the ibex vessel—as I was almost certain I'd do, tonight—what would happen to Takeo? I'd been angry at him the last two days, but now that our friendship had been restored, what I was going to do could turn out very badly for him.

"To being here. Together," Takeo added as an afterthought.

I joined him in clinking glasses. The sake burned my throat after the first sip, so I put down the glass. And while the carryout food was delicious, I found myself unable to eat more than a few bites.

"You've hardly eaten. Is there something wrong with the food?" Takeo said after a while.

"Not at all. I was just thinking I'd better—save it. I know there's not much for tomorrow, and what if—"

"What if we're here for days?" Takeo laughed. "There is a bag of rice in a kitchen cabinet, and we won't even have to go down to the beach to fish. The fish will be thrown up here—I remember that from the storm when I was a boy."

"And there's *daikon* growing in your garden, right? We'll be fine." Fine—except that the idea of playing house with a suspected international art thief made me feel queasy. Takeo's glass of sake was already empty, so I did what Japanese etiquette called for and filled it for him. Promptly, he refilled mine even though it was still two-thirds full.

"I saw a picture of this room in a magazine," I said. "It looks so different tonight, and I don't think it's just the lighting. Did you put a lot of the valuables away—I mean, things that were arranged in the room for the shoot?"

"I don't think we define valuable in the same way," Takeo said, instead of answering me directly. "To me, the first camellia I planted and raised as a boy is more valuable than any painting. Hey, why aren't you drinking?"

"I don't want to get a headache." It was interesting, but while I was away from Hugh, I was drinking about a quarter as much.

"I'm sure you won't," Takeo said. "Unless it's from that scream-ing wind outside. Shall I put on a new record?"

"All right," I said reluctantly. Maybe I'd gone too far with my questions.

This time, the recorded voice was that of a woman. As her sweet, high-pitched voice crackled from the old machine, I heard snatches of phrases about school, a school uniform, a lover. At the end of the song, the needle ran on, bumping again and again at the record's edge. Takeo seemed lost in thought and didn't move, so I got up and put the needle back on its rest.

"What did you think of the lyrics?" he asked when I returned to the table and sat down on the *zabuton* cushion.

"I caught something about a lover and pine needles and a school uniform, but that's about it," I confessed.

"The song is called 'Voice of the Pine.' It's the story of a young student who, after she lives away from her family for the first time, becomes corrupted."

Too close to home for me. I asked, "What about the rest of the lyrics?"

"She sings that she's forgotten all her teacher's lessons because of her nighttime lover. She wears a schoolgirl uniform wrapped around her shameless heart by day, but by night, she changes into fancy clothes, and wonders to whom she'll show those colors." Takeo paused. "It's a very sad ending, maybe not right for tonight."

"It sounds like a Japanese Lolita story," I mused aloud. "You've got to tell me the ending!"

"After her family and lover desert her, she knows there is nothing left to live for, so she drowns herself in the Sumida River."

"People must have died along the coast today. Flash floods like those I saw, flying tiles—"

"You're so pessimistic." Takeo leaned over and took my left hand, which I'd been using to shred up the paper doily from under the croquettes.

"You must be careful not to corrupt yourself," I said, finding myself unable to withdraw my hand from the caress. In a room this dark, with the wind howling outside, the feeling of Takeo's touch was electrifying.

"And what about you?" he asked. "When you started your perilous journey to this house, did you telephone your own fiancé in Washington to tell him whom you were going to see?"

"He's not my fiancé," I said defensively, as thoughts began to whirl through my head. Takeo thought I'd come to Hayama to see him. "This evening is starting to feel strange. I apologize if I have confused you."

"Wait a minute. Did you just say that you are not engaged?" Takeo's voice sounded strange.

"I'm not. There's no ring. Didn't you see that?" I extracted my left hand, the one he'd been holding, and waved it at him.

Takeo's expression, in the dim light, appeared almost dazed. "After missing you for three years, your hand wasn't the first thing I looked at. It was more—the rest of you—the whole person—"

"I'm sure I look older," I said drily.

"You look more sophisticated, actually. And the way you carry yourself—your body, it's quite—muscular and more firm now, isn't it?" Takeo finished his glass of sake and poured himself another, as if he'd forgotten all the rules about drinking.

"Emi is absolutely exquisite," I protested, suddenly noticing that my *yukata* was gaping open on one side, exposing a bit more than my trapezius.

"I agree. And sometimes I feel quite ready to be married to her. Other times, not so ready." He looked at me again. "What would happen if I kissed you?"

"I guess I'd have to knock you through the shutters out into the storm. Although of course, it's your house, not mine, so that doesn't seem entirely fair—"

"You are the one who's not fair!" Takeo said, his voice rising with emotion. "I didn't know that you decided not to marry. And look at what's happened to my life, in the meantime."

"You never loved me, and I remind you that you willingly entered into your *omiai*." I couldn't figure out whether Takeo was drunk or just a bit tipsy. I had barely had more than a few sips because I knew I needed to stay very sober for my night's work—if I ever got around to it.

"Forget the *omiai*." Takeo's voice cracked, and then he kissed me.

Hugh. I absorbed the kiss, and began to respond to it. *Forgive me.* It was odd; the more I tried to think about Hugh, the less clear his image was. He was like the faded illustration on the record jackets. Everything that I had feared, back at the Smithsonian conference table, had come to pass.

Was it really wrong to do this? I wondered as the wind howled outside. Quickly, I'd moved from nervousness to something entirely different. We weren't sitting at the table anymore, but were stretched out on the floor, the hallowed ground where nobody ever wore shoes and we'd made love. And if I stopped Takeo, what would become of the night, the vessel, the whole reason I was there?

This was good, I said to myself as Takeo discovered the navel ring, laughing softly before he moved lower. I dug my fingers into Takeo's straight, thick hair and closed my eyes, giving in to my rising level of excitement. It was about time I relaxed, because ever since my arrival I'd been anxious about everything: the theft of my phone, my lack of progress in the mission, and the beautiful young girl who'd taken my place.

Well, now I was the one with Takeo, not Emi, and that in itself was arousing. Takeo, as corrupt as he might be about antiques and love, was also bizarrely safe—a man on the verge of marriage who would never come after me with messy, emotional demands.

So I did it: everything that he wanted, and then the things that I wanted, too, things I'd been afraid to ask Hugh, because they seemed too—foreign. Too Japanese. It was fate, I told myself, as Takeo sank into me so deeply that the tatami matting underneath me indented my skin. Then I didn't notice the scratchy mat anymore, didn't notice anything except the desire inside me gathering and intensifying, a typhoon that had come out of nowhere but seemed incapable of lessening.

Afterward, Takeo led me into the bedroom, where I was stunned to see the Chinese altar bed made up with fresh linens. It was only then, when he asked me to lie down again, that I really heard the sound of the wind outside the house, and I realized it sounded like someone crying.

19

Afterward, Takeo fell asleep almost immediately.

Just what I wanted—time to work. I waited twenty minutes to be sure he wasn't going to wake up, then tiptoed back to the living room, where I wrapped up in the discarded robe lying on the tatami. The sight of it shamed me deeply. But what would have happened, I thought, if I hadn't followed Takeo's lead? We'd still be up talking—arguing, probably. There would have been no chance at all to look for the ibex ewer.

I walked the edge of the room, thinking about where it must have gone. Takeo might have placed it in formal storage—a bank vault, or something like that. I shook myself. No, that couldn't be. Takeo didn't take care of valuable objects in the manner that I did. To Takeo, the ewer was like any other object he used to arrange flowers. After he was done with the magazine shoot, he would have taken the old flowers out to the compost heap, rinsed the vessel in the house's deepest sink—the one in the kitchen—and put it away. It wasn't the right way to treat an old piece of earthenware, but then, Takeo was even less of a curator than I.

The kitchen. I hadn't really looked through it yet. I carried the hurricane lamp with me into the kitchen. I saw a flash of movement, and realized that a mouse had run across the floor. Well, we'd been too caught up in things to put away the original food containers, which lay open on the kitchen table.

Where would Takeo put a vessel that he used for flower arranging? My eye was drawn to the massive old cherrywood *tansu* cupboard along one side of the wall. I gently opened the first sliding wood panel and held the hurricane light close as I peered inside. Sturdy blue-and-white teacups nestled alongside various earthenware bowls. The second compartment held square plates of different colors, some old and decorated with elegant hand-painted designs, as well as plainer modern ones.

I got to my knees and opened the lower sliding compartment doors. A prosaic watering can brushing the edge of a colorful Dale Chihuly glass vase that I remembered was one of Takeo's favorites. As I touched the glass vase to withdraw it, it made a scraping sound. Something was shoved in, tight behind. I wiggled out the vase, and there it was: the ibex vessel.

For a moment, I just stared. Then I lifted it gently to the kitchen table. It felt so light, lighter than I'd expected—it could break so easily. I found myself trembling, after I'd gotten it to the table. I hurried to the *genkan* to retrieve my backpack, where I had my reference photos and notes about the characteristics of Mesopotamian pottery stored in an inner compartment.

The papers were dry, thanks to the fact that I'd kept them in a plastic zip bag. I also pulled out my measuring tape, because size was the first thing to check.

Takeo's vessel stood eight-and-one-quarter inches high, as did the piece taken from the museum. *Good for the government; not good for Takeo*, I thought as I continued my survey. The ewer was reddish brown, as Elizabeth Cameron had said it would be; it also had a pleasing irregularity at the top edge, something that she hadn't mentioned but that seemed consistent for an old, hand-shaped piece. I closed my eyes and held the ewer, trying to memorize its texture. Too bad I didn't have the camera-phone: I could have had a digitally enhanced picture to compare with the slide from the museum—just as, if I'd had a chance to get to a professional laboratory, I could have had its age checked through thermoluminescence testing. All I had was my magnifying glass.

I used the glass to help me focus on the slight crackle of the ewer's surface, and then ran my fingers lightly over it. Strange that the piece had survived so long without a chip—but that was consistent with the museum's description. I held it to my nose and sniffed inside, catching the faintest odor of something organic. Takeo hadn't cleaned it the way many *ikebana* artists would have, with a mixture of water and bleach. That was good for the ewer, at least.

A natural thief, I reminded myself. I'd been sent across the Pacific to find out the truth about an object, and I'd found out the truth about a man. What had I expected? I'd felt so torn, wanting to succeed at the mission of finding the vessel; now I'd done that, but I was on the verge of destroying someone's life. No, three lives. I'd screwed up things for Takeo and for his fiancée, not to mention Hugh.

What was the next step? I stared through watery eyes at the vessel, losing focus. I was tired. A flash of movement at the periphery of the room startled me. I refocused and saw that Takeo was standing in the doorway.

"You're awake," I said, starting to put away the pictures. "I was restless, so I thought I'd clean up the kitchen."

He sat down across from me at the table, the hurricane light and ibex vessel between us. "This pottery certainly doesn't need to be cleaned."

"I—I—noticed it in the magazine photo. I wanted to look at it a bit. I don't know much about Mesopotamian ceramics, and I'm interested, you know, branching out a bit into Near Asia, as the scholars are calling the region now—"

"You have some papers with you."

I shoved them back into my backpack. "Sorry, it's confidential."

"What?" Takeo's expression turned from curious to hurt.

"Where did you get it, Takeo? Who sold it to you?"

Takeo shook his head at me. "Sorry, that's confidential."

I looked at him and sighed. "It was a mistake. I'm sorry."

Takeo gave me a long look. "Well, I'm not going to be able to sleep again. I'll make some tea."

"But the gas doesn't work—"

"The gas heater light came on again. That means Tokyo Gas and

Electric turned it on." Takeo filled a cast-iron teakettle at the kitchen tap. "And we never lost our water, either. This typhoon was a big deception."

The rain was much lighter now, it was true. But I knew he was referring to more than the storm. I would have to talk to him somehow, without giving things away.

"You were about to mention who sold this vessel to you?" I asked when Takeo brought the teakettle over to the table.

"Nobody sold it. It was given to me." He placed the kettle precisely on a rush mat, so the heat wouldn't hurt the table. Then he moved back to the *tansu* and selected two mottled green tea bowls for us to drink from.

I hadn't expected that, although it could be an excuse someone would use if he'd knowingly trafficked in stolen goods.

"So who was the generous giver?" I asked, when he sat down across from me again.

"I think I've told you enough," Takeo said lightly. "Now it's time for you to tell me what I want to know, things like whether you even wanted to make love with me in the first place!"

"Why won't you tell me who? As I mentioned before, I'm really interested in this type of ancient pottery—"

"It's out of your league, Rei. You couldn't afford it. It's a thousand years old."

The vessel was at least twice as old, I thought but did not say. "Who gave it to you? Takeo, it's very important that I know."

"None of your business." Takeo poured the tea, refusing to meet my gaze.

"Emi. You must have received it from her, or her father—" What Mr. Watanabe had mentioned about her father's previous government posting in Turkey came back to me.

He gave me a long look. "It was from her father, to celebrate the engagement. And now I've given you what you so desperately craved, tell me what I want to understand—why you pretended that you wanted me when all you really were after was one of my possessions!"

"I'm not going to take it." I put my hand over Takeo's. "I can only suggest one thing to you, that this vessel might be better off back with Emi's family—at least until the wedding. Believe me, Takeo, I'm suggesting this for your own well-being."

"I can't."

"Why not?" I couldn't even begin to sip the tea Takeo had made. It was too hot.

"Because—because I had seen it in their home, and admired it, so he gave it to me. It was part of the *omiai* process. I don't think you can possibly understand—"

"Oh, but I do." I looked at Takeo steadily. "Mr. Harada gave you something very precious because he wanted you to ensure that you married his daughter."

"I didn't agree to marry her because of a piece of pottery!"

"Of course you didn't. You decided to marry because of her father and what he could do to advance your environmental causes."

Takeo's skin flushed with anger, but he didn't deny it. He just sat silently.

I thought again. "Okay, I understand now why you can't return it to the house. But maybe you should keep it somewhere safer for the time being, like a bank vault. I could assist you with setting something up."

"If you think I should put everything over three hundred years of age in a vault, this house would be half-empty."

"Takeo, I'll do it for you, if you like. Please, just believe me this once—"

"I'm afraid I've been too believing," Takeo said. "Our last evening—it was all a show, wasn't it?"

"It wasn't," I said, not wanting to think about the fact that I'd come twice, two betrayals of Hugh within seventy-two hours of my arrival in Japan. I shouldn't have felt this kind of pleasure with someone who was so bad for me.

When things were awkward, the best solution was escape. I stood up and said that I was going to pack up.

"But it's still raining," Takeo said. "Your clothes are wet and the floodwaters still must be high—"

"I've really overstayed my time here," I said. "I'm sorry. I wonder if you would be kind enough to lend me jeans and a T-shirt or something like that. I'll mail them back."

It was almost nine in the morning by the time I'd taken my shower and gotten Takeo to lend me a shrunken pair of drawstring farmer's pants, one of his many Greenpeace T-shirts, and thick wool socks that would protect my feet from the wet insides of the rain shoes.

"You forgot something," Takeo called after me as I unlocked and slid open the front door. There was no more rain, but everything, from the top of the bamboo fence to the leaves and grasses, glittered with teardrops of water. Along the driveway, there were large puddles, but I knew I could make my way out—even if I had to cross people's property to stay on high ground.

"I don't think so," I muttered, continuing down the stone driveway.

"Take it! I want you to have it as a memento, since this was what you were really after."

I turned and saw he was holding the vessel carelessly, a couple of fingers in the handle.

"Don't drop it!" I shouted, unable to hide my fear.

"You've always cared for things more than people, haven't you?" Takeo shook his head.

It was more than that. Maybe the anger was a face-saving move, I thought suddenly. Takeo could have finally understood that there was something amiss with his engagement gift and wanted out of the whole corrupt deal.

"All right, I'll take it, thank you very much." I strode up to him, thinking, this will settle it for all. It's not the way the people in Washington expected things to go, but I wouldn't look a gift ibex in the mouth.

Takeo placed the vessel in my hands. "I'm sorry, Rei."

"You don't have to say it—"

"You're right that what we did doesn't—work—anymore." He shook his head mournfully. "And I can never undo what I've done to Emi."

"It may sound unbelievable, but I do wish the two of you well. I wasn't trying to take you away—" I tried to blink away the tears that were forming.

"I understand," Takeo said shortly. "Well, we won't do it again. We've learned."

"I guess this will be good-bye, then," I said. We looked at each other for a long moment.

"I probably shouldn't see you again. In Japan, it's just—"

"I know. My aunt explained how things have to be." I paused. "Well, if I'm going off with your vessel, I want to travel safely. Could I trouble you for a good, strong box and lots of packing paper?"

We walked into the house again, and I set the vessel down on the tea table in the living room, while Takeo came up with a box and tissue paper. The sound of the unlocked front door sliding open startled both of us. We exchanged glances.

"Your father?" I asked nervously.

"He's in Kyoto. I don't know who it could be."

I had a sudden flash of fear, as if someone had come for the vessel, just as I'd finally gotten my hands on it.

Takeo gave me a last look and walked out of the room toward the entryway. After a moment's hesitation, I followed, reasoning that it would be better to present a united front against a burglar, if that's what we were up against. I took the precaution of picking up a telephone receiver, because even though it didn't work, the burglar wouldn't know.

I stopped short in the hallway when I saw the small, slim girl in a pink raincoat holding a Hermès print Kitty umbrella.

Emi had arrived.

20

"Emi-chan, how wonderful to see you. You came all by yourself? What a surprise!" Takeo, never good at pretending, didn't sound happy at all.

Instead of answering him, Emi stared at me, her eyes, if anything, larger than before.

"It was just a quick visit," I stammered. "I—I am just now leaving—"

"But you are wearing his clothes." She gestured at the Greenpeace T-shirt and baggy farmer's pants that I had rolled up a few inches over my ankles.

I thought quickly. "Yes, I was caught in the rain. My clothes were soaked through. He kindly lent these things to me so I could walk out to catch a train back to the city. In fact, I was just leaving—"

"You always say you're leaving."

I stopped, remembering what I'd said to her the last time.

"The rain stopped last night," Emi continued. "So you must have come yesterday."

"It was a surprise visit," Takeo said before I could muster up another faltering excuse.

"Oh, I see. Just as the auction was a surprise, and going to the Kaikan was a—coincidence!"

"I'm sorry," I said.

"Sorry!" Emi's voice cracked. "And to think I was so silly to ask my father's driver to go to the trouble of bringing me here. Everyone advised against it, so why did I come?"

"Are you saying that the floods have subsided, then?" Takeo said. I could have shaken him for his insensitivity.

"Not all of them. I was scared we wouldn't make it, but I really wanted to see you. I brought the painting that you forgot."

The handbag painting. She'd risked driving sixty kilometers in a typhoon-struck region to make sure Takeo saw the handbag painting in the house. Or maybe she'd done it because she'd had a sense that we'd meet in Hayama and things would happen.

"I'll bring in the painting. We'll all look at it," I offered, sliding into my shoes and starting out the *genkan* to the garden. I saw a long black car idling, and a blue-uniformed man standing in the garden, his hands crossed before him. When he saw me, he made a quick bow.

"Excuse me, but could there be . . . an honorable hand-washing place . . ."

I could imagine how long the car trip had been. I took the painting out of the trunk of the idling car and led the driver into the house and to the powder room off the hallway. After that, I thought I'd see if I could discreetly get the ewer out of the living room and into my backpack.

When I ducked my head into the room, I found that Takeo and Emi had gotten there first. Takeo had put his hands on Emi's shoulders, but she was twisting away. In doing so, she caught sight of me and gasped.

"Do you want him? Well, you can have him!"

"Please calm down, darling. Nothing has changed. Rei will assure you of the same thing." His eyes pleaded with me.

"I have no interest in Takeo," I said softly. "All he is to me is an old friend—"

"Oh, that story. Old friends, old times. Just because I'm young doesn't mean that I'm stupid. I know when it's time to go, and I'm leaving—" She broke away from Takeo. Passing the *tansu*, she grabbed up the vessel. She paused for a minute, then swiveled toward me.

"I'm sorry you're upset," I said. "I wish you all the best for your marriage, I was just telling Takeo."

"Everything's changed, since you've come. It's because of you—" and before I could realize it, the ewer was hurtling through the air, right at me.

I screamed and reached out my hands for it, but I was distracted by the sight of Takeo, in my peripheral vision, diving in front. We bumped into each other just as the ibex ewer hit the tatami.

"Oh, no!" I screamed, feeling my own world crash along with it. Emi dashed from the room. Takeo ran after her. A car door slammed and an engine started.

As if on cue, the chauffeur emerged from the powder room, drying his hands. At the sound of squealing tires, his head turned toward the open door. "What's that?"

"It sounds like someone went," I said, stepping clumsily into my shoes and hurrying out, just to see the limousine slaloming down the hilly driveway. Takeo and Emi were nowhere in sight—obviously, they'd gone off together.

"She's not driving, is she?" he asked, his face crumpling into an expression of panic.

"I don't know who's behind the wheel," I said.

"She must be driving. And if anything happens, I shall be held responsible. I should never have left the car to tend to my selfish personal needs—" The chauffeur gave me a little wave and started running down the driveway.

"You're not going to catch them!" I called after him. "They were going—really fast!"

"I must try!" His voice floated back to me faintly as he disappeared down the hill.

I wasn't going to join the chase. I had my own disaster to clean up. I stepped out of my shoes and dejectedly dragged myself back to the living room, where the vessel lay in pieces.

I sank to my knees, examining the fragments. It was terrible how easily the vessel had broken. Heavy clay usually broke in larger chunks, and perhaps might have even survived a fall onto a mat-covered floor. The only reason could be the force with which Emi had thrown it.

I took a tissue from my pocket and began to lay the pieces of pottery on it. I couldn't imagine how I was going to explain to Michael Hendricks what had happened to the priceless vessel. Suddenly, the loss of my visa to Japan seemed like nothing in comparison with my knowledge I'd caused the destruction of one of the oldest, greatest antiquities of the Middle East—no, of the world.

Ouch. A rough bit that I'd picked up broke through the skin of my forefinger, and I watched idly as a tiny drop of blood slowly formed through the open skin. Earthenware wasn't usually hard enough to cause damage when it broke, but it somehow seemed appropriate for me to have blood on my hands, mixed with the dust of one of civilization's ruined treasures. I left the ruins on the floor to get up to find some toilet paper to stanch the bleeding. In the process, I stepped on more broken pottery. Damn it. I crouched down to pick the piece out of my thick sock, and then I saw it— the interesting texture I'd felt in the night, patterned with light, rightward-swirling whorls from its time on the potter's wheel.

I stood there, my bleeding finger forgotten, feeling my heart hammer as I looked, shard by shard, to make certain about my conclusion. Yes, the ewer had been formed on a potter's wheel, an invention that wasn't part of ancient Mesopotamian pottery making. I examined it further, making mental notes.

Takeo's vessel was a fake. And for once, a fraudulent antique was a very good bit of news. No world treasure had been smashed. Takeo wasn't guilty of harboring stolen art; neither for that matter were Emi's parents. Everyone was off the hook, and I could shoot out of this hellhole of Japanese embarrassment back to Washington fast—tomorrow, maybe. I'd make a few calls to see if I needed to take the shards all the way back to Washington or whether Mr. Watanabe could accept them.

I used the box Takeo had found for me but had hastily abandoned upon Emi's arrival. Every sizable piece went in, and then I used a damp cloth to wipe clean the place on the tatami where the vessel had fallen. As I packed up the shards, I thought about whether I should leave Takeo a message telling him not to worry about the loss.

I couldn't, I realized: any note that Emi found might set her off in another rage. I would have to go incommunicado, permanently. But the important thing I could hold to myself was that their engagement present was innocent, even if their relationship wasn't, anymore.

21

The train system was running again, but slowly. While I was waiting at Zushi station, I picked up the pay phone and was happy to hear a dial tone. Guilt made me call Hugh first, but I was still cowardly enough to use his number at work, where I could assume—from the time of night—he would be absent. I left a voice message saying that I'd been cut off from communication because of the typhoon, and added that I'd lost my cell phone, so if he wanted to reach me, it would have to be by phoning the Grand Hyatt.

Next, I called Michael Hendricks; yes, it was two in the morning Washington time, but I figured he would rather hear something from me, after two days of silence, than nothing at all. He picked up his cell phone halfway through the first ring. Either he was already awake or he was as jumpy a sleeper as I.

"Well, what a dramatic surprise. I thought you'd gone AWOL," he grumbled after I'd identified myself.

"I have a really good explanation."

"I'm glad. I was beginning to wonder if I needed to send the JSDF after you."

"JSDF?" I asked, thinking Michael trafficked in far too many acronyms.

"Japanese Self-Defense Forces. Our friends in uniform."

"Michael, first I lost the cell phone. Then with the typhoon, I couldn't find a working phone, not until five minutes ago."

"And where is this phone?" his voice was clipped.

"At a station platform in Zushi. I know it's nonsecure, but I'm sorry. It was all I could get, and you were saying you wanted to hear from me—I've got good news."

"You made contact with Mr. Flowers?"

"Better than that." In a few sentences, I told him that I'd found the vessel and ascertained that it couldn't possibly be 3,000 years old. But Michael wasn't as pleased as I'd expected. He expressed horror at the breakage, and he seemed doubtful that I was right about its age. Also, he wanted to know more about the circumstances of the accident—chiefly, why Emi had been around and angry enough to throw it.

"It was all a misunderstanding. She drove up unexpectedly and discovered me talking with Mr. Flowers." There. I kept it short and simple.

"Hold on. You said you were at the house, but I didn't know Flowers was involved. Did you—tell him that you were interested in the Momoyama vase?"

"Of course not! He thought I was just there to get out of the rain. We closed up the house, had dinner, and afterward, I took advantage of the time he was sleeping to find the vessel." The hell if I was going to tell him what I'd had to do to get Takeo to fall asleep. "Unfortunately, he discovered me examining it, but I think he believes that I'm interested in Near Eastern art. And it was good that I talked to him, because he explained the thing was actually an engagement present from her parents."

"I see." Michael was quiet for a moment. "So when did they become engaged?"

"I believe it was last June."

"The photo spread came out in May," said Michael. "So he actually had the vessel well before this engagement."

"I don't know why," I said. "Maybe they gave it to him a little bit earlier, when they were hoping he would follow through with asking her to marry him."

"It strikes me as odd," Michael said. "There's too much mystery about the ownership, and we don't know the piece's age until the lab experts examine the fragments."

"I thought you hired me because I am an expert," I said. "But that's okay, I can hand over the shards to Mr. Watanabe to take wherever you like."

"No names, please. Have you told him that you have the vase?" Michael's voice was tense. When I replied in the negative, he said, "Good. Let's keep the situation between the two of us, for now. I'd like you to package up everything and send it by the fastest air service possible. I'll use the lab at the Sackler, of course."

"What's going on? I thought you and our—Japanese colleague—were partners in this project."

"His role was to make the phone calls to let you back into the country legally, and to assist you, should you have found yourself on the wrong side of the police, which fortunately has not happened yet."

"All right, boss. Or may I call you captain?"

"I retired as a lieutenant, okay? And I don't mean to snap at you. It's just I've been a little—worried, because of the botched call earlier."

"Which call?"

"You called me yesterday around two in the morning. I assumed because of the weather situation, the signal was lost."

"But I didn't call you," I said.

"You did. I saw the number of your government phone flash up on my phone's caller ID feature."

"Like I said a few minutes ago, I lost the cell phone. If a call was placed using it to you, it must have been made by whoever has the phone." Now I told him in detail about how the cell phone had disappeared from my backpack.

"Whoever had it must have broken your password," Michael said. "What the hell did you choose—your birthday or your first name, something that anyone could think of?"

"Why does it matter what I chose?" I answered, thinking sorrowfully that Take0 had been far too simple.

"When did you last use the phone? Think about whether anyone was watching you or listening."

"That night I called you from the bar—there was a guy, this an-noying Austrian, who came up to me wanting to see the phone. I said no, of course, and he wandered off, but he might have been listening when I was talking with my friends later on—not that I said anything about the mission or Flowers, but still—"

"Have you seen this guy again?"

"No. I remember him introducing himself to me as Jürgen. I could probably find out where he's staying—I'm sure it's one of those backpacker flophouses."

"Don't bother," Michael said. "You need to stay focused. I'll send you a new cell phone, but not to the hotel where you were. Can you find yourself a safer location?"

"My aunt and uncle's house in Yokohama is pretty far off the radar screen. But what's the point? I finished the job. I was hoping to call a travel agent today to get on a flight home."

"But the job's not over," Michael said.

"I found the vessel—"

"You found a Momoyama vase," Michael corrected. "It's not necessarily the right one, as you said. There could be two vases: a real one and a reproduction."

I sighed. "What if it was a fake all the time in the National Museum, and nobody knew it?"

"If that's the case, whoever bought it from the looters is still guilty of a felony. And as it stands, things definitely sound suspicious. Someone may have stolen your government phone to ascertain who your contacts are."

I didn't want to concede that Michael was right, but what he was saying fit into the troubled thoughts I'd had while walking to the Zushi train station.

"I don't want you calling this cell number or my office number anymore. I'll get a new cell for myself and give you that number the next time we speak at your aunt's house. Can you move there today?"

"I guess so. I was getting to like that hotel, though." Oh, for a hot shower there, and room service.

"You're being watched, Rei. Your current location is unsafe. Pack up, pay the bill with your government credit card, and discreetly make your way to Yokohama."

"But can't I find another place? I could maybe rent a room some-where."

"A rented room is not as secure as a family home."

But a family home meant protection, meaning I'd get nothing done. I said a depressed good-bye as the train pulled slowly into the station.

In Tokyo there was standing water at some street corners, and a lot of trash blown about, but none of the kind of devastation I'd seen on the Miura peninsula. I picked up both the *Japan Times* and the *Asahi* to read while I rode the last stretch, a bit of subway, over to Roppongi. The newspapers said that Japan's southeastern edge had been hit very hard, with billions of yen lost in property damage, and twenty people dead. At least five people had been swept over bridges similar to the one I'd crossed in Zushi—the account from eyewitnesses of how these people had been lost made me cringe at my misplaced bravery.

The Hyatt's desk clerk had noticed my absence the previous night and expressed relief that I hadn't been a casualty of the storm. I apologized for causing her worry, then asked her to please pre-pare my bill and call a private car to take me to the airport, as I'd be checking out shortly.

"Have you shortened your business trip?" the clerk asked.

Why did she care? And how did she know I was on business? Suddenly paranoid, I said, "It was always going to be a quick trip, but now at least the planes are able to fly, so I can get out."

When I made it up to the hotel room, it took a moment to re-member which switches operated the curtains and lights. While I stripped off Takeo's clothes and stuffed them into the plastic bag meant for laundry, I turned on the television to see what the ty-phoon had wrought.

After that I took the shower I'd been long awaiting, and dressed in Grand's suit, perfectly cleaned by the hotel's dry cleaner. Then it was time to pack. I was beginning to regret my various shopping sprees, because even tiny things like bras take up space, if you've bought six of them. Packing the underwear, so lacy and cheerful, made me think about Hugh. I toyed with the idea of calling him to tell him I was going to be at Norie's, then reminded myself that he was still sleeping. I'd check in with him later when things weren't so hectic. And I still needed time to figure out what I would say. The Japanese had a don't ask, don't tell policy toward infidelity. And Hugh might be happier knowing nothing—especially since this had been an infidelity that would never be repeated.

Emi Harada. Takeo Kayama. The names floated back into my consciousness, and I realized that it wasn't because I was thinking aloud. The television announcer was saying something about Emi and Takeo.

I turned back to the television, where the story had changed to the cost of typhoon damage. I began channel surfing and stopped on TBS, the sensational channel, which was showing a snapshot of Emi at her high school graduation.

Emi Harada, daughter of the current minister for environmental affairs, was in critical condition at Saint Luke's Hospital in Tokyo following an automobile accident in Hayama. The car in which she was traveling, witnesses said, had run through a traffic light, hitting one car, then crashing through a souvenir shop and out to the beach. Her companion had also been in the car but escaped injury and reportedly pulled Harada from the car. I saw a shot of Takeo from behind, following police officers into a sedan.

Emi was injured, and it was my fault. So what if she'd been at the wheel—her mind had been somewhere else, back at the house, where she'd seen me and instantly understood the horrible thing I'd done. It had been so upsetting that she'd had to flee, had no time to wait for the driver. She'd been a novice steering a huge sedan, and her mind had been crazed with rage and perhaps fatigue. And the crash must have been shattering. I suppose it was a miracle that Takeo hadn't been hurt; I'd clearly seen him walking away. But why away? He should have gone with his fiancée to the hospital. The police could have asked any questions they had there. Unless . . .

Unless, I finished thinking, Emi had been trying to kill them both.

Now my sorrow for Emi began to mix with panic for myself. If the police were investigating the accident as an attempted murder-suicide, the whole business about motive would come up. And how long could Takeo stave them off without telling what he'd done the previous evening . . . and with whom?

Everything had changed. I was out of my room fifteen minutes later, my hair still wet from the bath. Now I knew that I had to break all contact with Takeo. Sending back the clothing I'd borrowed was too much of a risk, so I balled up the shirt and pants in a plastic bag and threw it into the trash collection bag hanging on an unattended maid's cart in my hallway. The clothes were gone in an instant. Too bad the rest of my problems couldn't have gone there, too.

I sailed downstairs on the noiseless elevator, paid my bill, and slid into the backseat of the Mercedes the front desk clerk had summoned. I told the driver to take me to the nearest DHL office, where I went in and mailed the shards of the vessel—except for one piece that I'd wrapped in tissue and kept in the outer pocket of my cell phone holder. I had made a snap decision about the piece; I could be wrong. I wanted to hold on to something until I knew for certain.

After I'd paid, not flinching at the high overnight charge, I jumped back into the car and asked the driver to take me to Shibuya Station. Even though I could have paid him to take me all the way to Yokohama, I didn't want a record of the address where I was headed. Instead, I'd take my chances on the train, watching carefully when I disembarked at Minami-Makigahara Station to see if anyone was following me.

It turned out that I was the only one to get out at my aunt's neighborhood station. I walked slowly uphill, trailing my suitcase behind me. A major storm might have swept the region, tearing limbs from trees, but in the Shimura family's tidy neighborhood, the streets had already been swept clean of organic litter by the housewives. Aunt Norie even had taken advantage of a few particularly graceful pomegranate boughs and arranged them in a large Satsuma urn outside her front door. I studied the tranquil, undeniably practical arrangement as I waited for someone to answer the doorbell. After five minutes, I realized the bell might not be working, so I rapped lightly on the door.

Chika answered promptly. She looked from me to my suitcase, then back again. "What's this?"

"You're supposed to welcome me." I leaned forward to peck her cheek. My cousin smelled like baby powder and looked fresh as ever in a starched white T-shirt and low-waisted Burberry plaid pants.

"But you had a room in a great hotel! Why in the world would you come here? We have no electricity or gas, probably for another day."

"You're my relatives and I'd rather be with you, helping in any way that I can," I said piously, exchanging my rain shoes for a cheery pair of tartan slippers my aunt kept on hand for guests. "Why would I prefer to stay in some impersonal box of a hotel room?"

"A box with room service and privacy," Chika said. "If you don't want your hotel room, I do. With the band coming in, I want to be staying nearby, and have, you know, freedom of movement."

"Freedom?" Aunt Norie, carrying a pail of broken camellia branches, appeared in the entryway, a frown etched between her eyebrows. "What kind of freedom is that, can you explain to your mother?"

22

Chika looked down at the fuzzy balls on her house slippers, then at me, as if for help.

I cleared my throat and ad-libbed, "It's just what I was explaining to her, that I once believed freedom of movement was so important, but now that I'm older I know it is family that counts. I wish I'd followed your advice and stayed here during the typhoon."

"*Ah so desu ka!* Yes, you do understand." Norie turned her gaze toward me, fondly. "What a good surprise to see you today. I'm sorry that we don't have hot water for you, or any electricity at all—we are using the old things you like, though, lanterns and hibachis and such—"

"Does your telephone work?" I asked.

Chika answered for her mother. "Not yet, but our neighbor heard that it may be restored by evening. I'm so worried that, you know, the band will arrive and not be able to reach me."

"But Rei-san probably needs the telephone for work purposes, which is more serious. Especially since the cell networks are down." Norie frowned at me. "I hope that our conditions don't last so long they cause an imposition."

I assured my aunt that they wouldn't, and then, after I'd moved my suitcase into the downstairs tatami room and laid out the futon for myself, I started cleanup duty. For an hour I picked up branches in the garden, and then I ruthlessly cleaned out all the spoiled food in the fridge. Aunt Norie sent Chika and me on foot to the grocery store, because she wanted to conserve what gas was in the tank of the family car. Pumps wouldn't be operable at gas stations until the power came back.

Chika and I came back with less than we'd hoped to get. All the bread was sold out, and the grocery store had the same issues of spoiled cold foods that we had in the house. We wound up with packages of Japanese curry sauce, a few vegetables and fruits, and canned soup, coffee, and beans—all things I reasoned that we could put in a pan and heat over the hibachi.

To my surprise, Norie already had a pot of rice and hot soup made when we returned—she'd grated the dried bonito fish she kept in a wooden box, and mixed in the homemade *miso* she fermented herself and stored under the kitchen floor. She garnished this perfect soup with some *shiso* leaf she'd grown in the garden.

While Chika set to making a curry from the vegetables and a packet of sauce, I complimented my aunt on her ability to run a calm household during a crisis. She shook off the praise. "Being here is easy," she said, as she deftly peeled a potato she was holding in one hand. "Your uncle was stranded at his office for two days! I am looking forward to greeting him tonight after two days away. And Tsutomu, well, he should have come today, but he's stayed on. The hospitals in Yokohama and the smaller places without power are sending the medical emergencies to Tokyo, so it's quite a lot of work for St. Luke's and all the other hospitals. I plan to go tomorrow morning to volunteer."

"I'll go with you," I said, picking up the potato peels out of the sink and putting them in the trash.

"But what about your work?" Norie asked. "I don't want to interfere with it. What do you still need to do, exactly?"

"Nothing, really," I said. "I'm just hanging tight for a few days."

"Will you see Takeo-kun again?" my aunt asked. It was the first time my aunt had mentioned him since the afternoon at the Kaikan.

"I—I don't think I need to," I said. "That meeting took care of all our unfinished business. Thank you for your help."

"He didn't seem so—pleased at the surprise. I've been worrying about what I should do the next time I am faced with him at a flower event."

"There is no need to worry," I said. "Really. I think you were right, it's just about impossible for a man and woman in Japan to be friends. Especially after an engagement," I added.

"Well, so now you know."

Dealing with the electrical shortage had kept me from thinking about Takeo and Emi, but Norie's questioning had brought back all the horror of the infidelity, the discovery, and the car crash. I didn't have much to say during dinner, even though Uncle Hiroshi and Tom arrived home around eight, in time to eat with everyone around the hibachi. Now I watched the family eating the ready-made curry, proclaiming it as good as any from a restaurant downtown. To me, the sauce was too thick and overspiced, but I never liked Japanese versions of Indian food.

My cousin Tom glanced over, raising his eyebrows at my lack of appetite, but I didn't react, and he retreated back into his own distracted state. He'd been that way ever since he'd returned. The hospital was overflowing. People with chronic conditions who needed electricity to operate their ventilators and IVs had come in, along with those who had become dehydrated from lack of water, were cut by broken glass, or who had injured themselves falling over things in their dark houses. Tomorrow, he predicted grimly, there would be a new group with food poisoning. And to top it all, the victim of a bad car accident had been flown in by helicopter. The operating room had been completely full, so she'd had to be transferred by ambulance to a hospital on the east side.

The lights came back on midway through the meal, and everyone cheered. Norie rushed to turn on the television that usually formed the soundtrack to all household meals, and Chika excused herself to use the phone. Uncle Hiroshi was talking about floods at his favorite golf course, and while I nodded to show that I was listening, my thoughts remained focused on what Tom had said. The accident victim he'd mentioned sounded as if it could be Emi. I wanted to ask him about her, but not in front of anyone.

It took a long time to clean up, since the water was still off and we had to do things with a store of rainwater in the backyard. But finally, the dishes were as clean as they'd get, and I settled down with my relatives to watch the TV news at eleven.

There was news about Emi Harada. It wasn't good. Norie, who of course hadn't heard the earlier TV report, turned to me and gasped, but I kept my eyes on the screen, where a reporter was soberly telling the world that after three emergency surgeries and the efforts of eight doctors from two of Tokyo's leading hospitals, eighteen-year-old Emi Harada had died.

23

I had a premonition of bad media, so I expected to find a flotilla of TV vehicles outside Norie's house the next morning. But at six in the morning, I was still blessedly anonymous, albeit depressed. I'd do anything to undo my trip to Hayama; if I hadn't been there with Takeo, Emi would still be alive.

I tiptoed downstairs to make tea for myself but discovered that Tom had beaten me to the task. He was at the dining table, a steaming cup at his side and the morning paper in front of him. He'd been reading an article about Emi Harada, I deduced from the photo that I spotted on the lower half of the folded paper.

"Is she—the patient you couldn't admit?" I said, picking up the Imari teapot and pouring a cup of green tea for myself.

"How did you know?" Tom looked up at me, and I saw the pain on his face.

"I knew about her being airlifted to your hospital," I said. "So it was a guess."

"Well, you guessed right. But the fact was, we didn't admit her." Tom explained that the emergency airlift to St. Luke's had been disastrous. He, the ER chief, hadn't known she was coming in until the helicopter was ten minutes away. And both of the hospital's operating rooms were in use. There was no space to treat her, so he'd had the hospital radio back to take the patient elsewhere. The helicopter wound up landing, anyway, and Emi had been transferred by one of St. Luke's ambulances to Hiroo Hospital.

"What was it, actually, that caused her death? Bleeding or—"

"The article doesn't mention the specific cause." Tom shook his head. "Instead, there's lots of detail about how she was going to marry Takeo Kayama next month. No wonder Mother was so upset yesterday evening, because of that connection."

"Will you read the article to me?" I asked. Tom was one of the few people who knew that I had the reading level of only a Japanese third-grader.

"Certainly. But it doesn't say much." Tom read aloud the short article, which reported that Kenichi Harada had apologized for his daughter's accident to the owners of the souvenir shop and the chief of police in Hayama.

"I know that people here apologize about as often as they breathe, but this is ridiculous!" I fumed, thinking of how futile being sorry was. I'd said it to Emi, and it had just sent her rushing off to the car. "He's a man who's lost a child. Why should he be organizing apologies right now?"

"Rei-chan, her death caused a huge use of police and fire vehicles when they were needed for storm relief. Think about how the families of suicide victims pay if someone jumps the tracks and causes a commuting delay. Frankly, if anyone else needs to offer an apology, it's probably me," he said glumly.

"You? But why?"

Tom folded the paper up, as if he could store away the trouble, before he spoke. "I did not stabilize her before sending her on, and she was clearly in shock, from the paramedics' description." He took a deep breath. "The hour that follows a trauma is what we call the golden hour. A patient has the very best chance for survival, if treatment comes during that hour."

"But you had no available operating room, you said."

"I could have stabilized her for transit. Made sure she had adequate IV fluids, at least." He looked down at the folded paper, then back at me. "Why are you so interested in this, anyway? It is my problem, not yours."

"Actually, the problem is kind of—ours."

"How so?" Tom looked at me warily.

"I was introduced to her through Takeo."

"Really! Was she a nice person? Did you like her?"

I nodded slowly, because the truth was that I'd thought she was shallow, until the end when I'd realized that she actually loved Takeo. And now—she was gone. There was no chance for her to re-build her relationship with Takeo, or to reconsider her life and wait to get married to somebody who was really right for her. I felt terri-ble.

"You're crying." Tom grabbed a paper napkin out of the holder in the table's center.

"I don't mean to, I'm sorry."

"You must explain more, because this is not a normal reaction," Tom said.

"Emi thought I wanted to take him away from her. That's why she died."

"That makes no sense," Tom said. "How do you know what she was thinking, anyway? You just met her briefly at the auction house, right?"

"When she saw us—socializing—at Takeo's house, she became so upset that she jumped into her father's car and drove off." I spoke in a monotone, trying to keep from crying again. "She was so distraught, Tom, I wonder if she willfully crashed the car—"

"Just because you were socializing with an old friend?" Tom looked at me hard. "What form, exactly, did this socializing take?"

"We were just there, together." I couldn't bring myself to explain the full story. "But she mistakenly thought we'd become a serious romantic couple. Of course she didn't know about Hugh."

"Do you mean to say that—during the typhoon—you were in Hayama?" Tom interrupted, his voice incredulous. "You must have been. That's where the accident happened."

I nodded glumly. "Please don't tell anyone. I am still in a panic that the whole story will get out, somehow."

"Why? Do you think that she mentioned you to her parents? Or anyone else in her family?"

"She's an only child, and she couldn't have talked to her parents that fast. She literally saw me, put things together in her mind about what happened, started yelling at Takeo, threw—threw—a piece of china—and ran out of the house into the car." I paused. "But there was the driver of the car, who arrived at the house. He saw me."

There was a sound of movement upstairs. Aunt Norie was getting ready to come down.

"That's a shame," Tom said. "I'd say that we need to arm ourselves with a bit of knowledge about the causes of her death." Tom paused. "I have a colleague at Hiroo Hospital who may have some information."

"But that—that action could cause more attention," I said. "And why do we need to know the minutiae? She's dead, that's enough for me. I feel bad enough already."

Tom shook his head. "Emi's father is very powerful. We need to know who's at fault in the death, because he could ask for an investigation into the emergency transport for her medical care. And in any case, I'm going to make my own apology to him."

"Do you mean—you'll write a letter?" I cringed at this idea of Tom declaring himself at fault on paper. And given the mood he was in, he'd probably expose me, too.

"I'll see him at the funeral services at their home in Setagaya. It makes sense, because last night, after you went to bed, Mother was on the telephone with her flower arranging friends getting information about the memorial. I know she's going. I'll go, too, if I can find someone to cover for me at work."

The Japanese mourn quickly. Emi's cremation, which was attended by close family members, was set for the very next evening. And to my dismay, Aunt Norie was insistent that I also attend.

"It doesn't seem right that I go, Obasan," I said to her, when she first raised the issue with me. We were doing the laundry, for her a daily ritual that had been postponed during the time of the typhoon. Norie was ironing, and I was folding the ironed things.

"But you must. Already I've determined that Hiroshi and Chika cannot go because of his office schedule. For me to go alone, without family, is embarrassing."

"But your son Tsutomu's going to be there." Absently, I matched one of my cousin's black socks with a brown one, then caught myself.

"Yes, but he's a bundle of nerves. He won't do much good at my side, whereas you are like the elder daughter I never had. You will be a good reflection on us and the Kayama School." Aunt Norie kept her eyes on me as she ironed, completely in control.

"I don't want to go." But as I said it, I was thinking of what Michael wanted me to do, to find out more about the art and antiques holdings of the Haradas. This would be a way to get that done, all at once. But it felt like preying on Emi's family at a rough time—a time that had come about because of the injection of me into Emi and Takeo's romance. Emi's death was my fault.

"You look sickly, Rei-chan," my aunt said, expertly flipping over a pair of my underpants to iron its other side. I always fought against her ironing my underwear, but she always won.

"It's—it's the smell of that spray starch," I said.

"Well, you've not left this house—except once, to go to the store—since your arrival. I need you beside me. I can hardly believe that you would refuse to pay your respects to the young woman who was going to be the *iemoto*'s wife, the future of our flower arranging school."

And so it came to be that a few hours later, I was squeezed next to my aunt on the Toyoko Line train bound for Setagaya. Tom, who had gone into work hours earlier, would meet us on the platform promptly at 5:02.

"So, is everyone from the flower arranging school coming?" I hoped so, because if there was a large crowd I was less likely to be noticed by the people I was loath to see: Emi's family, their chauffeur, and Takeo.

"Oh, no," my aunt said. "Apparently, Takeo-san asked only the top administrators to be there—and of course, the few teachers who had been involved in Emi-san's training."

"Did you teach Emi?" I asked, startled by this revelation.

My aunt dropped her gaze to her lap and smoothed the black

wool crepe skirt she was wearing. I was in black, too—a business suit taken out of Chika's closet that was almost perfect, except that the skirt was a few inches too short. My aunt had given me a silk handkerchief she'd ironed that morning to spread over my knees to protect my modesty.

"Well, I was supposed to teach her."

"Aha," I said. "So it didn't actually happen?"

My aunt glanced around, as if she feared she might be overheard. The seats we'd taken together actually had some empty spaces around them, because although it was rush hour, we were headed into the city instead of out. "Emi-san was scheduled to take a private morning workshop with me twice a week, but actually, she didn't come after the first time. Maybe it was because she had so much trouble."

I felt a flash of sympathy for Emi. "She couldn't be worse than I was. Don't you remember all those embarrassing times for me at the school?"

My aunt shook her head. "It's true, Rei-chan, you do not have a natural gift for flower arrangement, but you can concentrate and follow directions. I don't like to speak ill of the dead, but Emi seemed—distracted. Not quite there. I imagine she was thinking exciting thoughts about her engagement, needed to shop for clothes and china—that kind of thing."

It was true that Emi loved to buy things. Maybe my aunt was right. I nodded and said, "Well, anyway, it will be good to go with you. I'm not the greatest at knowing what to do at funerals. I'll just follow your lead."

"Oh, I'm a very poor example to follow," Norie said. "I failed to involve her enough in *ikebana*. I just couldn't understand her." Norie put her hand in her purse and touched the *kouden*, a small envelope containing cash that she was bringing to the funeral. I'd contributed 5,000 yen of my own to the envelope, bringing the total to 15,000. I doubted that her family needed financial help with funeral expenses, but bringing *kouden* was important as a show of respect.

"You're an excellent teacher. It's a shame she didn't come back for a second lesson."

Norie sighed. "I just couldn't understand her, in the same way that I can't understand the situation with Takeo-san."

"Really," I said cagily.

"I find it strange that there has been so little mentioned in the media about Takeo-san. He was shown briefly on television last night; I recognized him. And surely, she was visiting him in Hayama, though why so soon after the storm, when the roads are bad, I don't understand. Unless . . ." My aunt's voice trailed off.

"Unless what?" I asked dutifully, wondering if she had guessed anything about my role. Tom wouldn't rat on me, I was sure of that.

"Unless Emi spent the night of the storm with him, in his house. Yes, that must be it!" Norie's voice was low, but strong with conviction. "No parent would ever want the news to be known that his daughter spent her last hours at an overnight visit with a boyfriend."

"I suppose not," I said, relieved that the heat was off. "But surely Takeo will be at the funeral?"

"I'm sure that he will. And he will need kindness from all of us, and who knows, perhaps in a year or so he will be ready to think about marriage again. Although it will be harder for him, with this scandal on his record."

24

My aunt had no idea of what scandal was, I thought as we got off the train, located Tom looking grim in a black suit, and took a taxi driven by a white-gloved septugenarian to the Haradas' house in Setagaya. As we rode along, Norie talked about the old Shimura family compound about a mile away, the house my grandparents had to give up after the war to American troops, and then never were able to afford to regain. Houses in the calm residential neighborhood filled with tall ginkgo trees were very expensive now—too expensive even for someone like Tom, a successful physician, to buy.

"Who lives here, then?" I asked, and to my surprise our gray-haired driver answered.

"Rich people! Television producers, senior government officials, actors. Do you know the actor in the Samurai Soap commercial? Yes? He lives the next street over. I have driven him once or twice."

Aunt Norie, Tom, and I all exchanged a quick, amused glance, and the man kept up a pleasant patter until we came to a long white wall with a paper lantern outside marked with the *kanji* character for mourning.

"Oh, a funeral. I'm very sorry," the driver said somberly.

"It's actually a memorial service. And thank you," Norie said, fumbling in her purse her reading glasses.

"Eight hundred yen only. And please tell me, when I shall return?"

"I'm not sure," my aunt said. "I thought we would just tele-phone for taxi service in a while—"

"Very few available this evening. And you won't want to incon-venience the mourning family by asking to use their telephone. Re-member, not all the telephone lines are restored in this area."

My hackles went up immediately; it didn't make sense that this man wanted to take us back. But Norie exclaimed that it would be very kind if he came for us in an hour's time.

After we'd gotten out and Tom had buzzed the entry button next to the gate, I whispered to my aunt that I thought we should use Tom's cell phone to call for another taxi to pick us up.

"But why, Rei-chan? It makes sense to have a car waiting, espe-cially in the evening hours. And that nice driver-san will be coming back. If we don't come out for him, he'll ring the bell and that will create a lot of trouble, you know, call attention to us."

"It's odd. I think he's too interested in us. You never know who he might be," I said as the gate swung open silently for us. A long walkway stretched ahead, with a few other black-clad mourners entering through a huge carved door that looked as if it had come from an Indian temple. It was unusual for a Japanese house, but then, so was the house itself—a newly built two-story cream stucco building with stained-glass windows. It looked like a cross between a church and a mosque, I thought, surveying the domed ceiling. No doubt the Haradas had chosen to re-create, in Japan, some of the things they'd admired most during their years abroad.

Inside, the memorial service was different too, chiefly because half the guests appeared to be twenty and under. Young women clutched each other and cried, too young to hide their emotions be-hind handkerchiefs. It seemed like a group, and I imagined most of them had gone to Tokyo International Girls School with Emi. One girl caught my eye, because she wasn't as painfully thin as the oth-ers; she was plump, in fact, and the loose black dress she wore, which reached to mid-calf, only made her look larger. She sat alone on a carved rosewood chair, her reddened eyes darting toward the living room door as each person entered—as if, I thought, Emi might suddenly show up and change everything.

The grown-ups in attendance were, of course, colleagues of Emi's parents. I recognized the chairman of one of Japan's automobile manufacturers, as well as various politicians. Mr. Harada was at the center of them all, grave-faced, wearing a black suit and his old-fashioned black-rimmed spectacles. He was a blur of motion, nodding and bowing to the callers. It hit me that the same kind of mob scene would have taken place a few months later, for the wedding. But then, everyone would have been smiling.

Feeling sick, I turned away and focused my attention on the Haradas' house. Like many upper-class Japanese homes, it had a number of square rooms that could be transformed into larger spaces by opening sliding wood-and-paper screens. But in this house, unlike the other Japanese homes I'd visited, the tatami flooring was covered with Oriental rugs—antique rugs, I realized, as I stooped down to pick up a card that I'd dropped on purpose, in order to get a close look. I couldn't tell a Tabriz from a Kerman, but I could guess that these rugs cost a lot.

The rugs also provided a buffer layer so that the Haradas could use non-Japanese furniture, like the great walnut dining table stacked with *kouden* envelopes and overseen by two unsmiling men in black suits, one of whom I instantly recognized as the chauffeur. I turned away quickly and studied the framed photos of the family with notables. I identified Japan's last prime minister and the host of the most conservative television news program. I thought about what was missing—regular family pictures. But maybe the Haradas didn't think it was right to place casual family snapshots on the same level as their most honored contacts.

I squeezed my way into the kitchen, where half a dozen women wearing aprons and head scarves were arranging trays of food. Everything was rose marble; the appliances were stainless steel, typical in the West but unusual in Japan. Someone had gone to a great deal of trouble to affix photographs to the fridge, which I knew from experience was resistant to magnets. But here, in tiny frames, were the kind of family pictures I'd been looking for: a young father holding a chubby toddler girl on his shoulders. A round-faced schoolgirl in a black uniform standing by the Great Buddha of Kamakura. A plump teenager making rabbit ears over a friend's head, as the two posed in front of the Sphinx.

I could see Emi's big eyes and smile in each girl, but I was stunned by how chubby she'd once been. It was hard to believe, given the Pocky Stick frame she'd shrunk into. Had she developed an eating disorder—and if so, when? Surely it had happened before she'd met Takeo, I thought, remembering the recent school photograph of Emi that had appeared on the television news. She'd been thin then.

One of the caterers asked me what I needed, and I answered vaguely—too vaguely, because I was instructed in no uncertain terms that if I wanted something to eat, it was available in the dining room.

I went out, trying to steer clear of the chauffeur, yet somehow inspect the quality of the Haradas' art and antiques. The problem was that there was almost too much to take note of: a ceramics collection that contained Korean celadon, Chinese blue-and-white and Japanese modern and antique pottery. I was drawn to a simple tea bowl made of a reddish clay that reminded me of the ibex vessel, and I gently lifted it to examine the bottom. Decoding pottery was, for me, much easier than decoding a newspaper; after about ten seconds' study, I had figured out that the bowl had been shaped by Kazu Sakurai, a famous Kyushu artist whom the government had recently named a living national treasure. I put the bowl down carefully, and after I was sure it was settled back into its place, I turned to go into the next room.

Yasuko Harada—Emi's mother—was regarding me with an uncertain expression. I hesitated, not knowing whether I should make some kind of explanation. But before I could do anything, two women descended on Mrs. Harada, bowing and murmuring. My opportunity was lost, but maybe that was a good thing. What could I possibly have said?

I walked purposefully into the next reception room, where a white brocade-covered coffin rested at the foot of a dais constructed in front of the *tokonoma*, the ceremonial alcove that was the focal point of the room. A type of altar had been made around a three- by three-foot framed photograph of Emi. Around it stood a sea of floral wreaths that all had identifying tags showing which company had given them.

I gazed at the portrait of Emi in a stiff brocade floral kimono, a kimono that I knew was typically given on a girl's eighteenth birthday. This "coming-of-age day" kimono was expensive—usually costing between 5 and 15 million yen. In Emi's case, I guessed it had been even more.

The young, sad girl I'd noticed when I'd entered the house was standing near me, looking at the picture of Emi. Then she knelt next to the coffin, folded her hands in prayer, and whispered something. In the end, she peered into the little window through which Emi's face showed. She got up rapidly, and backed off.

I had been avoiding looking at the corpse, but I did look now. Emi's eyes were closed, her long lashes lying neatly against her fair skin. She looked like a beautiful young girl asleep. I found myself having the same reaction as the other girl, leaving quickly. It was too sad to linger over this sleeping beauty who could never wake up.

"Did you know her from high school?" I asked the girl, when I caught up with her in the next room over the hors d'oeuvres table.

"Not really. I just started at Waseda, and she is—was not—in college." The girl had been aiming her chopsticks toward a piece of deep-fried tofu, but suddenly changed direction to a piece of sashimi. Was it guilt, because I was standing near her?

"That tofu looks good," I said mildly.

"Yes, but too oily."

Just as I'd thought. "So, how did you know Emi-san?"

"My family lives nearby. We attended primary school and junior high together. Then she went away to Turkey, and came back last year. Her parents sent her to Tokyo International Girls School. That's where those other girls are from." She tilted her head toward the other room.

Often, when Japanese families took their children with them to live abroad for a while, they felt that they could never again enroll the children in a traditional Japanese school. At such a school, discrimination against a child who spoke English too well, and had gotten used to certain freedoms, was too likely. I imagined that the Haradas might have thought this way—but it didn't quite jibe with what I'd expect from a family conservative enough to arrange a marriage for an eighteen-year-old daughter.

"How interesting," I said. "Well, you must be a true friend to have stayed in touch. My name's Rei Shimura. What's yours?"

"Nagasa Fumiko." She bobbed her head. "I would like to think she remained my friend, but I don't know."

"How so?" I asked gently.

"Well, Emi-san used to look more like I do. She became so—slim—in Turkey. And I think she was a little embarrassed to be seen with me."

"Oh, no, you're a lovely person—I envy your skin." I'd had to think fast.

Fumiko shook her head. "Everything had to be perfect for her. Not just the face, but fashion, slimness, manners. Even before she became engaged to that *ikebana* headmaster."

I noted the way she spoke about Takeo—rather flatly, with no special enthusiasm. Maybe she thought the arranged marriage was a bad idea. I wanted to ask her about it, but suddenly there was a swelling of noise in the next room, a raising of voices and the sound of someone male, shouting in poor Japanese. "Please. Just to see—"

The hubbub rose, and Fumiko and I exchanged glances. There was a sound of something breaking in the next room. I waved at her to follow me. If something was happening between people, maybe she could provide an explanation.

In one corner I saw a caterer bent over a smashed cocktail glass, and a huddle of women around her, trying to help. But all the action was heading out of the room toward the entryway. A beautiful foreign boy with dark curly hair, wearing a black shirt and black jeans, was being hustled out of the house by three smaller Japanese men, including the chauffeur. The boy's full lips were twisted in a grimace and his eyes blazed with wetness—tears? I was stunned. The sight of such naked emotion made me want to draw back, as if I'd intruded.

"He's here," Fumiko murmured.

"Is that one of Emi's old friends?"

She shook her head.

"Then who is he?" I persisted.

"I'm sorry." She looked at me, and I saw a mixture of sorrow and panic on her face. "I have to leave."

"I didn't mean to—" I started to say, but Fumiko had pushed her way through the crowd as if she couldn't get away quickly enough.

"Do you understand anything about what happened?" I asked Tom, when I'd squeezed my way through the throng to where he was standing.

"I don't exactly know. I saw that foreigner talking to the other young people. Then those men asked him to leave, and he tried to resist."

"Those were the men who guarded the *kouden* envelopes," Norie interjected. "Maybe he was trying to take some money. Now, Rei-chan, tell me, are you enjoying yourself? The house is so beautiful!"

I looked at her. "It's hard to have a nice time at a funeral."

"True, true, it's terribly sad, but the food is lovely. And I've gotten the chance to meet some nice young friends of Emi-san's, a few of whom are thinking of enrolling to study *ikebana* in one of our holiday mini-courses."

"Really." My thoughts about the boy who'd been thrown out vanished.

I was making my way back to the mourning room when I spotted Takeo Kayama, looking right at me as he wove his way through the crowd.

I gave him a warning look and shook my head slightly, but he continued in my direction. I'd known he would be at the memorial, but I'd assumed he would use good sense and stay away from me. Well, I had some choices of my own, and my choice was not to talk to him.

I made it through the doorway before he did and, spying hall stairs carpeted with an Oriental runner, hurried up them. Nobody would think of going into private living quarters during a memorial. I crouched against the wall under a painting by the French artist Balthus of an Asian nude, despite the barking dog behind a nearby closed door.

A Balthus painting, come to think of it, was a very significant personal asset. I turned around in my crouch and tilted my head back so that I could study the oil painting of the Japanese-looking woman who was standing at a mirror, her robe open, with a malevolent-looking dwarf peeking through an opened door at her. It looked like the cousin to a very famous Balthus painting, which showed a half-dressed Japanese woman reclining in a bathroom with Turkish tiles, gazing at herself in a hand mirror.

How could a civil servant afford an original painting by Balthus? I tried to memorize the details of the painting to check against the Art Loss Register, a website devoted to tracing stolen art. It had to be a real Balthus, didn't it, if there was a motion sensor above the frame?

My examination was suddenly interrupted by the soft waterfall sound of a flushing toilet. Before I could change my position, a door opened halfway down the hall from me. Mr. Harada came out. As he headed toward the stairs, he caught sight of me and stopped.

25

I bowed, but Mr. Harada was staring intensely. I wondered whether he remembered me from the auction house, and if he had even heard anything about me from Emi.

"There are dogs up here. You must not go inside," he said firmly.

"I was actually looking for a bathroom—"

"There is a facility downstairs," he said stiffly. "Any of the caterers can show you."

I was lucky that he believed that I only wanted to go to the bathroom. Quickly, I bowed my head again and apologized. Then I went into a short recitation of the words people used, at funerals, to convey sympathy for a terrible loss. At the end, I said, "I'm so sorry about your daughter's passing. She was much too young."

"She was our greatest treasure," he said, keeping a wary eye on me.

"Yes, there are many beautiful things in art and nature, but nothing as lovely as a child." After I said it, I felt a rush of pain. My private pain, the one I tried not to think about.

He nodded. "That's right. I'm sorry, I didn't hear your name."

He was trying to place me. I hesitated, remembering Tom's worries about liability, but also his desire to apologize. "I'm Shimura Rei. I'm here with my family, who are connected to the *ikebana* school—"

I didn't finish, because Mr. Harada had raised his hand to someone in the hall downstairs and moved on as if I didn't exist.

I spent the next fifteen minutes glued to my aunt, ducking behind her every time Takeo entered the room. I noticed that Mr. Harada motioned to Takeo several times, bringing him into one circle of men after another. The two of them had a strong relationship, it was clear. I noticed the way Takeo held Mr. Harada's arm, almost supporting him at times. Mr. Harada hadn't been exactly warm to me, but why should he be, under the circumstances? I saw now how shaky he was, and I was glad Takeo had moved on from pursuit of me to concentrate instead on his intended father-in-law.

It turned out that I was wrong about Takeo. When it was time for my aunt, Tom, and me to locate our shoes among the dozens visitors had left stacked in the shoe cabinet, Takeo descended on me again.

"Help." I heard his voice in my ear as I was bending to put on my shoes. As I turned to see him we bumped foreheads. It hurt, but that wasn't half as bad as my realization that Aunt Norie was right behind us, witnessing the encounter.

"Help me, Rei," Takeo repeated softly in English, as if to make his words less likely to be understood.

I could imagine the kind of help he wanted. Well, I wasn't delivering it again. I jammed my feet into my shoes and launched myself out the front door. Our taxi was waiting. I planned to get into it, lock the doors, and wait for the rest of my party to assemble.

But Takeo ran out after me, not even bothering to find his own shoes. He closed the distance between us, and once we were outside the house's gate, he grabbed my arms and faced me in the warm orange light of the funeral lanterns.

"Use some sense." I shook off his hold. "Your fiancée is lying in a box inside the house and you're trying to chase me down."

"Because I need to talk to you about—what happened with Emi."

The taxi driver had seen me, and had swung the black door open automatically for me; I bounded in, but unfortunately Takeo followed. I jumped out on the other side, so I was standing on the street, and he followed me out again.

"If you don't want to talk here, give me your cell phone number. I'll contact you later."

"I don't have one. My phone was stolen."

"Stolen! So you're having strange problems too."

"I may have my own problems, Takeo, but let me tell you, they're nothing compared with what *could* happen. We mustn't attract attention."

"Nobody can see with the taxi blocking us like this." Takeo ran a hand through his hair. "It's about Emi. I'm facing legal troubles because of the way she died, and I don't know what to do."

"You are?" I felt a twinge of worry mixed with guilt. I knew that the whole nightmarish scene inside had been caused by my own rash actions.

As if sensing he'd hit on something that affected me, Takeo spoke again. "We have to talk. You're the only one who can help me, at this point."

"All right, I'll talk to you," I said quickly. "But I don't know where we could possibly meet. I can never go back to your house in Hayama, and please don't suggest my aunt's house, because she really wouldn't approve—"

"If you are with your aunt in Yokohama, let's meet at Sankei-en. Behind the big teahouse, there's a forest trail. I will be waiting there tomorrow at eleven."

"Good-bye for now," I whispered and climbed back into the taxi just as its door swung open for my relatives.

Norie immediately wanted to know what Takeo had wanted. I told her that I was too upset to talk. The driver muttered as if to himself about the crazy younger generation.

We caught our train, and an hour later we were home. It was nine o'clock. Uncle Hiroshi had come in the door a few minutes earlier and was impatient for his supper. Norie started cooking, and I used the time to ask Tom about what had happened with Mr. Harada. We were downstairs in the corner of the dining room, where I had busied myself setting the table. Tom was leafing through a fax that had come in on the telephone-fax set up on a side table.

"So, how did the apology go?" I asked.

"It was fine," he said shortly. "He seemed more jumpy and distracted than angry. I suppose that's natural, given the situation."

"Did you actually admit that you were the one who said St. Luke's couldn't take her?"

"I told him I was in charge of emergency services that day, and the rooms were full. I said that we organized the taxi that took her to Hiroo Hospital." Tom picked up the second paper. "Looking at this medical note, it made sense that we sent her to Hiroo. It's one of the few hospitals in Tokyo with a unit for treating drug overdoses."

"A drug overdose?" I caught my breath.

"Technically, she died because her heart stopped. In fact, she lost consciousness before she crashed the car."

"Do you think it was an attempted suicide?"

"Not at all." He swallowed hard, then went on. "There were high levels of amphetamine in her blood."

"What kind of amphetamines?" I asked, thinking about a lot of things, all at once: how casual Simone had acted about the pills that she and Richard had shared. They hadn't made it seem much more dangerous than a few drinks. But Emi had taken amphetamines, and they'd stopped her heart.

"An autopsy will determine exactly what it was," Tom said. "Though chances are it will never be publicized. My guess is that it's just a kind of diet pill that's very popular with young women. Ephedrine, speed, maybe even Ecstasy, though that's still more popular with foreigners."

"I assume she was an occasional user?" I asked, thinking of Richard's laid-back attitude.

"No," Tom said shortly. "Her body was cachetic—the muscle mass and fat were wasting away. She'd been using for many months, if not years. And the pathology reports showed high deposits of lead—one of the by-products of synthetically made drugs like speed."

"Lead poisoning makes it hard for people to concentrate," I said, remembering how Emi hadn't been able to follow a flower arranging class.

"You're right about lead doing that, and the amphetamine itself makes people paranoid," Tom explained. "Ironically, the effects of amphetamines, at first, make the users feel that they can perform better at work, or on tests, or even with their sex partners. Many different versions of amphetamines are popular with gay men—"

"I know," I said glumly, thinking of Richard. I couldn't believe he had fallen into drugs, and so had Emi—a young girl gone, the result of paranoid rage that had sent her hurtling off in the driver's seat of a limousine, causing all manner of havoc before her heart finally gave up.

"What's going on in this country?" I moaned. "I leave for a little while and come back and find that everyone's gone crazy, being self-destructive—"

"It's true that Japanese behavior has become more similar to that in your country. Amphetamines are our most abused drug. This used to be more a problem limited to the military and businessmen, but now you can buy speed pills in almost any Tokyo nightclub, and if you're a girl, well, you often don't have to buy for yourself."

I nodded, thinking that this was a variation of the free drinks on ladies' nights at bars; young women didn't have to pay, because men wanted them to be eager sexual partners.

"Emi went to Tokyo International Girls School," I said. "Maybe she was able to get the drug there. Although from the photos I saw of her at the house, it looked as if she'd already started to slim down while she was living in Turkey. Of course," I said, remembering what Takeo had told me, "she went to the American school there."

"Is that so?" Tom sounded pensive. "Yes, we have had troubles here with Americans and drugs—but you know that." He turned his gaze on me. "You are from San Francisco, the historic center of recreational drug culture. It must have been hard for you to resist cultural influences."

"Oh, come on. Every other person in San Francisco is an ascetic who does nothing, whether it's drugs or meat or sugar." I hated it when my cousin pulled a *sempai* act on me, taking on the role of boss just because he was two years older.

"Well, in any case, it is doubtful that Harada-san is going to reveal publicly the cause of his daughter's death. On the other hand, it's a shame that justice can't be served," Tom grumbled. "I wouldn't be surprised if that foreign boy we saw at the party was a dealer of amphetamines."

"Don't be xenophobic," I chided him, but not too roughly, because I had a burning question. "Tom, is there a way to find out whether the amphetamine was contaminated?"

"What do you mean?"

"I mean, what if it was cut with something lethal?"

"Well, she took it in a tablet form, so that seems unlikely." Tom rifled through the papers. "No, no sign of anything but amphetamine. But as I told you, that in itself can kill."

I nodded, but my thoughts were elsewhere. There was still a chance that Emi's death wasn't accidental. I remembered Takeo's rushed words about the trouble he was in. Was he under suspicion for giving her the drug that had ended her life?

"You seem a bit tense," Tom said. "Now I worry that I shouldn't have told you what I know. And I want you to try to lift your mood. The bad weather must have kept you from running, but perhaps you can start again tomorrow."

"Now that's good therapeutic advice." I smiled at my cousin, who was looking at me anxiously. "All right, I think I will go to Sankei-en tomorrow and run through the gardens."

"Please telephone first to see if it is open," Tom advised. "If there was a lot of storm damage, the place might be closed."

"Of course," I answered, my thoughts still on Emi, the drug, and what Takeo might know.

26

My departure for Sankei-en was complicated by a special delivery of a new cell phone, which came with a padded black case that, in turn, had a steel clasp attached to it. As I hooked the holder into the front right-side pocket of my hooded cashmere sweatshirt, I was reminded of a child having to wear mittens on a string.

The return address on the box was the American embassy in Tokyo. This raised all kinds of questions from Aunt Norie, so I had to embroider yet more details about my job for the Smithsonian. The phone was, if anything, more complicated than the last one I'd had, and I spent twenty minutes figuring it out while I lounged in a quiet section of Minami-Makigahara Station—not a difficult spot to find, since rush hour was over. I was all alone as I finally got the numbers pressed in correctly and heard the sound of a phone ringing in Washington.

"I've been going through a report on the death of the bride," Michael said after we'd exchanged terse greetings.

"And what have you found?"

"The cause of death was never released by the hospital. Typical."

"Actually," I said, feeling a rush of pride, "if you'd like, I can give you some details from the medical record."

"What?" Michael's voice was sharp.

"You can't tell anyone because it could get my source in trouble.

But she died because of heart failure triggered by an amphetamine overdose." I told him about what the medical notes had revealed—and what I'd figured out about her unhealthy weight loss through my conversations with Fumiko and Takeo.

"That's good work," Michael said grudgingly. "I don't suppose—there's anything else?"

Using a minimum of words, I filled him in on what I'd noticed at the Harada house—from the mysterious young man who was thrown out to the expensive Japanese pottery to the Kazu Sakurai bowl and the painting that I thought was a Balthus. I didn't go into the business of Takeo chasing me down.

"I don't suppose you know what paintings by Balthus sell for at auction?" Michael asked when I was through.

I'd checked out all the sales statistics that I could find on the Internet the previous evening, after Tom had gone upstairs and I'd sneaked onto his desktop computer. "One Balthus painting sold in Paris a few years ago for over two million dollars, but that was an isolated case. Since then, the paintings of his that have come on the market went in the range of six hundred thousand to seven hundred thousand dollars. The Kazu Sakurai piece is in a lower range, but still very expensive—I imagine the bowl I examined would sell in the middle four figures, at least. Sakurai doesn't have a website, but I might be able to find out more about the prices directly from his business in Kyushu."

"I see." Michael paused, and I heard the sound of turning pages. "The bride's father—let's call him Mr. Harmony—his annual salary is probably about half of what one of those Balthus paintings you mentioned cost. Do you think he'd blow two years' salary on a painting?"

I'd once blown a year's earnings on a *tansu* chest, but I'd resold it at profit. Maybe Mr. Harada operated in a similar way. "Mr. Harmony could buy for several reasons."

"Such as?"

"Well, he might have inherited money, or he might have made successful investments or earned extra money from another job like consulting. I first saw him at the Meiwashima auction house, and he appeared to be known by the staff. Maybe he sells there as well as buys. He's definitely an art connoisseur. That's why his giving a reproduction historic piece as a gift to his future son-in-law makes no sense to me."

"Speaking of the vessel," Michael said, "I'm surprised you haven't yet asked what our contacts have to say about its provenance."

"It's been evaluated already?" I calculated backward, realizing that the broken ewer couldn't have arrived more than forty-eight hours earlier.

"They're still working on it in the lab, but I've already heard that your theory will likely prove correct."

"Well, thank you very much." This was an understatement. I was relieved to know that I was right, and that I hadn't caused a major loss to international art history.

"You've done fine so far," Michael said. "It must be around nine in the morning there. What's on your agenda today?"

"Tak—Mr. Flowers—wants to meet to talk about something. Legal troubles, he said."

"Well, hold his hand if you must, but don't lose track of the final objective. And don't get embroiled with the Japanese police, okay?"

"I won't even ask a cop for directions. And what's this about the final objective? I believe that I've delivered what you wanted. I should be on my way home now."

"I'd like to keep you around for a while. It seems to me there's something going on with the late bride's family and all their art. I want to know more about the painting, so I can check it against international police records."

I had written a full page of notes about the Balthus, as well as some of the other paintings and artwork. I relayed all the information in detail, then told Michael good-bye as the train rolled in. While using a cell phone was not illegal on trains, it was strongly discouraged—this meant I'd probably be the only person talking in the car, providing an earful of entertainment for whoever could pick up whatever language I was speaking. Until Michael and I developed a new version of pig latin, I was staying off the phone on trains.

• • •

It was this Japanese understanding of the importance of peace and quiet that had led to the establishment of Sankei-en, a lush walled garden in north Yokohama. Tomitaro Hara, a nouveau riche businessman who'd made his fortune in the early nineteenth century, had given his estate grounds so that the public could admire acres of purple iris each spring, followed in turn by cherry blossoms and azaleas. These flowers were out of season now, and the garden had suffered damage in the typhoon. Whole trees had been ripped out of the ground, and at the teahouse Takeo mentioned, the windows had been blown out. A crew of workmen wearing split-toe rubber boots were putting in new windows as I passed by. They called out a warning to me about the trail beyond being blocked. I pretended I didn't hear and continued on.

I'd expected Takeo to be waiting for me, but he wasn't there. I waited a full fifteen minutes before he showed up, looking unlike himself in a Tokyo Giants baseball jersey, oversize cargo pants, and a backward-turned baseball cap. He'd added sunglasses for good measure.

"Did those workmen talk to you?" he asked, shooting a look over his shoulder.

"They told me the trail was blocked," I said.

"Apparently it is. So why don't you proceed out by yourself over to—the pond where the irises bloom? I'll join you there a few minutes later."

I wasn't used to Takeo being as nervous about observation as I was, but these were hard times. I walked back toward the workers and held open the park map, consulting it as if I didn't know the gardens well. I strolled on to the pond. The iris had already bloomed and were just neatly tied bundles of dull green, but the pond was full of geese, which immediately left the water to surround me.

"I have nothing," I told them in both Japanese and English, but they remained around me, stubbornly calling, until I remembered a piece of cookie wrapped in a napkin at the bottom of the backpack and distributed it. But that only set off more excitement, keeping me busy until Takeo arrived.

"These geese are driving me crazy, and I'm tight on time, Takeo. Let's get to the point, okay?" I spoke while making useless shooing gestures with my hands.

"So, what's your next thing, a jogging date?" Takeo looked skeptically at my black yoga pants and tank top, over which I'd layered a hooded zip-front gray cashmere sweater, then sighed. "If only my life was simple."

"No, jogging was my cover to get away from my family. Though you look like you're off to a baseball game, not very smart because I don't believe the Giants ever play this early on a weekday morning."

"There are people who dress like this," Takeo grumbled. "In any case, I don't want to look like myself. The police might be following me."

"Why are the police concerned about you?" I was almost afraid of the answer. Takeo had slept with me because he hadn't been in love with Emi. Her death would have freed him. The facts laid out baldly looked bad for him.

Takeo swallowed hard, looked down, then looked up at me again. "Drugs. Emi actually died from a drug overdose. The police think that because I was the man with her, I gave her the drugs."

"Well, you knew what she was doing, didn't you?"

He looked at me warily. "What do you mean?"

"Did you see her take the pills?"

He shuddered, then nodded. "It happened very fast. She swallowed three pills in the house without even taking water. I tried to stop her, but it was impossible."

I remembered Takeo's arms around Emi. What I'd thought was his effort to comfort her might have really been an attempt to stop her from taking the drugs—if he was really telling me the truth.

"So you knew she was using drugs. The obvious thing would be to tell the police."

"As I told you, they think I was her supplier. Of course you know I'm not."

"Okay, I believe you. Then who could it be?"

"No idea." He shook his head. "Maybe one of her high school friends. There were always a lot of friends stopping by to visit her, or she'd drag me to those ridiculous clubs in Roppongi. I didn't realize she was taking anything until after the *omiai* was set. Then it was too late."

"What do you mean, too late? Better to break an engagement than a marriage."

"Well, I didn't realize it was—serious. A lot of girls take these pills as a diet thing and for energy. I thought that after the wedding, either she'd stop taking them on her own or I could convince her to do so."

He was in a dreamworld. I said, "Let's get back to the accident. She was high—"

"Well, yes. She drove like someone who was crazy, I guess because of the drugs and also not really knowing what she was doing—I'd been trying to steer myself, but I wasn't able to change our course toward the shop, and we hit." He bowed his head. "It was actually my fault."

"But not the death," I said, trying to console him.

"Oh, but it was." Takeo's expression was anguished. "I didn't mention the drugs to the paramedics. And I asked them to send her to St. Luke's because your cousin's in the emergency room there, and I thought that when it came out about the drugs, he'd be sympathetic and figure out a way to help without getting us into trouble."

"Oh, my God. You were behind that decision to go to St. Luke's?" I was stunned.

"Yes. I made a mistake." Takeo's voice was bitter.

"Why didn't you go along in the helicopter? I saw you going off with the police instead, when I was watching the news broadcast."

"They demanded that I go. They wanted all the details of the accident, who was driving and so on. And the reason I'm late is—just this morning, new police officers came to my apartment. They'd found out from the doctors at the hospital that she'd been on amphetamines, and they wanted to search both my apartment in Tokyo and the house in Hayama."

"Did they find anything?"

"In her handbag, she had a lipstick case containing some tablets. I immediately took a drug test." Takeo looked at me steadily. "I tested negative, which should have been enough, but they've been questioning me about my friends in the environmental protest movement, insinuating that I run around with criminals."

"Have you gotten your family lawyer involved?" I asked. The way things worked in Japan, connections and backroom talk were everything.

Takeo's voice was deadly quiet. "If I talk to that lawyer, it means he goes to my father. If my father catches a breath of scandal, he'll take away my right to run the Kayama School. I'm thirty-one, Rei. I've worked all my life to run this school, and I—I was going to be able to do so much more for Japan—"

"That's right. You were about to become the son-in-law of the minister for the environment, and you were going to influence government policies on land and pollution." I remembered how ambitious it had all seemed, a few days ago. Now it just seemed sad. "And speaking of Emi's father, I think—I think you must still have an ally. Certainly, Kenichi Harada would want the fact that his daughter died from amphetamines to remain quiet."

"I went to the house early yesterday, before the memorial, and we talked. He wanted to know if I'd known, because he hadn't. I told him how I thought it was a phase, and how very sorry I was not to have been more—active—about stopping things." Takeo put his head in his hands.

"Was he angry with you?"

"He was upset, but he told me, in quiet strong language, that he wants nothing to be known about what happened. While I was there he telephoned the detective in charge of the case to reiterate the point."

"Well, that should take care of the problem—"

"It won't. The detective in charge said he wouldn't expose the cause of Emi's death, but he is trying to identify whoever provided the drugs, as part of a larger crackdown."

"Do you know anything about the young man who was thrown out of the funeral?" I asked.

"The foreigner with the curly hair?" Takeo sounded pensive. "I know I've seen him before. I didn't make the connection that he knew Emi until the funeral. Who is he?"

"I have no idea. We should find out. Perhaps that's the drug connection."

Takeo shook his head. "You, not me. I don't want to implicate anyone falsely. I mean, if you knew what I've had to say already to protect you—"

A light flashed, startling the geese, who rose up in a mass flurry. Caught off balance, Takeo pitched forward. I reached out my arm to catch him, but his weight caught me off balance and we both tripped into the pond.

The water was only about knee-high, but cold.

"It looks like I'm the one who needs protection," he said. I laughed, because I couldn't help myself. The situation was so ludicrous.

"Yes. I once had a much better time with you underwater in Hayama. Remember?" Takeo asked as we stepped back up onto dry land.

"Yes, I remember." I paused. "But you know, it can never happen again. I don't want it to."

"You're right." Takeo looked at me for a long moment, then dropped his gaze. "We can never go back to being lovers. But at least we can help each other."

"All right, then," I said, taking off my Asics sneakers one by one, pouring out the water, and putting them back on. "You were saying you had protected me from the police. Why did my name even come up?"

"It wasn't your name. Emi's father's chauffeur told the police that a woman dressed in man's clothing had been at the house, and her presence had agitated Emi. When the police asked me about it, I told them a woman had come by to ask for some assistance after the storm. I said I didn't know her."

So he'd lied. I should have been relieved, but this news set off a new storm of worries. "I hope that lie doesn't come back to haunt you."

"Well, now you know how deep I'm in. By the way, there's something I want to ask you about," Takeo said. "You mentioned that you had a cellular phone stolen. When?"

"The day I went to talk to you at the school. I think someone may have grabbed it when I was going home after the storm, because I know I didn't leave it downstairs at the baggage checkpoint. I called to ask."

"What did it look like?"

"It was one of those camera phones. It was dark blue and there was a brand name on it, Linxar."

"Emi had a dark blue telephone that I didn't recognize. I saw it in her purse when she was taking out the pills."

"Oh! So maybe I left the phone by mistake when I was talking to you in the headmaster's study." I thought about the password that had been broken—Take0 would have been an easy guess for Emi, and my choice of it as a password would have made her believe I was obsessed with her boyfriend.

"Now the police have it, because they have her purse."

So the Japanese police would find, in the phone's memory, the list of numbers I'd called, including Michael and Hugh in Washington, my aunt in Yokohama, and Mr. Watanabe in Tokyo. The numbers wouldn't lead them to drugs, but would lead to everything I'd been bound to keep quiet. I looked at Takeo, then away. I had to get out. I was so panicky, suddenly, that I couldn't stay in the park another moment.

Across the pond, a group of schoolchildren, mothers, and teachers were walking; someone in this group had probably flashed a camera, startled the geese, and caused us to fall into the pond. Now I needed them. I was still a little younger than the casually dressed mothers, but I'd make myself blend in.

"I'm going to try to slip out with that school group," I said to Takeo. "I think it'll attract less notice, just in case someone did follow you and is waiting on the outskirts of the park."

"What if I need to talk to you again? I'm really worried."

"I have a new phone." Grudgingly, I gave him the new number but instructed him to purge it from his phone's memory, once he'd completed a call. Then I said, "Can you try to do something for me?"

Takeo shot me an exasperated glance and did not answer.

"When you go back to the Haradas' house, I want you to keep your eyes open for another piece of pottery that looks like the ibex ewer you had in your house. Don't say anything, just be aware."

"Why?" Takeo asked fiercely. "Why is that vessel so important?"

"I could tell you, but then I'd have to kill you." I said it lightly, as a joke, but he didn't laugh.

"I'll do what I can. I'm expected to pay a call there anyway in the early afternoon. We're all going to the cremation."

The cremation. I'd been to the cremation of my Japanese grandfather. I'd seen the coffin slide into the oven, seen the big metal doors latch closed, and then heard the sound of the flames. I'd been so terrified that I'd run outside, but there I saw a plume of gray smoke rising from the chimney. I couldn't escape the horror of the death, no matter where I went.

"I'm so sorry," I said now to Takeo. "I haven't gotten a chance to tell you yet how sorry I am for everything that happened, and that you lost her."

"It was a short engagement," Takeo said. "But I did care for her. I understand now that it would have been a terrible marriage. But I did care."

After I took my leave of Takeo, I sent an e-mail to Michael giving him a brief message about the Japanese police having custody of the telephone. Then I closed up my phone and clipped it into the lining of my sweater pocket, deciding this was safer than my backpack.

I caught a bus to Yokohama Station, and as I stared at the bustling traffic around me, I thought more about what Takeo had said about caring. It was a word he'd always used a lot: he cared about social justice, endangered butterflies, and so on. He'd even continued to care about me, since he'd decided to keep my name from the police, or was it more that he cared about losing his flower arranging empire?

He might have cared about me, but he never loved me.

A familiar face with dark green eyes swam before me, but I closed myself to that image, and tried to think happier thoughts until we reached the train station.

27

Waseda! I'd spent a junior year abroad here, so I felt a small explosion of nostalgia to be back in this paradise for smart, unconventional young Japanese. Waseda University was one of a kind in the city; it was tough to get into, and its graduates went not only into business but into advertising, media, and other creative fields. It also boasted the highest population of foreign students at any Japanese institute of higher education—that was why I'd gotten in.

From Waseda Station, I took a narrow curving road toward the campus, where I was quickly surrounded by a mix of prewar and modern academic buildings. I had to pause at the Okuma auditorium, a golden brick building topped by a medieval-looking tower. I used to meet my friends from Waseda's art study club in the peaceful garden next to the tower, because we thought art could flow only from tranquillity—and student life in Tokyo was not, on the whole, tranquil. As I walked closer to look at the tower, it made me think about how the European castle style remained popular for love hotels. At the Haradas' house as well, with its stained-glass windows and fancy furniture, Old World European aesthetics prevailed. Given Kenichi Harada's worldly views, it seemed strange that he hadn't wanted Emi to study at a university before marrying.

I was annoyed to learn that the international students' center was no longer in the center of campus, but in a section of off-campus buildings; I made the trek over, then discovered the administrator was at lunch. I had to shift to plan B and visit the registrar's office, where I found an exhausted-looking woman sunk behind a computer terminal with a stack of folders at her side.

The woman listened warily to my story: that I was urgently trying to get in touch with a student I was currently mentoring.

"Her cell phone must be off, because she's not answering," I said, taking out my new phone and waving it about, as if it contained the proof of my efforts. "My best thought is to meet her outside the classroom. I thought you could tell me where she is, geographically, at this moment."

"I'm so sorry," the woman said in a standard apology that brooked no rejoinders. "We cannot allow anyone to enter the classroom and disrupt the schedule."

"I won't go into the class, I swear. If I could just wait outside the door, I could catch her in time so she doesn't miss her interview."

"Interview?" the girl repeated dully.

"Yes, at the Diet. For an internship there."

She blinked, because I was talking about Japan's parliament. It was the most important place I could think of, offhand, and not a place I could ever remember a Waseda student interning.

"It's very important for her to have this interview. Her future depends on it." I spoke earnestly, hoping the jogging clothes I was wearing wouldn't dissuade her from thinking that I was an important person.

"I'll check for you now. But please don't disturb the professor." The administrative assistant closed the screen she was working on, and replaced one sea of *kanji* characters with another. With lightning speed, she pressed keys and flipped through web pages. At the end, she printed out a sheet for me.

"Here you are."

"I'm so grateful. Thank you very much. You've been very kind." I bowed a thousand times and backed out of the office, running into a stocky sixty-something professor, whom I recognized at the last minute as the person who'd given me a C in linguistics.

"*Gomen nasai,*" I apologized, turning to bow. My mistake.

"Shimura?" Professor Morito didn't use an honorific with me, as was typical for older professors toward students. "Well, I never thought I'd see you again. The last thing I heard was that you'd become a salesperson of old things—"

"She's a mentor," said the secretary. "She's arranged for one of our students to have an interview at the Diet."

"Yes, yes, I'm hurrying to meet a student. Excuse me for being rude, but I really must run!" I said over my shoulder despite Professor Morito's continued grumbling commentary on students who squandered lost opportunities. The truth was that Professor Morito was right. I hadn't worked hard enough at linguistics or learning *kanji*, and as I walked down the boulevard, studying Fumiko's class schedule, I wished desperately that I was fluent in written Japanese. Here was the time, 13:00; the name of the topic she was studying was unintelligible. The only thing I could tell was that she was studying at the Information Technology Center, a place where I wished now I'd spent more time during my year overseas.

There was a little glass window in the door of the Fumiko's classroom, so I peeped through it a few times, looking for her in the class of about fifty, before I realized that I was attracting the attention of several students. I slunk back to the opposite side of the hallway. Nobody was around, so I made a phone call to the Meiwashima Auction Gallery to find out whether Kenichi Harada ever brought things to auction. No, he hadn't sold anything, but he had been a longtime customer. I thought about calling Kazu Sakurai's studio in Kyushu to ask him whether Kenichi Harada had been a customer, but I didn't know the name of the town the studio was in. I'd have to research it later.

I looked again through the classroom window. All the students had their laptop computers open, hindering my inspection of their faces. I was a bit shocked to see students using laptops in the classroom, but I guessed that was a reflection of my age. It would have been nice to have had a laptop during Professor Morito's class, so that I would have missed his myriad cranky expressions.

I hoped Fumiko wouldn't be a dead end, because I needed information. I didn't have time to follow false leads, when the Japanese police were probably close to figuring out I was a player in Emi Harada's death. To derail them, I had to get Takeo the information he needed about the drug supplier.

Finally, I heard the snap of all the laptops closing. There was much scraping of chairs and a babble of voices, and then the students streamed out. Fumiko was wearing a generous sweatshirt and jeans. She did a double take when she saw me, letting me know that I didn't need to worry about reintroducing myself.

"*Ohisashi buri desu,*" I greeted her. *Long time no see.* It had been less than twenty-four hours, but so what?

"Do you teach here?" she looked at my clothing with seeming confusion.

"Please tell me I don't look that old," I said, falling into step with her. We passed out of the building and started our way down the campus's main pedestrian boulevard.

"I didn't mean a professor. I thought you might be a teaching assistant. I mean, why else would you be here? You told me you'd finished your studies."

"I came today because I need to talk to you about Emi. It's starting to get out about the amphetamines—"

"Don't say that word!" she whispered, panic in her voice. To think a college student was this paranoid about drugs! It reminded me that I was in another country.

"Sorry. Let's talk about it in a quieter place. May I take you to lunch?" I was starving, despite the stress.

"I only have about thirty minutes." She looked at me anxiously.

"I know a great, quick *okonomiyaki* shop nearby." I knew that *okonomiyaki*, the delicious Japanese savory pancake, was as essential to the survival of Waseda's students as pizza was to American undergraduates.

"Omori-san's shop? Is it even open for lunch?"

"Yes. I know most students go in the evening. It won't be crowded and we'll have the privacy we need."

• • •

Feeling as if I'd been away from Waseda for only a semester, I walked into the restaurant and I led Fumiko straight to the old table of the art study club, close to the restrooms—a good location because of the amount of Kirin we drank in those days. The lacquered pine table was well worn from many student elbows. The center of it had been cut out and had a round electric cooktop, which was quickly turned on by the cook-owner, an old grandma type who greeted me with a smile of recognition. Omori-san asked us a few questions, then carefully poured a mixture of egg, soy, scallions, and octopus onto the hot surface. It was up to us to poke at the pancake, from time to time, to see if it had set.

I liked the pancake fully done, but I deferred to Fumiko when she decided to start cutting it up for eating a scant five minutes after it had started to cook. She was obviously in a rush.

"So, you seemed to understand what I said about the—substance." I opened the interview, keeping my voice low and calm.

"Did her parents find out?" She watched me anxiously.

"Yes. They need to know who the supplier was."

"It wasn't me! I never—"

"I believe you. But I think you might know something. When that boy ran out of the funeral yesterday, some people were wondering if he had something to do with the drugs. It seemed as if you recognized him."

"I do," she said in a low voice. "He's a student in the foreign exchange program. His name is Ramzi Birand."

"Birand?" I sat up straight. Birand was the name of the Turkish art dealer Michael Hendricks had mentioned during the slide show about Takeo. "How do you spell it?"

"If you want to see the spelling—" she touched her backpack—"I have our student list with me. He's auditing a history class."

Fumiko rummaged through a folder and handed me a piece of paper. The list was typed in English, signaling that this was a cross-cultural class with a high number of foreign students. Birand's name was spelled right, and his nationality was listed as Turkish. There was also an address, with a telephone number.

"You mentioned to me that Emi never studied at Waseda—or any other college. So why did Ramzi attend her memorial?"

Fumiko pressed her lips together and shook her head.

"Please," I said. "If you're keeping a secret for Emi, there's no point anymore."

"He—he was her boyfriend at the American school in Istanbul. This past summer, he came to Japan and enrolled at Waseda to be near her."

Another man. Something I hadn't expected from the innocent-looking Emi. Trying to readjust my thinking, I asked, "What was their relationship like?"

Fumiko closed her eyes, then opened them. They were slightly wet with tears. "She—she sent me a lot of e-mail from Istanbul about him. He was two years older, and they met at a school party. She was always talking about how smart and handsome and funny he was. She was crazy about him! Then, her parents found out."

"I gather they were nervous about it?" What parent wouldn't be nervous about a teenager embarking on a serious relationship?

"Not nervous—furious. Her father was angry that she'd gotten so seriously involved—and he moved their whole family back to Japan. He put her in a girls' school and told her that she could go only to a women's college after she was done. But she kept writing to Ramzi, and he found a way to gain admission to Waseda."

"Oh! So they carried on their romance here—"

"Only for a little while. When the parents found out Ramzi was here, Emi was forbidden to see him again." Fumiko pressed her lips together. "Emi's father couldn't force the university dean to make him leave, so he and his wife decided to make Emi completely un-available to Ramzi. They made her have an *omiai.*"

"In your opinion, was the arranged marriage to Takeo an at-tempt at—punishment?" I was skeptical, remembering how posses-sive and passionate Emi had seemed toward Takeo.

"Not punishment, but control. They just thought that it was time to get her safely married. They said she'd gone too far."

"Are you sure about all this? I saw Emi together with her fiancé. She seemed really excited to be with him, happy to be furnishing their house." I didn't add how I'd overheard the sounds of her and Takeo settling into each other for a serious snog, just a few days ear-lier at the flower arranging school.

"She kind of liked him, I guess. There were many advantages he could offer her."

"What kind of advantages?" I asked, wondering if she'd been as calculating as Takeo.

"Well, she did have choice about the man she married. She thought Takeo was the best of the men she met because he was so successful. He was so busy with the *ikebana* school that he told her he'd spend a lot of time away on business but he'd provide her a generous allowance, and she could stay at the apartment in Tokyo or the house in Hayama, whatever she wanted."

"But—but what about the physical nature of marriage to a man so much older?" I tried to express it delicately. "Wasn't that frightening to her?"

"Oh, she'd done it lots of times, with Ramzi and then—with Takeo. She told me all about it. She said it was quite nice, actually. She also said that one day my time would come. But look at me—who's going to want to sleep with such a big fatty?"

"Please, don't talk about yourself that way!" I said gently, but my mind was racing. Takeo and Emi had embarked on their traditional marriage plan with complex and mercenary agendas. But being typical modern, young Japanese, they'd had sex along the way—and that had changed everything, at least for Emi. Takeo's charisma had led to her undoing, to the start of her falling in love. And perhaps the drugs she took made the decision easier.

"Did she start taking drugs in Istanbul?" I was beginning to think that Emi had changed from a good Japanese girl into a teenage libertine while she was abroad—just as Japanese people were wont to say about "foreign-returned girls."

"I think so, but it got a lot worse here," Fumiko said. "She was already slim enough when she arrived. I told her she shouldn't keep taking pills, but she insisted it was the only way to keep the pounds off. And after her parents found out about Ramzi, I think the pills made her feel better, emotionally."

"So," I said, studying the list of students in the class that Fumiko had showed me at the beginning of our conversation, "I don't recognize this address where Ramzi lives, and it's not right here in Takadanobaba. Did you ever go there with Emi?"

"No, and she didn't go there either. He lives with his uncle over their shop in Omote-sando. Actually, if that's all you need, I should go now. I must not be late for my next class." Fumiko held out her hand for the paper.

Thanking Fumiko profusely, I copied the information onto a napkin and snuggled it in the cell phone holder. I gave her back the student roster and declined her attempt to help pay the lunch check.

"Please, it's on me. You've been very, very helpful," I said.

"Why? What are you going to do?" Fumiko looked at me anxiously.

"I'm not sure exactly. But I'd like to talk to Ramzi."

"If I'd known you were going to talk to him, I would never have told you anything—"

"Why? Are you scared of him?"

She shook her head. "Of course not! But he was always hanging around, trying to spy on her during the times she was with Takeo. He's a little bit strange. He will be upset if he knows I was talking about him."

"Thanks for the warning. I'll be quite careful," I said as we parted. And I would be, because a new theory was forming in my mind. Ramzi and Emi had a plan for the future, but it had been dashed by Emi's growing attraction to her betrothed. Who would want to stand by while a beloved girlfriend prepared to marry— and then have all hopes of seeing her again forever dashed by her death? Ramzi had probably stormed the memorial because he wanted to say something to her parents, make them pay for what they'd done.

28

Omote-sando had always been my aunt Norie's idea of shopping heaven. There wasn't much I could afford on the long boulevard lined with tall zelkova trees. It had become a satellite Paris; the street was home of the highest-grossing Louis Vuitton store worldwide, and there were also lavish boutiques devoted to Chanel, Yves St. Laurent, and Christian Dior, very close to an older, Japanese-owned tourist haunt, the Oriental Bazaar—which obviously had been named in less politically correct times.

Normally, I would have passed the Oriental Bazaar by, but today I paused between the huge porcelain lion-dogs that guarded its entrance. There were a few things inside that might be of use to me, and the prices would definitely be the best on the block.

I hurried past the furniture sections crowded with Korean-made replicas of old Japanese chests and into the books section, where almost everything was published in English. I skimmed the new edition of *Born to Shop Tokyo* and came up with the town, Umeda, where the Japanese sculptor Kazu Sakurai was based. The author recommended that foreigners visit his shop by making an appointment ahead of time and bringing plenty of cash—a minimum of $3,000 for the smallest piece. Well, that was the value of being a Living National Treasure, I thought wryly, scribbling down the phone number on a shopping circular and sliding it into the cell phone case. Maybe I could live without a backpack after all, I thought, leaving the books section in search of toys for my niece and nephew in Washington. Having mixed-sex twins to shop for was a challenge, but I ultimately settled on a pair of Japanese police officer dolls—one a man and one a woman, a sign of political progress. And the dolls weren't just for play—they would teach fine motor skills. Win especially would have fun taking off the dolls' black lace-up shoes, though he'd need his mother's help to put them on again.

How soon would it be until I saw Kendall and the twins again? I wondered as I tucked the package containing the dolls into my back-pack and continued on my trail to Ramzi Birand's address. I had to come up with something here. I didn't know what I was looking for, but if I didn't find it, I didn't know when I'd ever get home.

For now, my business was the Birand family. The address was easy to find, because it was in a pretty lane that ran behind a small street containing my favorite coffee shop, Appetito, right across from the Hanae Mori building. Right now, stretched across the street's entrance, there was a huge banner stretched bearing the cryptic acronym FCUK. It wasn't till I got to the other side that I learned that this stood for French Connection United Kingdom.

I'd try to get Ramzi to come out to Appetito with me for a quick private talk. If he lived nearby, it was probably his favorite place. While Japanese students lived and died for *okonomiyaki*, foreign students were addicted to coffee and pastry.

When I reached 17-11-2A Kawashima, a couple of turns past Appetito, it didn't look like the apartment I expected. The address was that of an antiques shop named Treasures of Tabriz, according to the curly gold letters on the door. Ali Birand, proprietor, was the name listed underneath. Ali, not Osman.

I peered through the plate glass window at a ceiling dripping with baroque-style light fixtures. Under the soft electric candlelight I caught sight of a tasteful grouping of Ottoman and French regency furniture. The floor was covered by an Oriental rug with a minute hand-knotted pattern of flowers in delicate creams and blues.

My mother would have gone mad for this shop. It was her decorating taste exactly. I didn't believe in lusting after things too rich for my budget—I'd gotten into trouble that way before. Still, it wouldn't be hard to feign enthusiasm for what was in stock at Treasures of Tabriz.

A soft chime announced my arrival as I opened the door and stepped inside. I hadn't seen anyone through the window, but once I'd made myself known, a slender woman who looked like a Japanese equivalent of my mother—expensive fur-trimmed sweater, stylish boot-cut pants, and socialite pageboy—popped up from behind a large cardboard box. With her long manicured fingers, she'd been uncrating an ancient-looking terra-cotta horse from a wooden box. Wood shavings spilled over its edge, marring the perfection of the shop. It even smelled expensive here, I thought, taking a whiff. It smelled like Russian tea, a blend of orange and cloves and black tea that had been all the rage in San Francisco when I was younger. I remembered my mother and her book club in the living room with a pot of Russian tea on a Chippendale table, discussing Toni Morrison's novels. I looked around Treasures of Tabriz for a teapot, but saw none except for a gorgeous blue-and-gold Sèvres piece set on a high shelf amid an entire tea service for twelve.

"Welcome," the woman said, her voice politely modulated but a bit curious, perhaps because of my appearance. The only kind of woman my age who would walk into an elegant antiques shop wearing Asics running shoes, a cashmere hoodie, and yoga pants would be a confused backpacker or a wealthy expat wife who didn't yet understand how women were supposed to dress for shopping in Tokyo.

"I came from Waseda." A semitruthful statement. "Is this—is this the place where Ramzi Birand lives?"

"He lives upstairs with his uncle—the owner of this shop." She inclined her head gracefully, revealing sparkling diamond studs. "I am so glad that you came to visit. Ramzi's been very sad, and we are worried that he has no friends. Would you care for some tea while I call him?"

"I don't want to put you to the trouble," I said. But, of course, I did. A cup of tea would hit the long-lost Russian tea receptor in my brain, and it would also busy her for a minute so that I could inspect the shop more thoroughly.

"It's no trouble at all. Please, wait just a minute." She disappeared behind a hanging tapestry.

I strolled around the room. There were plenty of nineteenth-century European antiques of the sort that used to be sold in Baltimore's Howard Street shops where Grand took me, every now and again during my childhood visits, to educate my eye. In the Birand shop, these pieces of furniture were nicely offset by Middle Eastern serving pieces of filigreed silver and brass, which bore hefty price tags that signified either valuable metal or age.

I walked back to look at the Chinese terra-cotta horse that was standing on the counter. It had a stick-on price tag on it that said 6,000Y. Was that yen or yuan? I didn't know the current value of Chinese currency, and the box was stamped as coming from Shanghai. As I bent to look at it, I saw the ears of another horse sticking up through wood shavings. Without looking any further, I knew the horses were reproduction pieces, because real Tang dynasty horses sold for about $500,000 a piece.

"May I help you?" A man's voice this time, in what I would call newcomer's Japanese—slow, measured, accented with the sounds of another land. I straightened my posture and turned to regard the speaker: an olive-skinned man with closely cropped hair, a hooked nose, and piercing hazel eyes. Fifty-something and foreign, I decided, looking at the fine business shirt he wore tucked into wool gabardine slacks.

"Hello, sir. May I ask if you are Mr. Ali Birand?" I asked in excessively courteous English, trying to make up for the way I looked.

"Yes, I am. And you, who are you?" He beamed, as if the English I'd used had been a welcome surprise. As he spoke, he picked up the box of horses and moved it back behind the counter.

"My name is Rei Shimura. I was in the States before, but I'm at Waseda right now." Again, very close to the truth.

"Ah, that explains your so beautiful English." His smile deepened. "So you came to see Ramzi?"

"Yes, we've all been quite worried about him. I've brought some papers for him from class."

"Really?" The thick brows pulled together. "I wasn't aware he had many friends. In Istanbul, he was so popular, but here—he just hasn't tried enough, I think."

The danger would be if Ramzi emerged and looked at me without recognition. I had to prepare myself. "Actually, he doesn't know me very well at all. I'm an older student, you know—"

"And he only had eyes for one girl, didn't he?" Ali Birand sounded rueful. "With age there is wisdom—something my nephew certainly lacks, in his own character and those of the friends he's chosen."

Ali Birand's allusion to Emi made me want to jump right into some questions, but the saleswoman interrupted us. She was carrying a tray containing two tall Middle Eastern tea glasses, each resting in an engraved brass holder. Mr. Birand took the tray in his own hands and settled it down on a marble-top table in front of a pale blue velvet sofa. He indicated that I should sit down.

"That's for sale, isn't it? I don't want to make it dirty." The bottom half of my pants were still damp with dirty pond water.

"Please, please! You are an honored guest. You must enjoy Miss Iwada's tea. It is something I have taught her."

I'd never thought anyone could out-Japanese the Japanese at courtesy. Giving up, I took the glass and settled down, making sure to stretch my legs out so they didn't rub against the sofa.

The tea had been brewed at least ten minutes earlier, I judged by the rich taste of orange and cinnamon and the drinkable temperature. It seemed almost as if they'd been expecting a visitor.

"I hope it's not too hot," Miss Iwada, the salesclerk, said to me in Japanese. I could tell from her face that she was figuring out which side of the Pacific I really belonged to.

"It's delicious. I must say that I didn't expect this beautiful shop, and to have tea as well. Thank you so much." I spoke in Japanese to her, wondering how much Mr. Birand understood.

"Oh, no, I am so glad you are here. Ramzi-san has missed all his classes since the—accident," Miss Iwada said. "His uncle told him to go, but he just refuses. He would stay in his room all the time if he could."

"It's so convenient to have the apartment over the shop. What a beautiful space it is—for how long have you been here?" I switched back to English, so I could better include Ali Birand.

"We've had the building for a year, but it took a lot of renovations to make a place for the shop—which opened last month. But it's not our only place; my brother and I have other antique stores in Istanbul and Cairo and, once upon a time, in Baghdad." He smiled wryly. "I'm afraid your army put a dent in that business."

"I can certainly understand why you would want to be here, in Tokyo. And I'm intrigued by the store name. Isn't Tabriz a city in Iran?"

"It was the cultural center of old Persia. The rug near the window was made in Tabriz one hundred years ago. It took eight artists two years to create it."

I sighed in appropriate admiration, then said, "But are you Turkish?"

"We are. But you know, everyone in Japan thinks of Turkey just for rugs, not for high-class antiques. So we chose the name Tabriz, and we offer treasures from all over the Middle East, including Turkey. Not just the Middle East, but Italy and France and England—that is an Italian marble table, where you just put your glass."

"Ooh, sorry!" I picked it right up. "I hope I didn't damage anything. It looks so antique!"

"That table will be fine." He smiled graciously. "My brother acquired it from the Italian ambassador, whose family had owned it for two hundred years. Other objects—like the tea glasses and rugs—were made recently but by skilled artists carrying out a generations-old tradition."

"And the terra-cotta horses you were unpacking?" I couldn't resist asking.

"I was just opening them when you arrived," Miss Iwada said, turning to look at Mr. Birand, as if for guidance.

"A Chinese museum has fallen into some financial difficulty, so we were able to purchase these Qin dynasty horses. They are quite valuable, so I thought I would bring them to this market first. But if they don't sell here, I'm sure they will be of interest to our clientele abroad." Ali Birand spoke so confidently that for a minute I almost believed him. But if these were real warrior tomb horses, they would have been hand-carried by Mr. Birand himself from China instead of shipped by crate with the price tags still affixed, and he'd know their real value. He obviously thought I knew nothing about Asian antiques.

"Oh, dear. I fear that I could never afford anything here, except maybe a tea glass." I ran a finger along the glass, and it made the light singing sound of fine crystal.

"You chose a nice reproduction set. We have a special price. Ten thousand yen for a set of five," Ali Birand said.

One hundred dollars for five gorgeous tea glasses. Aunt Norie would like them, and none of the other housewives in the neighborhood would have anything comparable. Tea glasses would be the perfect present for me to bring after my mysterious day away from her home; hopefully they would distract my aunt from asking what else I'd done in Tokyo.

"I'll take the set," I said, fishing into my backpack for my wallet.

"For a student, you have exceptional taste. Now, I fear, I have an appointment across town. It was lovely to meet you, Miss Shimura."

Mr. Birand pulled on an inky black cashmere coat and disappeared out the front door and down the street. I watched him set off, thinking about the charming, poised way he'd presented himself. And what of Ramzi? He had the Birand looks, with the advantage of youth. But last night, when he'd been thrown out of the Haradas' house, he had been awkward, unsophisticated, emotional—the very opposite of his uncle.

The salesclerk was dexterously wrapping up the package in gold paper when Ramzi finally slouched into the room. He wore a stained rugby shirt and Levi's that hung low at the waist, exposing a flash of boxers with an American flag pattern. He looked around expectantly, then settled his lazy, long-lashed eyes on me.

"Ramzi-san! How are you doing?" I asked, looking him over. He was lean, but not too thin. He didn't look at all like my idea of a drug user.

"Iwada-san, didn't you say a friend was here?" He looked blankly from me toward the saleswoman.

The Japanese Ramzi had spoken was broken—understandably, because it was still a very new language for him. I switched to English.

"My first name is Rei," I said. "I was at Waseda today, and I bring you some papers and a message from Kashima-san."

"Kashima-san? You mean that nerd in my Internet class?" he said in quick, perfect English, but with a slight accent that seemed to curl upward like the steam from my cup of tea. The English had worked. He had become interested in me, as I could tell from the way he'd turned his lanky body toward me.

I couldn't comment any more on Kashima-san, having never met the person whose name had been smack in the middle of the roster Fumiko had shown me, so I tried to move on. "I've got the information with me. Why don't we go to Appetito just around the corner? We can eat while we talk."

"I'm not hungry," Ramzi said.

"You must eat! You haven't had anything in five days!" Miss Iwada said.

Ramzi scowled at her, and the tension was broken only when a Japanese man started to come into the shop, but backed out, as if the sight of the two of us in our jeans and sweats had made him decide that this shop was not a proper one after all. I hadn't gotten much of a look at the man, but he must have looked like a good customer, because Miss Iwada hustled out to the street to entreat him to return.

"Did she put you up to this?" Ramzi said to me as we watched, through the window, while Miss Iwada bowed to the man and implored him to return.

"Iwada-san? Absolutely not. How could she, when I've never met her before?"

"Just as I've never met you. You're not in any of my classes. I don't understand why you're here—"

"I saw you at the memorial gathering." I took a deep breath. "You're right, it's not about schoolwork. It's about Emi."

29

"Emi?" He turned to me with eyes filled with pain. "What business is she of yours?"

"As I said, I was there and I saw those men make you leave. It was terribly unfair, I thought."

"Yes, it was." His voice was bitter. "I was thrown out while her murderer stayed sipping whisky, the bastard—"

"Who's a murderer?" I asked, picking up the box of glasses I'd paid for.

"Her fiancé. The one who crashed the car that she died in." As he spoke, I saw Miss Iwada coming back.

"Let's talk about this outside," I said, taking Ramzi by the arm, figuring that gentle force would work better than words.

"I don't understand who you are! Why do you care about this?" Ramzi practically exploded when we were out of the shop. I remembered that Fumiko had said he was strange, so I answered as calmly as I could.

"It's complicated. I knew her, but I knew Takeo Kayama, the person you think murdered her, first. He was the one who introduced us."

"Oh! I suppose he sent you here to plead his case. Frankly, I don't know why he even bothers." Ramzi's voice rose sharply, startling a German shepherd, who barked mercilessly, almost dragging his owner, a small woman, forward.

"Stupid dog. Reminds me of the ones Emi's parents have," Ramzi said as we passed along.

"Keep your voice down. More people understand English than you might think," I cautioned as we turned another corner and the yellow-and-red awning of Appetito appeared. "I suppose you come here all the time, living as close by as you do—"

"I don't know the area at all. And I'm not eating," Ramzi said stonily.

He was firm. I couldn't even get him to agree to coffee, because he said the substance served in Japan was nothing like what he was used to in Turkey. I could see his point, so I got myself a cup of steaming milk tea, even though I'd had half a cup of Russian tea just minutes earlier, so I would be buzzing for hours. I also put two chocolate croissants on two plates, just in case.

I carried the tray over to a table at the window, where Ramzi was staring out at a boy wearing a stovepipe hat and polka-dot pants who was locking a bicycle. At second glance, I realized that the person was a girl.

"Crazies," Ramzi said, but his tone was almost warm. "I'm going to miss seeing Japanese crazies."

"At least she isn't a Lolita," I said, watching the whimsical person disappear into the Shu Uemura makeup boutique. "What do you mean by missing them, though?"

"I'm going back to Turkey. There's nothing more for me here."

"I can understand why you feel that way." I had an urge to put my hand over his, but instead, I put a plate with a croissant in front of him. "Chocolate helps."

"So, who are you really, Chocolate-Tea-and-Shopping Lady?" He used the words lightly; clearly he thought I was a phony.

I had to make an impact, and get him to feel allied with me. "I'm Takeo's ex-girlfriend. From some years ago."

He sat bolt upright. "So you came to see me because you were jilted, too?"

Jilted. Interesting choice of word, but I couldn't ask him about that yet. "I came because I'm confused and concerned about a lot of things that happened, starting with the fact that you were forcibly removed from Emi's house by those men. Why did that happen?"

"Those men told me I was upsetting her parents. Apparently, I always did. But for them not to let me even see her one last time—" He passed a hand over his eyes and turned away from me.

"Why were they so hard on the relationship? Didn't your parents meet at some point while you were both in Istanbul?"

"Our fathers did business," Ramzi said. "Lots of business. A Japanese will do business with foreigners. But not personal relationships. Not even my father's money made me good enough for Emi."

"The Haradas are very traditional," I said, choosing my words carefully. "It's not the way most Japanese are. The arranged marriage for Emi, right after high school graduation, seemed—almost medieval to me."

"Yes, the Haradas like the old world." He sank into silence.

"I gather your father sold antiques to the Haradas?" I ventured.

"Yeah. There are plenty of my father's wares in his house—so ironic, when he throws me out!"

"Your uncle mentioned to me that he and your father sell more than just Middle Eastern pieces."

"Yes. They carry everything—lots of French and Italian, which sells to the Turkish buyers; and of course Turkish and Middle Eastern, for the Europeans who want something ancient and exotic." He made quotation marks with his fingers to emphasize the seeming silliness of those adjectives. "The mix of pieces that you saw in the shop just now is pretty much like our shop in Istanbul. Only the shop in Istanbul takes up half a city block. It's huge."

"How does your father obtain the French and Italian pieces?"

Ramzi shrugged. "He does a few scouting trips a year. But more often people bring things to him to sell. He runs in diplomatic circles, and those people sometimes want to sell or exchange their pieces for something my dad had in the shop."

"I saw a Balthus painting in the Haradas' house. Did that come from your father's store?"

"Who?" Ramzi looked at me blankly.

"Balthus was a recently deceased French painter who did most of his work in the mid-twentieth century. Upstairs at the Haradas' house, I saw a portrait of a young Japanese woman, with a kind of dwarf in the corner. It looked like a Balthus, but I wasn't certain."

"I went upstairs in that house just once. I'm afraid that I didn't spend the time looking at anything on the walls." Ramzi gave me a tight, mirthless smile.

I tried a different approach. "Did you know Emi when she was chubby?"

He cocked his head to one side. "She told me she'd been heavier, but I could never imagine it. She came to our school in her sophomore year when I was already a senior. By the time I met her at a party, she was perfect. Like a doll."

"I agree," I said. "She was very beautiful."

"Oh, but you didn't see her at her peak. When she came here, and all that crap went down with the engagement, she got thinner. Too thin, I think."

"Do you know why she became so thin?"

"The way everyone does: by not eating. She was unhappy, just like me."

"Did you ever see her take any tablets?"

He started to shake his head, then paused. "Well, there were always vitamins. She sometimes took them in front of me."

I looked at him hard. How could a college boy not know about drugs? He hardly struck me as the sheltered type.

"Those vitamins," I said. "Where did she buy them?"

"I don't know. Maybe her mother bought them for her. Who cares?" Ramzi paused. "What do you know that you're not saying?"

"I think she may have been taking amphetamine tablets. They're popular with young women who want to lose weight."

"Oh." He sat for a minute, the shock registering on his face. "Who said Emi was taking that? How do you know?"

"It's apparently what the police think. They asked Takeo all about it. Haven't they asked you about it yet?"

Ramzi's voice grew cold. "I know the stereotypes about—my country. But people in my social class—we have better things to do than buy and sell drugs. My uncle isn't smuggling them in his furniture crates, and I'm not selling them on the campus at school, okay? And what you're talking about—amphetamines—it isn't a Turkish thing. People take hash and opium in Turkey, but not people in our class."

"You mean—your class in school or your social class?"

"Social class. The American kids, well, there was a segment that loved drugs. I knew those kids and I went to their parties, but it was just for the girls. Nothing else."

"Thanks for explaining," I said. "I meant no offense to you. It's just that—it would be safe for everyone concerned if we could figure out who sold the amphetamines to Emi. Like I told you, the police are asking around."

Ramzi shook his head. "This is so—new to me. I just can't believe she would do a thing like buy drugs. Buy handbags and pretty clothes—yes. But not drugs! What if Takeo provided them?"

I shook my head. "He didn't provide them, I'm certain, but he did know something was going on, and he was worried. He'd hoped he could get her to quit after the wedding."

"After the wedding," Ramzi said, his voice soft. "Emi said things would be better after the wedding. He'd be working, so we'd have time to relax together at the country house. We could even travel together, if the situation was cool."

"That sounds like a plan," I said. A plan I would have hated, if I were the cuckolded one.

"Well, that plan went to hell when he killed her! I can't help thinking—" Ramzi's voice broke off.

"What did you think?" I asked gently.

"Maybe he found out about me, and he was so angry that he—he just—"

"He never knew about you," I said, meaning to reassure him, but instead seeing tears form in his eyes. Well, of course. Ramzi was in the process of learning that he'd been even less visible and less important than the Haradas had made him feel.

"When was the last time you spoke to Emi?" I asked.

"Three weeks ago. I knew from—from a friend who helped us— that she had an appointment at the bridal salon at Matsuya. I was waiting by the escalators when she came out, but her mother was there. I had to walk away. It wasn't until an hour later that Emi phoned and asked me to stop following her."

"That must have hurt terribly."

"I couldn't understand it. We've had arguments before, but this was—this was unexpected. She said she wanted to concentrate on the wedding and get on with life. I know she really didn't mean it. She was probably confused." He paused. "Maybe because of those pills that I thought were vitamins. How stupid can a person be, not to have known?"

"Well, it sounds like she'd started on the path much earlier. How could you have suspected anything, if her baseline of normality was actually a drugged state?"

Ramzi seemed to struggle with an answer. "I really don't know if what you're saying is true. I just know that I loved her, and if her family had stayed in Turkey like they should have, we'd still be together."

"Do you think her parents brought her back here because—because they were so upset about the relationship?"

"That's what they said to Emi, and she told me. My father didn't care about me seeing her—just that I really told him where I was going at night, came back when I said, that kind of thing."

It sounded reasonable to me. "So your father was pretty supportive. Is that why he let you come to Japan to study?"

"He wasn't excited about it. He thought, after the Haradas left, that it would be better to leave things alone. But I knew my uncle had gotten the visa and had rented a building here. It was the perfect situation for me, and my father had to let me go. I was nineteen, and I'd come into my trust fund the year before."

"Must be nice," I said automatically.

"No, it's not nice," Ramzi said stonily. "The reason I have that money is because my mother died five years ago."

So he'd lost a mother. No wonder he'd clung to his girlfriend so desperately. Feeling as though I'd really put my foot in things, I said, "Ramzi, I'm so sorry about all that you've suffered. Of course the trust fund is something you never wanted—"

"My mother's death is nobody's fault."

His choice of words was interesting, I thought as we parted a few minutes later and I began my damp-footed trek home. Whether he was conscious of it or not, he hadn't absolved me of Emi's death—something I wasn't ready to do, either.

30

My journey back to Yokohama seemed to take forever. Outside the grimy train windows, the late afternoon sun illuminated mud-stained roads, toppled signs, and sagging power lines. How odd it was to see my beloved, immaculate Japan looking like an unmade bed! But Typhoon Nigo's damage would take time to clean up. I supposed the scenery along the route would eventually, perhaps within a few weeks, be almost the same as it had been before the floods and winds. Still, for the people who knew and loved Emi, life would always be divided into "before the typhoon" and after it.

Ramzi had complained about the injustice of Yasuko and Kenichi Harada's attitude toward him. He had a point, but I pondered what it might feel like to see one's daughter plunge headlong into sex at sixteen. I remembered how furious my father had been when I'd told him, as an eighth-grader, that I wanted to go with some girl-friends and a group of much older boys to a midnight screening of *The Rocky Horror Picture Show*. He'd been outraged that I'd even asked. I dated covertly, and with considerable fear of discovery, until I'd left home at age eighteen for college.

Covert dating. Spying and sexual infidelity. My terrible behavior of recent days probably had its origins in my own family history, but I had no time for self-analysis. I needed to remember what

Ramzi had said about the art, and his father's relationship with Kenichi Harada.

Emi's father must have done business with Osman Birand more than once, because Ramzi had recognized several pieces in the house. There was a relationship. The ibex ewer could certainly have gone from the Birands to the Haradas. I knew that a fake vessel lay in its fragmented state in Washington. Did a genuine ancient vessel even exist?

A recorded female voice sweetly reminded me to take all my personal belongings with me as I disembarked at Minami-Makigahara Station. I was glad of the reminder, given my distracted state. The train was so crowded that I'd had to stand the whole way, and endure the slightly disapproving looks of people who saw how much space my backpack, stuffed with the gifts, was taking up on the overhead luggage rack. Now I took it out, opening room for someone else to stow a carry-on suitcase.

I squeezed through the bodies and made it out to the platform at Minami-Makigahara Station. It was ten minutes by foot to my relatives' house, and during that time I would be blessedly free of people crowding around me. I checked behind me for company—no, nobody was following me up the quiet hilly street that led to my aunt's home—and took out my cell phone.

"I received your e-mail," Michael Hendricks said, after I'd greeted him.

"I didn't think you'd have read it already. It's what, six in the morning?"

"That's right. What I want to know is whether you wrote rather than calling because you thought I'd yell at you."

"Actually, I thought I'd avoid being overheard. You can't imagine what it's like always being surrounded by people."

"I can't," Michael said. "It's pretty quiet on the Japan desk."

"I suppose if worse comes to worst, we can bring in Mr. Watan—"

"No names please," Michael said crisply. "The colleague you wanted to mention—let's call him Mr. Ito—is one of Mr. Harmony's colleagues. Because of that relationship, Ito is no longer an asset to this operation. And now, let's talk about something else."

Watanabe was Ito, Harada was Harmony, Emi was "the bride," and I was—what? A bungler, at the very best. Feeling rather subdued, I said, "Did you know that the antique dealer's brother recently opened an antiques shop in Tokyo?"

A long pause. "No, I didn't. When?"

"A month ago."

"So what's the place like?"

In short order, I described Treasures of Tabriz, and the reproduction Chinese horses I'd seen. And mindful of Michael's new insistence on aliases, I called the dealers "Brother A" and "Brother B," and Ramzi "Robert."

At the end of all this, Michael said, "Rei, as we know now, the vase Flowers had wasn't genuine. But that doesn't mean it passed from the brothers to Mr. Harmony. Why would a successful dealer sell a fake to a connoisseur?"

"It happens all the time. A connoisseur can't be an expert in everything. There was a significant Japanese bowl that I noticed in the Harmony household, and really, that's the only thing I'm positive is authentic. It makes sense that Harmony would be more aware of fine modern Japanese ceramics than ancient Middle Eastern work—just as I am."

"What you're saying, though, is only half of it. You're telling me why Harmony might have taken the piece. But what would the motivation be for the dealer to scam a well-connected diplomat? Brother B would risk losing his entire international clientele if word got out that he was a cheat."

"It could have been a matter of anger."

"Why? Did the son say there was an argument?"

"There was no fight between B and Harmony that Robert mentioned, but the fact is that the bride's parents refused to let her see Robert. They even shipped her back to Japan. This could have wounded Robert's father's pride enough for him to give Harmony a fake in exchange for payment."

"Hmm," Michael said. "It's an interesting theory, but it puts a lot of importance on a high school relationship. How likely is that? I mean," he said, "maybe you remember your first boyfriend, but were your parents vested in how that relationship turned out?"

"They were vested in destroying my relationships," I said, remembering.

Michael laughed, the first time I could remember him doing so. "And now that you're over thirty, it's probably the reverse."

"You're right, but don't let me lose my train of thought. I can make sense of Emi's parents' actions more than I can understand Brother B's laissez-faire parenting. Apparently Brother B wasn't thrilled that his son wanted to study in Japan, but because Brother A had already moved to Tokyo to open a shop, and Robert was of legal age and had his own trust fund, B didn't try to stop him."

"Ah, the trust fund left to him by his late mother?"

"Oh. You know about the mother?"

"I have done some research," Michael said. "What I've learned is that she was Iranian, was wealthy, and fled Iran with her parents for Paris during the revolution. She met her husband when he was taking a course there in arts and antiques. They married, and Robert was actually born in Paris. He holds two passports: E.U. and Turkish."

"I bet he used the E.U. passport for his student visa," I said. For a Turk to get a student visa would be much harder. "What about the mother? Do you know when and why she died? Robert was shaken when we talked about her."

"There was a car accident four years ago," he said. "The Mercedes she was driving was hit by a speeding bus on a mountain road near a resort. Not only did she die, but five people on the bus did, too."

"Oh, my God. And the bride was lost in a car accident, too." I was silent for a moment, thinking about how painful this coincidence must have been for Robert.

"You still there?" Michael's voice had a hint of anxiety.

"Yes. The main reason I called—I want more background on why the Harmonys left Japan. As you were saying, a high school romance is hardly reason to jump ship from an important ambassadorship. I wonder why he came back and took that other post. I think Mr. Ito would be our best source here—"

"You can't talk to him. I told you that already." Michael's voice was impatient.

"But why?" I challenged. "If you trusted him enough to bring him into the conference room at the Smithsonian and to arrange for my reentry into the country—why can't I ask him what I really need to know?"

"The father of the bride is a colleague of similar rank in the government. If we ask Ito about Harmony, there's a good chance he'll feel that the loyal thing to do is call the guy and warn him of our interest."

"I don't know about that. I liked Mr. Ito."

"Yes. You liked Mr. Flowers, too."

I bit my lip. "What are you insinuating?"

"Nobody said that you had to sleep with our suspect."

A slow flush spread through my body as the words registered. At last I said, "I'm trying to decide whether to hang up on you."

"Please don't. I'm sorry if you're embarrassed, but I have suspected this for a while, and I have to know. There aren't supposed to be secrets between us."

When embarrassed, go for sarcasm. "Actually, I'd think you would be delighted about what I did. The sacrifice of my virtue, or whatever you want to call it, meant that I was able to remain in the house overnight and locate the vessel. In fact, I answered the question you sent me out to answer, yet I still haven't been released from active duty—"

"I haven't called you home because you're doing so well," Michael said. "By all means, Rei, find out what you can by using the underground channels you seem so good at working. And I know you came onboard pro bono, but—this job has turned out to be more difficult than we all thought. I've put in a request already to arrange for some financial compensation."

Yes, I was a real whore.

I hung up, knowing that I should feel good about both the money and the praise, but I was only more depressed. How would I know the job was finished when the job description seemed to be changing daily? And I was disturbed that Michael knew about Takeo. Somehow, it gave him more power over me, and I didn't like that feeling at all.

I put the phone back into my sweater and rounded the corner, entering the residential neighborhood where Norie and Hiroshi lived. A Japanese policeman was standing alone in the center of the street. I continued on, but the policeman stepped directly in my path.

"This is an identification check," he said, in a voice that was all business. "May I see your foreigner registration, please?"

So the police had found me.

31

Identification check. The only thing I had going for me was that I didn't have my card with my name—although that in itself was a violation of the law. Foreigners were supposed to carry foreigner registration cards. Nobody really did in the old days, because the police didn't run around hassling people. But that was then. This was now.

"I'm just visiting on a tourist visa. I'm not a resident, so I don't carry a card," I said, eyeing the street for signs of life. A block ahead, a salaryman was turning into his walled garden. There was nobody else around, just a big black car purring gently in a no-parking zone. Maybe that was what had brought the cop here—a chance to ticket the car, which some trusting Japanese person had left with the keys in the ignition. And now it was time to ticket the foreigner.

"When did you arrive?" the officer demanded.

"October fifth."

"And when is your departure date?"

Why had I bought Jackie and Win police dolls? This man was the farthest possible thing from cuddly. "I'm not sure. The next week or two."

The officer shook his head. "You must show me your passport and embarkation card."

Now I was in trouble. The fact was, fine print on the embarkation card said I was required to carry it with me at all times while in Japan. In the old days, nobody ever did that either.

I looked up at the tall officer, trying to establish a human bond. He looked so stern. He hadn't even demanded my name; I guessed that was because he knew it. The whole thing was a setup.

Damn, damn. I lowered my head and began, very slowly, to unzip my backpack. I certainly wasn't carrying my passport—after my bad luck with the first cell phone, I had stashed it in my suitcase in Aunt Norie's house.

I couldn't decide whether to admit to him that I didn't have the passport with me or to feign surprise about its absence. This man would show no mercy, and under Japanese law he had the right to take me into police custody and postpone telling the American embassy about my whereabouts for as long as suited police purposes. I was screwed.

I crouched down as if to grope in my backpack. All I wanted was for the ground to open up and swallow me, I thought as I looked at the policeman's large feet, in black suede running shoes. I blinked and looked again. Yes, he was wearing Nikes, not black leather lace-up boots like the police dolls in my backpack.

Why would a Japanese policeman wear the wrong shoes to work? A policeman would never do that. But an imposter might.

Trying to seem unsure, I rose up slowly and then hurled the backpack as hard as I could at the man's groin. He doubled over, swearing, as I sprinted up the street toward Norie's house. But before I knew it, I heard the big black car start up. He'd recovered enough to get himself into it. I now realized that it was his.

As I pounded the asphalt, I thought about the cell phone in my pocket, and the impossibility of pausing to make a call to 119. The man was probably a gangster, and he might even have a gun. In the land of gun control, gangsters seemed to be the only ones with guns.

I heard the car creeping around the corner I'd just turned. My only hope was to go where the car couldn't, over the walls and into the private gardens that surrounded the houses. But where was an entry point? I ran past one house with a six-foot stucco wall, knowing that it was too high and had nothing for me to grasp. The next one was bordered by a shorter bamboo fence, though, and hand over hand I pulled myself up, using the muscles that had previously been tested only in gym classes.

He'd seen me go over that garden fence; but now he couldn't see me anymore, and I had two other garden walls to choose from: one garden on the left, and one on the right. I ran for the higher one, which I knew bordered a house catty-corner from my relatives' house. It was high, though—about seven feet. I stood in front of it, breathing hard, trying to assess whether I'd make it. Fear made me feel as though I'd been running for an hour, but no more than a couple of minutes had passed. If only I had the power to get to the house.

Powerhouse. I remembered the pet phrase of my trainer at the gym in Washington. Women's strength was always in the belly. I just had to concentrate and pull my belly to my back. Feeling long, straight, and strong, I moved quickly upward, using the ivy that covered the garden wall for footholds. The top was in sight. The narrow, powerful wedge that I'd shaped myself into pulled over the top and then dropped down easily on the other side.

I was running through a garden, feeling the crunch of flowers under my feet. Sorry! I apologized between breaths as a woman peered at me out of her brightly lit dining room.

Another wall at the back of the garden, a little bit higher; I struggled more, scraping my hands as I climbed this one and half fell into the next garden. This was Aunt Norie's neighbor's garden, three houses away; I recognized the neighbor as she peered out at the intruder running through her bed of chrysanthemums.

I hoped she would call the police. Maybe the presence of real cops would scare away the impersonator. I had no inclination to make the call myself, right now—it was such a quiet night that I was sure my ragged voice would carry. I couldn't give myself away.

I couldn't run much more, but I was almost home, I thought as I faced the stone wall where, on the other side, I knew Aunt Norie's few remaining camellia bushes were planted. I took a deep breath, preparing to climb, then paused.

He'd know I was going home, I thought with a feeling of awful certainty. If he'd lain in wait for me in the Shimuras' neighborhood, he certainly knew my address. I imagined myself inside, and him knocking on the door—or, even worse, him presenting himself to Aunt Norie and getting in by pretense or force. I could make out headlights on the road, outside the other garden wall—the one that fronted the street. He was probably already there, waiting.

Norie's street was a cul-de-sac, so I could make my way out of the neighborhood by running through all the walled and fenced gardens, and back down to the main road where he'd found me. That was about the best I could do. I still had my train pass zipped into the cell phone holder, so I could board a train and get out of the neighborhood. Maybe Richard would take me in for the night, because all my cash and credit cards were in the backpack. I wondered what my pursuer would make of all that, and the police dolls and the boxed tea glasses, which I'd heard smash after the backpack bounced off his body.

I escaped the residential section, but I still felt vulnerable on the main road. I took a parallel path, down a smaller street crowded with little restaurants, to reach the train station. Then I jumped onto the first train heading back to Tokyo. It was rush hour, but I was too frazzled to observe any etiquette. My phone had switched itself into e-mail mode, and I had to press the "enter" button over and over again to get back to a telephone menu. At last I was able to dial my aunt's home number. Norie picked up. Her tone was impatient.

"Where are you? I've been so worried. A policeman was here just a few minutes ago. He wanted to return your backpack, which you apparently lost and a kind person turned in at the police station."

"Obasan, listen carefully. That man is not who he says he is. Tell me if he's still there—yes or no."

"No. He's not here. But as I was saying, Rei-chan, he would like to bring you your backpack when you return—which will be when? You're an hour late already."

"Obasan, if he really was a cop, why wouldn't he have just left the backpack with you to give to me?"

She paused. "He was a little strange, I suppose. His shoes—"

"Yes, they were the wrong ones, because it was the only part of his costume he overlooked." I gulped, because my throat was so dry. "His coming to you proves that he won't give up looking for me."

"Ara!" Aunt Norie exclaimed, the reality finally dawning on her. "I should call the police."

"Tell them there's an impersonator lurking in the neighborhood," I said. "Give them a physical description, including the shoes. If he's lingering around, they might find him. Oh, and tell them he's got a big black car. I couldn't identify the model, but it was a large sedan."

"Rei-chan, you are the one who noticed the most. You must be the one to give the description—"

"I'm sorry." I dropped my voice. "I'm in a situation where I just can't talk to them right now. I can only promise that I'll be careful and call you when I reach safety."

"Where are you going?" Aunt Norie's voice broke. " Not back to America. I know that place is not safe. Chika told me about the men who tried to beat up Angus-chan in your neighborhood—"

"My passport's at your house, remember?" I tried to sound reassuring. "I'm not going anywhere. I'm just looking for a quiet place where I can figure out the next step."

"A police station. That's where you should go!"

"I will call you later. Good-bye. And you must take care, too."

After I clicked off the phone and tucked it back into my pocket, I sat, gazing out the window and thinking. My retreat would have to come tomorrow, after I'd gotten more money. In the meantime, I'd need to find somewhere to spend the night, with no more than a fifty-yen piece in my pocket.

In actuality, there were several old friends and colleagues I could ask, but none of them had a spare room to put me in—and I was ashamed to ask for a favor when I hadn't bothered to pay them a social call on this visit. No, the only people I'd already visited, whom I could ask straight out with no worrying, were those paragons of responsibility, Richard and Simone.

I disembarked at Shibuya amid the evening bustle. As gray-haired salarymen in gray suits swarmed toward the trains, they were nearly knocked over by a reverse migration of young partyers. Twenty-something boys with hair the shade of Marilyn Monroe's and hot pink sneakers on their feet, teenage girls who'd worked their school uniform skirts to breezy new heights, fashionistas of both sexes in cowboy boots and shearling—they seemed to curve around me and lift me into their current. We were like a flock of birds, flying westward to where the best stores, restaurants, and nightclubs lay.

I remembered meeting friends at the statue of Hachiko the dog right outside the west exit; and a bit farther on, I remembered once feeling almost paralyzed with pain as I glimpsed Hugh sitting at a trendy wine bar with another woman. The bar was still there. I had an urge to stop in for a glass of something to calm my nerves, but then I remembered that I had exactly fifty yen to get me through the night.

I pressed on toward Language House, the school where Richard and Simone had set up a partnership. They'd chosen the location well, on a small side street loaded with comic book shops, bars, clothing boutiques, and record stores.

An animated billboard advertisement for Panasonic's new camera featured the singer Ayumi Hamasaki smiling down like an angel of the Tokyo night. Keep me safe, Ayumi, I thought to myself. And don't you dare take a picture of me in these clothes.

I was just going into the language school when the cell phone vibrated in my sweater pocket. I answered and heard Michael Hendricks's voice.

"Hold on a sec." I was relieved to hear from him, but I needed to find a really private place, so I headed for the ladies' room, which I knew had a door that locked. An English conversation school was not a place I wanted to be overheard having an English conversation.

"What's going on? What's happening to you?" Michael said.

"How—how did you know something happened?"

"It looked like you were trying to send e-mails. Lots of short messages came over with nothing on—"

"Oh. All I can think is that I accidentally bumped the phone when I was climbing!"

"Climbing?"

I explained about the man who'd been waiting for me, and my narrow escape.

"I'm concerned about what happened to you," Michael said slowly. "Still, I can't help wondering if, in this case, he might be the genuine item. It's fully within a policeman's rights to pursue an un-cooperative person. And perhaps there's more flexibility about shoe style than you think."

"His sneakers aside, no Japanese cop would lie in wait like that. If he was on a mission to bust illegal foreigners, he would be in certain Tokyo neighborhoods, not middle-class suburban Yokohama. And how would he know to show up at my aunt's house when there was no information in my backpack containing that address?"

"What if he was a real cop sent on a private job by someone higher up?" Michael asked, not pausing for an answer. "We know the police have custody of your old cell phone. I'm sure they've gone through it. Maybe you've become a person of interest to them, which is just what I was hoping would not happen."

"It's true, but . . . who would that someone higher up be? Mr. Harmony?"

"I'm thinking of Ito."

"Poor Mr. Ito. You're so untrusting of him—"

"He left a lot of gaping holes in the information he was supposedly providing us. Things like the engagement and the shop opening. For that reason, I can't trust him anymore."

"But you were so proud of your investigative skills. Now you're putting the onus of investigation on him, and I don't think that's fair."

"My business was to investigate you," Michael said bluntly. "He was responsible for the Japanese intelligence—and as you have pointed out, we had precious little, which compromised your work. Tell me, when's the last time Mr. Ito had contact with you?"

"After the auction. And he did explain exactly who Emi was, when I asked him afterward." But, come to think of it, he hadn't returned the calls that I'd made after Emi's accident. Why not?

Michael broke into my thoughts. "I bet he's headed back to Washington. I'll check on it. In the meantime, what can I do to help you?"

"To help?" I was incredulous. "Right now, I'm alone in the city with fifty yen in my pocket, and I'm not sure whether I should run to or from the next cop I see. What the hell can you do about that?"

Michael's voice remained cool. "I'll arrange for you to pick up some cash at the embassy tomorrow morning, when it opens at eight-thirty. Now, what about your passport? Was it in your back-pack, too?"

"Nope. It's still safe and sound in my suitcase at Aunt Norie's."

"Great. We can send a courier to pick up the suitcase and bring it to you at the airport. You'll get your ticket there, too. Now, the question is where you're going to sleep tonight."

I'd caught a whiff of something that made me uneasy. "What ticket are you talking about?"

"Your airplane ticket home. As you've reminded me ad nau-seam, I've kept you on active duty too long. You'll come home to-morrow."

"No! I know I sounded—stressed—a minute ago, but that doesn't mean I want to run away."

"Why wait? As you pointed out, you're in serious danger."

"But—" I broke off. It was hard to explain, but the incident with the cop had changed everything. All my old feelings of humiliation at being at the mercy of the Japanese law had come back. But this time, I had the possibility of revenge. If it was true that some gov-ernment bureaucrat had ordered my abduction, I wanted him ex-posed and brought down. I wouldn't be chased out until I knew the answer.

"Rei, can you hear me?"

"Yes, I can. And I'm sorry I snapped at you. I'm not ready to go, not when I'm so close to finding out what happened." I leaned against the tiled wall for support, because it felt stronger than I did.

"Come on, Rei. There's a time to exit gracefully. And don't worry about the mission. We can work on getting a warrant to get into Bi-rand's shop, Harada's house, wherever the damn vessel might be. But it's too high a risk for you to stay in Tokyo."

"I agree it's a bit dicey at the moment," I said, seeking to mollify him. "After I get the money from the embassy, I'll jump on the first train out. Don't send a courier for my suitcase. I can get it myself."

"Out to where?"

"I'm thinking of Kyushu. It's quiet, and I want to visit a pottery studio. After that, I'll think seriously about whether I should come home."

"Kyushu," Michael said, sounding mystified. "I suppose you want to make the most of your trip and bring home some pottery?"

"Not exactly." Men could be so dense. "Don't you remember that I said the Harmonys own a bowl from a Kyushu artist?"

"Yes, but I don't understand its significance in light of what's going on." He paused. "Go there if you want. Get the hell out of the city. I'd say go tonight, but I can't get the financial arrangements together quickly enough. What I'm going to do is have money wired to you through the State Department. I'll call the duty officer at the embassy in Tokyo right after I'm done. Where will you sleep tonight, if not at your relatives' house?"

"I'm going to ask Richard if I can sleep on his spare futon. Right now, I'm at his language school, waiting for them to finish teaching."

"Your gay ex-roommate?" Michael said.

"Right. There's no danger that I'll do anything stupid with him."

Michael sighed. "If that arrangement falls through for any reason, call me back. I'll come up with a safe house for you."

Safe house. Powerhouse. Language House. It all ran together in my head as I clicked off and went back into the reception area, looking for my friends.

32

While I was talking, classes had ended. Richard and Simone had taken the students on a field trip to Smoke Hose, I heard from one straggler who was still putting on a coat.

A language discussion group in a nightclub? I shook my head at the seemingly unlimited creativity of my friends. What did they really think the students would gain by struggling to hear foreigners shout casual English at each other in a loud setting?

"The goal is to be able to understand lyrics!" Richard shouted in my ear when I arrived at the club twenty minutes later. Smoke Hose was on the fifth floor of one of Roppongi's quintessential nightclub towers. There was a different club on each of the nine floors. Club Isn't It had been the hottest dance club in this particular tower three years earlier, but now hardly anyone had gotten out of the elevator on its floor. Richard and Simone had picked the noisiest, most crowded place, the new bar called Smoke Hose. The name was not a misspelling but a reference to the exposed ductwork on the ceiling and walls, and of course to the haze of cigarettes.

The students in the language class were seated at two round tables right at the front. Everyone had the same kind of ruled notebook, a sharp pencil, and a cocktail. Even the cocktails appeared to be the same—cosmopolitans, which by now I'd figured out were the city's drink of the moment. The goal, Richard explained, was for the students to attempt to transcribe what they were hearing. I couldn't catch more than the singer's refrain, "pounding rain and I love you again," but maybe that was the point. For anybody, this show was a critical test of language comprehension.

"She's Canadian," Richard informed me after the interminable performance finally terminated. "It's perfect for Simone's students doing French, and mine as well. Though it turns out she's mostly singing in English, which is pissing off the French students. And then it's Angus and company, just like you told me."

"The Glaswegian Hangover?" I caught my breath, trying to remember when Chika had told me the band was going to arrive.

"Of course. You told me they were coming in, and I checked the schedule, and it was delayed a couple of nights because of Nigo. Remember, you wanted to go out and see them?"

"It's just that I'm—I'm somewhat embarrassed to see Angus after—after Hugh and I haven't spoken for a while." I spoke fast and low, because a couple of the students were leaning in to listen, with pencils poised to write down my words.

"What's going on?" Richard scrutinized me.

"The fact is, I don't know if I have the stamina to make it through the whole performance. Like I told you and Simone, I need somewhere to crash tonight and I'll be forever grateful for your spare futon."

"I can understand you not wanting the news getting around about how you look tonight." Richard paused, then delivered the bad news. "Like a soccer mom who was left out in the rain—but this business about not talking to Hugh? Please explain."

I sighed and said, "It all started with a stupid little argument we had on the phone the night you met me at Salsa Salsa . . . and it kind of continued. I shifted places where I was staying, so, well, . . . we haven't been in touch for a while."

Richard pursed his lips and said, almost primly, "How would you feel if he did this to you?"

"I'd be angry, unless there was a good reason."

"Precisely. And whether or not you have a good excuse for what you did, you can think one up now. Where's your cell phone?"

"Did you smoke something tonight? You seem awfully forceful," I said in a low voice.

"No, I'm not. It's a casual, every-now-and-then thing. And don't distract me from the topic of this conversation. You've got a phone call to make."

Richard was right. The time had come to make the call, and there actually was a lull in the noise because the Canadian singer was gone and the roadies were redoing the stage layout for the Glaswegian Hangover to come on. Chika came in, though, and sat down next to me.

"I'm so glad to see you," I said, giving her a hug.

"Yes, I—I'm surprised to see you. Mother said you were in trouble. She called me about it. And it turns out all you wanted to do was get to the show!" Chika giggled, putting her hand over her mouth.

"That's not it at all," I said. "Chika-chan, I am mainly here because I'm hoping to stay with Richard afterward. I can't stay at your house any longer because someone's looking for me there."

"Who?" Chika looked alarmed.

"I don't know. That's the problem."

We'd been speaking in English, and I realized now that the students at the table were listening with interest, some taking notes. Christ. How could I call Hugh in this environment?

When Chika went to the stage, answering Sridhar's call for help moving a speaker, I made my own move to the edge of the room to escape the eavesdropping students. I punched in the number for Hugh's office.

When I asked to speak to Hugh, Rhiannon, his personal assistant, sounded surprised. "Rei, it's such a relief to hear from you! Hugh's been a real pain for the last week, let me tell you, worried out of his mind. Neither of the phone numbers you gave him worked, and I triple-checked as well, with no luck. What happened?"

Feeling deeply guilty, I mumbled something about the typhoon and moving around.

"Now, if only I can get him. He's in conference with a gentleman from the Treasury Department, but I know he wouldn't want to miss you—"

"I could call back in an hour."

"No, no, he'll have my head on a platter if he misses this. And I know he's off to New York for something later on. This is the only time to catch him. Hold on, love, I'll ring his private line."

Half a minute later, Hugh was on, his voice sounding as if he were in a tunnel.

"Hi, Hugh! Is your telephone okay? Can you really talk?" I asked by way of greeting.

"I put you on the speakerphone because I have to go through some e-mail while we talk. So what's doing?"

"Ah, won't the speakerphone disrupt you and your client?"

"He just left. It's okay."

Hugh's words were reasonable, but his manner put me on edge. He hadn't called me darling, as he usually did, or given any inkling of the reaction that Rhiannon had led me to expect. He was reviewing e-mail while talking to me, for God's sake.

"What's doing, Rei?" he repeated.

"Well, I'm in a new nightclub called Smoke Hose, and your brother is about to take the stage. Right now he's tuning up his guitar, and my cousin Chika's helping move a speaker on the stage—"

Hugh interrupted me sharply. "What are you trying to do, establish the fact that you're in an actual location with witnesses?"

"Not at all. I was just answering your question. Why the interrogation?"

"You're no longer registered at the hotel where you said you'd be. The cell phone number you gave me was answered by another woman the first time around, and now is disconnected. You were at your aunt's fleetingly, but not anymore. If this is your idea of a business trip, I can only hope that your client has better access to you than I do."

Did his words have a subtext, or was that idea just my paranoia? "Hugh, I apologize. I did call you several times, including once in the night when I thought you'd be in bed, close to the phone. But all I ever seemed to get was your voice mail. Didn't you hear those messages?"

"Of course I did, but you left no information that allowed me to contact you. Anything could have happened, and you'd never know. We had a bomb scare in the building last week, for instance—"

"The apartment building?" I asked, struggling to hear. Angus and the boys were onstage, tuning their instruments.

"No, at my office. Andrews and Cheyne. You didn't read about it in the papers?"

"Hugh, I've been so busy I've barely had time to look at the papers."

"I'm busy, too, but I check the papers every day. The *Post* and the *Times* and also the Japanese papers I can find online, just so I have an inkling of situations that might affect your safety—"

"If you're reading the Japanese papers, you must realize that the typhoon we had last week affected everything. I never had a phone that worked to call you. I'm just trying to make amends—"

Hugh sighed audibly. "For that to happen, I need you to stop all this evasion. Tell me the truth about why you went."

"You know it was for the Smithsonian Institution."

"I was so frantic about you that I called over to the Smithsonian to find a contact. Nobody there knows your name."

"That must be because the Smithsonian is so large. They can't keep tabs on every museum's activities, and the Sackler is one of the smallest."

"You're lying to me. Because when I called the Sackler, nobody there knew of you either—"

With an ear-shattering bar of electric guitar, The Glaswegian Hangover were on.

"Hugh," I shouted, "your brother's started playing. I can't hear you."

"Well, bloody well step outside the club for a minute."

"If I do that, they might not let me in again, and I have no money." And if I lost contact with Richard, I'd lose my bed for the night.

"Priorities . . . mine . . . wrong place . . ." I could make out only a few of Hugh's words. It was like trying to understand the Canadian singer all over again.

"I'll call you later, Hugh!" I called into the receiver. "I love you!"

"Go to hell," Hugh shouted in return.

33

The saving grace, as the night rolled on, was that the music was so loud. I didn't need to speak; I could just sit there and nod every now and then. I could not smile, though I mustered up an approximation of something like a smile when Angus raised his bottle of Kirin to me from the stage. Even when Chika and part of the language class took to the front of the club to execute a line dance to the song "Loved You Last Night, Hate You Today," I couldn't laugh and cheer the way the rest of our group did.

I'd lost Hugh, just as I'd lost him time and time before. We fought as much as we loved each other—if you looked at it objectively, our union had really been one long disagreement broken by spells of remarkable sex. I remembered the last four passionate nights before I'd left. Maybe we'd both been so eager because it was a way of suppressing the lie that lay underneath us. Hugh must have sensed that something was up, but he had not dared to pursue it until I was gone.

Angus and his friends performed two forty-five-minute sets. I went with everyone to Café Almond afterward, and we walked back to Shibuya amid a throng of excited students, drunken musicians, and my two old friends. Chika slipped in beside me and we linked arms, like Japanese schoolgirls.

"Do you want to stay with us?" asked Chika, who was bunking

with the band at their hotel, the Roppongi Lily. She'd already called her mother to report that she had found me safe and sound, and the two of us were staying at a girlfriend's apartment.

"Thanks, but I really do want to stay with Richard."

Chika cocked her head. Her long, striated black-and-gold hair fell across her eyes, and she pushed it back impatiently. "You're so lucky you don't have to make excuses. You can do just what you like."

"Well," I said carefully, "I've actually found that lying's worse. I don't recommend it at all."

Chika's pretty face flushed. "My parents don't want to know the truth. This is easier on everyone."

We paused, momentarily, because there was an obstacle in our path. A Japanese girl in her late teens, eyes closed, was lying on the damp sidewalk in front of us with her legs and clothes askew. Behind her was the doorway of a nightclub; the bouncers standing there seemed to be jeering at her.

"Drunk. The poor thing!" Chika said, stepping around her.

"Wait a minute. Who's taking care of her?" I called out so the bouncers would hear. They looked away from me, so I called it out again.

One of the bouncers said, "Who knows? She had too much drink. She just fell down." He didn't look at me as he spoke.

"How do you know? It could be an overdose, something really dangerous!" I said, crouching down and adjusting her clothes. Seeing my action, the last remaining students in the group formed a knot around the girl and me and began murmuring expressions of concern.

"Excuse me, but who brought her here? Where are her friends?" One of the female students spoke up.

"She stepped out with a man. He went off to get a cab, I think—"

"Maybe he won't come back," someone else in the crowd said in a knowing voice. The others murmured in agreement.

"It's the way things are," the bouncer said, throwing up his thick hands helplessly. "This thing happens every night."

"We could call her parents." I opened the small Kate Spade bag at her side to look for a piece of identification. There was nothing;

just a pack of tissues issued by a loan shark, a Shiseido lipstick, ten thousand yen and change, and a small red pill.

"This! Look at this!" I held it up for everyone to see. "She could have OD'd. She needs to be seen at a hospital—"

"Rei, put that thing away," Richard interrupted. "You don't want the cops to take you in."

It was true that I didn't want any face time with the police. I let my group carry me along, but not before I'd made certain that the bouncer had called an ambulance.

The sight of the collapsed girl haunted me as I lay on Richard's mildewed guest futon, trying to get to sleep. I'd been to the bathroom, looking for a sleeping aid but finding nothing on the bathroom shelf except Richard's amphetamine tablets. I flushed the tablets down the toilet, and left a tiny note inside the foil where they'd been wrapped: *Sorry. But it's because I love you.*

In the dim glow of his clock radio, I stared at the Marky Mark poster on the wall across from me, the famous Bruce Weber shot of him in Calvin Klein underwear, leaning against a pillar, shading his eyes. It was almost as if he didn't want to be identified, though of course he did; the picture had made his career.

Nobody had known who the girl on the sidewalk was. Nobody had cared. I would have been the same, dead, without a passport to even identify me, if I hadn't gotten away from the man near my relatives' house. I really had no safe haven. I had to leave.

The band had a car and driver, so one of the last things I'd asked for, before we parted, was that the driver pick me up at Richard's address at ten minutes to eight. He was too early to be of use to the boys, but he would be able to offer me a safe passage to the embassy, and then on to Tokyo Station.

The boys had been so giddy the previous night that I wasn't sure if my request would really make it to the driver, but sure enough, just before eight the next morning the same Lincoln Continental was waiting for me with the same man who'd ferried Chika and the boys off after Café Almond. I told the driver where I wanted to go, and he sped me there quietly. We didn't break our silence till we reached the huge, boxy gold building that was the U.S. Embassy. When I'd tried to get the cab to wait for me alongside the chancery's long black fence, a Japanese police guard had come up and refused to let him even stop. It was because of security, they said. As a compromise, I told the driver I'd look for him at Hotel Okura across the street.

Michael had told me to be there at eight-thirty, but a line of about 100 people—Japanese and others—were already waiting for admission. Feeling depressed, I joined the end of the line. When a blond woman backpacker walked straight to the guard post at the front of the line and was instantly waved through, I turned to the Brazilian-Japanese man waiting behind me.

"Did you see how she went ahead of everyone?"

"Americans can go ahead. Even if they don't have their passports."

Feeling guilty, I thanked the man for the information and went straight to the front. There, things didn't go as smoothly as I hoped. For one, because I didn't have my passport, I had to convince the guard that I was actually American, not Japanese. Of all the times to fit into Japanese society, this was not the time I wanted. I persisted and remembered something Michael had said about a so-called duty officer knowing my name. At last, the guard gave me a long look, then went into his booth and made a phone call. I heard him speaking into it, saying that my English was almost perfect, but my name was Japanese, so he didn't know. He listened for a minute, then hung up and nodded at me.

"Miss Shimura, you may step through the metal detector."

I did that and practically sprinted along the short path to the next security checkpoint, which was yet another metal detector at the embassy door. Once I passed through it, my gaze turned from a room packed with visa applicants to a small, intense Caucasian man with his shirtsleeves rolled up, who held out his right hand to me.

"Miss Shimura. I've been expecting you. I'm Jim Renseleer, the vice consul. I'm going to walk you through the passport replacement process, and then I'll bring you on to your next meeting."

Shaking his hand, I said, "I don't actually need a new passport. I'm really here about—money."

"But you didn't have your passport at the gate."

"I couldn't bring it with me this morning." I wished I could say more, pour out my nightmarish last twenty-four hours to this concerned-looking man, but I knew that I should not.

"All right, then. There's an army officer here on temporary duty who wants to see you. I believe she'll be handling whatever transaction the State Department has decided is appropriate."

He was suspicious of me, I thought, as he led me down a gray-carpeted hallway. I knew that I was a contradiction in terms: the American citizen who looked Japanese, the person without a passport who didn't want a new one but simply wanted money.

"Here you go. Good luck." He opened the door to a conference room crowded with desks and computers. I stopped at the threshold and gaped at the officer who was sitting at the conference table.

The woman at the table had tawny skin, hazel eyes, and a commanding manner. This time, she was out of uniform and in a plain blue suit, but I would have known Brenda Martin anywhere.

The colonel inclined her head at me. "Good morning, Ms. Shimura. I see our receptionist hasn't gotten you coffee yet. How do you like it?"

I remembered our first meeting, when I'd arrived dressed well enough, but wrecked from my night at Club Paradise—I'd sensed she could tell. Today I'd again had a hard night, and I was wearing wretched, filthy clothing. Did I need coffee? Incredibly. But I was not about to admit I was collapsing.

"Oh, that's okay. I don't need any coffee."

"Here, sit down." She motioned to a chair pulled up on the other side of her desk. "You look exhausted. Michael said you've been through a lot in the last few days."

I wanted to change the subject. "Do you work in Tokyo now, Colonel Martin?"

"Not exactly." She sipped from her own cup of coffee. "I'm in Army intelligence, though, so I travel quite a bit. I arrived a few days ago, after I'd reviewed the evidence you sent. I'm still getting adjusted to the time—which is why I was glad you wanted to come in first thing this morning."

"I see." I shifted uneasily in my chair, knowing I should feel reassured, but feeling only more nervous.

"I have the money for you right here. Do you wish to check the amount before you go? I need you to sign a receipt for me." She slid an envelope across the polished desk, along with a thin paper slip and a pen.

"Intelligence," I said, thinking it over. "I had thought this was just—State Department stuff. Does that mean Michael's in Army intelligence, too?"

"Michael is ex-Navy, remember? And I'd rather have him discuss the specifics of his organization. But he's a good man to work with, I'll tell you that much." She smiled at me.

"Really." A chill settled over my skin, despite the warm, even heat of the building. If she wouldn't tell me, that probably meant Michael was part of the CIA. Now I thought about all the things—the monitoring that had been done for me, the ease with which an official passport had been issued, Michael's insistence on code names, the spontaneity with which he offered me a bonus.

"I love my work." Brenda looked at me intently. "I've been able to combine an interest in foreign relations with justice. And believe it or not—I got where I am starting out in a capacity similar to what you're doing now, though it was less dangerous."

"That's right. My job wasn't supposed to be dangerous at all."

Brenda lowered her voice. "I understand there has been a casualty. Michael offered you the option to go home, but said you wouldn't. We can still get you a ticket, any time you say the word."

A casualty. She made Emi's death sound like a small event in a big war. But I wasn't giving up on that war. Resolutely, I said, "I'm not going until I've accomplished what I promised."

"What if it's not here, after all? The interviews you've done so far have added to the case that the brothers are selling fraudulent merchandise, but not the original we were worried about."

"Yes, they are selling some new pieces that they're pretending are old, but why would they sell copies of stolen artworks? That would be utter insanity for their business. It would draw the police straight to them—"

"That's why our plan is to pass on what you've found out to organizations that can better investigate the complexities of suspected art theft. And as I just mentioned, you could return to the United States as early as this afternoon."

"But what about Emi's father?" I didn't mean to interrupt, but I couldn't help myself. "What did he do during his time in Turkey that got him bounced back here? And how did he get the funds for the world-class art collection in his house?"

"Even if some of his art was obtained through shady connections, it seems clear that he didn't steal any. Remember the original mission, Rei: it was to locate a stolen work of art that was taken out of Iraq. The mission was not to embarrass the Japanese government, our longtime friends who actually agreed to give you, a persona non grata, a chance to resume life on Japanese soil."

I listened to Brenda Martin's words, and I had to admit that she had a valid argument about not wanting to cause unnecessary trouble with the Japanese. But the fact remained that a Japanese man had been lying in wait for me the previous evening. I told the colonel what had happened, and my suspicions about who was behind it.

"I think I know why that incident happened," she said when I'd finished.

"Why?" I sat up straighter in my chair.

"Your experience last night came about because you blew your cover." Brenda Martin's voice was suddenly cold. "You flew to Japan in the guise of a museum consultant, but instead you turned yourself into a one-woman, legal task force asking people too many questions about drugs and their sex lives. Obviously, you teed someone off, and that individual sent an enforcer to find out who you're working for."

"I've told no one," I said.

"Good," Brenda answered. "Now, in accordance with Michael's wishes, I'm not going to try to force you to leave the country. I do think it's a good thing that you're at least going away from Tokyo for a while."

We looked at each other. I'd won the skirmish, but barely.

"Thank you," I said.

"Absolutely. That's why I'm here. Now, I understand that you have a new cellular phone?"

"I do." I patted my pocket. "One of the few things I didn't lose yesterday."

"You're lucky you got into the building; it's against the regs," she said crisply. "Let me give you a few phone numbers where you can reach me, although you should feel free to continue to call Michael. How long do you expect to be away?"

"Just a day or two." Long enough to see the potter, and have the questions answered that had been at the back of my mind.

"And during this time, may I have your word that you won't try to speak with anyone in the Japanese government, whether it's someone as lowly as a cop or as high up as a government minister?"

I nodded glumly and signed the receipt. I wanted to get out of there.

"This is the best number to call, if you want to discuss something personally with me." A long, French-manicured fingernail tapped the first number on the card. "The other ones will allow you to leave a message with a human being."

"Okay. Well, I'm actually hoping to be out of town within the next few hours—that is, if I can get a ticket—so I'd better go."

"*Gambatte*, Rei." She held out the envelope, which was still lying on the desk. "And don't forget to take the money."

It wasn't until I was in the limousine ten minutes later that I opened it and saw how much there was. A million yen—the equivalent of $10,000. And an unsigned note inside: *Michael said for you to keep the change.*

34

I'd been planning to travel to Kyushu on the bullet train, taking the whole day, but I was now rich enough to take an hour-and-a-half flight direct from Haneda Airport to Fukuoka. First, thought, I'd need my passport, and that would involve retrieving it from Yokohama. I weighed the risks of taking the train to my aunt's station and then walking to her house, but I decided that would be foolhardy.

I asked the driver to give me the name of a trusted colleague, and by the time we'd reached Angus's hotel, I'd booked my own car and driver and reserved a seat on the one o'clock flight to Fukuoka. Feeling supremely organized, I used the house phone and called from the lobby to Angus Glendinning's room.

"Hi, I'm calling up from downstairs. I just wanted to say I'm done with borrowing your driver. He's in the hotel drive, awaiting your next command."

"Command? What the hell time is it?" Angus croaked, sounding exactly like his brother first thing in the morning.

"Nine-thirty. Too early, huh?"

"Christ, I'm exhausted. Your cousin's a madwoman. Kept me up all night."

"Really?" I'd thought Chika was interested in Sridhar. Had she leapfrogged to Angus?

"Yeah." Angus laughed richly. "She just, like, wanted to give us all Japanese lessons all night to make a good impression on TV today."

"That's right, your chauffeur said that you need to be at TBS at eleven for an interview," I said, vastly relieved that all he was talking about were language lessons.

"There's still time. Come up for a coffee or something. Chika made it already."

My second offer of coffee this morning—and this one was worth taking up, I decided. I hadn't had any time to catch up with Angus, and now he was fully available and sober. I thanked him for the invitation and rode the elevator up to the tenth floor. Outside Angus's room, the *Japan Times,* the *Asahi Shinbum,* and a Japanese tabloid popular with male readers, *Tokyo Supootsu,* lay waiting. I picked them up to bring in before I knocked.

Angus answered, half-dressed in a hotel towel and with wet red hair standing on end.

"You must have just gotten out of the shower," I said, feeling shy in the presence of all that Glendinning skin. "I'm sorry to have come this early. Shall I leave and give you time to dress?"

"Why so formal?" Angus said, imitating Hugh's upper-crust Edinburgh drawl. "Come in, darling. You look like you could use wee kip on the sofa."

I put the paper down on the coffee table in front of a cheerful striped sofa. The Roppongi Lily was a decent hotel, not as luxurious as the Grand Hyatt, but with Western amenities like the sofa, a desk with cables for a laptop, and a double bed. I looked for evidence that two pillows had been used by two people, but there was no way to tell. All the pillows were on the floor.

I looked around for Chika. "Where's my cousin?"

Angus yawned. "Off to work, Sridhar said. But she was good enough to spirit herself around and make everyone's coffee."

As I poured cream in my own cup of coffee, I pondered the meaning of Angus's statement, which seemed to suggest that Chika had slept in Sridhar's room. Well, I liked the prospect of Chika with Sridhar more than the thought of her with Angus.

"I'll take another cup, Rei. Make mine black as your beautiful hair," Angus called. He'd slipped on his jeans while I'd been fixing my cup, and he was now lounging on the sofa, leafing through the newspaper.

I took him the black coffee, figuring it was the least I could do after borrowing his car. And I wanted to use his bathroom, too. "Do you mind if I spend a few minutes freshening up?"

In the bathroom mirror, I evaluated myself. Not pretty at all, even after I'd washed my face. I was still wearing the same bedraggled clothes as the day before—and my hair was so awful. I was an ugly, easy mark for the cop who'd stalked me. And where was the policeman from hell today—still looking for me?

I scrutinized Angus's many grooming aids tossed across the vanity table. There was a surprising amount of makeup to play with, and a bottle of temporary hair coloring. The shade was flame red.

I stuck my head out of the door and called, "Angus, do you mind if I try out your hair color?"

Angus was on the phone, talking with someone. "Yeah, yeah, tonight's great," he said, not noticing me.

I waved and held up the bottle questioningly. Angus smiled. I decided to take this as a yes. Besides, it was an economy-size bottle; there'd be plenty left over for him.

I read the instructions quickly. The redness achieved would vary, depending on one's original hair color and the amount of time the dye was left on. Black hair, I figured, would fall at the longer end of the waiting time. I washed my hair in the sink with Angus's Aveda shampoo, and then applied the color, using the provided plastic comb to distribute it evenly. Then, I donned a little shower cap—it amused me to imagine the macho Angus wearing this item—and waved a blow-dryer around my head. This wasn't part of the instructions, but I remembered my mother sitting under a giant bubble dryer when she had her blonding treatments. Heat could only help speed the process or intensify the color.

I thought about asking Angus—after all, he was the expert at this—so I turned off the dryer, adjusted the towel I was wearing around my shoulders to protect my sweater, and went back into the bedroom.

Sridhar, dressed in drawstring pants and a striped turtleneck, had joined Angus and had his own copy of *Tokyo Supootsu* in hand. When he saw me peep out, his eyes widened.

"Excuse the shower cap, I'm just working on restyling my look." I winked at him.

"Is it—because of the picture?"

"What picture?" Angus asked from his lazy perch on the couch.

"Chika saw it while she was riding the train. She called to warn us," Sridhar told Angus in a low, angry voice.

"So someone snapped a picture of us behaving badly last night?" Angus laughed lazily. "Well done. The timing's great, with the TV bit about to happen—"

"That's right," I chimed in. "People say that there's no such thing as bad publicity. How much trouble did you boys get into, after we parted last night?"

"We weren't the problem," Sridhar said, staring at me in a way that seemed almost reproachful. "You were."

"Oh," I said, starting to feel worried. If my face was in the paper, it would probably fan the flame of the man who was chasing me, and any of his colleagues as well. But who would have photographed me? "Did somebody take a picture of us standing around that poor girl who was passed out on the street?"

"I can't believe you haven't guessed." Sridhar's tone had turned from cool to frigid.

"I don't want to guess. Let me see!" Suddenly, I was frantic.

"Yeah, where's the infamous snap?" Angus was rummaging through his own copy, a perplexed look on his face. Apparently he hadn't known that in Japan, the back page of the paper is the front.

"Page three," I said, feeling dead. "That's usually where the scandal stories and photos are placed."

"Bingo," Angus said as I leaned in to inspect the close-up black-and-white photo of a man and woman.

It was bad. The couple in the picture were Takeo Kayama and myself, at the very moment at which Takeo had tripped toward the duck pond and I'd attempted to stop him and wound up in the water, too. The photographer had captured the two of us in each other's arms, laughing, and improbably surrounded by fluttering ducks. I didn't have enough time to decipher all the writing underneath, but I did make out my name and Takeo's, both spelled correctly.

"Who's the arsehole?" Angus finally said.

"His name is Takeo Kayama. He's an old friend."

"A boyfriend, according to the papers," Sridhar chimed in. "Son of the eighth richest man in Japan, who only the day before was mourning the death of his fiancée."

"I didn't know you could read Japanese," I said.

"I can't!" Sridhar retorted. "Chika translated the story for me over the phone."

"I had no idea someone was watching us with a camera," I said. "If only they'd come up and asked for an interview, I could have easily explained. We weren't hugging. It was actually an accident— he, we, fell into the pond. The ducks took off because of a light— damn it, that probably was the first camera flash! I remember more light going off when we were in the water, but I just didn't make the connection."

"Why were you having a walkie-walk by a duck pond with a guy who just lost his fiancée?" Angus demanded. "You're making a bloody fool of my brother, not to mention yourself."

"Takeo needed help, Angus. I'd just gone there to help him. And this picture—well, it will be even worse for him than me, if you can believe it." I put my face in my hands, wishing everything would go away.

"Go on, hide your face!" said Sridhar. "I would too if I committed such a devious deception!"

"The way Hugh talked about you to us . . ." Angus drifted off, sounding heartbroken. "He loved you more than life itself, and I know he thought you were going to Japan to work, not to become a total slapper!"

I looked at both of them, knowing the worst part was that I couldn't protest. There had been a one-night stand, and that was essentially the same thing as an affair. I stood up and attempted a wry half smile. "I never thought I'd get a moral lecture from two guys in a rock band. *Sumimasen.* I'll just get this crap out of my hair and I'll leave."

"So, where are you going?" Angus asked. "To this Takeo dude?"

I wiped away a bit of the foamy substance that had dripped underneath the shower cap onto my forehead. "No, I'm actually leaving town for a while. This kind of—misunderstanding—and the snap judgments of people I considered my friends make me realize I'd rather not stay around. I'll—I'll just go into the bathroom and rinse this stuff out—I'm supposed to rinse it out, right?"

"Yeah," Angus answered, not even looking at me.

"So that's why you're changing your hair color." Sridhar snapped his fingers. "New bloke, new look, eh?"

"It's not because of him."

"Like I said before, I liked your hair the way it was," Angus said.

When I came out of the bathroom again, they were gone: to Sridhar's room, maybe; or to one of the other guys, I wasn't masochistic enough to hunt them down to say good-bye.

Aunt Norie silently answered the door when I rang. I'd said *"Tadaima,"* the phrase that meant, "I've returned home," but she had not answered with the corresponding *"Okaeri nasai."* I was not welcome. My suitcase had been packed and was standing next to the front door.

"You changed your hair color," my aunt said dully. It figured that even if she didn't want to talk to me, she couldn't resist criticizing my appearance.

"I did it because of the man who followed me last night. It's supposed to wash out after a week or two." I hadn't left the color in long enough, or combed it through right, because the end result was a horrible hodgepodge of black and red chunks.

"Oh? You mean you didn't do it because of what's in the papers and on television?"

"Obasan, please understand that Takeo and I are not in a relationship," I said, choosing my words carefully. "We had met at the park to chat and didn't know we were being followed by a paparazzo. I was trying to help Takeo when he tripped into a pond, and that's all the picture shows."

"On the TV news this morning, they called you the ducky lovers,"

Norie said, her distaste clear. "A reporter even interviewed the taxi driver who took us to Emi's memorial service. He said you and Takeo had a passionate discussion right outside the family house!"

"I didn't want to keep that driver waiting around. I knew he was a gossip—"

"Oh, don't blame him. It would come out anyway that you were the girl who was banned from Japan, the girl whose return resulted in the death of a young bride-to-be—"

"I didn't kill Emi," I said, my heart pounding. "Is that what they're saying?"

"No, but it's just a matter of time before someone asks. That policeman yesterday evening was probably genuinely looking for you to question."

"Maybe so, but I doubt it. And the truth is, through this all I was only trying to help—"

"To think that I let you convince me to arrange a meeting with Takeo-san at his office, which started all the trouble!" Aunt Norie's voice rose into hysteria. "I've already spoken with your uncle and cousin about this. I fear we'll never be received socially again, and it could affect their jobs—"

The sad thing was that she was right. "Well, there's one way Japanese people have always survived socially, when a family member misbehaves."

"I'm not going to kill myself over your—your ridiculous actions."

"Of course you won't," I said. "But you can cut me off. Disown me. Not have me as a niece anymore."

Norie blinked, and I could see tears in her eyes. "I would never do that."

"I think you should if things are as bad for you as you've just said."

"Rei-chan." My aunt took a shuddering breath and seemed to calm down slightly. "I didn't intend to speak so sharply. You are one who makes mistakes. But you weren't brought up here. There's so much we should have taught you, that we haven't done."

"It's not your fault. And I'm sorry I dragged you into the matter with Takeo." I picked up my suitcase. "Do you know if my passport's in here?"

"I double-checked that it's in the front pocket. But where are you going? Not back into Tokyo, I hope, because that's where the press is crawling, looking for another chance to catch you doing something silly."

"I'll be miles away, where nobody expects to see me," I assured her. "And when I come back, I promise that I'll figure out a way to make things right."

35

When I first visited the island of Kyushu, I was on a holiday with my parents, buying pottery. The part of the daylong train ride I remembered best was passing Mount Fuji—how the faraway snow-capped mountain grew in size as I badgered my parents about getting out to climb it. But the train raced by, Fuji was gone, and I was heartbroken. So all the time we'd been in Kyushu, wandering through tiny, one-restaurant villages that did not serve the Italian pasta I craved, I'd griped to my parents about not stopping at Fuji-san to climb it. With the typical hubris of a seven-year-old, I was certain that I could make it to the top—and I wanted the walking stick, stamped with the milestones, that each successful climber brought home.

As the All Nippon Airways jet passed near Japan's most revered landmark, the pilot encouraged us to look for it through the windows on the left side of the cabin. I strained my eyes but couldn't see Fuji. The season was cold enough for snow to have covered the mountain, making it difficult to spot against the thick white clouds that enveloped it.

I was looking for something that, just like Fuji and its cloudy cloak, was masked by cloud cover. But I was highly doubtful that my trip to Kyushu would result in a revelation. I'd meet the potter, if I was lucky, and perhaps he could tell me something about how

Mr. Harada had paid for his artwork. That's all I might gain: a little more information on how the sophisticated collector did business, a tiny glimpse through the clouds.

The touchdown in Fukuoka was smooth, and my passage through the airport was just as uneventful. Nobody was on the lookout for me here, I realized with relief as I made my connection at Hakata station to a limited express train bound for Karatsu, the famous pottery region. A train attendant hawked copies of all the national papers, including *Tokyo Supootsu*, along with little cans of coffee, beer, and *bento* box lunches, but nobody who bought a paper glanced accusingly at me.

When the attendant came to me, I bought a lunch. Quickly, I demolished the picture-book arrangement of rice, sake-glazed salmon, and pickled bamboo shoots. I'd eaten nothing until now, and so I had been dangerously nauseated on the plane. I'd survived that flight, but barely, and now I was determined to arrive in Umeda in good condition. I'd taken the time, back at the airport, to change my clothes; now I was wearing Grand's smart St. John suit, which seemed a little incongruous with my hair but was the best thing I had in my suitcase. I also had a large box of Belgian Leonidas chocolates, which I'd bought for the equivalent of $100. That's what my expense account was for: I had to present Kazu Sakurai with a valuable gift that he couldn't possibly find locally. Judging from the tourist materials I'd picked up in Fukuoka, there wasn't much shopping near Umeda. Sakurai's pottery studio was the entire shopping scene.

My phone vibrated. I picked it up reluctantly and, remembering what I knew about phone etiquette on trains, answered in a low voice.

"Rei-san! What's wrong with you?"

It was Chika.

"It's not the way it looks," I said. "And I wish you hadn't gotten the boys all upset for nothing—"

"Hugh's wonderful. How can you do such a thing to him?" Chika was crying.

"It was a picture taken out of context—"

"Lie to him, but not to me." Chika's voice was hard.

"You're as tough as your mother," I said.

"And you—you're just—American!" Chika hung up after that.

Trying to calm myself, I read the artist's brochure, which was illustrated with color photos and had text in English, German, and Japanese. Kazu Sakurai was the ranking descendant in a family of pottery artisans—pre-Christian potters, if one was to believe the claims in the brochure.

I was skeptical about some of what I was reading, but not all. The history of Japanese pottery, I knew from my studies, originated in Kyushu as early as 10,000 BC. Kyushu potters made cooking vessels and female figurines that were different from the pottery found by archaeologists in other parts of Asia. This pottery style most probably came from Mongolia; thus, the early Kyushu pottery had more in common with Middle Eastern work than with what was commonly regarded as Japanese. Sakurai, the brochure told me, had spent twenty years studying the archaeological fragments of these pots, and had experimented with firing methods. When he felt he could produce pots that were almost identical to the earliest, lost works, he produced a collection of urns that won the grand prize in Japan's foremost pottery competition. After that, he turned away from the sophisticated glazes of his father and grandfather in favor of rustic historic forms. His fame grew, and within a few years he was designated a Living National Treasure, recieving an annual stipend to pay his apprentices' salaries.

There was nothing as tacky—or helpful—as a price list in the slick brochure. I figured that if you had to ask what it cost, you clearly couldn't afford it. The brochure explained that visitors would be granted access only to the studio shop. Should someone wish an audience with the master, he or she was advised to secure an appointment.

So I needed an appointment, I thought with a sinking feeling. At least I had the benefit of a little more than $9,000 in my backpack. I hoped that I wouldn't have to blow it all. I took out my cell phone, studiously bypassing the announcement of accumulated voice mail messages from Chika, Hugh, and Michael Hendricks. They were all probably calling to criticize me for my photographed embrace with Takeo. It was the last thing I wanted to discuss in a quiet train compartment.

A woman who sounded a good deal older than me answered the

phone. I pitched my voice into the high, polite register, saying that I was in from Tokyo and needed to see the master for guidance on choosing a piece of pottery.

"I'm very sorry, but my master is not available on short notice. However, I am happy to offer you personal assistance while you visit us. Is it a wedding gift that you seek?"

Why had she asked about a wedding? The thought of Emi and Takeo made me press my lips together. Then I remembered that I'd pitched my voice to resemble a Tokyo office lady's. She'd probably assumed that I was unmarried and had pooled resources with my colleagues to be able to afford something from a Living National Treasure.

"I'm not sure if it's going to be a present or not. But I do want to shop."

"*Ah so desu ka*," she said gently. "Well, perhaps I can give you some ideas about what we have in your particular price range."

"Thanks. Is there anything for about fifty thousand yen?" That was just a bit less than $500, and seemed a generous starting point.

"I'm so sorry, but at that price there is only one item we have: a *hashi-oki* service for five. And it would be made by an apprentice in our workshop who is under my master's direction, but not, you understand, custom-made . . ."

I winced. She was talking about chopstick rests, little pieces of porcelain used to hold the business end of chopsticks during a meal. "Did I say fifty thousand? I meant to say five hundred thousand."

"Oh." She laughed lightly. "In that case, you have another choice. We have at the moment a set of teacups made in the ancient style. And if you have a bit more flexibility in price, you will have the chance to commission something specially, though you said you needed to buy quickly."

"I don't know," I confessed. "What I really would like is to see what is in the studio, and humbly request your master's advice."

"Yes, I understand your wish. My master would like to meet with everyone who comes through the studio, but regrettably, in order to meet customers' deadlines he cannot do that. And since the typhoon, we have been very busy repairing the property."

"It's such a shame. I heard lovely things about the esteemed master from Harada-san, and that's why I was interested in a commission."

"Harada Kenichi-sama? The minister for the environment?" Her voice warmed.

"Yes."

"Ah, he is a very special friend to the studio. I think—my master may want to send his greetings to him. Your name is . . ."

"Matsuda Reiko," I said sweetly, taking the name from a real estate ad pasted near the train's ceiling. Matsuda was a very common name; if word of my visit reached Mr. Harada, he would probably scratch his head and remember a Matsuda from somewhere.

"Matsuda-san, we are delighted to hear from a friend of our honorable customer. I am Sakurai Nobuko. I apologize for not introducing myself earlier."

The potter's wife? I sucked in my breath because all through the conversation, I'd thought she was some kind of employee. Nobuko Sakurai had consistently referred to her husband with the feudal term *danna-sama*, which literally meant "master," and that could have been a term used by an employee instead of a wife. I understand now what people had told me about southern Japan—it was more antiquated than anywhere else in the country. In fact, as the train had passed the gardens of small houses, I'd seen men's and women's clothes hung on separate lines, something I'd heard was done so that the male garments would avoid contagion from the inferior female clothing.

"Well, I must prepare something for you to bring to Harada-san," Mrs. Sakurai said. "At what time would you like to visit the studio?"

I looked at my watch. "I'm about two hours away. Would a four o'clock visit be inconvenient, though?"

"Oh, no. Four is usually the time for our tea break, anyway. You must join us."

After hanging up, I tried to put my worries aside for a few minutes and take in Kyushu, one of Japan's most famously beautiful islands. It had been devastated by the typhoon, even in the inland area where we were traveling. Citrus groves were littered with fallen *mikan* tangerines, and the rice paddies were brimming with muddy brown water. Almost every tiled roof had large blocks missing, and downed power lines were everywhere. The damage here, while similar to what I'd seen in Tokyo and Hayama, was worse for the local residents because so many of them were farmers. Mrs. Sakurai had said the pottery studio had suffered damage, too. No wonder she had warmed up when I'd talked about spending half a million yen. Visitors to Kyushu would be fewer, and times harder, in the winter ahead.

The stationmaster at the closest town to Umeda advised me to take the number 8 bus, which was just about to depart, so I did. Once aboard, I thought about whether I should have taken a taxi; I had the funds. No, I thought, taxi drivers talked. Taking the bus would make me less memorable. I'd already begun to regret dyeing my hair, because while the streaky look was common in Tokyo, it wasn't in the village of Kyushu.

"This is the stop for Umeda. Please don't forget your things," a recorded female voice said from the bus's loudspeaker. I decided I'd better get out, because it looked as if the town was essentially a single road, spanned by a few shops. I stepped off the bus with my suitcase, and my feet crunched into something. I looked down. Pots. Everywhere, the earth was mixed with the shards of *kuromon*, as black pottery was called in this community. It wasn't new pots that had been lost in the typhoon, I realized; those shattered urns were close to the houses, where I could see they'd held things like farm tools, umbrellas, or plants. What lay underneath me, I thought with a thrill, was the town's centuries of life as a pottery village.

I raised my eyes a bit higher and started scanning the houses for something that looked like the studio. From the brochure, I knew it was located on this road, about an eighth of a mile away. Vacant, overgrown fields stood on either side of the houses; here, undeveloped space—which was a luxury in most of Japan—was running rampant with weeds. I'd seen very few people as I'd walked, just an old grandmother in baggy *monpe* work trousers pushing a wheelbarrow packed with freshly pulled *daikon*. She'd offered me a bag to take back to the city as a souvenir, and I'd been caught un-prepared. People didn't usually solicit that way in Tokyo, and I was unsure what the right, unmemorable response should be. In the end, I agreed to take a 500-yen portion, which I hoped would make her think favorably of me, though I had no intention of taking them back to the city.

"Are you going to see Sakurai-san's studio?" the woman said while tucking the coin I'd given her into her blouse. I'd nodded, and left it at that. It made sense; the only reason anyone from far away would come to this one-street town would be for a glimpse of the Living National Treasure.

Sakurai's studio was marked only by the *kanji* characters making up his name, placed on the wall surrounding the house, which looked to me like a typical middle-class tiled-roof house—except that many tiles were missing. They lay haphazardly scattered around the garden. As I approached the door, I realized that a thick black snake was lying in front of the steps. I halted, wondering how in the world I could bring myself to step over it.

As I stood deliberating, a young man with a rakish hairstyle, baggy jeans, and a black sweater turned the corner with a wheel-barrow of his own; it was filled with broken tiles and debris. The apprentice, I guessed.

"Good day. Excuse me, but are you Miss Matsuda?" he asked. His accent was different from the Kyushu dialect I'd heard spoken in the train station and aboard the bus. He was probably a trans-plant like myself.

When I nodded, he bowed. "The master is expecting you. How was your journey? You must be very tired."

"Yes. I mean, no. It's just—" I gestured toward the snake.

"Oh, I'm sorry! In Kyushu, these snakes are everywhere. So an-noying." He rolled his wheelbarrow toward the snake, and I caught my breath. Was he going to run over it?

That turned out not to be the case; the snake raised its head and slithered off into the bushes.

I gave a sigh. "Thank you."

"There's a peaceful way to do everything, the master says."

I smiled and said, "This is turning out to be a very exciting day."

"It is also an excitement for us. When one of Harada-san's friends comes to call, it is a special opportunity indeed," the apprentice said effusively.

"Oh, please don't say that, I'm getting embarrassed." I paused, thinking about the meaning of his statement. "Actually, have many of his friends come before?"

"Yes, he's sent us several friends from around the world who became customers."

The young man opened the front door, ceremoniously standing back so that I could be the first one in. A slender woman in her sixties dressed in a simple wool sweater and skirt appeared and sank to her knees, pressing her forehead to the polished pine floor.

"Welcome to our humble studio. I am Sakurai Nobuko." Mrs. Sakurai was smiling, causing her wrinkles to stand out in deep relief. Despite her fine clothes, I could see evidence of the years, and the environment, in her face. She looked like someone who had worked, and lived, hard.

I knew I wasn't supposed to reciprocate as dramatically, so I just gave the deepest possible standing bow, such as a disgraced executive would make at a press conference, and murmured my name and my apologies for disturbing her. When I stood up, I saw that she'd been staring at my hair.

I pretended not to notice. "I'm sorry to have disturbed you so much. I don't suppose that it is still possible for me to see the master?"

"Yes, yes, he's just finishing up at the wheel. I apologize for his lateness."

This was all very confusing to me, the fact that a Living National Treasure and his wife would be so obsequious to a stranger with some, but not much, money to spend. Maybe in Kyushu, the strong Japanese tradition of hospitality was even stronger. Or, I realized, it could boil down to simple Japanese reasoning: if the Sakurais gave excessively to me, I would have to outdo them. As I followed her into the studio, I wondered how much Mr. Harada's other international friends—perhaps even the Birand brothers—had spent.

36

I'd been expecting a luxuriously appointed shop, but the studio was more akin to a Japanese home. An idealized Japanese home, of course—a room large enough for fourteen tatami mats, its expanse of grass-covered flooring broken only by a low *kotatsu* table and three *zabuton* cushions covered in Kyushu indigo cotton. The only way you could tell it was not a typical tidy reception room was that the *tokonoma* alcove held a statuesque greenish brown *ikebana* vase that in turn was holding a branch of *mikan*, to which a few tangerines elegantly clung. The shoji doors were open to the garden, which was the only source of light in the semidarkened room.

Mrs. Sakurai followed the direction of my interest. "We lost our tree in the storm."

"I'm sorry to hear that, but you've made a lovely, spare arrangement. Have you studied *ikebana*?" I asked.

She laughed, putting a hand over her mouth. "No, I never had that kind of time. I've spent my life helping the master. There has never been time for flower studies." She paused. "Harada-san's daughter, she will marry a flower master soon, *neh*?"

Her words confirmed my thought that the Sakurais must not have learned about Emi's death. The remoteness of Kyushu from Tokyo—not to mention the loss of television during the electric outages—made that likely. Certainly national newspapers were available at the next town over, but there hadn't even been a convenience store in Umeda—and who had the time to sit and read newspapers when there were pots to be shaped, a roof to be retiled, and a destroyed orange tree to be disposed of?

I fretted inwardly about how I could break it to Mrs. Sakurai about the Haradas' tragedy. Then a sliding door in the back of the room moved and the gray-haired master entered, his shoulders slightly stooped under a thin burgundy sweater. He wore loose *gumue* trousers like those Takeo favored for gardening, and thick green socks with a split toe.

The simplicity of the potter should not mislead me, I reminded myself as I decided to go for broke and bow, on the floor, the way his wife had bowed to me. He was a Living National Treasure, so if I wasn't humble enough, he might be offended.

"Please, there is no need," he said gently, urging me up.

I gave my introductory greetings and offered my shopping bag, which contained the expensive chocolates.

"No, no, we cannot accept it. Please, this is too much." This time Mrs. Sakurai spoke, but as the courteous protest sprang forward, so did her slim hands. She took the bag and laid it gently to the side.

"It's just a few handmade chocolates from Belgium," I said apologetically. "Really a very small thing. I'm not sure if you like sweets."

"Oh, Belgian chocolate is very delicious. Thank you. Tell me, you must be very tired from your travel. The train takes all day, *neh*! How about some tea to restore you?"

"I flew," I said. "I took the train only from Fukuoka. I'm not tired at all. On the contrary, I'm so excited to see your great works."

"I'm terribly sorry, but there is not much here at the present moment," Mr. Sakurai said, sliding open the doors of a long cabinet set against a wall. I remembered doing the same thing at Takeo's country house, where the cabinet was neatly organized with boxed-up pottery. In the Sakurais' cabinet, extra shelves had been set in, to hold a copious amount of ceramics, all unboxed and arranged for display. Overhead were spotlights illuminating the ceramic treasures in gentle hues of green, brown, and black. Now I knew why Mrs. Sakurai had kept the room dark—to give the pottery, which itself was on the dark side, an almost magical glow, once the cupboard was opened.

No price tags, I thought, as my gaze ran over the breathtakingly simple plates, teacups, bowls, and vases. I saw the snake from the garden reincarnated in a *choka* or spouted sake ewer, which had an applied clay pattern of a snake curling up the side that formed a handle. It was too big for me to take home, let alone afford, but I thought I'd ask him about it.

"That we call *haritsuke*," he said. "It's an old method that had almost vanished from use among today's potters."

I knew from my own studies that *haritsuke* was a technique popular from the 1700s through the mid-nineteenth century, but I asked a question about its age so that I could lead into my next query. "So, what do you think about this controversy that the earliest potters in Kyushu were not Japanese at all?"

"Well, of course the Koreans were brought here from the 1600s onward," he said. "But there are some of us who were here much earlier. It's not a legend, but reality."

"That makes sense. I heard there is more in common with Middle Eastern pottery than Asian," I said. "That *haritsuke* technique—I feel as if I've seen examples of similar work in ancient Near Eastern pottery."

He nodded, smiling. "You're right. And I recently had the opportunity to explore more ways to work with *haritsuke*. If you're interested, I can show you some smaller examples for sale."

He disappeared from the room and came back with a box, which he set on the table. I sat down across from him and watched him open it. There, against a padded backing of brown silk, were the chopstick rests—five little brownish gray eels upon which one could set down dining implements. I found myself looking away from them immediately, and forced myself to concentrate. What was my problem? I realized that because these eels were so small, they were closer to looking like worms. Five hundred dollars for wormy chopstick rests; I tried not to recoil.

"How charming," I said, then wanted to bite my tongue for using a word they might find patronizing. It felt so odd to me to play the role of a dressed-up person with money; I was always on the other side. "I would like to buy something a bit larger, if it's possible. Your wife had mentioned teacups."

"Yes, I think we still have the set of cups. I'm slow." He gave a slight, self-deprecating smile. "You know, it takes about a full week for me to make a set. That's why there isn't much for sale. But I do have these."

The next box he opened held five cups, all of the lovely, brownish green color that came from skipping the bisque stage before the pot was fired in a wood-burning kiln. It was another historic method come back to life in Sakurai-san's weathered, skilled palms.

"Please hold them, if you like," he urged, and I put a hand out toward the box, silently praying that I wouldn't do anything as stupid as dropping a thousand-dollar teacup on the polished *keyaki* wood table. The feeling, in my hand, was good—oddly familiar, though. I studied the almost invisible whorls on the piece, thinking. Then I turned the cup over and saw the little indentation I'd seen on his bowl at the Haradas' home, and on the ibex ewer.

"You must hold them all. See what you think, please."

He wanted me to buy them, I thought as I put the first cup down and picked up the second. Now I knew he was complicit in Mr. Harada's deception. What to do?

I glanced away from the cups and saw that Mrs. Sakurai had come back holding an earthenware teapot and teacups similar to the one I was holding.

"I'm sorry. Shall I wait to serve the tea?" Her voice was apologetic.

"Please, I wish you hadn't gone to the trouble for me," I said. Secretly, I was glad to see her. I needed a break before I committed myself to spending thousands of dollars, and I also thought it would be advantageous to ask my questions before the deal was closed.

"She's very tired from travel. Of course she will drink tea," the master said. "Why did you take so long to prepare the tea?"

"So, please tell us the news of Harada-san and his family," Mrs. Sakurai said.

I couldn't keep going any longer. In a low voice, I said, "I apologize for the sad news I must bring you. Last week, his daughter passed away."

"Oh, dear," Mr. Sakurai said softly. He dropped his head for a minute, as if praying. Then he looked up at me again. "I'm so sorry. I didn't know. Please tell us about the situation."

"It seems impossible. She was such a young girl, about to become a bride—" Mrs. Sakurai choked and set down, on the tray, the cup of tea she'd been pouring for her husband.

"So you met her, then?" I asked.

"Oh, yes. Her whole family came last spring to see about having the groom's gift made," Mrs. Sakurai said. "Emi-san was such a lovely young girl, so slim and with so much energy, yet complete refinement—just what you'd expect from an ambassador's daughter. If I may be so bold to ask . . . what happened?"

"She was in a car accident," I said. "The street signals were out because of the typhoon."

"A car accident," Sakurai said, his voice heavy. "Life can be taken away, just like that. Having children ourselves, we can imagine her parents' grief."

"They drove to see us that last time, remember?" Mrs. Sakurai said. "Emi-san was their only child. I remember Harada-san's wife saying that she wasn't sure she was ready to let her daughter go. I told her that she would be young enough to enjoy her grandchildren. I shouldn't have tempted fate with my words."

"I'm sure you didn't do that. I am truly sorry to have brought you such bad news," I said.

"No, please don't worry. You came here for other reasons, happier reasons, and we asked you about Harada-san. We are distracting you with our grief! I apologize." Mrs. Sakurai bowed her head.

No, I thought with a mixture of chagrin and hardness, they were not distracting me. They were clearing the way for me to ask what I needed to ask. "You mentioned that they commissioned a groom's gift. Was it a set of cups similar to these?" Ever since I'd seen the cups, I'd had a suspicion they were an order for someone that hadn't come to fruition.

"No, it was something not so Japanese," Mr. Sakurai said. "A kind of *choka* using the *haritsuke* technique I mentioned."

"A *choka*?" I repeated. He had used a word for a spouted vessel for liquid, such as a ewer.

"Yes, a *choka*." Mr. Sakurai shook his head sorrowfully. "I completed it in the spring, in time for the engagement ceremony."

"I wonder if I've seen it," I said carefully. "Does it resemble a goat, by any chance?"

"Why, yes." Mr. Sakurai looked surprised, but nodded. "I didn't know anyone would recognize it as my work, because Harada-san was quite specific about my following the model of an existing ancient piece. I don't usually do that kind of thing, but, well, he is a very special customer."

"I think I saw it in a magazine," I said. *Special customer* might mean that Mr. Sakurai would call Mr. Harada after I left, raising his suspicions. "So, ah, do you still have the original model here?"

"No. Mr. Harada took it with him when he picked up his *choka*." Mr. Sakurai cocked his head at me, the grief he'd shown earlier replaced by a wary interest. "I wish I could show you a photograph . . . but Harada-san requested that I not photograph it for my artist's record. I agreed because the piece was not an original design."

"Speaking of original designs, I am quite enthralled by the set of cups you showed me. Are they really available for sale?" I decided to swing back into consumer mode, to allay any suspicions that might be forming.

"Of course. I mentioned them to you on the telephone."

"I would like to buy them." It was part of my cover—and now I had hard evidence of where Takeo's ibex ewer had come from.

"I am honored by your choice." Mr. Sakurai bowed his head, and so did his wife.

Feeling completely awkward when they faced me again, I said, "Will it be possible to arrange the details this afternoon?"

"Of course. Matsuda-san, are you returning home this evening?" Mrs. Sakurai inquired.

"I hadn't anticipated finding a perfect set of cups like this, so I didn't book a flight. And it's quite far back to Fukuoka—I don't think I could make a connection, even if I left now."

"Flying is convenient," Mrs. Sakurai said. "Harada-san usually flew to see us, but the last two visits he drove."

He drove. Had he been worried that airport luggage inspectors would come across the ibex vessel as he brought it to Kyushu and then carried it back? Why didn't he take the train instead? Driving seemed hard—but it might have been the method for someone who didn't want to be noticed.

"In case I can't catch my flight this evening, can you recommend a nice place to stay?" I asked, changing the topic.

"Oh, please stay with us. It's very humble here, but we would be honored . . ."

Ordinarily, I'd have delighted in the opportunity to spend a night under the same roof as a master potter and his wife, but not tonight. "Oh, I wouldn't dream of inconveniencing you. I wonder if you know where Harada-san liked to stay, while he was in the area . . ."

"I really don't know. The last time he was headed for his country house, wasn't he?" Mrs. Sakurai turned to her husband with a questioning look.

His country house. Something Ramzi had said came back to me. Emi had promised him that they'd have time together at the country house after her marriage. I'd thought it was Takeo's place, but maybe it was somewhere completely different.

Mr. Sakurai broke into my thoughts. "So, how did you say you knew Harada-san? Is it because of your husband, or . . ."

Husband? I wore no ring. Was it the fact that they thought no woman my age would still be single? I would have to go for something vague. I just said, "That's right."

"Ah, another diplomatic couple. I noticed your accent was different, and you have that special hairstyle. You must have been to so many interesting countries!" Mrs. Sakurai smiled at me.

"Matsuda-san, forgive me, but I must return to the wheel in my pottery." Mr. Sakurai stood up. "My wife can help you with the necessary details for the teacups. I hope you enjoy the efforts of my poor labor."

I bowed and murmured my thanks, wondering how the payment process should go. As Mrs. Sakurai carefully wrapped the box containing the cups in three layers of handmade *washi* paper, I realized that the rectangular plate next to the wrapping table was where I should lay my payment. I laid down the equivalent of

$6,000, allowing for the tax. After she finished the wrapping, she excused herself, taking the tray into the next room. She came back with some change and a receipt, which I slid into my wallet with some relief. A thousand dollars for a teacup—I almost felt that I was getting a bargain.

37

There really was no chance of leaving Kyushu that night. My suspicions about the length of the trip were confirmed when the local bus finally got me to the nearest train station, and I realized there was an hour's wait for the next limited express train to Fukuoka. The agent for All Nippon Airways said that the final plane to Tokyo left Fukuoka around seven. Given that I'd be getting to Fukuoka around nine, the agent offered to make a reservation for me at the ANA hotel. I told her I'd decide on hotels when I arrived and make the reservation myself. Actually, I planned to use a different name and stay at a different hotel, paying cash to protect my anonymity.

I checked my watch again and bought a can of hot Georgia Coffee from the station's vending machine. As I sipped, I congratulated myself for seeking out the Sakurais. What I'd learned about Kenichi Harada commissioning a reproduction of the ibex vessel had been fascinating. But it still left a question—why had he done it? Takeo had said that he'd been given the vessel—the fake one, though he didn't know it—after he'd admired Mr. Harada's possession. But why hadn't Mr. Harada given him the real thing—especially if the piece was going to stay in the family?

I drank more coffee, and as the caffeine shot through me, so did a new idea. Mr. Harada might have felt that he should not burden his future son-in-law with an illegal piece. On the other hand, he obviously knew he was in possession of a priceless artwork, and he simply might not have wanted to give it up. Famous artworks that were stolen had to remain under wraps; they were too well known to be sold, and they usually remained in the original thief's hands or were traded to another underworld figure.

And as far as the underworld went, I'd always assumed that Mr. Harada was a customer—but maybe he had played a more active role. He was a diplomat who'd traveled freely through the Middle East before the war, and because of his status, he was probably exempted from luggage screening more rigorous than the basic security X-ray.

I looked around the station and spotted a deserted row of seats. I sat down, took my cell phone out of my backpack, and punched in Takeo's private number.

"It's me. Can you talk?" I asked when he picked up.

"Yes, if I can fit you in between TBS and NHK and the other news organizations I never knew existed! Have you been busy, too?"

"Not that way. Nobody knows where I am."

"Well, where are you?" He sounded impatient.

"In southwestern Kyushu."

"Oh! So you've run away. I wish I could do that."

"Takeo, I need to ask you something. Did you ever go to Emi's family's summer house?"

"Twice. Why?"

"Do you remember the address?"

"Certainly. If you went all the way to Kyushu to find it, you're in the wrong place. The house is on the Izu Peninsula, about an hour and a half from Tokyo."

If Mr. Harada had driven all the way from Kyushu to Izu, perhaps it was because he didn't want the vessel to be noticed by the airport security staff—since now that he was a government minister, he wouldn't have the blessing of diplomatic clearances anymore. Why he hadn't used the train seemed mysterious, though. Maybe he just didn't want to be noticed, especially if the country house was where the vessel wound up. I asked Takeo if this was the place where he'd first laid eyes on the vessel.

"Yes, but—Rei, you're not thinking of breaking in, are you?"

"Of course not. But I would greatly appreciate learning the address from you."

"I don't believe it! You're up to the same business as when you came to my house during the storm."

"I'm sorry, Takeo. But if you let me know about this place, I might be able to do something that—shifts attention from you, and the whole horrible misunderstanding may resolve."

"How will it shift attention from me if you get caught as a burglar again? There's high security at the place—it's not like my country house."

High security, because there had to be priceless treasures within. Things were coming together in my mind. Knowing what Takeo had told me, I wouldn't go inside, but I'd feel I'd done all I could if I could give the address to Brenda and Michael quickly and let them get a search warrant. Now there was enough information to get a warrant, I was almost certain. But I couldn't tell Takeo about my plan.

"Takeo, please. Just tell me the name of the town. You won't be implicated for helping me in any way, if you just tell me that—I can do the rest."

"No, I won't."

"You just care about yourself, don't you?" I said, utterly frustrated.

"No." His voice cracked. "It's because I still care about you that I won't tell. Can't you understand?"

Takeo hung up, and I sat there with the phone in my hand, watching the crowd of people across the room board the train. The train. It was finally here.

I grabbed my carry-on suitcase and made it onboard just before the conductor blew the whistle.

By the time I got into Fukuoka, the moon was high. I was starving, so I stopped at a little ramen shop for a bowl of steaming noodles topped with a raw egg. Moon-viewing noodles, they were called. The egg cooked slowly atop the noodles, and I ate slowly, savoring the rich taste of the noodles, the broth, everything. Then I felt fortified enough to search for a hotel. I wanted a place where I would be totally anonymous, where no desk clerk would look at me or ask for identification or a credit card. The obvious answer was to stay at a love hotel, where check-in was self-service, in a curtained booth.

I'd stayed in a love hotel once with Hugh, but never with Takeo. Takeo was far too dignified for pop-culture sleaze. Tonight, I chose Love Palace, a hotel in the form of a Gothic castle. I knew that there was still a vacancy because not all the twinkling exterior lights were turned on. I walked quickly into the lonely lobby and then into the check-in booth, drawing the curtain. I realized that I was embarrassed, not just because I might be recognized, but because it was a sorry situation to be checking into a love hotel all by oneself. Still, once I had followed the blinking lights that lit up on the carpet and directed me to my room, I decided that I'd made a very good choice. The room was almost as large as my space at the Hyatt, and the bed was huge and had fresh linens. As I was unpacking my bags, the cell phone rang and I snatched it up.

"Rei." The voice was husky, full of pain, and maybe slurred with alcohol. Hugh's voice.

"Oh!" I dropped the phone in surprise, but it just landed softly on the bed.

"Where are you?" he asked.

"A love hotel," I blurted, before realizing the implication. "I was just looking for a cheap, quiet place to spend the night. I'm actually alone—"

"I'm sure not for long," Hugh said darkly.

"You must have heard from Angus?"

"Yes. But I already knew the worst. I read the Japanese news on-line, Rei, and when I Googled your name it led me to a site with scandal pictures—and I saw it there."

"You would Google the woman you love, rather than just ask her what's going on?"

"Well, that's why I called you, actually. To ask." Hugh's voice dripped with politeness. "Did you shag him?"

I sucked in my breath, shocked at the hardness of his language. But I couldn't lie, not for another moment. "Just once. And I'm sorry."

"Christ." Hugh was silent for a minute. "I don't—I can't believe it. You betrayed me."

"You must understand that I didn't go to Japan for that purpose—it was a terrible mistake—"

"You're asking me to *understand*?"

"It was a mistake!" I repeated. "That picture doesn't express any kind of intimacy that continued after—the incident, which was really just a one-night stand. In the picture at the pond, it was an accident, I was just trying to help him out—"

"I'm sure you helped him very nicely. And now, Rei, I'm off to work, where I'll be sitting down with people who actually need my help, and whom I can count on to behave like decent human beings."

For the second time that day, a man hung up on me.

After I was done crying, I splashed my face with water and looked at myself in the bathroom's tiny mirror, which had illuminated cherub light fixtures.

There was one last person I could call, someone whom I was reasonably sure would not hang up on me when he heard what I wanted from him.

I dialed Ramzi Birand.

38

It was noon when I'd transferred from Haneda Airport to Tokyo Station, where I'd promised to meet Ramzi outside the Japan Railway ticket office. However, I found him in a different spot, leaning against a pole plastered with ads for a loan shark agency. It was a wonder I located him. I'd just left my carry-on and the teacups in a storage locker, then paused to scrutinize the tomato and carrot sandwiches at Vegetaria, and it was there, when I was peering into the distance, that I saw him. Despite the crowding at the station, there was space around him, the usual arm's length Japanese commuters gave a foreign man, even a good-looking one with dark curly hair, a modish peacoat, and flared jeans.

"Let me buy your ticket," I said after I'd greeted him and thanked him for meeting me. After the way we'd left things, I wasn't even sure he'd be willing to give me the address of the country house. It turned out that Emi had taken him by train, and while he thought he could retrace their steps, he couldn't give me an exact address. Ramzi knew nothing of *kanji* or even the easy *hiragana* alphabet; it was a wonder to me that he'd made it through a semester at Waseda. But then again, he was planning to drop out.

"How do you know which platform is correct, when there are so many?" Ramzi asked in frustration as I led him two platforms over to the place from which the Odoriko limited express trains departed.

"I studied the big map by the ticket machines. You know, the map that looks like a lot of colored spaghetti?"

"Your hair looks like spaghetti," he said, looking me over.

"It's a change of pace," I said. My whole look was different. Back in Fukuoka, I'd had an hour to search the teen boutiques and put together my own version of the Lolita look. I bought a short red pleated skirt, blue-and-yellow striped tights, a yellow sweater with a Doraemon appliqué, and Minnie Mouse barrettes that I'd used to randomly clip strands of my multicolored hair. The salesgirl loved the look. If this was what twenty was supposed to look like, I thought as I surveyed myself in the dressing room mirror, I was actually glad to be ten years older.

The change of costume had been inspired by my conversation at six in the morning with Brenda Martin, whom I'd phoned out of a sense of duty.

"Why go all the way to Izu? You could just give me the address," she'd said immediately.

"My contact doesn't know an exact address, but he thinks he can show me the way. Then I'll share the address with you." I tried to sound more confident than I felt.

"And who is this contact?"

"It's nobody in the government, okay?"

"Who is it?" she repeated.

I hesitated before answering. "Ramzi Birand."

"Do you mean Emi's ex-boyfriend, with whom you made contact two days ago?"

"Yes. He went there a few times with her, and he's willing to show me the place. As I mentioned earlier, all things are pointing toward the original ewer being there."

"I'm concerned that this is too high a risk," Brenda said. "Especially since your face has been in the newspaper and on TV. How can you expect to do anything anonymously?"

"I already changed my hair—I'll change more. And Michael didn't think it was a bad idea." The fact was that he hadn't said it was a good idea, either. He'd just told me not to go into the house, and I'd agreed.

"I'm going to call over to him now to get his take on it, because it sounds risky to me. Can you wait until I get back to you?"

"It's too late. I already made my plan with Ramzi. I can't let him go out there alone."

"God help you if you're not being straight with me," she grumbled. "In any case, keep your cell phone handy."

"Come on, I'm at the end of the journey. I'm just getting the address. Then I'm out of here."

Out of here, I thought, as Ramzi and I waited for the train. In a way, I wanted out—but another side of me wanted to stay. I had wanted to visit a particular temple with Aunt Norie, and to spend hours at a Sunday morning flea market. I wouldn't get the chance to do any of this on my visit—or perhaps ever again.

"Why did you do that to yourself with those stupid clothes?" Ramzi's disapproval of my Lolita look interrupted my brief, self-pitying wallow.

"I wanted to look more your age, so people wouldn't be surprised at our traveling together." I paused.

"Emi never dressed like that."

"Well, she may have had better taste than I do. She definitely had more money." I changed the topic. "Do you see that train coming in? It's the Odoriko line. Does it look familiar to you?" I was hoping so, because there were a couple of railway lines that went to Izu, and if I got the wrong one, we would never locate the right town.

"I'm not sure—wait. Dark blue seats. Yes, I remember blue seats," he said, looking through the windows of the empty train as it rolled up to the platform.

It figured that he would remember a sensory detail and nothing else. After we settled ourselves into two velour seats in the very back—I wanted to be able to see everyone who was sitting around us—I asked him if he remembered the station where he'd disembarked in Izu. Quietly, I told him the names of the stops we had ahead.

During his time with Emi, he explained, he'd always let her be the guide. But he did have an important piece of evidence: a snapshot in his wallet of the two of them grinning, with a historic black ship in the bay behind them.

The black ship made me think of Shimoda, where the U.S. Navy commodore Matthew Perry arrived in 1853 in a black ship and demanded entry to a country that had shut out foreigners for the previous 220 years. Shimoda was the place, Ramzi said, where they'd spent an hour looking around before catching a bus for a thirty-minute ride out to the town where Emi's parents' place was. I bit my lip, thinking about how many small towns and villages there might be within half an hour of Shimoda. And who knew if he was even right about the timing of the bus ride?

Fortunately, he had correctly remembered the bus platform, near the Lawson's store next to the station. He pointed to a bus that showed its destination, Dogashima, in English.

It was ironic, I thought as we rode quietly along, both of us gazing outward, that I'd made it all the way to Shimoda, a place of historical intrigue. An American diplomat, Townsend Harris, had arrived here in 1856 to start the United States' first consulate in Japan, completely against the wishes of the Japanese. Much diplomatic wrangling followed, but what most Japanese remembered with great distaste was that Consul Harris had asked for the services of a young local woman called Okichi, who reluctantly obeyed the shogunate's request for her to become his personal maid for several years. Okichi served Harris faithfully as a nurse—and perhaps a mistress—until he retired from duty and returned to the United States, leaving her unprotected from the community's scorn. Okichi then tried to run a number of businesses, but by the time she was in her fifties, she had become an alcoholic. She finally committed suicide by drowning herself.

Shimoda had numerous memorials to Okichi in its temples and shrines, to remind everyone of the sad sacrifice made by the Japanese people to the future of international relations. I'd read the literature and thought that the real villains had been the community people who'd called Okichi a barbarian, but my sentiment wasn't shared by many. Everyone thought the tragedy was Harris's fault, for conscripting her to his service and tainting her reputation.

Foreigner's cruelty kills Japanese beauty. That was the way the story had played out 160 years ago in the Japanese popular press. Come to think of it, that headline could have been used in yesterday's tabloid.

"This is it. I remember getting a bottle of water at that machine." Ramzi pointed out the window at a Dydo soft drink machine set next to a bench.

The tape recording on the bus had announced this place as Osawa Onsen, where there was a hot spring.

"Did she ever speak to you of the town being called Osawa?" I pushed the stop signal as I spoke.

"I'm not sure." He frowned. "I'm sorry. I think I heard that word somewhere. Is that this town's name?" He squinted at the station sign, which was written in *hiragana*.

"Let's jump off. We can always catch another bus, if we're wrong." I was already standing up and following a couple of back-packers who were getting off.

We paid our fares—$11 apiece for just a thirty-minute bus ride—and disembarked. The backpackers walked off, clearly following signs for a hot spring resort.

"Did you take a taxi from this point?" I asked Ramzi.

"No, we walked this way," Ramzi said, sounding confident. As we walked alongside a rice paddy and then cut through an orange grove, Ramzi explained that Emi had led him on a circuitous route so that people wouldn't talk. It was a summer house, and the Haradas weren't there very often, but still, the risk that someone would notice Emi with a boy was too great to bear.

After passing through the fields, we reached a wall at the back of a house. The wall, covered with black tiles fixed in a diamond pattern with thick white plaster, was a fortified style particular to Shimoda, to fortify its houses against strong sea winds. Over this beautiful wall a succulent vine trailed, making it picture-postcard perfect.

"This is the back of the house, I think. I'll know for certain in a minute," Ramzi said, leading me along.

"I heard there's a security system in the house," I said, eyeing the wall with some nervousness.

"Yes, there's an alarm system, but I've got the code."

"Really? I wouldn't want to chance anything," I said. After he'd revealed his trouble remembering directions, I couldn't imagine that he'd know any code.

"No, I have it. Here, in my calendar." He patted his pocket.

"Why did you write down the code?" I asked suspiciously.

"I told you that we had plans to meet here again. It made sense for me to know."

I shook my head. "We mustn't go in. If two foreigners like us are caught—well, it could mean jail or deportation. Believe me, I have experience in these things."

"Why did you ask me to bring you here, if you didn't want to go in?" He sounded impatient.

"As I said to you on the phone, I just wanted to see the place from the outside."

"Well, I came because I plan to go inside." He scowled at me.

I hesitated. I supposed my only option was to abandon ship and not go a step farther. If Ramzi stormed the house and something went wrong, the police would come and we would both be in the soup.

"Ramzi, if you go in, it's your decision. But I'm not going to stay on the premises if you do that. I'm not willing to take the risk."

He pressed his lips together. "Then why don't you just go?"

He'd called my bluff. He knew I had to see the house. "Please, Ramzi. Let's just walk there, and I'll give you time to mourn, I really will, and then we'll go back."

"It's a left turn ahead, I think. This looks familiar."

I took the turn with him, and then he stopped. Ahead of us was an especially high wall of diamond tile, with *kanji* characters making up the name Harada on a mailbox, followed by the numbers 2-17-1 and the *kanji* for Isobe. I copied down both the *kanji* characters and my translation to call in to Brenda Martin as soon as I had some privacy, away from Ramzi.

"What are you writing?" Ramzi asked. He'd walked over to a pair of tall, iron gates that barred entrance to a long driveway disappearing into what looked like a small forest. The property was huge; I'd thought only Japanese aristocrats lived that way.

"Two-seventeen-one Isobe Street, in Osawa. That's the full address," I said, walking over to join him. "It looks like a beautiful place."

"Ten hectares of forest. Emi took me around. It's great," Ramzi muttered. Then he stepped to the right and flipped open a small box, revealing a keypad. He punched in a code, and slowly, the gates opened.

"You can't go in," I said quickly.

Ramzi turned to me. "I told you what I was going to do. Why else did you think I came here?"

As I stared at him, a sense of foreboding started to grow inside me. "Ramzi, what are you planning to do inside the house?"

"It's not your concern."

I could hardly choke out the words. "Are you thinking of . . . ending your life?"

"Suicide? I've thought of it before, yes, but not now." His manner was brisk. "I'm here to take back something that belongs to me."

"Okay, but let's—let's just wait a moment, maybe go around the corner to talk. We shouldn't just hang around right in front—" I had been thinking that the way we looked was fine for the train, but I was worried that in this exclusive neighborhood, we might attract suspicion.

"Well, if you're going, I'll just say good-bye now!" Ramzi shot over his shoulder as he walked through the open gate. I held my breath, imagining motion detectors or another force that would spring to life at Ramzi's invasion. But nothing happened. He continued up the long pebbled driveway and disappeared around a bend.

I'd thought Ramzi was helping me, but what he really wanted was an assistant of his own. Now I wondered if he was about to deface the house, or steal something from it—perhaps the ibex vessel. Ramzi had never answered me straightforwardly about whether he'd seen the piece; and now, because I'd asked about it, maybe he'd gotten an inkling of how important it was, and how its loss could devastate Emi's father.

I had promised Michael that I wouldn't go into the house, but I couldn't let Ramzi get away with the vessel. And that could be done, if there was anther exit from this large property. I picked up the cell phone and called the first number Brenda had given me, then the second. She didn't answer either. Well, so much for support. As I listened to her recorded voice tell me to leave a message, I decided against it. I'd come up with a plan.

I was going to walk onto the property, but I would wait in a hidden position outside the house, to see what Ramzi was up to. And then, if things looked bad, I'd call Michael Hendricks. So with a flutter of excitement overlying fear, I nipped through the opening Ramzi had left me, positioning the gate so it looked closed but still would allow me passage out.

39

I jogged up the wide driveway, which led through a naturalistic garden filled with tall pines and cedars. The Emerald Forest, I thought to myself, because in my girlish frock, I felt a little bit like Judy Garland going up the yellow brick road toward Oz. My expectation that this house would have magical qualities was confirmed when I turned the bend that Ramzi had taken and saw a long, single-story stucco house, elegant in the same East-West style as the Haradas' home at Setagaya. Under a tiled-roof carport, two cars were parked: a black Mercedes and a white Toyota Camry, both with Tokyo plates.

Two cars. I immediately got off the path and went behind a stand of trees. As I stopped and tried to still my breath, I thought frantically about possibilities. Had Mr. Harada received a call from the loyal potter and come here to spirit away the ibex ewer? I hadn't believed that I'd given Kazu Sakurai the impression I was any kind of police officer or agent, but the fact that Harada was probably inside the house had to be connected to my visit. But why two cars, instead of one? And had Ramzi dared to go into the house when it appeared to have people inside?

He probably had, I realized when I heard dogs barking within the house. Kenichi Harada must have brought the guard dogs that had been shut up in his house during the memorial service in Setagaya. And judging from the timbre of their bark, they were not a small breed. Also, Ramzi had said something to me about the dogs. What was it—that they were German shepherds? Perhaps Mr. Harada might not call them off if they attacked an intruder.

I slipped my phone out of my bag and programmed in the digits 110. At the first sound of something ugly, I planned to call Japan's nationwide police emergency number. The prickling feeling I'd had when I'd encountered the fake cop had come back. Something terrible was going to happen; I felt it.

The door slid open with a crash and two huge, furry beasts bounded out. The gate was too far away for me to get back to it. The only way I could go was up, and I'd always been rotten at climbing ropes. Still, I did my best, flailing my way four feet off the ground on the lean cedar. Why hadn't I raced over to one of the large maple or ginkgo trees nearby? I cursed myself because the cedar had no large, sheltering limbs. The dogs surrounded me, barking raucously and jumping. The phone. I still had my lifeline to the outside world, even though I had to deal with it one-handed, because my other hand was hanging onto a limb. It was a fidgety thing to handle, and as I was searching for the "talk" button I lost my grip on it. The phone fell to the ground, and the larger dog took it, then spit it out a few feet away. The other one raced over, made a few circles around it, and then came back to me.

Did they think I was playing? I began feeling around the tree for a furry cedar branch I could snap and throw. If I got them far enough away, I could slide down and get my phone, which lay half-buried in a heap of red maple leaves.

Before I could attempt anything, I heard the crunching sound of leaves and someone walking. Timberland boots came into view before I saw Ramzi. I was getting ready to call to him about the phone, but then realized that he was not alone. He was followed by his uncle Ali Birand and Kenichi Harada.

Harada said a few words and the dogs came to stand behind him, their tails wagging. I was not a dog person, I thought to myself. Never had a dog, never wanted one. But now I wished I had the kind of dog savvy to befriend them, trick them into letting me get away.

"Oh, hello. Thank you. I didn't know if they were playing," I said in Japanese, striving to act normally—as if it could possibly be normal for a thirty-year-old Lolita to be climbing a tree in a locked-up garden.

"Why don't you come down? Please." The tone of Harada's voice was anything but courteous. I also noticed that he'd spoken English—was it because he wanted to make sure the Birands understood?

I slid down faster than I intended, scratching my legs as I went. I smoothed down my short skirt as I landed, unable to stop feeling ridiculously vulnerable. I thought about picking up my phone, then thought better of doing something that seemed so obviously panicky. Instead, I continued in my faux friendly tone. "Well, then! What a coincidence to see Mr. Birand is here with you, Harada-san, when Ramzi and I had come out to the area to—pay our respects."

"I called Birand-san here because I thought I needed to solve a faraway problem. But the problem's right here." Kenichi Harada spoke English and looked straight at me.

"And we found another problem in the house!" Ali Birand cuffed his nephew on the ear. Ramzi flinched but didn't do anything in return. He looked as frightened as I felt.

"What have you explained, so far?" I asked Ramzi. I needed to know the basic framework of what our excuse was going to be.

"I told my uncle that I was here to get what was mine," he said stonily. "I said nothing about you. Why are you even here? You said you were staying outside."

Now both men were staring at me, waiting.

"As I was saying, we traveled to Izu so Ramzi could pay his respects. I came into the garden because I was afraid for his safety," I explained, wishing now that I had worn my usual clothes. It was hard to act convincingly like an adult while dressed like a Polly Pocket doll.

"I doubt that entirely. From my conversations with Birand-san and others around the country, it seems clear that you want to take something from me." Harada watched me as he spoke.

"I'm not sure what you're talking about," I said mildly. "All I've heard about is a gift from Ramzi to Emi that he wants back for his own personal sense of peace."

"My nephew has no right to give away anything from our shops or storage areas," Ali Birand said hotly. "This vessel was a gift my brother made to the ambassador. That's all there is to the matter!"

"Please, that's enough information. She knows too much already," Harada said reprovingly to Birand.

"Who would say such a thing?" I asked, watching him.

"A colleague showing proper respect," he said. "That's all you need to know."

Mr. Watanabe. He had become a mole, when it turned out that the scandal over the ibex vessel could taint a government official. The situation had turned out just as Michael had predicted. But Mr. Harada didn't know that I knew Mr. Watanabe, or he wouldn't have spoken the way he had. He still thought I was clueless. I would have to use that fact to my advantage.

"Which vessel are you talking about?" Ramzi seemed to have regained a bit of confidence. "All I wanted was my watch, which I left here by accident—the last time."

"Really? What kind of watch?" I asked skeptically.

"A Tagheuer. It has my initials engraved on the inside. You know, Uncle—my watch!"

"Yes, yes, he does have a watch of that description—a gift from his father, his last birthday." Ali Birand spoke in a placating way to Mr. Harada, who seemed to bristle a bit less.

Well, maybe. Maybe a Tagheuer was the kind of thing you wanted to take with you, no matter what. Or was it that Ramzi was trying to annoy Emi's father by making it clear that he'd taken off his watch and clothes and slept with Emi in this house?

"The watch is irrelevant. You are not to disturb my household anymore. I know that your father and uncle made that clear." Harada spoke to Ramzi firmly. Then he turned to Ali Birand. "So, this is what we will do. You and your nephew will go into the house and retrieve this watch, and then the two of you may drive back to the city. In the meantime, I will take Shimura-san out to the gate."

Ramzi cast an awkward last look at me and went inside with his uncle. Obviously, Harada trusted the uncle in the house. But he didn't trust me to walk to the gate.

"I can go alone."

"I don't think so." Then he pointed me not toward the driveway at all but toward the woods behind the house.

"That's not the way to the street," I said, and for the first time I felt fear. Ramzi and his uncle wouldn't know what had happened. Even if they came out in five minutes, it would be too late.

"It's—how do you say it in English? A shortway."

"Shortcut," I said, and then switched to Japanese. "And it's not a shorter way. It's the wrong direction."

"Ah, so Shimura-san thinks she knows the boundaries of my property better than I do."

"I know the way out. After all, I just followed Ramzi in." I thought about running down the path toward the gate, but there wasn't enough space between us. And he had a small bulge in his pants pocket, something that couldn't possibly be part of a Mae West joke. It might be a weapon. In Japan, there was gun control, but there were still guns. Gangsters had them, and diplomats who could travel without having their luggage examined might have them too. I knew for sure that this man, not Ali Birand, was the dangerous one.

"If you're sure that I'm a thief, why don't you call one-ten?" I asked. My two goals were delay and distraction. If only I could stay in place until the Birands emerged. Why was it taking so long to find the watch?

He didn't answer, so I tried again.

"Yes, you went to great lengths to try to get rid of me. I almost wonder at times if it was revenge because of Emi. You know, I'm very sorry about that—"

He wrinkled up his nose. "Revenge? Because you desire to take her former fiancé, now that he's free? That's not of interest to me."

So he didn't know about that night. He wasn't out to avenge Emi. But he still felt strongly enough to want to walk me into the woods, away from the Birands, and get rid of me.

Why was he so worried about the vessel? It was more than a gift. Something my aunt had taught me early on came back, all of a sudden; that once you gave someone a present, he was duty-bound to give you one in return, something that was worth the same.

I wondered what the Birands might have received in exchange for an ancient, indescribably gorgeous piece of pottery. A favor, perhaps. What had it been? I tried to recall how long Ali Birand had been living in Tokyo. When was it that Ramzi had said that his uncle was granted a visa?

The visa. I remembered Simone and Richard talking about visas, and my own hassles. It was very difficult for most foreigners except Americans and northern Europeans to get visas to live and work in Japan. Ramzi had used a French passport to get in. Yet Ali Birand, a citizen of Turkey, had gotten a visa and been able to secure a business address in a top-flight section of Tokyo. That was what frightened Kenichi Harada—the threat of exposure of how he'd abused his government privilege for a gift.

"Go," he ordered me, in the imperative form used with inferiors. "If you don't do as I say, I'll set the dogs on you!"

I eyed the dogs, judging my chances against the two of them. If they attacked me and the Birands came out, he'd say it was my fault. And even if they doubted him, they'd be afraid enough of the dogs—and of what might happen to them as foreigners in the Japanese judicial system— to agree with whatever he wanted them to do, or say.

My survival was contingent on the Birands' coming out before I was dragged into the woods. Delay was the only strategy I had left. If I could get Kenichi Harada invested in finding out more about what I knew, I'd live.

In a steady voice, I said, "The Birands were able to give you the ewer because they couldn't possibly sell it. But I feel worried that maybe it was an unfair thing that happened to you—how could you know its origin?"

"Obviously, there's something important about it, if you came all the way here to take it from me. But that is not the point. All I know is that you have invaded my property with the purpose of theft, and I plan to exercise my right to order you to leave." Again, he waved his hand in the direction of the woods.

Keeping my gaze on him, I asked, "As I was trying to explain to you, the history of the vessel is unusual. It was stolen from the National Museum in Iraq."

Kenichi Harada's face flushed deep red. "I never heard that. I'm completely innocent in this situation. As Birand told you himself, it was a simple gift—"

"You must have had some inkling it was stolen property, because you didn't exhibit it in your house in Setagaya with all your other beautiful, legally acquired things." I paused. "I wonder what other treasures are in your house. Was that your game? Gifts of art and antiques in exchange for visas?"

"Whom do you work for?" Harada asked quietly.

"I work for people who know my suspicions about you. If you take me into the woods and shoot me, the first person they'll interview will be you." At least, I hoped so. Mr. Harada would find a way to pin things on the Birands, who had the bad luck of being on the scene in Izu, too. The foreigners, not the government minister, would make the police suspicious.

"I want you to start walking now, quietly. Don't make me angry."

"I won't go," I repeated. "You shouldn't, either. You should call the police and tell them you want to turn over something that you've just discovered is a missing international treasure—"

I'd meant to give him a way out, but I'd gone too far. He reached his hand into his pocket and pulled out something small and hard and wrapped my hand around it.

I opened it up and saw a vial of pills—lots of them, small and red and stacked almost to the top.

"I want you to swallow them. My idea about taking you through the woods was to make it easier. There's a stream there; you could have had water. But now, you'll have to swallow them without. Take them all. I tell you it will make you happy for a short while— or if you'd rather, I'll tell the dogs to do their job."

I did then what I should have done the minute the Birands disappeared into the house. I screamed, yelling the names of Ali and Ramzi, beseeching them to call the police. Then I shouted out again, this time in Japanese, in the unlikely event that anyone in the neighborhood would help.

"You fool. Give it to me—" He came at me, and I turned and hurled the vial as far as I could. I expected that the dogs would go after it, and the pair of them did, joyfully.

My plan was working. With the dogs and Harada diverted, I started my run for the gate. Behind me came Ramzi's voice. "What's going on, Rei?"

"Yes, what did you do?" Ali called out.

I heard the sound of crunching leaves and realized that one of the dogs was heading right for me. Kenichi Harada had made good on his threat, but to my delight I noticed that the dog had, in its jaws, something red. To him, my cell phone was a toy. He dropped it at my feet and stood waiting, as if he wanted me to throw it. I glanced over to see what Harada was doing; he was scuffling around with the other dog in the pile of leaves for the vial. To think that all my terror had ended up in a search for dropped tablets. I was reasonably sure I could get away from this situation.

"Good boy. Just a minute," I said, putting the phone to my ear and pushing through on the 110 exchange I'd set up earlier, in anticipation of trouble.

"No, no!" Ali Birand was shouting suddenly. "Don't do it!"

A competent-sounding Japanese woman's voice came on the line. "Emergency services; do you require the police?"

I was about to answer her when I heard Ali Birand scream.

Something had happened, and I could barely bring myself to turn and see what it was.

40

Kenichi Harada had tossed down his own throat all the tablets in the vial: enough amphetamines to kill two men. Six doctors, a week in the hospital, the attentions of his wife, and an anxious nation would aid in his recovery. Mr. Harada had already offered his resignation from government service for reasons of health. Nobody had to know that he'd been the one who'd lived for years with an on-again, off-again amphetamine habit to cope with the stress of long working hours. It was by raiding her father's well-stocked medicine cabinet that his daughter had become hooked, too.

A quick resignation was prudent; in the eyes of Japanese society, the minister for the environment had gone to the rural area he loved best and, stricken by grief over his daughter's death, attempted to end his own life. This played much better than the reality that was emerging after government intelligence agents interviewed Ali Birand, who maintained that Kenichi Harada had streamlined the approval of twenty visas to Turkish citizens in exchange for the gifts. All the immigrants had paid special fees to the Birands, who personally handed over their passports to Kenichi Harada. As a result, the Birands had made plenty of extra money, and instead of having to share a portion of those fees with Kenichi Harada, they'd been able to unload a dangerous asset on him that they didn't dare sell.

On paper, it looked as if the Birands were the worse villains, but the truth was that they hadn't played any role in trying to track and terrorize me, nor was the vessel even in their custody. It was back in Iraq, in a box that had been mailed from Tokyo in care of the provisional director of the National Museum in Iraq.

We'd done it together: Ali Birand, Ramzi, and me. It was my idea; after the police and ambulance had roared away with Kenichi Harada, I'd suggested that the three of us drive back together to Tokyo and, along the way, figure out our next step.

As I drove, Ali's defenses tumbled down. He was worried enough to tell me all that I needed to know. He'd driven to the house under the direction of Kenichi Harada, who'd asked him to get rid of the ibex vessel. So he had wrapped it in bubble wrap inside a plastic shopping bag; the whole thing was in the trunk of the Camry.

Ali was indeed desperate to get rid of the piece; he'd known that it was stolen, of course, and he understood that sooner or later the police would come calling for it. As we drew closer to Yokohama, he begged me to make a quick stop so that he could throw it away. I refused, telling him I had an idea that would set everything straight.

I drove all the way to Yokohama Station, where I asked the men to stay in the car while I took the bag with me into the station. I retrieved my luggage from the locker, and stopped in at a shop in the station's arcade. There I bought a set of cheap everyday soup bowls because I liked their sturdy wooden packing box, and the larger cardboard carton that the saleswoman gave me, upon request. I retreated to the ladies' room, did some packing, and in the end had made up a secure parcel that contained within it the ibex vessel and its bubble wrap tucked in the Oriental Bazaar box that had once held the police dolls. I also included Kazu Sakurai's cups in their own brown satin-lined box, plus the receipt for them. Then I walked again through the crowded station to its busy postal station, where I addressed the package to the museum and gave as the return address Brenda Martin at the American embassy in Tokyo. On the customs declaration form, I described the contents as contemporary Japanese tea bowls and a rustic pottery pitcher, valued at $5,050. I'd thought there might be some fuss about the high value of the package, which I insured, but the clerk either didn't notice or didn't care about the irregularity. I was just another Lolita in a line of twenty customers, all of them anxious to get their mailings completed before their trains came in.

And that's how my last few days in Japan went. I hustled around, making peace with my aunt and Chika, who were outraged most about my actions with Takeo. Following their advice, I didn't see Takeo in public again, but we talked on the phone several times. Takeo expressed horrified surprise about where Emi's drugs had really come from and told me he was going off women for good. Jokingly, I offered to have Richard bring him to one of the cool gay clubs in Tokyo, but he told me that he'd already been accepted at a Buddhist monastery in India. He'd take a brief break from Tokyo and flower arranging, and then return, if the situation suited him.

The other man in my life wasn't as easy to say good-bye to. I'd called Hugh from Japan to apologize again, and he'd said that he'd already packed up my clothes and sent them to Kendall's house in Potomac. Moving the furniture would be harder, because there were some things we had chosen and bought together. "It's like a common-law marriage, practically," Hugh said, when he started trying to explain the legal ramifications of our furniture. I shook my head, thinking it was so like him to say that—to find a marriage, even when it had never been.

I was back in Washington a week later. It felt colder than before, and winter seemed to be setting in. But there was a bit of a thaw with Hugh. He'd finally agreed to meet, face to face, for a cup of coffee before we started allocating the furniture. He'd suggested going to the Evergreen, a new coffee bar that had opened in Adams-Morgan just after I'd left for Japan. Probably, this was the reason that Hugh had suggested it; we had no shared history here, and the shiny espresso maker and the assortment of inexpensive scones and sandwiches couldn't possibly trick us into thinking we were having a dinner date.

Striving to seem as though I didn't care, and also to show that I was ready to lift furniture, I came in my trusty yoga pants, as good as new after a thorough laundering in Kendall's washing machine.

With them, I wore a trendy argyle sweater that had shrunk and was too small for Kendall but was perfect for me. On my feet were the same trusty Asics that had gotten me away from the phony cop. Hugh disliked the American habit of wearing running shoes everywhere; I thought about that as I put them on. I was going to make it as easy as possible for both of us to say good-bye.

I arrived at five-thirty and found that Hugh had gotten out of work early and was already there, in a black Italian business suit and wing tips. He looked sharp but somber. His only item of color was a red-and-gold Aquascutum tie that I particularly loved.

"Right on time," he said when I joined him at the counter, where he was scrutinizing the assortment of pastries.

"I try my best." I kept looking at the necktie, because I was still too nervous to look into his face.

"Well, it doesn't really matter, I suppose. The crowd's huge here in the mornings. But now . . ." Hugh glanced around. "We could have any table we like."

Hugh ordered Earl Grey tea and two blueberry scones. I settled for hot apple cider. I paid for both of us before he had a chance to get out his wallet. I figured it was the least that I could do with my extravagant payment from the U.S. government.

"You may wonder why I picked this spot instead of a restaurant," Hugh said after we'd sat down.

"Because it has no memories?" I asked.

"They offer no alcohol," Hugh said. "I stopped drinking ten days ago."

This was the length of time that had elapsed since my confession. I asked, "Do you mean that you think you are an alcoholic?"

"I don't know. I ran into bingeing problems before back in Scotland. And with my brother and his mates, the rock-band lifestyle . . . I think I forgot who I was." Hugh smiled without warmth.

"I never thought of your drinking as anything more than—fun. But I guess that at the end, things spun out of control." Just as the typhoon had spun me into Takeo's arms, changing everything over the course of a few horrible hours.

"Even before you left for Japan, I felt as if you'd already checked out of my life." Hugh's words came slowly. "That party—I know it wasn't your thing, but I felt that if I did something really grand—made a statement that hundreds of people saw—you'd understand how much I loved you. But I buggered up so badly that night that you shot off for Tokyo almost immediately. Not wanting me to go with you—well, that was the final blow for me."

I wanted to stretch my hand out to comfort him, but didn't dare. "The irony is that while I was there, I wished I weren't. I never felt like that in Japan before."

"My brother phoned me yesterday to say that apparently the picture was mix-up. The tabloid even printed a retraction, at the behest of Takeo's family—"

"So, the Kayamas intervened and saved everyone's reputation." I sighed. "But I'm not going to make excuses. As I said over the phone, I really did sleep with Takeo."

"I wonder," Hugh said slowly, "if that was some kind of mix-up, too."

"What do you mean?" I eyed him suspiciously. Hugh had made it clear over the phone that he wanted me out of his apartment. This meeting was supposed to be about arranging the logistics of my move. Was he trying to offer forgiveness instead?

"I wonder if you went into the situation with all your faculties intact," Hugh said.

"I wasn't drunk," I said tightly. "But I was—desperate in a way that I hope never to be again."

"I appreciate your honesty."

I stared at the grain of the pine table between us. "I suppose you're being like this because you want to part cordially."

"I do want that," Hugh said. "The truth is, I realize that I've got to separate myself from the situations and people that led me into trouble. I've asked for a transfer, Rei."

"A work transfer?"

"Yes. Right now it might be Europe or Latin America. I was passed over for partner, so I don't really care where I go." He paused. "So the flat . . . the reason I want you to move the furniture is that I'm moving out myself. Very quickly."

"It's a good thing you never bought," I said, feeling hollow. Of course I should have known he'd run. He'd done it before, when we'd both been in Tokyo, and once before that, in Washington. Both times, I'd wound up winning, but not on this occasion.

Hugh's mouth was moving, and belatedly I realized that he was asking about my own plans.

"Well, I'm staying with Kendall till I can't stand it anymore—that'll probably be three days, tops—and then I'll go to Grand's in Baltimore or somewhere like that. It depends on the job I take up next—"

"You're staying here? Rather than decamping to Japan?"

I shrugged. "It depends on the job I take. And as far as Japan goes, my visa status is back to normal again. I'm sure I'll go back, but there are a lot of other places I want to see, too."

"So you'll be in the Washington area, still." Hugh picked up a scone as if he meant to eat it, then put it down.

"I don't know. I stayed here because of you, and now that's changed." I stared at the scones, unable to wipe away the tears welling up in my eyes.

Hugh didn't speak again. And when he left the coffee bar, I stayed resolute, not turning to look after him. Grimly, I remembered what Chika had said about her parents not wanting to know the truth—and realized that maybe my young cousin was the wisest one of all.

Michael Hendricks had known about the package I'd mailed to Iraq before I left Japan, but I wasn't sure what his reaction was until I met him for lunch a few days after my disastrous parting from Hugh. Michael had suggested Zola for lunch; his choice of the restaurant, which sat right over the American Spy Museum, was a gesture that made me smile at a time when smiles were in scarce supply. Even though it was early November, the weather felt like winter. I had on Grand's suit, which I decided looked surprisingly hip when worn with a tight black tank top underneath it, thigh-high black stockings, and the strappy high-heeled Manolos on my feet.

Michael was wearing another fade-into-the-background Brooks Brothers suit, but he looked different somehow. Maybe it was because his ice-blue eyes, as they regarded me, finally looked like those of a friend, rather than an adversary.

"I swear to you that from this day forward I'm never going to talk about the Momoyama vase anymore," he murmured after we'd been seated in one of the best places—a red velvet booth with a porthole window, so you could see who was behind you. In our case, it was Italian tourists lost in an argument only they could understand. I sat down, reassured.

"Did you hear what I said, Rei? About the Momoyama vase?" he raised his voice slightly.

"I did. And it sounds as if you are still talking about it."

"I can call it an ibex ewer now," Michael said. "And it's back where it belongs without so much as a chip, which is fortunate, given how it was sent."

I shrugged. "It must be that the sender was an expert at packing antiquities."

"That's right. The government held a news conference showing the vessel in its glory. Three elementary-school classes came to see it. The public knows that it's back."

"I'm glad." And I was, despite all that had happened.

"The ewer's return precludes any prosecution of the Birand brothers for its theft. Did you know?" Michael asked.

"But they're still in trouble for the passport-brokering, I bet." I laid down my menu to pay full attention.

"They're out of Japan for good, and Turkey doesn't want them back. But I understand they want to resettle in Morocco because of the tourist trade. Ramzi, you may be glad to hear, had not been charged with anything. He's going to finish his studies in France."

I'd kept in touch with Ramzi, so I knew that already. But I was anxious to understand more about the situation for Ali and Osman Birand. "Are you saying that the Birand brothers don't face any criminal prosecution?"

"Did you think things should be otherwise?"

"Well, they didn't do anything to hurt me or anyone I know of. And from what Ali said to me, the vessel was a gift to his brother from one of the people seeking a visa in the first place." I suddenly felt anxious. "I'm sorry there was no exposure of an art theft ring, but the fact is that these gift-giving chains, in the Middle East as well as in Japan, are hard to understand and trace."

"Yes. That reminds me of the way the ewer arrived. Apparently, a set of five tea bowls made by a Living National Treasure had been sent along with it. That was a clever touch, leading the customs inspectors who opened the package to concentrate on the known value of one thing, and completely bypass the other. Over at the museum, they're still trying to decide who gets the tea bowls. Any ideas?"

Of course Michael knew that I'd done it; he was just teasing me. "How about the next seriously wounded Iraqi child? Maybe they could parlay it into a visa to a safer country."

I'd expected Michael to protest my partisan political statement, but instead, he looked at me and said, "What about you?"

Vehemently, I shook my head.

"You lost everything, didn't you? Both the men, your place to live in Washington, and the support of your relatives in Yokohama."

"Oh, nothing's irreplaceable." I amended my hard words. "Well, maybe I don't mean my relatives. But I think they've all decided it was just a matter of crazy Rei being a little crazier than usual. They've forgiven, if not forgotten."

I'd given my cousins a sketchy but honest report of the situation: that Takeo had been racked with anxiety over Emi's death, and I'd comforted him. The fact that I'd left Japan proved I had no real interest in resurrecting our relationship, and by now, the media's attention was long gone from me. The truth had gotten out about the drugs that Emi had taken before her death, and the press furthered the idea that the shame and horror her father had faced because of his daughter's drug overdose had led to his attempted suicide.

On the bright side, Tom had told me, there was a sudden increase in serious media coverage of the dangers of Japan's most popular drug, and the warning signs parents could observe. And it seemed that Takeo was no longer a social pariah; he was seen as a sad, flawed hero who had tried in vain to prevent his fiancée's death.

"But what about Hugh?" Michael was like a dog who wouldn't drop a bone.

"It's over, though I haven't retrieved all my things from his apartment because I'm not sure what I'm doing next."

"In terms of work, you mean?"

"Exactly." I watched him closely, because he'd hinted about having more work for me, and I wondered if the offer still stood.

Michael folded his arms and regarded me. "You know that I'm pleased with the way your first job for us went. My bosses are pleased, too. They hope you'll work for us again."

I felt myself flush. "You mean, join the C-I-"

"No names," Michael said in a low voice. "But you're in the right arena. I'll show you my credentials later on, when we're outside."

"I can't believe you could possibly think the job went smoothly," I said. "My mistake with Takeo led to a chain of events that were nearly disastrous."

"What you did the day and night of the storm—getting to the beach town, and finding a way to stay in the house and discover the fake—verged on the heroic." Michael's gaze was warm. "Hugh understandably has a different reading of it, but rest assured that in our line of work, you aren't the first agent to have done that sort of thing."

"But I wasn't an agent—"

"You could be," Michael said, studying me. "If you were willing to sign a secrecy agreement, we could formalize our relationship."

I laughed shakily. "No, thanks. I'm too liberal, and I'd never pass the physical."

"I disagree with both." Michael grinned. "And I promise you that because you're still remaining something of an independent contractor, the training is minimal. For instance, there would be no paramilitary training, although you probably should take some more *kanji* classes, since your difficulty reading Japanese is really the only weakness I see."

Michael was still watching me, so I was relieved to be interrupted by the waitress. I ordered the corn and mussel soup and the vegetable stack.

"Anything to drink?" she asked.

I hesitated, thinking that this was a business lunch, and also thinking about Hugh's problem, but Michael interjected, "Did you know that they serve wines by the glass? I'm having a glass of Pinot Grigio."

Wines by the glass! A brilliant idea. A tiny bit of golden joy in a glass, not too much, just enough to make the flavors of the food rounder, and my back rest a little more comfortably against the banquette.

"Is this a typical workday lunch for you?" I asked after the exquisite food had arrived and I'd taken a few bites.

"This meal is not on the government's tab," Michael said. "Although my time talking to you will be. Getting back to our conversation, I want you to consider taking on some jobs that I might hear about, dealing with cultural treasures and delicate human situations: situations that could be peacefully solved, to use one of your infamous expressions."

"It sounds like the right idea, philosophically," I said, "But I still don't feel I could do things like that. I wouldn't know where to start."

"Consider how things worked out in your debut operation. The ibex ewer is back in Iraq and relations between Japan and the United States are intact, despite our apprehending one of their citizens."

"But has justice been served? Mr. Harada's probably going to retire without going to jail, and the Birands are free to keep running their dubious business in another country. And what about Mr. Watanabe, that double-dealing bastard?"

"Early next year, apparently, he's rotating out of the embassy and retiring to go into private industry." Michael took a sip of wine. "Obviously, the scandal that he tried to prevent wound up tainting him, too."

"Well, frankly, I'm glad he's not staying in office. I can hardly stand to live in the same city as the man who betrayed me to someone who hired a thug to do away with me—"

"Yes. I made a sorry choice in recruiting him to help, although he probably would have been fine if it had not turned out that our real suspect was one of his colleagues." Michael looked at me. "I'm sorry, Rei."

I shuddered. "Well, you did start warning me to be cautious, pretty early on. And at least it's over."

"Yes. And even though there won't be newspaper clippings this time around telling the truth about what you did over the last few weeks, you must feel satisfied knowing that you've uncovered corruption within immigration circles."

"I was lucky. I guessed the truth at the critical moment." I felt uncomfortable with all the praise.

"I disagree, and I'm writing an analysis of your experience, to be shared agencywide. You're the first person in our employ who's pointed out that governments must be highly vigilant to make sure diplomats don't foster immigration fraud. Just think how terrorists might get into our country, if we had an ambassador who operated the way Harada did."

"You're very kind to make such a big deal about it," I said.

"Rei, I want you to work for us again." Michael was looking straight at me in a way that made me drop my own gaze. It was too intense, too close.

"I promise that I'll think about it," I said. Kendall was sure she could find work for me decorating her friend's new restaurant, and my grandmother had cooked up some kind of an opportunity to catalog a famous netsuke collection in North Baltimore. But I'd keep Michael's offer in mind. It was bound to be the highest-paying, and it had the advantage of travel—something that sounded good to me, now that I no longer had a home.

When I left Zola two hours later, I discovered that the sun had completely vanished, obscured by what looked like snow clouds. Snow in early November in Washington? It could happen, though it was unusual.

Much of my trip back to Bethesda was underground, so when I got out of the station, I was pleased to see a faint dusting of white everywhere. The bus to Potomac was delayed because of the weather, so I decided to walk.

The two miles to Kendall's house went rather slowly because of my impractical shoes. But I didn't mind. As I picked my way along the path, I looked heavenward and let the flakes fall on my cheeks, eyes, lips, and hair.

The snow kept falling. The dull suburban landscape was now

completely frosted in white, except for the black asphalt roads and the tiny holes that my heels were making on the snowy sidewalk. Tomorrow I would teach Jackie and Win how to make snow angels.

I had the time, because it would be a snow day—and because I finally understood that my own winter years were nothing to be afraid of.

Girl in a Box

Sujata Massey

1

It's taken me almost a whole lifetime to become a decent liar.

I still endure stabs of good-girl guilt about it, even though lying has started a brilliant second career for me. I tell stories easily, rarely missing a step as I switch between English and Japanese. But I often wonder how I ever got to this crazy place in life, and where I will go next.

This day had been like all the others: a cool winter day in Monterey, with eight hours of classes at the Defense Language Institute, followed by my usual routine—a run out to Lover of Jesus Point in Pacific Grove. On days like this one, I felt that the Pacific was my constant friend. The water was the divider between me and Japan, between my old life and the new one. I'd have to cross it to go home.

It was odd that I felt this way, I thought as I ran along the dirt trail that paralleled the coast. California was my birthplace—San Francisco, to be exact, about two hours to the north, where my parents still lived. But Japan, where I'd lived so briefly but happily teaching English and selling antiques, always beckoned. The sensation had been stronger on this day than at any time so far in the two months I'd been studying at DLI, preparing for the kind of career in which you couldn't tell anyone what you did, but that would get me back to Japan.

Good things are worth waiting for. I reminded myself of this truth as I ran, dressed for the winter in a long-sleeved black shirt really meant for bikers, and shorts, because I was too vain to wear sensible running tights. The wind on my legs didn't bother me; but on my way back, my knee started throbbing, and I thought about how much I wanted to replace the Nike Airs. In Monterey, there were a few places to buy running shoes, but nothing with the vast array of choices that a thirty-year-old with fading knees required. Of course, I could go up to San Francisco and easily get my favorite Asics style, but I wasn't in the mood. I'd been there at my family home for Christmas and New Year's, a time when I found myself fending off a combination of unhealthy foods and intrusive questions. As much as I loved my parents, I couldn't tell them about the Organization for Cultural Intelligence—OCI—the super-secret spy agency where I'd been hired as a special infor-mant. I also couldn't explain why Hugh Glendinning, the man to whom I'd once been semi-engaged, had thrown me out of his life and Washington, D.C., apartment for-ever. But I wouldn't lie to my parents—that would be completely against my internal code. So I chose not to talk.

I actually liked the solitude of the Monterey coast, with its jagged rocks set against the turbulent, frigid Pa-cific: home of sardines, surfers, seals, and whales. Now I glanced toward the ocean, just to make sure I wasn't go-ing to miss the sunset. Another great blessing of my post-ing in Monterey was my proximity to sunsets over the Pacific: performance art in vivid shades of red, orange, and purple, each sunset unique, like the kanji characters I was studying.

The sun took its leisurely time slipping down to the ho-rizon, but as closely as I looked, I missed the green flash. I always seemed to miss it, even on the days when I'd been with Hugh, vacationing in beautiful parts of Japan and Thailand, and he took pains to point it out. I never saw the same things he did. Perhaps that had been the problem.

I shifted my gaze forward in the direction I was run-ning, coming close to the Hopkins Marine Station, a research outpost connected to Stanford University. It had a beautiful rocky lookout point, but I'd never gone out because the station had a high wire fence and many signs saying "keep out." I was getting quite used to barriers, fences, and warning signs; usually, the Department of Defense identification card that I carried would get me in most places, but I had no business at the station.

Someone else did, though; a solitary sightseer, who was out on the rocks with field glasses close to his face.

I had noticed the same man half an hour earlier, because of what he was wearing: a business suit, which was a rarity in Monterey. I assumed he had to be some muckety-muck, though in my experience, marine scientists were more likely to wear jeans than gray flannel. Not that I could tell what the suit was made of: I was much too far away to make out those details, let alone the guy's face. I imagined for a minute that he was a spy, watching the coast for his contact to come in. He was probably an out-of-control tourist who just wanted to take pictures—though why he wasn't looking seaward rather than at the recreation trail didn't make sense.

It took me a couple of minutes to pass the rocky outcropping, then the rest of the fenced station, and then its exit. My knee was really bothering me, so I moved to the side and tightened my shoelaces—anything for more support. As I finished tying the knot, I turned around to look for bikers, always a liability on the trail, and I was stunned to see the man in the business suit running out of the marine station's parking lot. Now I knew that what I'd sensed earlier had been correct; the field glasses had been trained on me, not on any form of sea life.

I was fairly breathless because I'd already been running for about half an hour, but I mustered an extra bit of power and began running toward the American Tin Cannery Outlets. The first place I saw was a Reebok outlet, but I ran on, figuring I wouldn't get much sympathy there when I was wearing Nikes. I also passed by Isotoner and Geoffrey Beene, on the assumption that these were not brands that would draw a young, fit crowd ready to aid in my defense. The students at DLI, mostly young enlisted men, were certainly buff enough help me out against an assailant, but I was the last woman they'd want to help. I don't know whether I'd ticked them off by screwing up the academic curve, or because I'd refused any and all romantic propositions. It was impossible to know—and actually of no consequence at a time like this.

Damn, I thought, after glancing backward. He was gaining on me, and the glasses were now hanging around his neck, hitting his chest as he ran. No normal jogger ran in a business suit; he was a lunatic. I broke into a full-throttle sprint. He was still so far away that I couldn't see his face, but from what I'd seen, he had gray hair. This fact—that he was significantly older than I—should have made me calm down, but did not.

There was a little restaurant at the end out the outlet strip brightly painted red, white, and blue, probably in an attempt to cater to both Monterey's military population and foreign tourists. I jogged up the steps and burst inside, finding the place absolutely empty; of course, it was before the dinner hour.

At the far end of the room, a couple of young men in T-shirts and jeans were sitting together conversing in Spanish. They looked at the runner in their restaurant and said nothing. I didn't know if it was because I looked so disheveled, or because there was a language barrier.

"I have a problem. Can you call the police?" I said between heavy breaths.

The two men hesitated a moment, glancing each other. Then they ran back through the kitchen.

"It's a misunderstanding, I didn't mean—" I called out, wishing I had spoken in Spanish the first time. Spanish was the first language of Monterey, I should have thought to speak it right away and not use a trigger word like "police."

A banging sound told me they'd gone out the back door. Now I was all alone. I quickly threaded my way through the restaurant, looking for a telephone. The man had obviously seen me go in; there was no point in hiding. I'd just be on the phone with the cops when my stalker arrived.

I found a phone at last, and as I pressed "talk," I finally got a close-up view of my pursuer through the window. And shakily I put the phone down. I had been right when I'd briefly daydreamed about the figure on the rocks. He was a spy—a spymaster, to be correct. The man I'd run from was the chief of OCI's Japan desk: Michael Hendricks, my boss of the last three months.

"Michael! What a surprise," I said, striving for normality as he stepped through the door.

Michael Hendricks must have become extremely bored with his duties in Washington, because he'd been e-mailing me jokes almost daily, silly lightbulb riddles like *How many spies does it take to screw in a lightbulb? Answer: Twenty. One to do it, and nineteen to develop a distraction.*

However, in Michael's numerous e-mails, he'd never once mentioned that he was planning a cross-country trip to California.

"Why were you running away?" Michael was breathing hard and pulling his tie out of his shirt collar as he spoke. Michael was not a conventionally handsome man; he was too thin, and although his features may have started out

patrician, he looked as if he'd had his nose broken somewhere along the line. But his salt-and-pepper hair was cut
well, in a classic military buzz, and his ice-blue eyes were
so appealing that I often had to look away.

I decided to answer honestly. "I was scared. Wouldn't
you be, if someone watched you with field glasses and
then started running after you?"

"I was looking for you." His breath was gradually
slowing. "When I made the positive ID, I decided to catch
up with you. By the way, did you know that you pronate
when you run?"

"Yes. The shoes make it worse." I flushed, embarrassed
that I'd been seen not only running away, but running
away with bad form.

"You mentioned once that you ran in this area, so
that's why I came, after I found you weren't at your
apartment. I picked that point, on the rocks, just to make
sure I'd see you before you went home, or into town, or
wherever." Michael tugged off his suit jacket. I looked
for huge sweat stains on his oxford shirt, but it was crisp
and dry. Either he was a very cool customer or he wore
an undershirt.

Michael spoke again. "Actually, I've been trying to catch
up with you all day. There's something we have to discuss,
as soon as possible."

"What could it be?" I asked grimly, because I was sure I knew. He had learned the results of my embarrassing polygraph test a few days earlier, and come to tell me that my very short career in government intelligence was over.

"It looks like there's nobody here to take an order, so let's talk about it back at your apartment." Michael reached into his jacket pocket and pulled out a car key with a rental company tag. "There's plenty of room in the Impala they gave me."

A Chevy Impala? "No, thanks. I'd prefer to finish my run. It's barely a half mile back to the apartment. And then I've got to shower."

"Of course," Michael said smoothly. "Hey, I'll get us some take-out food, and meet you over there. That'll give you enough time, I hope."

An Impala was a ridiculous car for a man not yet forty to be driving, I thought as I jogged up Spaghetti Hill to my apartment. I had a feeling that Michael was going to beat me in the car, but I needed the time to clear my head.

But he wasn't there after all. I unlocked the back door to the Spanish-style bungalow on Larkin Street with the key I'd tucked into the inner pocket of my shorts. I went immediately into the small bathroom, took a superfast shower, and dressed, this time in a pair of jeans and a silk kurta I'd bought in one of the little boutiques downtown. I decided against putting on makeup and blow-drying my hair—I rarely bothered with those things these days—but I did attempt to straighten up the apartment a bit before he arrived. The apartment had been converted out of the back end of a modest two-bedroom bungalow built in the twenties. At one time it must have been lovely, but now the stucco walls were crumbling, and the landlord had covered the old terra-cotta tiles with vinyl and had provided only cheap wicker garden furniture. I was rearranging the cushions on the love seat and chairs that made up my living room suite when I heard a knock on the door. I checked the peephole, identified Michael, and opened up.

He was carrying a bag from the Paris Bakery, one of my favorite haunts, and two cups of coffee. But behind him, lying against the small porch railing, were more than a dozen large, flat cardboard boxes—moving boxes, I realized with a start. After handing the food to me, he began hauling the boxes into the room.

"You brought—cookies? What kind of a dinner is that?" I asked as I looked at the enticing mixture of checkerboard cookies and raspberry butter cookies. I was trying to figure out both the meal and the moving boxes.

"There's not enough time for a sit-down meal. But I thought the sugar could carry us both through what we need to do tonight." Michael cleared his throat. "You're probably wondering why I came all the way to see you."

"Yes, I'd say Monterey is a little out of the way from D.C.," I said.

"I took a military hop. Nonstop, on a Learjet. Really a pleasure."

"So it's urgent." I sipped the coffee and winced. He had added plenty of sugar, but no milk.

"You wanted milk?" Michael's gaze was keen.

"Yes. A latte with just two sugars would have been perfect, but you'll know that for next time." I caught myself. "Actually, I guess there won't be a next time, from the boxes you've brought. Something's wrong, isn't it?"

"I wouldn't say wrong." Michael paused. "And I am sorry to pull you out before the academic course is over. Your instructor told me that you were doing really well, the top of the class."

"Little else to do around here except study." But I was secretly pleased that he'd heard how well I'd done.

"Well, maybe you can come back to Monterey later in the year." He paused. "I need you in D.C. I came out to explain the situation personally, because you have the option to accept or decline."

Obviously he expected me to accept, because he'd brought moving boxes. Carefully I asked, "Do you mean it's an OCI job?"

He nodded. "We have about a month to prepare for the mission. Then, it's back to Tokyo for you."

"Excellent." My spirits rose for the first time in weeks. I didn't mind leaving Monterey if it was for Japan. I knew where I was going to find my replacement running shoes—in Shinjuku!

"I'm going to explain as we pack, because you've got to be out of here, on my flight, tomorrow at ODT."

"What does *that* mean?" I'd noticed that Michael's years in the Navy and then the federal government had resulted in his speaking a language of abbreviations that was as complex as Japanese.

"Oh-dark-thirty. It means very early, before daylight." He paused. "Our flight to Langley leaves at six-thirty. You've got to be packed tonight, and we'll leave everything here for one of our people to move out tomorrow. Your personal shipment will be airmailed space-A after we go."

Another one of his abbreviations, which I'd learned meant "Space available," probably later than sooner. I glanced around my untidy apartment. "How can I possibly . . ."

"I'll help you." Michael was starting to fold and assemble the first box. "I've done this kind of pack-out many times, and yours should be a snap. All you've got are clothes and books, correct?"

"And music. And cooking stuff, and . . ."

"No problem," Michael said, pulling a thick roll of tape from his jacket. "As we pack, I'll tell you everything."

BOOKS BY SUJATA MASSEY

GIRL IN A BOX

ISBN 0-06-076514-3 (hardcover)

Rei Shimura takes on a freelance gig with a Washington, D.C., alphabet agency that might have ties to the CIA. Her mission is to go undercover as a clerk in a big Tokyo department store.

THE TYPHOON LOVER

0-06-076513-5 (trade paperback)

Through her chaotic twenties, antiques dealer Rei Shimura has gone anywhere that fortune and her unruly passions have led her. *The Typhoon Lover* takes her on her biggest adventure yet, a perilous journey that only Rei, with her experience in antiques and her foothold in two countries, can handle.

ZEN ATTITUDE

ISBN 0-06-089921-2 (trade paperback)

When Rei overpays for a beautiful antique chest, she's in for the worst deal of her life. The con man who sold her the *tansu* is found dead, and like it or not Rei's opened a Pandora's box of mystery, theft, and murder.

THE PEARL DIVER

ISBN 0-06-059790-9 (trade paperback)

A dazzling engagement ring is an added bonus for antiques dealer and sometime-sleuth Rei Shimura, who is commissioned to furnish a chic Japanese-fusion restaurant, where, in short order, things start to go haywire.

"A riveting story." —*Library Journal*

THE SAMURAI'S DAUGHTER

ISBN 0-06-059503-5 (trade paperback)

Antiques dealer Rei Shimura is in San Francisco tracing the story of one hundred years of Japanese decorative arts through her family's history. Before long, Rei uncovers troubling facts about her own family's actions during the war.

"Absorbing cross-cultural puzzle." —*Publishers Weekly*

THE BRIDE'S KIMONO

ISBN 0-06-103115-1 (mass market paperback)

Rei Shimura has managed to snag one of the most lucrative jobs of her career: a renowned museum in Washington, D.C., has invited her to exhibit rare kimonos and give a lecture on them. Within hours one of the kimonos is stolen, and then a body is discovered in a shopping mall Dumpster.

THE FLOATING GIRL

ISBN 0-06-109735-7 (mass market paperback)

During research for a comic-style magazine, Rei stumbles upon a disturbing social milieu of pre–World War II Japan. It evolves into something much darker when one of the comic's young creators is found dead—a murder that takes the tenacious Rei deep into the heart of Japan's youth underground.

THE FLOWER MASTER

ISBN 0-06-109734-9 (mass market paperback)

Life in Japan for a transplanted California girl with a fledgling antiques business and a nonexistent love life isn't always fun, but when the flower-arranging class Rei Shimura's aunt cajoles her into taking turns into a stage for murder, Rei finds plenty of excitement she's been missing.

THE SALARYMAN'S WIFE

ISBN 0-06-104443-1 (mass market paperback)

Rei is the first to find the beautiful wife of a high-powered businessman dead in the snow. Taking charge as usual, Rei searches for clues by crashing a funeral, posing as a bar-girl, and somehow ending up pursued by police and paparazzi alike. In the meantime, she manages to piece together a strange, ever-changing puzzle.